OBSESSED

Books by Jo Gibson

OBSESSED

TWISTED

AFRAID

And writing as Joanne Fluke

Hannah Swensen Mysteries

CHOCOLATE CHIP COOKIE MURDER
STRAWBERRY SHORTCAKE MURDER
BLUEBERRY MUFFIN MURDER
LEMON MERINGUE PIE MURDER
FUDGE CUPCAKE MURDER
SUGAR COOKIE MURDER
PEACH COBBLER MURDER
CHERRY CHEESECAKE MURDER
KEY LIME PIE MURDER
CANDY CANE MURDER
CARROT CAKE MURDER
CREAM PUFF MURDER
PLUM PUDDING MURDER
APPLE TURNOVER MURDER
DEVIL'S FOOD CAKE MURDER
GINGERBREAD COOKIE MURDER
CINNAMON ROLL MURDER
RED VELVET CUPCAKE MURDER
BLACKBERRY PIE MURDER
JOANNE FLUKE'S LAKE EDEN COOKBOOK

Suspense Novels

VIDEO KILL
WINTER CHILL
DEAD GIVEAWAY
THE OTHER CHILD

Published by Kensington Publishing Corporation

OBSESSED

JO GIBSON

KENSINGTON PUBLISHING CORP.
www.kensingtonbooks.com

KTEEN BOOKS are published by

Kensington Publishing Corp.
119 West 40th Street
New York, NY 10018

All Kensington titles, imprints, and distributed lines are available at special quantity discounts for bulk purchases for sales promotion, premiums, fund-raising, and educational or institutional use.

Special book excerpts or customized printings can also be created to fit specific needs. For details, write or phone the office of the Kensington Special Sales Manager: Kensington Publishing Corp., 119 West 40th Street, New York, NY 10018. Attn. Special Sales Department. Phone: 1-800-221-2647.

ISBN-13: 978-1-61773-238-6
ISBN-10: 1-61773-238-9
First Kensington Trade Paperback Printing: June 2014

eISBN-13: 978-1-61773-239-3
eISBN-10: 1-61773-239-7
First Kensington Electronic Edition: June 2014

10 9 8 7 6 5 4 3 2

Printed in the United States of America

Contents

The Crush

One

Deana Burroughs beat her fists against the steering wheel in pure frustration. This had been the absolute worst day of her life, and now her car had conked out on her. The old black Nissan had started making strange chugging sounds right after she'd turned left from Olive Street, and she'd barely managed to make it over to the curb before the motor had given a gurgling cough and died.

She stared out at the deserted residential street with small, one-level bungalows that were so common in Southern California and thought about the horrible day she'd had. For starters, she'd overslept. And then, when she'd hopped out of bed, knowing she'd be late for her summer session Spanish class, she'd stubbed her toe on the dresser. That little incident should have warned her. She should have gone back to bed, pulled the covers up over her head, and slept the day away. But she hadn't. She'd raced to the shower, turned on the water, and the cold water knob had twisted right off in her hand. She'd wasted valuable time attempting to re-attach it, so much time that the hot water had run out and she'd finished washing her hair in an icy stream. And from that point, things had just gotten worse.

Deana rested her forehead against the fake sheepskin steering wheel cover and mentally added up the disasters. The zipper on her favorite pair of jeans had broken, her left shoelace had snapped, and the watch band she'd been meaning to replace had finally given up the ghost. And all that had happened before she'd even left her room!

She had arrived at summer school twenty minutes late, and found her class taking a surprise quiz. Since it was oral, she'd missed the first fifteen questions, and ended up flunking. So much for her first class. Algebra had been next, and naturally, she'd forgotten her homework . . . again. Miss Berman had been so angry, she'd called Deana's mother at work, pulling her out of an important conference.

Deana had been ready to give up right then and skip her last class. But Miss Berman had personally escorted her there, forcing her to sit through another of Mr. Scharf's boring lectures. She'd dozed off a couple of times, but to her surprise she had managed to answer the three questions he'd written on the board at the end of the period.

Deana had stared at the questions, and groaned along with the rest of the class. *What was the date of the Battle of New Orleans? Who led the American troops? Which river did they travel?* It was all Greek to her. But then she'd remembered their last rehearsal at Covers, the teenage nightclub their speech and drama teacher owned. Michael Warden, the featured singer at the club, was fascinated by vintage rock 'n roll and he'd sung a number called "The Battle of New Orleans." The lyrics had been so catchy, Deana had remembered them.

> *In 1815, we took a little trip,*
> *Along with Colonel Jackson down the mighty Mississip.*
> *We took a little bacon and we took a little beans,*
> *We fought the bloody British in a town called New Orleans.*

Deana had written down the answers. 1815, Colonel Jackson, and the Mississippi River. And Mr. Scharf had been so pleased, he'd complimented her in front of the whole class. Deana had walked out of the room with a smile on her face. Could her luck be changing?

No. She'd gone down to Chuckie's Wagon for a burger with a

couple of girls, and Sally Hornaby had squirted catsup all over her new peach silk shirt, the one she'd been planning to wear the next time she went out with Michael.

Surprisingly, Deana's afternoon hadn't been all that awful. The cable had gone out during Oprah, but she hadn't really been into interviews with women who beat their husbands anyway. And she'd remembered to put in the roast and baked potatoes the way her mother had asked her to. Of course she'd forgotten that the oven was fifty degrees hotter than it said on the dial, but she'd turned it down just as soon as she'd remembered. Naturally, her bratty brother had complained, but her father had said he didn't think the roast was *that* dried out, just a little crispy around the edges.

Deana's mother had come home late. She'd been crabby because she'd had to work overtime, and she hadn't forgotten about Miss Berman's call, though Deana had hoped she would. Deana was grounded—for a solid month. She couldn't sing at Covers again until her summer school classes were over. And if she got into any more trouble with Miss Berman, or any of her other teachers, she could forgot about that new guitar they'd planned to buy her for her birthday.

Even though her mother had been angry, Deana had tried to appeal to her sense of fair play. Yes, she'd messed up. And she wouldn't do it again. But she'd made a commitment to perform at Covers. Couldn't her mother see that it wouldn't be fair to quit now, without any notice or anything? Deana's mother had pointed out that her commitment to pass her summer school classes was a lot more important than singing at a teenage nightclub. First things first. Then she'd marched Deana up the stairs like a naughty child, and locked her in her room to do her homework and go to bed.

Deana had watched the clock. Her parents always went to bed early on Thursday nights. When they'd come up the stairs at nine-thirty, she'd hopped into bed with all her clothes on, and waited until her mother had opened the door to check on her. The minute she'd heard the television click on in their bedroom, she'd gone into action. The old apricot tree outside Deana's window had been her secret escape route for years. She'd shimmied down without doing too much damage to her clothing, hopped in the Nissan which was parked a couple of houses down the block, and headed for Covers. She hadn't been scheduled to sing until ten-thirty, and she'd figured she could get there by ten at the latest.

But the fates had conspired against her. The Nissan needed gas. Deana stopped at the Shell station on the corner, charged the gas to her father's account, and arrived at Covers at ten-twenty-five. But she'd forgotten to look at the new schedule they'd posted at the last rehearsal. She'd missed her first set, and someone had been forced to fill in for her. Mr. Calloway had been very upset with her, and he'd told her that if she was late again, she was out. And then Michael Warden had positively glowered at her when she'd told him she hadn't had the time to learn the lyrics to the duet he'd planned to sing with her.

Deana glanced at her reflection in the rear-view mirror and frowned. Now Michael was mad at her, and she had to think of some way to make it up to him. They'd gone out the past three Sundays in a row, and she was crazy about him. He wasn't that much older, only two years, but he'd just finished his freshman year at U.C.L.A. All her high school friends were envious because she was dating a college guy, and it had given her some real status around the high school campus.

Michael was tall, dark, and handsome, and the best singer Deana had ever heard. There was no doubt in her mind that he'd make it big someday. Since Covers was in Burbank, only a stone's throw from the studios and the big record companies, Michael had managed to make some good contacts. Mr. Calloway had connections and he sent out tickets to lots of people in the biz. When you got up to perform at Covers, you never knew who might be in the audience.

Had she blown it with Michael tonight? Deana frowned. She'd had plenty of time to learn those lyrics, and now she could kick herself for putting it off. When she got home tonight, she'd do it. *If* she got home tonight.

Deana's frown deepened. She didn't dare call her parents to come and get her. They'd be mad she'd sneaked out of the house in the first place, and when they found out she'd spent the money they'd given her for the auto club on clothes, she'd never be allowed to leave her room again! But what should she do? She couldn't sit here all night. It was almost midnight, and there was no traffic. That meant there were no cars to flag down. This area was relatively safe, but she still didn't want to try to walk home alone.

A car rounded the corner, its bright headlights illuminating the interior of her car. It pulled over to the curb to park behind her, and Deana shivered. A rapist? A murderer? But then she recognized the car, and she smiled in relief. Her luck was changing. Help was here!

It took Deana only a moment to grab her purse and lock up her car. Seconds later, she was standing by the open passenger door. "Boy, am I ever glad to see you!" she said. "My car conked out. Can you give me a lift home?"

"No problem. Climb in."

Deana climbed into the passenger seat with a smile on her face. She'd be home in a couple of minutes.

"What's wrong with your car?"

"I don't know. It just died." Deana frowned. "It sounded like it was out of gas, but I know that's not it. I just filled the tank."

"Do you want me to stop at a gas station?"

Deana shook her head. "Don't bother. I'll take care of it in the morning. All I want to do right now is get home."

As they headed down the street, Deana glanced at her watch. Eleven-forty-five. This awful day was almost over, and tomorrow was bound to be better. Things were always rushed in the morning, and if she was lucky, her parents wouldn't even notice the Nissan was gone. One of the guys from school could help her fix it, and her parents would never know.

But this wasn't the way to her house! Deana turned to the driver in surprise. "You know where I live, don't you?"

"Yes. I'm taking a shortcut."

"Great," Deana said. Anything was fine with her, as long as she got home as fast as possible. An experience like this could make her swear off sneaking out of the house for life!

But suddenly they pulled over to the side of the road, and Deana frowned. "What's the matter?"

"Car trouble."

Deana almost groaned as she looked at her watch. Two minutes to midnight. This day wasn't over yet, and this area was really deserted. No houses, just warehouse buildings that wouldn't open until morning. Her rotten luck was still with her. But at least she wasn't alone.

The trunk opened, and then the hood popped up with a solid clunk. Deana didn't bother to get out to help. She didn't know anything about cars, anyway. What good would it do?

"Deana. Come here a second, will you?"

Deana sighed as she got out. She supposed she was expected to hold tools or something, and she'd get her hands all greasy. She might even break a nail and she'd just spent a fortune having them done. "What do I have to—"

Deana's question died on her lips as something hard struck the middle of her back. There was a burst of horrible pain, and she fell heavily to the pavement. The last thing she saw was the bright moonlight glinting off a heavy tire iron as it arced down toward her head.

Two

Judy Lampert put her eye to the screen and peeked out through the mesh at the audience. It was a full house tonight, but that wasn't surprising. Covers had been very popular since it had opened last year. She'd really lucked out when she'd landed this job.

There was a mirror on the back side of the screen, and Judy checked her reflection. She looked good tonight. Her wavy blonde hair was pulled back into a high ponytail, and she was wearing her usual stage manager's outfit, a black turtleneck sweater, black jeans, and black sneakers. She was responsible for adjusting the microphones, prepping the stage between numbers, and handling the props. They didn't have a curtain, so they cut the lights between acts, and no one really noticed her up on the stage as long as she wore black.

"Ready, kid?" Michael Warden walked up behind her and slipped a friendly arm around her shoulders. Judy felt such a rush of pure pleasure, she knew she would have purred if she'd been a cat. But Michael was only being friendly. She'd lived next door to him for enough years to know that he wasn't interested in her, except as a sort of kid sister. He hadn't paid attention when her hair had grown long and wavy. He hadn't commented when her braces had come off and her smile had turned out picture perfect. He hadn't even noticed when she'd lost her awkward baby fat, and started wearing the clothes that would show off her new svelte figure. Sometimes Judy felt like the invisible woman. Michael never seemed to really see her. It was frustrating to be in love with a guy who didn't seem to know that she existed.

Judy glanced at her watch. Michael was right. It was time to start. She gave him a quick hug. He didn't seem to mind that, and then she walked to the old-fashioned light box on the wall. During the year she'd been working at Covers, Judy had learned a lot. The first time she'd brought up the lights, they'd clicked and blown a fuse. Now she knew the right way to handle the finicky old equipment. She brought the stage lights up slowly, gradually illuminating the painted flat that formed the backdrop—dark green with a pink Covers logo. Several students from the Burbank high school art class had completed it last summer.

When the lights were up all the way, Judy cued Michael. He gave her a thumbs up gesture, and walked quickly to the black stool that sat on the apron. Michael was tall, and he didn't have to climb up on the stool. He just slid on with one fluid motion, crossed his long legs, and grabbed the hand microphone while the audience applauded. All the regulars knew Michael. He was the closest thing to a star they had, and there were rumors about possible singing and acting contracts coming his way.

For a moment Judy felt almost jealous of Michael's success. But that was ridiculous. She knew she had no performing skills. She couldn't sing, act, do stand-up comedy or play a musical instrument. She didn't know how to juggle, and she couldn't do magic tricks. But she was good at her job, and that was all that counted. Mr. Calloway had told her that she was the best stage manager he'd ever had.

"I'm Michael Warden. Welcome to Friday night at Covers." Michael grinned and went into his opening speech, the one he gave every night except Sundays during the summer. When school reopened in the fall, Covers would only be open on Saturday nights. But it was summer now, and they were in full swing.

"I see some regulars out there," Michael said as he waved at a group of people he knew. "I'm glad you're back, Bill. Hi, Mary. Nice sweater."

Judy tuned out for a minute. Michael always greeted the regulars by name. It made them feel important. But she started listening again when he went back to the script.

"It's always good to see new faces in the crowd, and that's why I'm up here . . . to tell you about Covers."

That was Judy's cue to bring up the back-lighting on the Covers logo. It began to gleam vividly against the dark green background, and she smiled. Back-lighting the logo had been her idea, and once she'd shown Mr. Calloway the effect, they'd used it every night.

"Covers is our nightclub, staffed by teens with teen entertainment. But Covers isn't owned by a teen. I'm telling you that right up front, because sometimes my former teacher, Mr. Stan Calloway, tries to pass himself off as a high school sophomore. Stand up, Mr. Calloway, and show everybody how young you look after that last face lift."

Judy swept the spot toward Mr. Calloway, and he stood up to take a bow. The audience applauded, and there were a few predictable chuckles from the regulars. Stan Calloway was a short, bald-headed man in his forties, and absolutely no one would mistake him for a teenager.

"Covers serves the best burgers this side of the Burbank River." Michael paused, waited for the puzzled expressions, and continued, "That's the concrete drainage ditch that runs right by the back of the building."

There was a burst of laughter, and Judy nodded. Michael had given this speech so many times, he could probably do it in his sleep. But Michael was a good actor, and he had the ability to make it sound fresh each night.

"But seriously folks, our burgers are great. Andy Miller, our short order chef, just won several prestigious awards from the California Council of Intestinal Medicine."

There was another burst of laughter and Judy was ready with the spot. As he did every night, Andy poked his head out of the kitchen and waved a spatula at the crowd. He was a high school senior who looked like he enjoyed his own cooking. His face was freckled, and his curly red hair was almost hidden under a high chef's toque that Judy had found in a gourmet shop. Andy hated the white, puffy hat, and he only wore it when Michael did his introduction.

"Your menu's on the table, under the glass. Order from Ingrid Sunquist, she's the stunning Scandinavian blonde in the pink blouse. Or you can flag down our lovely Latin beauty, Nita Cordoza. Nita's brother, Alberto, will also take your order. He's the big, dark-haired guy in the pink shirt. And I wouldn't say anything about the color of Berto's shirt, folks. He's a fullback on the Burbank High football team."

Ingrid curtsied, Nita waved, and Berto gave one of his tough-guy smiles. Judy held the spot on them for a moment, and then she dimmed it.

"And now for the good news. Just in case you didn't know it, we have a bar!"

The audience burst into applause, but they stopped abruptly when Michael followed it up with his next line. "The bad news is, it's a non-alcoholic fruit juice bar. But our bartender, Vera Rozhinski, makes a very mean virgin Piña Colada, so belly on up between acts and tell Vera your troubles."

Judy swiveled the spotlight to Vera, a classic Slavic beauty with coal black hair and blue eyes so dark, they were almost purple. Vera was short, only a little over five feet, and Mr. Calloway had built a slatted platform behind the bar so that she could reach the glasses.

"It's almost time to say 'on with the show.' But first, Mr. Calloway has a few words. As some of you may know, one of our best singers, Deana Burroughs, died last night." Michael's voice faltered and he cleared his throat. "Mr. Calloway would like you to join us in a moment of quiet reflection."

Judy picked up Mr. Calloway with the spot, and followed him to the stage. Then she dimmed, and leaned back, half-listening to the words of praise about Deana. Just last night, Mr. Calloway had been mad enough at Deana to kill her. She'd thrown them all off schedule by being late. But now he was praising her, and telling the audience how much they'd all miss her. It was ironic, and Judy almost smiled until she realized that smiling would be terribly inappropriate. One of her first nannie's favorite phrases had been, *"Don't think ill of the dead."* But Miss Hopkins had never been able to explain why. Judy had never liked Deana, and she thought it was wrong to claim she'd liked her, now that she was dead.

Mr. Calloway had prepared a touching speech, using words like *sweet,* and *beautiful,* and *talented.* Judy frowned as she thought about her own experiences with Deana. As far as she was concerned, Deana had been a bitch. Deana had always complained about the way Judy had lit into her, and she'd been positively nasty one night when she had worn a yellow blouse that looked orange under the lights. Judy had tried to explain that it wasn't her fault. Deana had bought the blouse that afternoon, and she'd been late so there hadn't been time for a light check. But Deana had blamed her anyway. And what she'd tried to do to Michael had dissolved any positive feelings Judy had begun to harbor for Deana.

Judy glanced at the stage. Mr. Calloway was still speaking about what a wonderful girl Deana had been. Maybe she'd been wonderful to other people, but she certainly hadn't been wonderful to Michael. Of course, Michael hadn't been in a position to know Deana's plans for him. But Judy had been.

She knew she'd never forget the day last month, when all the girls at Covers had gone out to lunch. Summer school hadn't started, so Deana had been with them in the corner booth of the little Mexican restaurant down the block.

"So what do you think we should do with Michael?" Vera had asked. *"He's been really depressed since he broke up with that college girl he was dating."*

Nita had shrugged elaborately. *"What can we do? I've tried to cheer him up, but nothing works."*

Judy had nodded. She had noticed Michael's depression, but she didn't have any idea what to do to cure it. But then Mary Beth Roberts, the tall blonde dancer, had spoken up.

"I think we should all make a big play for him. If we all treat him like he's the sexiest thing we've ever seen, he'll perk right up."

Mary Beth had leaned forward across the table, and a bus boy had almost dropped his water pitcher. Mary Beth had been wearing a blouse with a scoop neckline, and when she'd leaned forward the tops of her breasts had been clearly visible.

"You think all of us should come on to Michael?" Vera had looked confused.

"Why not?" Mary Beth had warmed to her plan. *"We can have a contest. And the winner will get the biggest prize at the club. Michael Warden."*

Carla Fields had frowned. She was the student manager at Covers, a thin, quiet girl with glasses and mousy-brown hair. Carla did all the office work, and no one really knew her very well. They'd only invited her because she'd happened to be standing there when they were making their plans. *"Are you sure that's a good idea?"*

Mary Beth had laughed. *"Why not? I'd like to go out with him, and so would every girl at this table. Am I right?"*

"Of course." Nita had flashed a big smile. *"Michael is* primo."

Mary Beth had grinned, and then she'd started to poll the girls at the table. *"How about you, Vera?"*

"Well . . . sure." Vera had looked slightly uncomfortable.

"Me, too." Ingrid had sighed. *"I'd love to date Michael."*

"Becky?"

Becky Fischer, Covers' short, dark-haired resident comedian, had shrugged and nodded. Even Linda O'Keefe, the pretty red-head who sang torch songs, had blushed and smiled her agreement. The only girl who hadn't agreed was Carla. And Judy, of course.

"Are you in, Carla?" Mary Beth had grinned at Carla, a mean sort of grin that let everyone know she didn't think Carla could get a date with Michael if she was the last girl left on earth.

"No." Carla had folded her napkin and stood up. *"I like*

Michael. *He's a very nice person. And I don't think it's fair to treat him like a prize we're all competing for.*"

Judy's eyes had widened as Carla had turned and left without another word. She'd been thinking the same thing, but she hadn't had the nerve to say it.

"*Carla knows she couldn't get a date with him anyway.*" Mary Beth had given a nasty little laugh, and then she'd turned to Judy. "*Come on, Judy. You haven't said anything. Are you in?*"

Judy had taken a deep breath. She'd wanted to leave, right along with Carla, but then Mary Beth might say the same thing about her.

"*Not me.*" Judy had laughed, a laugh that said she didn't care one way or the other. Of course she wanted to go out with Michael. She'd been trying to attract him for the past two years. But she'd never admit it in front of the rest of the girls.

And then Linda spoke up to save her. "*Michael treats Judy like his kid sister. He'd know something was up if she started coming on to him. Maybe she could be the scorekeeper or something.*"

Mary Beth had given Judy a long, hard look, and then she'd nodded. "*Okay. If you don't think you could get him to ask you out, we'll let you keep score. Deana? How about you?*"

"*Count me in.*" Deana had grinned at them all, and then she'd turned to Judy. "*Mark me down as the winner. I've got a late date with Michael on Saturday night.*"

There had been absolute silence at the table, and then Mary Beth had spoken up. "*That's only one date, Deana. You haven't won yet. I think we should agree on a definite time limit. Michael has to date you for two solid weeks before we declare you the winner.*"

"*And it has to be exclusive.*" Ingrid had declared. "*If Michael goes out with anyone else during that time, you lose.*"

"*That's fine with me.*" Deana had laughed, and tossed her head. "*Why should Michael look at any of you, when he's got me? You girls might as well give up right now, because you don't stand a chance!*"

Several of the girls had exchanged glances, and then Mary

Beth had snorted disdainfully. *"I'm not giving up. And neither is anyone else . . . right, girls?"*

"Right!" Nita had leaned forward to glare at Deana. *"Don't count your chickens before they're hatched."*

One by one, the girls had turned to glare at Deana, but it hadn't seemed to faze her. She'd just fluffed her hair, lifted her eyebrows, and laughed. *"Knock yourselves out, girls. It doesn't bother me at all. But I'm warning you . . . I'm going to play dirty. And I'm going to win. Michael's so handsome, he's to die for!"*

"Would you?" Judy had given Deana a long, level look. She hated that stupid phrase.

"Would I what?"

"Would you die for Michael?"

Deana had stared at Judy as if she were crazy, and then she'd laughed. *"Don't be silly, Judy. That's just an expression. But I'm going to win that contest. You can count on it!"*

Judy shivered a bit as she remembered that conversation. Deana had said that Michael was to die for, but she hadn't known she'd actually wind up dead. It was scary to think that a careless slang phrase could foretell the future, but it had.

Suddenly, Judy realized that Mr. Calloway was introducing Michael's first number. She'd almost missed her cue! She flicked a switch and the Covers logo began to change colors, all the way from red to violet and then back again. Judy called it her rainbow effect, and Mr. Calloway had loved it when she'd tried it out at rehearsal that afternoon.

"And now . . . the star of Covers . . . Michael Warden!"

Judy dimmed the lights as Mr. Calloway left the stage, then rushed out to move Michael's stool into position. When Michael was seated, his guitar in his lap, and his microphone live, she hurried back to the light box to bring the lights up again.

Michael strummed a series of chords on his guitar, and then he pulled the microphone closer. "This is a song I wrote for Deana. I'd like to think she's listening, wherever she is right now."

Judy blinked back tears as Michael started to sing a slow, dreamy ballad about a beautiful girl with ebony hair. There were tears in Michael's voice, too, and they made his voice deep and almost foggy. It was clear he'd liked Deana a lot; maybe he'd even started to love her. Her death had been a blow to Michael, and Judy wished there were some way she could comfort him. Then she thought about the contest, and she didn't feel like crying any more. Deana had used Michael, and he was much better off without her.

Was there some way she could tell Michael about the contest? Warn him that the girls were all after him, like vultures fighting over a choice piece of meat? No. It would only hurt Michael's pride if she told him. He probably thought Deana had loved him, too. It would be much too cruel to tell him the truth.

Carla slipped behind the screen to join her, and Judy turned to give her a smile. Carla always watched the first song that Michael sang, and then she went to the office to total the receipts from the ticket sales.

"Is he all right?" Carla leaned close to whisper in Judy's ear.

"I think so." Judy whispered back. "It's a song he wrote for Deana."

"She didn't deserve it!" Carla sighed deeply. "Do you think they're going to call off that contest now?"

"I don't know. I hope so."

"Me, too." Carla nodded, and then she frowned. "You're not in it, are you?"

"Of course not! You were right, Carla. The girls don't really care about Michael. He's only an object to them, the prize they'll collect if they win the contest. I just wish I'd had the guts to say it like you did."

Carla looked surprised, and then she smiled. "Sometimes you have to stick up for what you believe. And I knew that stupid contest would end up causing everybody a lot of grief. I just hope the girls learn a lesson from Deana, and drop it!"

"What do you mean?" Judy felt a twinge of alarm. "Do you think Deana's death had something to do with the contest?"

"Of course. Deana wasn't supposed to be here last night. Her mother grounded her. But she sneaked out of the house. Deana didn't dare miss a performance. She was afraid somebody else might move in on Michael if she wasn't here to look after her interests."

Judy nodded. "I see. If Deana hadn't been so determined to win that contest, she would have stayed home. And if she had, she'd still be alive."

"Right." Carla sighed deeply. "I tried to warn them that the contest was a bad idea, but nobody listened. And now Deana's dead, and they're still going on with it."

Carla left, and Judy thought long and hard about what she had said. She agreed with Carla. There was a lesson to be learned from Deana's death, but she didn't think any of the girls were smart enough to learn it.

Three

After Covers closed at eleven, everyone sat at the big round table in the center of the room, waiting for Mr. Calloway's nightly critique. But he didn't seem up to the task tonight. He just sat down, and sighed.

"The show was fine . . . considering. You're all troupers, and I appreciate the effort you made."

"But, Mr. Calloway . . ." Linda looked puzzled. "I was flat on my second number. Didn't you notice?"

Mr. Calloway shook his head. "I guess I was too preoccupied, thinking about Deana. Did any of you girls drive here alone tonight?"

"I think we all did," Judy volunteered. "We always drive our own cars. We live in different directions."

"Okay, let's have the guys split up and follow you home. I want to make sure you all get there safely."

"Do you really think that's necessary?" Carla frowned. "I live over on the other side of the freeway, Mr. Calloway. It's out of everybody's way."

"It doesn't matter, Carla. I'll follow you myself. I just don't think you girls should drive alone until they find the guy who killed Deana."

"But that could be months from now!" Ingrid said. She looked upset. "We're not babies, Mr. Calloway. And Deana didn't get into trouble because she was driving alone. She ran out of gas, and she was hitch-hiking."

"How do you know that?"

Andy spoke up. "I told her. And that's what my uncle told me. He's a detective with the Burbank Police Department."

"Your uncle's a detective?" Mr. Calloway looked surprised. "You never mentioned that before."

Andy nodded. "I know—it's something I don't usually talk about. I'd never get invited to any parties if my friends knew I had a cop in my family."

"I see." Mr. Calloway looked amused for a moment, but then he turned serious again. "What else did your uncle tell you, Andy?"

"He said they found Deana's car about two miles from where she was killed, and the gas tank was empty."

"But that doesn't make sense," Mr. Calloway frowned. "Deana told me she was late because she had to stop for gas."

Judy looked thoughtful. "Somebody could have siphoned the gas from her tank. That happened to me a couple of weeks ago."

"Here?" Mr. Calloway looked surprised when Judy nodded. "I guess we'd better keep an eye on the cars in our parking lot."

Judy nodded. "I already do that. I go out a couple of times every night, between numbers."

"Well . . . keep it up." Mr. Calloway smiled at her approvingly. "And I want everybody to check to make sure they've got plenty of gas before they leave, okay?"

Everyone nodded, and then Judy turned to Andy. "Did your uncle tell you if they had any leads?"

"Not really." Andy hesitated for a moment, and then he sighed. "But I can tell you more if you want to hear it. It'll all be in the paper tomorrow anyway."

"Tell us." Michael looked upset as he leaned forward. "I want to know what happened. Maybe there's something we can do to help the police."

"Okay. I'll tell you everything I know." Andy took a deep breath and began. "They found Deana about two miles from her car. Somebody hit her over the head with a blunt instrument, and then they..." Andy stopped and swallowed hard. "Are you sure you want to hear this?"

Judy nodded. "We're sure. You said it was going to be the papers tomorrow, anyway."

"Right." Andy swallowed again. "Well...after she was dead, somebody stuck... uh... they stuck an arrow in her chest."

Mr. Calloway's mouth dropped open. "An arrow? But... why?"

"That's what they're trying to figure out. They think it might be some sort of gang symbol."

"They didn't...uh...rape her, did they?" Michael looked horrified.

"No. They just hit her and killed her, then stuck in that arrow."

Berto winced. "I'll ask around on the street, but I've never heard of any gang that uses arrows. That's weird...unless they're Indian or something."

"Maybe it's part of some kooky new religion." Carla looked puzzled. "Was it a real arrow?"

Andy nodded. "It was the kind you use for archery practice. You can buy them at almost any sporting goods store."

"Did they shoot it from a bow?" Mary Beth shivered slightly.

"No. They just kind of stuck it there."

"Maybe it means she was targeted." Vera's face was white. "You shoot arrows at a target, right?"

"That's what I thought." Andy nodded. "It must mean something or they wouldn't have left it there. And my uncle says they've never had any trouble with an Indian gang before."

"Who else uses arrows?" Nita looked puzzled. "Indians, and sportsmen, and...I can't think of anyone else."

Judy frowned slightly as she answered. "Cupid uses arrows."

"Cupid?" Andy raised his eyebrows. "I bet they didn't think of that. Do you mind if I tell my uncle?"

Judy shrugged. "Go ahead. I just thought of it because Michael sang that song about Cupid last month."

"How about Robin Hood?" Linda frowned slightly. "Did they steal anything from Deana?"

"Her wallet's missing. You might be onto something, Linda. But Robin Hood stole from the rich and gave it to the poor. And Deana wasn't rich."

"But they might have thought she was." Ingrid sighed enviously. "She sure spent a lot of money on clothes."

Mr. Calloway glanced at his watch. "Okay, guys. Let's break this up. It's almost midnight. Who's going to follow Ingrid home?"

"I will." Michael spoke up. "I'll do a caravan with Mary Beth, Ingrid, and Becky."

Mr. Calloway looked puzzled. "But they're in the other direction. Wouldn't it be better if you followed Judy home? She lives right next door to you."

"I have to go to Becky's house anyway." Michael explained. "We're going to take a couple of minutes, and go over her new material."

"Tonight?" Carla looked surprised.

"We have to do it tonight," Becky said to all of them. "I've got an audition at Laughs Galore tomorrow night."

"Congratulations!" Mr. Calloway looked pleased. "It's a good club, Becky. I've met the owner and he treats his people right. But we're going to miss you if you get the job."

Becky laughed. "No, you won't. If I get the spot, he only wants me for Sunday nights. And that means I can still work at Covers . . . if you want me."

"Of course I want you. You're the best comedian we've ever had, and the audience loves you."

"Let's just hope they love me at Laughs Galore." Becky looked a little nervous.

"They'll adore you, just like we do—I already told you that." Michael slipped his arm around her shoulders and gave her a little squeeze. Then he turned to the group. "She's on at ten-thirty tomorrow night."

Carla spoke up. "Do you want us to come and laugh at all your jokes?"

"That's really nice of you, but . . . well . . . it's really not necessary." Becky looked slightly embarrassed. "Michael's coming, and he's really all the audience I need."

Mr. Calloway shook his head. "Nonsense! The more laughs you get, the better your chances are. I'll be there."

"Me, too." Vera nodded.

"I'll bring Nita, and we'll invite our older sister and her husband." Berto spoke up. "That'll be four more."

Ingrid nodded. "I'll come. How about you, Mary Beth?"

"Sure, if I can ride with you. Are you in, Judy?"

"Of course," Judy nodded.

One by one, everyone promised to come to Becky's audition. It was the first time one of their group had auditioned for an outside job, and they were all prepared to give Becky lots of support.

"Okay." Mr. Calloway stood up. "Does everybody have rides arranged?"

Carla nodded. "We're all set, Mr. Calloway. Judy? Will you help me lock up the office?"

"Sure." Judy was slightly puzzled. Carla had never asked for help before. But when they got to the office, Carla turned to her with a frown on her face.

"They're going on with the contest, aren't they?"

It wasn't a question. It was a statement. Judy looked at Carla in surprise. "What makes you say that?"

"Becky. Deana's only been dead for twenty-four hours, and she's already moving in on Michael."

"I noticed that. But maybe Becky's just nervous about her audition. Michael's always helped her with her new material."

"At midnight?" Carla raised her eyebrows. "Well . . . we'll see. She hasn't said anything to you about giving her points, has she?"

"Not a word."

"If she does, I think you should warn her to be very careful. I've been thinking about what you said about Cupid, and it makes some kind of crazy sense. It's possible Deana was killed because she was going out with Michael."

"You think one of the group killed her because they were jealous that she was winning?"

Carla shrugged. "I don't think anything. I just pointed out that it's a possible connection if your Cupid theory is right. I'd warn her myself, but . . . well, you know how the other girls feel about me."

Judy nodded. It was true. The other girls really didn't like Carla, and they'd laugh in her face if she tried to warn them.

"Will you just think about it, Judy? The girls all like you, and they'd listen."

"I'll think about it," Judy promised. She smiled at Carla. "It's really nice of you to be so concerned, especially when the other girls have been so nasty to you."

Carla shrugged, and then she grinned. "Well, I have an ulterior motive. If any more girls get killed off, Mr. Calloway might decide to close Covers down. And I really like this job."

Four

When Judy pulled into the Laughs Galore parking lot, she was surprised to see Becky's yellow Toyota parked by the rear door. Michael's old white Lincoln was parked next to it, so they hadn't driven here together. Perhaps Carla was wrong, and Becky wasn't planning on trying to snare Michael, after all.

Judy found a space between Mr. Calloway's big black Cadillac and Andy's full-sized red Blazer, and squeezed her gray Volvo in. It had been a sixteenth-birthday present from her adoptive parents, the safest car that money could buy. Of course, Judy would have preferred some wheels that didn't make her feel like a well-to-do, middle-aged matron. The expensive Volvo set her apart from the rest of the high school crowd, but Judy solved the problem by telling everyone that she was using her mother's car.

Getting out of the Volvo was a slight problem since the spaces were all designed for compact cars, and she was flanked by two huge American vehicles. It took some maneuvering, but she managed to wiggle out without getting any grime on her best jeans and sweater.

The back door was locked, and Judy walked around to the front entrance on Ventura Boulevard. The bright blue Laughs Galore building had been a small theatrical playhouse for most of its existence, and it had been converted to a comedy club several years ago. Mr. Calloway had once told her that location was everything, and Judy could see why Laughs Galore was so popular. This wasn't the ritziest area of Ventura Boulevard, but it was only a short drive to the famous restaurants and shops. Judy doubted that the rent was very expensive—after all, Laughs Galore was right next door to a cut-rate muffler shop. But the building had easy access to several freeways, and it was in the right location to attract a lot of business.

"Judy! Wait up!"

Judy turned and waved as she saw Linda and Mary Beth racing across the street. Mary Beth had driven her lime green Volkswagen Bug, and she'd found a parking spot in front of a dry cleaners with the slogan, *We're sixty years old but we don't have wrinkles.*

"This is very nice." Linda gazed up at the marquee, and sighed. Laughs Galore was featuring the comedy of Hank Brothers, a comedian the girls had never heard of. "Do you think I'll ever see my name up in lights?" she asked.

Mary Beth grinned at her. "Of course you will—especially if your parents buy a sign."

"Very funny." Linda glared at Mary Beth, but then she started to laugh. "I just hope Becky's as funny as you are tonight."

When they got inside the lobby, they found Mr. Calloway waiting for them. He'd arrived early and reserved three tables for the Covers crowd. As he led them through the crowded showroom, Judy gazed around her in awe. There had to be at least a hundred people here. At five dollars a head, Laughs Galore was pulling in some decent cash, especially since every table seemed to have a round of drinks, and waitresses were hurrying back and forth, filling orders.

Judy was pleased as she joined the middle table. Everyone who worked at Covers had shown up to watch Becky's audition. Berto and Nita had brought their older sister and her husband, Vera was there with a handsome guy she said was her brother, and even Carla had shown up. Naturally, Carla was alone.

Mr. Calloway ordered a round of soft drinks, and Judy

nursed hers slowly, like everyone else. Although she had plenty of spending money, she knew none of the others could afford to pay for more than one outrageously priced Coke.

Mr. Calloway table-hopped between acts, and when he came back to their table, he looked a little nervous. "Now remember, girls . . ."

"We know, Mr. Calloway." Linda grinned at him. "We're supposed to laugh at all of Becky's jokes, whether they're funny or not."

"You got it." Mr. Calloway sat down next to Judy, and took a deep breath. "What time is it?"

Judy glanced at her watch, which was difficult to see in the dim light. She stretched her arm toward the candle on the table and finally managed to read the dial. "It's ten twenty-five. They should be doing Becky's intro any minute now."

Just then the lights came up, and Howie Thomas, the owner of the club, came out. He'd been a comedian in the fifties, and he was still pretty funny.

"We've got a little surprise for you tonight. One of my best buddies is here, and he owns a teen club in Burbank called Covers. Stan Calloway and I have been good friends for years, and he's got a real eye for upcoming talent. Stand up and take a bow, Stan."

Mr. Calloway stood up and everyone applauded. Then he sat down again, and muttered to them in an undertone. "That's show biz, girls. I only met him once, and that was ten years ago."

"Stan brought us his best stand-up comic, Miss Becky Fischer. Becky's a doll, folks, and she's a very funny little lady. Let's all give a hearty Laughs Galore welcome to . . . Becky Fischer!"

"Where's Michael?" Carla leaned close to Judy to whisper.

"I don't know. I haven't seen—there he is!" Judy pointed to the best table in the room, only inches from the stage. "He just sat down. He must have been backstage with Becky."

Before Judy could say any more, Becky came out on the stage. She was wearing a sweater three sizes too large for her, and a shirt that was a hopelessly awkward length. There were huge horn-rimmed glasses on her face, and she peered at the audience near-sightedly. Her beautiful blonde hair was covered with an ugly brown wig, and she walked flat-footed in her brown lace-up oxfords.

"Hi?" Becky's voice was small and tentative, as she looked out over the crowd. "My name is Ludmilla Grooch, but you can call me Lud."

There were titters from the crowd. And then Michael called out, "Hey, Lud. You doing anything after the show tonight?"

Becky smiled, fluffing her awful brown wig. "Sorry, but I'm busy. I've got an appointment at the car wash. They let me go through for half price, because I walk."

The audience started to laugh, but Becky kept a perfectly deadpan expression on her face. "It's great for my hair, and it gets my clothes clean, too. And sometimes I even . . . but I suppose I shouldn't tell you this."

"Tell us!" A table of guys sitting in the back of the room started calling out at her. "Come on, Lud. Tell us!"

"Well . . ." Becky gave them an eager smile. "Sometimes I even take off my clothes. And the attendants are so nice. They leave because they don't want to embarrass me."

This time, the whole audience roared. But Becky frowned. "No, honest. The guys at Benny's car wash are real gentlemen. They even cover their eyes when they run for their cars. And after they leave, I just press that little button for the hot wax. You see, I met this girl, and she said it cost her fifty dollars to get her legs waxed. So I figured . . ."

Becky didn't have time to finish her sentence before the whole audience roared again. But something about Becky's routine was beginning to bother Judy. She glanced over at Carla and winced. As usual, Carla was wearing a shapeless sweater, a baggy skirt, and her horned-rimmed glasses. Her hair wasn't as awful as Becky's wig, but it was the exact same color. And Carla was squinting at the stage, the same way Becky was squinting at the audience. Was it a coincidence? Judy hoped so. If it was intentional, Becky was doing a very spiteful imitation of Carla.

Judy looked over at Linda, her best friend at the club. Linda was frowning, too. They exchanged worried glances, but Carla was laughing, right along with the rest of the audience. Perhaps they were wrong?

Becky's routine lasted another ten minutes, and Judy winced all the way through it. When Becky left the stage to a burst of thunderous applause, Judy felt sick. Becky's routine had been excellent. She'd been funnier tonight than she'd ever been at Covers. But Ludmilla Grooch was Carla. Judy was sure of it, although Carla didn't seem to realize that. She was clapping right along with the rest of the audience.

Becky came out to take a curtain call, and the audience applauded again. Then she hopped down off the stage, ran over to Michael and kissed him. On the lips.

Judy frowned. Michael seemed surprised at the kiss, but he didn't pull away. He just hugged Becky tightly as he kissed her back, and then he pulled out a chair for her so she could sit down.

There was one more routine, and then a fifteen minute intermission. During the intermission, the Covers group met in the lobby to congratulate Becky. She'd taken off her brown wig and horned-rimmed glasses, and she was beaming as she accepted everyone's congratulations.

"That's a great routine." Mr. Calloway patted Becky on the back. "Why didn't you do it at Covers?"

Becky grinned and slipped her arm around Michael's waist again. "Because it's new. Michael's been helping me with the jokes almost every night. And I didn't want to do it at Covers because it's based on Carla."

Judy glanced over at Carla. Had she heard? Apparently not, because she was still smiling. Judy couldn't believe Becky was being so cruel. She hadn't even bothered to lower her voice.

"Becky?" Howie Thomas came rushing up, his round face flushed with exertion. "They loved you, kid. Can you work Sundays at nine?"

Becky absolutely beamed. "I'd love to, Mr. Thomas."

"What do you say we go to my office right after we close, and work out the details? It shouldn't take more than a half hour or so."

"Sounds good to me." Becky turned to Michael with a smile on her face. "I'll meet you at the apartment in a couple of hours, okay?"

"Don't you want to go out for a celebration?" Mr. Calloway asked. "I'll take you all out for pizza, my treat."

Becky shook her head. "We'll have to take a raincheck. My older sister's gone for the weekend, and I've got the keys to her apartment. Michael's heading over there right now to put a bottle of champagne on ice."

"You drove here? By yourself?" Carla looked worried.

Becky nodded. "Of course I did. And I've got a full tank of gas with a locking gas cap, so you guys don't have to worry. I'll see you all tomorrow night. And thanks for coming, okay?"

Everyone started for the door, but Becky called out to Judy. "I need to talk to you, Judy."

"Yes?" Judy hung back as the others began to leave.

"You might as well mark me down as the winner right now. After I get through with Michael tonight, he's going to be in no condition to even look at another girl!"

It was past midnight by the time Becky left Laughs Galore, but she was so happy, she wasn't a bit tired. Mr. Thomas hadn't offered her the salary she'd hoped to get, but it really didn't matter. She'd be working at two clubs instead of just one. Twice as many people would see her now, and the audience at Laughs Galore was older, which meant she might be able to make valuable contacts.

The moon was almost full, and Becky smiled as she walked across the parking lot. It was a perfect night for romance, and she had her bases covered. Her parents thought she was spending the night with a girlfriend. Since they left for work at seven in the morning, she wouldn't have to be home until tomorrow afternoon. Twelve hours with Michael should be enough to win that contest.

There was only one other car in the parking lot, and Becky was sure it belonged to Mr. Thomas. Who else would drive a silver Jaguar with a license plate that said YUX? She walked past the Jaguar, wondering when she'd be able to afford a luxury car, and headed toward her bright yellow Toyota. It was a hand-me-down from her mother which her parents had given her at the beginning of the summer when her mother had replaced it with a newer model.

Becky looked into the window to make sure that no one was hiding inside before she unlocked the door. Michael had made her promise to be extra careful since she was driving alone and she'd forgotten her cell phone. She was pleased by all the extra attention she was getting from Michael. He was an absolute hunk, and she was crazy about him. Of course, she was also crazy about Bill Emmerson, and Craig Jensen, but they were seniors at Burbank High, so she'd have plenty of time for them next year.

Becky got into the car and locked the doors behind her. She wasn't really worried. Deana had been killed miles from here, but it couldn't hurt to be careful. She started her Toyota, put it into gear, and drove out of the parking lot with a triumphant smile on her face. When she arrived at Covers and confirmed that she'd spent the night with Michael, the girls would have to declare her the winner.

She didn't hear the noise until she'd turned on Sepulveda and was heading up the pass. At first she hoped it was just the uneven road, but the bumping got worse with each passing second. A flat tire. And it was almost twelve-thirty in the morning. The houses in the pass were set back from the road, and she doubted that anyone would open their door at this hour. Why hadn't she taken the freeway, where there were call boxes every mile for emergencies?

Becky got out to look at the tire, and confirmed her worst suspicions. It was as flat as a pancake. She wasn't even sure how to use the jack, but Michael was waiting at the apartment and she'd just have to figure it out.

A horn beeped, and Becky turned to watch as a car pulled up behind her. She remembered what had happened to Deana, and she opened her car door, intending to get back in and lock all the doors. But then she recognized the car, and she gave a big sigh of relief. What luck! They could leave the car right here by the side of the road, and pick it up in the morning.

But no. The driver was carrying a tire iron. That was even better. If they changed the tire now, she wouldn't have to leave her car and risk getting a ticket. Becky walked around to the back of the Toyota and opened the trunk. The jack was in here someplace.

She had the jack in her hands, and had just turned to say thanks when she saw the moon glinting off the raised tire iron. A blunt instrument. Deana had been bludgeoned to death with a blunt instrument!

Becky panicked and adrenalin rushed through her veins. She had to get away! She started to run, but her foot slipped on a patch of loose gravel, and she fell heavily to her knees. Then she heard the tire iron whistle through the air, and before she could even raise her arms to ward off the blow, everything went black.

Five

Judy turned to Michael in alarm. "Are you okay?" she asked. He looked horrible, and that was quite a feat for someone who was as handsome as Michael.

"Yeah. I guess." Michael sighed, and shook his head. "It's awful, isn't it?"

Judy just nodded. Mr. Calloway had told them the news when they'd arrived at Covers for their Monday rehearsal. Becky was dead, bludgeoned to death just like Deana.

"Mr. Calloway wants everyone in the showroom at five o'clock sharp. Some detective from the Burbank Police Force is coming to talk to us."

"But why does he want to talk to us? The police don't think one of us killed Becky, do they?"

"Of course not." Michael draped a friendly arm around her shoulders. "Relax, Jude. Detective Davis just wants to find out more about Becky's personal life."

Judy snuggled up a little closer to Michael. Was he beginning to think of her as more than just the kid next door? But he gave her a quick, friendly squeeze and dropped his arm. Judy stepped back, and did her best to keep the disappointment from showing on her face. "I really didn't know that much about Becky. Did you?"

"I knew a little. Her favorite color was blue, she loved pizza with anchovies, and she was afraid of dogs. That's about it."

"Really?" Judy stared hard at Michael, but he seemed totally sincere. Perhaps he really hadn't been as involved with Becky as everyone had thought. "But . . . Becky told me she was going to spend the night with you last night."

Michael looked very embarrassed as he nodded. "Uh . . . yeah. That's true, Jude. Can I be honest with you?"

"Of course you can!"

"Becky arranged the whole thing. It was supposed to be a sort of celebration, with champagne and everything. She . . . uh . . . she kind of sprung it on me at the last minute. Becky was pretty young, and I usually don't . . . are you sure you want to hear this?"

Judy nodded. "You can tell me, Michael. I won't repeat it. I promise."

"I know you won't." Michael smiled at her. "I trust you, Jude. And I really need someone to talk to."

Judy nodded. She wanted to say that she'd always be here for him, but that could come later. "Tell me, Michael."

"I didn't want to do anything that might upset Becky before her audition, so I just nodded and said whatever she wanted was fine with me. I'd like to think I would have talked her into going home, that I wouldn't have taken advantage of the situation, but . . . I just don't know. Becky was an attractive girl. I'll never know what would have happened if she'd met me at the apartment."

It was clear that Michael felt terribly guilty, and Judy wanted to reassure him. "It doesn't really matter now, Michael. Becky didn't get to the apartment. And you didn't do anything wrong."

"I guess you're right. I just don't want anyone to know. Please don't mention it to Detective Davis, okay?"

"Are you afraid you'll get into trouble?"

"That's part of it, sure. But there's another reason. I don't think it's fair to ruin Becky's reputation over something that never happened. Her parents don't know, and well . . . they might be even more upset if they found out."

"You're right." Judy nodded. Michael was a totally nice guy. He cared about Becky's reputation and her parents' feelings; even though Becky was dead. "I won't say anything, Michael. And don't worry. I'll explain it to everyone else, and they won't say anything, either."

"Thanks, Jude. You're a real pal, you know?"

Judy sighed as Michael walked away. *A real pal.* Michael was still thinking of her as the little kid next door. But it was clear he liked her. And he trusted her, too. Now all she had to do was get him to see her as an attractive woman, the woman he wanted to date. Perhaps it was terribly wrong of her to even think this way, but attracting Michael would be a lot easier now that Becky was gone.

Judy frowned deeply. Of course she'd never confess her inner thoughts to anyone at the club. It had been perfectly all right to dislike Becky when she was still alive, but now that she was dead, everyone at the club seemed to regard her as some kind of saint. Judy knew that Becky hadn't been a bad person, but she had been terribly thoughtless. Becky had never stopped to consider anyone else's feelings. Basing her routine on Carla had been a very unkind thing to do, especially since Becky had come right out and admitted that Carla had been the model for her character. And even worse, Becky had taken that silly contest much too seriously. She'd wanted to win so much, she'd lied to her parents and arranged to spend the night with Michael. Becky had tried to trap Michael, and that hadn't been fair at all.

One of the spots was a little off, and Judy started to climb up the ladder to fix it. Mr. Calloway had a rule about using ladders. One person was always supposed to steady the ladder while the other person climbed. But heights didn't scare Judy, and the ladder was sturdy. She'd already climbed up five steps when she saw Linda racing toward her.

"Judy, wait!" Linda hurried to the base of the ladder, and steadied it. "Call me next time, okay? You could fall and get hurt up there."

Judy smiled down at Linda. "I'm fine. Don't worry, Linda. I do this all the time."

"Well, you shouldn't." Linda still looked worried. "You might have a terrible accident."

Judy smiled as she climbed the rest of the way up the ladder and stepped out on the catwalk. It was silly, but Linda had really been scared. Her face had been white, and her voice had been shaking when she'd called out to wait. Linda seemed to really care about what happened to her.

The rest of the girls at the club were very nice when they wanted something from Judy, like a prop they were too busy to find, or some fancy lighting to show off a new outfit. But most of the time they didn't seem to know that she existed. They were stars, and she was just a girl who worked backstage. Judy had grown used to the division between the stars and the rest of the staff. It was the sort of division that always existed in show business. Linda was a true exception. She was a star who was also a friend, and that made Judy feel very good.

Detective Davis wasn't the type to inspire confidence. He was a short, heavy-set man in his fifties with grey hair, a grey complexion, and spots on his tie. Judy's eyes widened as he emptied five packets of sugar into his coffee. With his weight problem, a little Equal or Sweet n Low would make more sense.

"I'm looking for possible connections between the two victims." Detective Davis looked around the table. "Any suggestions?"

Mr. Calloway nodded. "They both worked here. Deana was a singer and Becky did stand-up comedy."

"Right. Any more?"

"They both lived in Burbank and they were seniors at Burbank High School." Mary Beth spoke up.

Linda nodded. "They lived in the same housing development. I live there, too."

"Okay. That's good." Detective Davis made a note.

"They were both female. And they were very sex—uh . . . attractive." Andy's face turned red. "Of course, that's probably not important."

Ingrid reached over to pat Andy's arm. They all knew he'd been trying to date both girls, but he hadn't gotten anywhere with either of them. "I just thought of a connection. Deana drove a Nissan and Becky had a Toyota. They're both Japanese cars."

Detective Davis nodded. "Right. We've got that. Any more?"

Carla frowned. "Both girls were driving alone, late at night. And they both had car trouble. Maybe nothing would have happened if they'd had a passenger with them."

"Good." Detective Davis smiled at her. "Now here's a difficult question, but I have to ask. Is it possible that they were involved with any gang members?"

Everyone looked stunned for a moment and then Michael spoke up. "I'm sure they weren't, sir. Deana and Becky were here almost every night. We were all friends. We would have known if they were involved with people like that."

"Maybe. Maybe not." Detective Davis turned to Berto and Nita. "According to your earlier statements, you live only a few blocks from a borderline area. Did either of you ever see Becky or Deana in your neighborhood?"

"No, sir. They never came to our neighborhood." Nita sounded very definite.

"My sister is right," Berto nodded. "And I'm almost sure they had nothing to do with the gangs. They weren't the type, you know what I mean?"

"Okay," Detective Davis said as he nodded, then turned to Vera. "How about you? Can you think of any more connections?"

Vera started to shake her head, but then she frowned slightly. "They both drank piña coladas. I know. I'm the bartender."

"You serve alcohol here?" Detective Davis asked.

"Oh, no, sir! We serve non-alcoholic fruit drinks, and Becky and Deana always ordered piña coladas."

"I see." Detective Davis nodded. "How about when the girls weren't here? Did they drink then?"

Mr. Calloway shook his head. "If they did, it was only an occasional thing. I watch my employees very carefully, and we've never had a problem with alcohol."

"Drugs?" Detective Davis turned to look at each of them, and one by one, they shook their heads. "Wild parties? I wouldn't ask if I didn't need to know."

"Becky didn't go to wild parties." Ingrid spoke up. "We usually went out together, and she had a curfew. Her parents were very strict."

Carla nodded. "I don't think Deana did, either."

"How do you know that?" Detective Davis turned to Carla. "Were you friends?"

"Not at all. Deana didn't like me. But she loved to brag about the places she went and the exciting things she did. She would have told me to try to make me jealous."

"Is that true?" Detective Davis looked straight at Linda.

"Well . . . yes. Carla's right. Deana did like to brag."

Detective Davis made another note, and Judy winced slightly. She hoped Carla hadn't landed on the suspect list by being honest.

"All right. Are there any other connections we haven't mentioned?"

Judy sighed deeply. There was another connection, but there was no way she'd mention it. It would only embarrass Michael. Deana had dated him, and so had Becky. And both of them had been trying their best to win that stupid contest.

"How about you?" Detective Davis turned to Judy. "You just thought of something, didn't you?"

Judy nodded, and thought fast. "Yes. I did think of something. Deana's father was a lawyer. And I think Becky's Dad was a parole officer, or something like that. I was just wondering if they might have been involved with the same court case."

"Young lady, that's a winner! I'll have my men start checking the court records right away. It's possible the girls were murdered because someone had a grudge against their fathers."

Detective Davis beamed at her, and Judy smiled back. She was glad she'd thought of something to say, and Detective Davis seemed to think it might be helpful.

"Okay. That's it. You can all go back to your work now." Detective Davis stood up and tucked his notebook into his pocket. Then he turned to Mr. Calloway. "I'll give you a card with my telephone numbers. Do you have somewhere you can post it?"

"How about the office bulletin board?" Carla suggested.

"That's good." Detective Davis nodded. "If you think of anything else, just call and tell me. Even if it seems silly to you, it could be important."

Mr. Calloway stood up, too. He hesitated for a moment, and then he asked the question everyone was thinking. "Do you think the same person killed Deana and Becky?"

"Sorry. I can't give you that information. But I want all you girls to be very careful. Set up a car pool or something, and don't go anywhere alone."

"We already did that." Andy leaned forward. "Do you have any leads you can tell us about?"

"Not at the moment, but something could break any day. We'll catch him, don't worry."

Mr. Calloway walked Detective Davis to the door, but no one made a move to get up. As soon as they were out of earshot, Andy motioned them closer. "They think it's the same killer. My uncle told me. There was an arrow stuck in Becky's chest."

"That's horrible!" Linda shuddered. "I know it's crazy, but those arrows bother me almost more than the murders."

Ingrid nodded. "Me, too. If you hit somebody over the head and kill them, it's terrible. But if you stick an arrow in them afterwards, it makes the whole thing really creepy."

"But they were already dead!" Andy looked puzzled. "The arrow didn't hurt them, Ingrid."

"I know . . . but I still think it's creepy."

"I think the arrows are very important." Judy spoke up. "I'm almost sure there's a reason the killer used them."

"What reason?" Michael turned to her.

"The killer could be leaving us a sign. All we have to do is figure it out, and the murders will stop."

"If you're right, the police will figure it out," Andy declared. "They're trained to make connections like that."

Carla glanced at her watch, and stood up. "We've got a show to do in less than three hours. Mr. Calloway says he'll order in pizza if anyone's interested. That way we don't have to go home to eat."

"Great idea!" Vera grinned. "I want anchovies on mine."

Ingrid nodded. "I'll split with you, Vera. I love anchovies. Let's order anchovies, mushrooms and fresh tomatoes on ours."

Everyone began to crowd around Carla, giving her their orders. In the confusion, Michael turned to Judy. "Do you really think the arrows are a sign from the killer?"

Judy nodded. "I do. But no one else seems to be taking me seriously."

Michael slipped his arm around her shoulders and gave her a hug. "Well, I'm taking you very seriously. If you're right, you might be able to figure it out, Jude. You've always had a good head on your shoulders."

"Thanks." Judy smiled at him. "Maybe we can get together and talk about it sometime?"

"I'm not sure I want to. Just thinking about it makes me feel sick. And speaking of feeling sick, what do you want on your pizza?"

Judy hesitated. She was crazy about sausage and pepperoni, but Michael always ordered Canadian bacon and pineapple.

"Make up your mind, Jude. We don't want to be stuck with someone else's leftovers."

"Okay." Judy nodded. "I'm really in the mood for Canadian bacon and pineapple tonight."

"Great! Let's share. I'll tell Carla to order an extra large for us."

Judy watched as Michael got up to give Carla their order. She hated pineapple, but it was worth it to share a pizza with Michael. And he'd told her that she had a good head on her shoulders. If she could just get him to notice more than her head, this could turn into her lucky day.

Six

Judy dimmed the spot as Linda's last note died away. What a performance! Linda had sung one of Michael's original songs, a sad ballad about lost love and tearful goodbyes. The audience broke into loud applause as Linda left the stage, and Judy clapped, too. But when Linda reached the screen where Judy was waiting, she didn't smile as she usually did after a good performance. Instead, she reached for a tissue and dabbed at her eyes.

"What's the matter?" Judy stared at her friend. Linda looked absolutely miserable.

"I . . . I don't know." Linda wiped her eyes and blew her nose. "I feel just awful, Jude!"

Mary Beth was on next, and she arrived just in time to hear Linda's comment. "But you were fantastic, Linda. It was much better than rehearsal. How did you get that wonderful little quaver on your last note?"

"I started to cry, and it just came out that way. I kept thinking about Deana and Becky, and . . . and everything."

Judy nodded. "If I were you, I'd think about Deana and Becky every time I sang that song. Just listen to that applause."

"But, Judy!" Linda looked shocked. "That's selfish, isn't it? I'd be using their deaths to sing better."

"That's true. But something good should come out of all this tragedy. And every singer uses personal emotion to enhance a song. Becky and Deana were troupers. If they were here right now, they'd tell you to do whatever works to make your performance better."

Mary Beth nodded. "I agree with Judy. It's sort of like a tribute, you know? I heard an interview with Rhonda Bourelle, and she said she thinks about her dead sister every time she sings, *'Angel On My Shoulder.'* "

"Well . . . maybe." Linda didn't look convinced. "But Rhonda Bourelle's sister died in an auto accident. She wasn't murdered like Deana and Becky."

Judy smiled sympathetically. "That's true, but there's nothing you can do to change what happened. And you might as well use the situation to your advantage. It's not like you killed them, you know."

Michael walked up, carrying his guitar, and the three girls fell silent. They knew that Michael felt bad about Becky and Deana, and they didn't want to talk about the tragedy in front of him.

"Ready, kid?" Michael smiled at Mary Beth, but the smile didn't quite reach his eyes. "We'll do it just like we did in rehearsal. I'll go out and introduce you. Then I'll start playing, and you come on."

Mary Beth took off the kimono she was wearing over her costume, and handed it to Judy. "I'm ready. What do you think of my costume?"

"Wow!" Michael raised his eyebrows. "It's great, Mary Beth!"

Judy exchanged a quick glance with Linda. Mary Beth's costume looked very authentic for her Flamenco number. She was wearing a black satin dress with a huge red ruffle at the hemline. It was cut low in front and even lower in back, and it was so tight, Judy didn't see how Mary Beth could keep from popping the seams when she moved. Her auburn hair was piled on top of her head and held in place with two combs, and she was wearing bright red lipstick. The costume made her look much older, and very sexy.

"I left my castanets in the dressing room. Run and get them for me, will you, Judy?"

Judy sighed. Mary Beth was always asking her to fetch something she'd left behind, and she wasn't supposed to leave the light board unless it was an emergency.

"I'll go," Michael offered. "Judy's got more important things to do."

Judy turned to smile at Michael, but he wasn't looking her way. He was staring at the top of Mary Beth's costume as if he hoped it would fall down.

Linda spoke up. "I'll get the castanets. Judy has to bring up the spot, and you're due on stage in less than two minutes. You know how nervous Mr. Calloway gets when we're behind schedule."

"Right." Michael nodded. He tore his eyes away from Mary Beth's costume, and turned to Judy. "Are you going to use your strobe effect when Mary Beth goes into her finale?"

"Sure. If you want me to."

"I liked it." Mary Beth spoke up. "Mr. Calloway said it added excitement."

Judy nodded. "Okay. I think I should warn you, though. It won't be exactly the same as it was in rehearsal. It was light out then, and now it's dark. And there won't be any other light on stage. It's very tricky to dance under a strobe light."

"I can do it." Mary Beth gave a careless shrug. "We've been rehearsing this number for over two weeks, and nothing's going to throw me off."

Michael frowned. "Judy's got a point, Mary Beth. We've never tried it at night, and it might distract you. Maybe we should wait until we have a chance to rehearse it on a totally dark stage."

"No. It's my number and I want the strobe." Mary Beth glared at Judy. "The performer always gets what she wants, right, Judy?"

Judy frowned. She had the feeling that Mary Beth was talking about more than the strobe light. Could she be referring to the contest? But she didn't have time to think about that now, so she turned to Mary Beth and nodded. "Whatever you say, Mary Beth."

"Okay. That's settled." Michael patted Judy on the shoulder, and then he grinned at Mary Beth. "It's on your head, kiddo. If you fall flat on your face, don't say we didn't warn you."

Judy glanced at the clock. "Ten seconds, Michael."

"Okay, Jude, I'm ready. Bring up the spot. It's show time."

As Michael walked out on the stage, Judy found herself almost hoping for disaster. Perhaps Linda would be late with the castanets. Or maybe Mary Beth would trip when she danced under the strobe.

There was a round of applause. and Michael began his introduction. It took only a few moments, and then he was taking his place on the stool at the side of the stage. Linda raced back with the castanets just as Michael began to strum his guitar, and Mary Beth grabbed them. A second later, she was dancing out on the stage.

"She didn't even say thank you," Judy griped as she turned to Linda with a frown.

"Oh, well. That's Mary Beth." Linda shrugged, and started for the dressing room. "I hope she marries rich, and has a full staff. Lord knows she's getting plenty of practice bossing us around like servants!"

About halfway through Mary Beth's number, Carla came to stand beside her. They watched in silence for a moment, and then she turned to Judy. "Mary Beth's really good tonight."

"Yes. She is."

"I saw them rehearsing this afternoon, but she's even better now."

Judy nodded. Mary Beth really was good, and Michael's guitar accompaniment was perfect. They were going into their finale now, and Judy switched on the strobe and dimmed the rest of the stage until it was totally dark. Mary Beth didn't falter or miss a step. And the audience was clapping along with the beat as she whirled and clicked her castanets. It was very impressive and very exciting. Then Michael struck one final chord, and the dance ended.

"Listen to that!" Carla looked surprised as the audience stamped their feet and whistled. No one had ever received such a huge ovation before.

Judy got ready to dim the spot, but Mary Beth raced over to Michael and kissed him on the lips. The audience cheered again, and Carla turned to Judy with a frown. "Do you think Mary Beth's making a play for Michael?"

"I don't think so. She's already got a steady boyfriend. I heard her tell Linda they were practically engaged. That's just a stage kiss, Carla. It probably doesn't mean anything at all."

Carla didn't look convinced. "I think it's more than that. Don't forget that stupid contest."

"But Mary Beth's boyfriend is in the audience. He always comes to watch her dance."

"Not tonight. I checked off all the complimentary passes, and Mary Beth's boyfriend is very conspicuously absent."

Judy nodded. "That fits. Mary Beth said something very strange right before she went on."

"What did she say?"

"She said she always gets what she wants, and I know she wants to win that contest. I think you're right, Carla. Mary Beth is trying to pick up where Deana and Becky left off."

After the club closed, they all sat around the round table in the center of the showroom for Mr. Calloway's comments on their performance. Andy had just passed out soft drinks, and they were all mellow and relaxed.

"Nice show," said Mr. Calloway. "You all did very well tonight, considering the strain we're all under. Linda? That last song of yours was a winner. And Mary Beth . . . what can I say? You brought down the house with that Flamenco."

Mary Beth grinned. "Thank you, Mr. Calloway. Michael and I worked very hard on it. We're going to work up a hula number next. Right, Michael?"

"Sure." Michael smiled at her. "That means long rehearsals, though. I don't know that much about Hawaiian music."

Mary Beth shrugged. "Don't worry about it. I've got lots of

tapes we can listen to. Maybe we could do something really original this time. I know you could write Hawaiian music."

"Well, maybe. If I can find the time."

"That's what I wanted to talk to you about." Mary Beth looked suddenly serious. "My dad's out of town for a week, and my mother's working the late shift at the hospital. She doesn't get home until two, and she's worried about me staying in the house alone. Maybe you could take me home, and we could listen to some tapes and work out a routine. That way I won't have to be all alone."

"I don't know, Mary Beth," Michael said. "I can't stay at your house until two every night."

"But it's only for a week. Then my Dad'll be home. And think of all the work we could get done on the new routine. I wouldn't ask, but after what happened to Deana and Becky . . . I'm afraid to stay alone."

Michael seemed to be wavering, and Judy spoke up before he could agree. "How about your boyfriend? Can't he come and stay with you for part of the time?"

"I broke up with him today." Mary Beth looked very depressed as she blinked back tears. "He . . . he found another girl."

Mr. Calloway reached out to pat her shoulder. "That's too bad, kid. Think of it this way. He's a loser if he didn't appreciate you. You were the star of the show tonight. Right, gang?"

Everyone nodded, and Mary Beth gave them a trembling smile. "Thank you. I don't know what I'd do if I didn't have friends like you to help me through this . . . this awful time in my life."

Carla sighed. "Come on, Mary Beth. People break up every day. I'm sure you'll find someone else."

"Oh? How would *you* know?"

Judy stifled a gasp. Poor Carla. Mary Beth shouldn't have made a nasty comment like that. But before Judy could think of any way to smooth over the situation, Michael stood up.

"Come on, Mary Beth. I'll take you home. And I'll stay with you until your mother gets off work."

"Thank you, Michael!" Mary Beth jumped to her feet and hugged him, and Judy noticed that she didn't look the least bit upset about her boyfriend now. "I'll try to arrange something soon, I promise. Mom's asked them to change her shift, but until they do . . . do you think you could possibly . . ."

"No problem." Michael interrupted her. "I don't have anything going, anyway. Come on, let's go."

Judy watched as Mary Beth and Michael left. She was doing a slow burn. Mary Beth had clung to Michael's arm like some frail little thing, and Judy was sure that she wasn't really afraid to stay alone. She probably hadn't even asked her mother to change shifts. It was just a trick to trap Michael and win the contest.

"Okay." Mr. Calloway looked up from his schedule. "Who's driving who home? I need to know."

"Nita and I are taking Linda and Ingrid." Berto spoke up.

"Good." Mr. Calloway checked the names off his list. "Who are you taking, Andy?"

"Judy, Vera, and Carla."

"Wrong." Carla spoke up. "I drove."

Mr. Calloway frowned. "But I told you not to."

"I know. I'm sorry, Mr. Calloway, but I had an appointment with the dentist this afternoon, and he's only four blocks away. It seemed really silly to drive back home so Andy could pick me up."

"But aren't you afraid to drive home alone?" Ingrid looked shocked.

"Not anymore. I've got this." Carla reached in her purse and pulled out a portable phone. "My uncle works for L.A. Cellular and he let me borrow one of their phones. If I have car trouble, all I have to do is stay inside the car with the doors locked and use my cell phone to call for help."

Mr. Calloway looked impressed. "That's a very good idea. I'd like to talk to your uncle, Carla. Maybe we could rent cell phones for the girls until this whole thing is over."

"I've got his card." Carla opened her purse and handed him a business card. "And I'm sure my uncle would be happy to help. He works nine to five in the customer service office."

Vera began to grin. "Wow! A car phone! I've always wanted to drive down the freeway and call somebody, just like one of those big executives."

"Maybe this isn't such a good idea." Mr. Calloway looked worried. "I'm willing to rent a phone for each of you, but calls from a cell phone are expensive."

Judy frowned. Mr. Calloway had a point. Most of the girls spent a lot of time on the phone. "I think we should pay for any non-emergency calls we make. Right, girls?"

The girls looked disappointed, but they all nodded. It was only fair.

"Okay. I'll call Carla's uncle first thing in the morning, and order phones for all the girls."

"How about us?" Andy spoke up. "We might be in danger, too."

"Okay, okay, If I can write it off as a business expense, you guys get phones, too."

They all walked out to the parking lot together, and Judy found herself next to Carla. "You're really not worried about the killer, are you, Carla?" "

"No. I'm not worried." Carla looked very serious. "He couldn't possibly be after me."

"Why not? You're female, you work here, and you drive home alone."

Carla gave a bitter little laugh as she unlocked her car door and opened it. "Don't be silly, Judy. Deana and Becky were performers, and they were very pretty."

"That's true, but I still don't see what that has to do with it."

"Just look at me and think about it." Carla slid in behind the wheel. "Compare me to Deana and Becky. I don't exactly fit the victim profile, do I?"

Judy was frowning as she walked to Andy's car. What Carla had said was true. Carla wasn't a performer, and she wasn't pretty, although she would be much better looking if she took off those awful glasses and wore her hair loose instead of pulling it back in that old-fashioned bun.

"Come on, Judy. Let's go."

Andy opened the side door to his Blazer and Judy climbed in. She was still puzzled by Carla's reaction. Instead of being relieved that she didn't fit the victim profile, Carla had sounded almost sorry that the killer wouldn't find her attractive enough to murder.

Seven

Judy brought up the house lights and watched as the audience filed out of Covers. It was Saturday night and the show had gone well, probably because they were much more relaxed. There hadn't been any new murders, and everyone was beginning to think it was over . . . everyone except Mary Beth. She'd told them that she was still afraid to stay alone, and Michael had taken her home every night.

Mary Beth had left her castanets behind the screen again. Judy picked them up and threw them in the prop box. Mary Beth was a total airhead, but Michael didn't seem to mind. Since she lived next door, Judy knew what time Michael got home. And he hadn't come in before three in the morning for the past five nights in a row!

"Here—let me help you." Andy rushed up as Judy started to drag the heavy prop box to the front of the stage.

Judy stood back as Andy lifted the box and carried it easily to the locker they'd built at the side of the room. Andy enjoyed showing off his muscles for the girls, and Linda and Carla were standing at the edge of the stage, watching. "Thanks, Andy. Are you still taking that body building course?"

"Can't you tell?" Andy laughed as Judy opened the locker. "I never would have been able to lift this last year."

Judy nodded, but she didn't say what she was thinking. Andy

was trying to impress the girls, but it wasn't going to work. Everyone liked Andy. He was a good friend, but nothing more. Poor Andy had been trying to date the girls for a whole year now, and so far no one had agreed to go out with him. Michael was the real attraction, and Andy was just a boy they worked with.

Carla frowned as Andy set the box inside the locker. "You should wear a weight belt, Andy. You could hurt your back that way."

"This is nothing." Andy grinned at her. "I'm bench pressing three times more than that little box weighs."

Linda looked a little worried. "Carla's right. You should be more careful. You could hurt yourself."

"But would you care?" Andy grinned at her.

"Of course I'd care! You're the best kicker on our football team. Who's going to punt if you hurt your back?"

"At last! I've done it!" Andy let out a whoop. "Linda wants me for my body!"

All three girls started to laugh, and Andy joined in. Then Mary Beth walked by and they quickly sobered. Linda waited until she was gone and then she turned to Judy. "Is Michael taking Mary Beth home again tonight?"

"Probably. He's been spending every night with her."

Andy scowled and then he gave a deep sigh. "I called Mary Beth and offered to help out. I said I'd come over to protect her if Michael couldn't make it."

"That was very nice of you," Carla said.

"Mary Beth didn't think so. She said if Michael couldn't make it, she'd rather stay alone."

The girls exchanged glances. Mary Beth shouldn't have been so mean.

"What's the big deal with Michael, anyway?" Andy looked puzzled. "You girls are all crazy about him."

Linda did her best to explain. "Well . . . he's already in college. And everybody thinks he's going to be a big star someday. Going out with Michael is sort of a status symbol."

"And going out with me isn't," Andy finished. "Okay, Linda. I get it. But I don't like it."

The three girls stared after Andy as he walked away. Then Carla shrugged. "Poor Andy. I'd probably go out with him if he asked me. But he won't. Andy's only interested in the girls he can't have."

"Do you think that's why we're interested in Michael?" Linda raised her eyebrows. "Because we know that we can't have him?"

Carla snorted. "The only reason everybody's interested in Michael is because of that stupid contest. Mary Beth is pulling out all the stops to win, and I bet she's not one bit afraid to stay alone."

"Are you sure?" Linda didn't look convinced.

"I'm sure. What's the killer going to do? Break into a locked house just to get her? Mary Beth's taking advantage of the situation so she can spend every night with Michael."

Judy was deep in thought as they took their places at the round table. Carla was right. Mary Beth had bragged about her parents' new state-of-the-art security system. She'd told them that if anyone tried to break into the house, bells would ring, sirens would blare, and armed guards would respond in a matter of seconds. All Michael had to do was take Mary Beth home and wait until she'd turned on the security system. Then he could leave. Mary Beth would be perfectly safe inside the house. There was no real reason for him to stay until her mother got home.

"Judy? Can I see you for a minute?"

Judy turned around to see Michael beckoning to her. She got up quickly and joined him at the deserted bar. "What is it, Michael?"

"I need a favor. It's kind of embarrassing, Jude. I hope you don't think I'm a louse, but I need some help getting Mary Beth off my back."

"What do you mean?"

"We're dark tomorrow night, and I have to go to U.C.L.A. to accompany someone at a student performance. Mary Beth just told me that her mother has to work, and I really don't want to take her with me."

"Why not?" Judy was curious.

"Look, Jude. I know I can trust you not to say anything, right?"

Judy nodded. "I promise."

"Okay." Michael looked very uncomfortable. "Mary Beth is getting a little too serious about me. Part of the problem is that we're together every night, and last night . . . things got a little heavy, if you know what I mean. I'd really like to cool it off before Mary Beth gets the wrong idea."

Judy nodded. "I understand, but what can I do?"

"Will you invite Mary Beth to your house to watch a movie or something? You wouldn't have to take her home or anything. Her mother could pick her up."

Judy nodded. "I'll ask her, but I don't think she'll go for it. Andy already offered to fill in for you if you couldn't make it, and Mary Beth turned him down."

"She did?" Michael frowned slightly. "She's not really afraid to stay alone, is she?"

"I don't think so."

Michael gave a sheepish grin. "You think I've been taken?"

Judy nodded. "Yup."

"How about that! She actually set me up?"

"I think so."

"Oh, hell!" Michael laughed. "Well . . . I'll think of something. Thanks, Jude. You're a real pal."

Judy frowned slightly as Michael walked over to the round table and took his usual place next to Mary Beth. He hadn't seemed that upset when he'd found out that Mary Beth's frightened little girl act was a scam. He'd seemed almost pleased that she'd cared enough to try to trap him. Perhaps those six nights with Mary Beth had worked. Michael might be beginning to care for her. And that meant Mary Beth had a good chance to win that stupid contest!

* * *

Judy pulled up the circular driveway in the most exclusive part of Sherman Oaks, and got out of her car. The moon was almost full, and the large, two-story house looked beautiful in the dim light. The house always reminded her of the one they showed on The Brady Bunch, except her adoptive parents, the Lamperts, weren't anything like the Bradys. And Judy wasn't part of a bunch. She was their only child, and the only reason Buddy and Pamela Lampert had adopted her was to fulfill the terms of Buddy's father's will.

She had been almost ten years old when she'd arrived at the Lamperts' home, and Judy had heard plenty of rumors from Marta, their housekeeper. Grandfather Lampert had rewritten his will. If Buddy was married at the time of his death, and if he had a family, Buddy would inherit the corporation. It was Grandfather Lampert's way of insuring that his son would settle down and become a family man. Of course, Buddy hadn't settled down. He'd married Pamela Thornbull, his private secretary. She'd always wanted to be in the social register, and it was a marriage of convenience for both the bride and the groom. Of course their marriage wasn't quite enough to fulfill the terms of Grandfather Lampert's will, so Buddy and Pamela had rushed to the nearest orphanage and filed the papers to adopt Judy.

The adoption couldn't have come at a more opportune time. Six weeks after Judy had moved into the huge house in Sherman Oaks, Grandfather Lampert had died. Buddy and Pamela's careful planning had paid off in spades. Pamela had wanted to be a society wife, and now she was. Buddy had wanted control of Lampert International, and he was now the president of the company and the chief stockholder. The only one who'd lost was Judy. She'd wanted a loving mother and father, and Pamela and Buddy were much too busy with their own lives to pay attention to her. Judy had been cared for by a series of nannies and maids. She'd had all the advantages that money could buy, but she would have traded it all for a normal family life.

There was a light downstairs in Buddy's office. He was up late, probably pouring over some corporate report. Pamela's bedroom was dark. She'd taken her sleeping pill and she was already asleep. Marta had told Judy that Buddy was flying off to Tokyo in the morning for some corporate meeting. Pamela wasn't going along. She was jetting to Paris for a summer fashion showing, and then she was spending a week as a guest of some countess at a villa in the south of France.

As she let herself in, Judy tiptoed past the office door. Buddy didn't like to be disturbed when he was working. She'd done that once, when she'd wanted to tell him that she'd won a school essay contest. Buddy had stared at her with a puzzled expression on his face as she'd told him, and then he'd congratulated her very nicely. But Judy was sure he'd forgotten all about the fact that he had a daughter until she'd appeared to remind him.

Judy sighed. She didn't really play a part in Buddy's life, or Pamela's, either. She'd never even called them Father or Mother. They'd told her that they preferred to be addressed as Buddy and Pamela, and Judy had never broken that rule.

At first Judy had tried to get their attention, to prove that she could be a good daughter. She'd made the honor roll in school, she hadn't caused a speck of trouble, and she'd kept her room immaculate. But Pamela and Buddy didn't seem to care what she did—as long as she didn't bother them. Her adoptive parents were strangers who just happened to be living at the same address, and growing up had been very lonely for Judy.

Judy still remembered her thirteenth birthday. Marta had planned a party and all her friends had come, but Buddy had been in Europe on business, and Pamela had spent the entire week shopping in Paris. When Pamela had come home, she'd given Judy a lovely designer outfit, all gift wrapped for her birthday. Judy had been delighted until she'd tried it on and realized that Pamela hadn't even known her correct size.

Of course, there were a lot of advantages to living in luxury. Judy never had to cook or clean, and she always had plenty of money. Buddy and Pamela had enrolled her at Vassar, and she'd be going there right after high school. Judy wasn't delighted about Vassar. Her grades were good, and she could have gone to any college of her choice. But Pamela had patiently explained that Lampert women always went to Vassar. It was the only place for a young woman of her standing to meet other people from suitably similar backgrounds.

Judy walked down the carpeted hallway and peeked into the kitchen. It was dark. Marta was already in bed. She opened the refrigerator, took out a Diet Coke and carried it upstairs to her room. If Pamela had been awake, she would have insisted that Judy use a glass. Drinking out of a can wasn't the sort of thing a Lampert did.

As Judy flipped on the lights to her suite, she wondered what Pamela and Buddy would do if they knew she was working at Covers. Naturally, she hadn't told them. And they hadn't even noticed that she'd been gone every night until almost midnight. There were some advantages in having absentee parents. Of course, Marta knew. Judy had convinced her to sign the parental permission slip that Mr. Calloway had put in her personnel file. Marta hadn't wanted to do it, but Judy had persuaded her by promising she wouldn't mention the boyfriend that came to stay with her when Pamela and Buddy were gone.

Judy walked into her living room and used the universal remote to switch on her large color television. Then she sat down in the swivel rocker and kicked off her shoes. Even though it was past midnight, she didn't feel like sleeping in her king-sized canopied bed. She couldn't see Michael's house from her bedroom, but she could from here.

A touch of the remote control dimmed the lights. Another button opened the floor-length drapes. Michael's house was right next door, and his bedroom faced hers. She'd sat here almost every night last year, watching him study at his desk, his head bent over his books. Every once in a while, a lock of hair would fall over his eyes and he'd brush it back with an impatient gesture. That gesture had always made Judy smile. Her hair did the same thing when she sat at her desk and studied.

But Michael wasn't home tonight. His room was dark. He was with Mary Beth. Judy tried to imagine what they were doing. Michael had said things had gotten heavy. Did that mean what she thought it meant? She'd been at Mary Beth's house once, a small two-story place with an addition built over the garage that they used for a recreation room. Two white leather couches lined the room, and there was an entertainment center with a stereo and a color television. Were Michael and Mary Beth on one of the long leather couches right now, watching television? Or were they wrapped in each other's arms, sharing passionate kisses, too interested in each other to even notice what was on the tube?

Judy couldn't help but feel a little jealous. What about her? Michael had told her that she was pretty. He seemed to like having her around, but he still treated her like a kid. Judy wished she could think of some way to make Michael realize that he had the perfect girl living right next door to him. She was tired of waiting, tired of being a pal and a buddy. Judy knew she could give Michael all the love he needed, if he'd only give her a chance.

Eight

It was Sunday night and Mary Beth was alone. She'd been as nervous as a cat all night, and she was beginning to wish she hadn't decided to stay alone. She hadn't been the least bit afraid when this whole thing had started—she'd just pretended to get Michael to stay with her. But she'd pretended to be frightened for a whole week now, and she was beginning to believe her own act. She had to calm down and stop being so jumpy. She was perfectly safe. No one could get inside the house without setting off the new security system her parents had installed.

The phone rang, and Mary Beth sprinted across the room to answer it. It could be Michael, saying he was coming over early.

"Hi, honey. Are you all right?"

Mary Beth frowned in disappointment. "I'm fine, Mom. How's work?"

"Busy. There's a couple of knife wounds coming in the door right now, so I've only got a minute."

"That's okay, Mom." Mary Beth crossed her fingers for luck. "Do you think you'll be home on time?"

"I doubt it, honey. It's been a madhouse all night. We've got all twelve rooms in emergency filled, and we're stacking them up in the hallway."

"But you'll call before you leave?"

"Sure, honey. I'll try to get off by two, but it'll probably be

closer to three. Keep the security system on, and don't let anyone in, okay?"

Mary Beth nodded. "I won't, unless it's Michael. He
promised to drop by later to check on me."

"You're very lucky to have a friend like Michael. He's a nice
boy, much nicer than that awful—"

"Oh, Mom!" Mary Beth interrupted what was sure to be a
lecture about Kevin Mallory. "I know you don't like Kevin.
That's the reason I broke up with him."

"That was a wise decision, honey. He was much too old for
you. You might not realize that now, but when you look back
on it, you'll know you made the right choice."

"Yes, Mom." Mary Beth nodded obediently, even though she
knew her mother couldn't see her.

"They're paging me—I've got to go now. I love you, honey,
and I'll see you about three."

Mary Beth winced as she hung up the phone. Her mother
didn't know it, but she was still seeing Kevin. She didn't like
sneaking around and lying to her parents, but she planned to
keep on dating Kevin for as long as she could.

Her mother definitely had a point. Mary Beth realized that.
Kevin wasn't as nice as Michael, but that didn't seem to matter.
A nice boyfriend like Michael wasn't very exciting, and she was
dying for some excitement in her life.

There were lots of fun things that Michael wouldn't do. He
wouldn't take her to a real nightclub like the Palace, and he'd
never buy her a fake I.D. so that she could order drinks. He
wouldn't tear down the freeway at ninety miles an hour with the
stereo blaring, and he'd never invite her to a wild party where
everybody went skinny dipping. Michael wouldn't suggest that
she tell her parents she was staying with a girlfriend and spend
the night with him, instead. Michael was trustworthy and reliable, the type of guy she wanted to end up marrying. But Mary
Beth intended to have some wild and crazy times with Kevin
first.

There was a picture of Kevin in her wallet, and Mary Beth
took it out. She loved his dangerous eyes with thick, black

lashes that never quite opened up all the way. Kevin was older. He'd been out of high school for five years now, and he knew plenty about women. She could see it in his eyes. Kevin knew how to drive her wild when he kissed her, and he wasn't the type to stop with just kisses. She'd fantasized about spending the night at Kevin's apartment, and she'd imagined what it would be like to stretch out on his waterbed and feel satin sheets against her bare skin. Of course things hadn't gone that far . . . yet.

Mary Beth gave a little shiver of excitement. She was glad she'd hedged her bets. Michael had career plans, and he was very serious about school and work. Kevin lived every day as it came, and being with him was always fun. She didn't want Kevin for life. She just wanted to borrow him for the summer and learn how to live on the edge. Then she'd settle down and go back to school and be Michael's nice girlfriend and her parents' good daughter again.

There was nothing but news on the television, and Mary Beth clicked it off. It was ten o'clock and Michael had promised to try to make it by midnight. That meant she had another two hours to wait, and Mary Beth hated waiting. She was just thinking about finishing the lemon meringue pie her mother had baked when she heard a loud crash in the front yard. Was it a burglar? Their neighbors had been burglarized a month ago, and that was why her father had installed the expensive security system.

Even though she was almost afraid to look, Mary Beth walked to the window and peeked out through the drapes. At first she didn't see anything out of the ordinary, but then she noticed that their garbage can was tipped over on its side. As she watched, she caught a glimpse of a big black dog running down the street. It was nothing to get worried about. Tomorrow was garbage day, and the neighborhood dogs had been in the trash again.

The wind had picked up, and Mary Beth saw several sheets of newspaper fluttering down the sidewalk. Should she go out and pick up the trash before it was scattered all over the yard? Mary

Beth thought about it for a moment, and then she shook her head. She didn't want to go out alone at night. It would be stupid to leave the safety of the house when there was a killer on the loose.

There was a loud rattle, and Mary Beth jumped. What was that? The sound seemed to be coming from the bathroom, and she remembered that the vent on the roof always flapped when it was windy. Maybe she should put on the stereo. Their house always made creaking and groaning sounds when the winds were blowing. It had never really bothered her before, but she was all alone tonight, and the noises seemed almost ominous.

It was only five minutes after ten. Had the clock stopped? Mary Beth walked over to look, but the second hand was sweeping around in endless circles. Time passed so slowly when she was bored, and Mary Beth was definitely bored. Maybe she should have taken Andy up on his offer to stay with her. Andy was a nice kid, and she could have told him to leave the minute Michael arrived. She would have felt a lot safer with Andy here, but spending the evening with him would be even more boring than being here alone.

Mary Beth thought about all the invitations she'd received for tonight, and that made her feel much better. The girls were definitely worried. Judy had suggested watching a movie at her house, Linda had asked her if she wanted to come over to spend the night, Nita and Berto had offered to take her out for pizza, Vera and Ingrid had said they'd come by to keep her company, and even Carla had called to say she'd be glad to drive over to check on her. Of course, Mary Beth had turned down every one of their suggestions. She knew exactly why the girls had seemed so concerned about her. It was their strategy. They were trying to keep Michael away from her because they didn't want her to win the contest.

But their strategy wasn't going to work. Mary Beth was determined to win. Michael would be here at midnight, and that meant she'd have three hours alone with him. Tonight was almost like a final exam, and Mary Beth had spent hours preparing for it. She was going to do her new dance for Michael, and if that wouldn't convince him to make her his girlfriend, nothing would!

Mary Beth walked out of the rec room, and down the hallway to her bedroom. Her costume was hanging on a hangar behind her door, all ready for action. She'd blown two week's salary on a sexy gold satin stripper's outfit, complete with gloves and black lace lingerie. And that had been only the beginning.

Her mother left for work at five-thirty every day, and Mary Beth didn't need to be at Covers until seven. She'd spent every minute of that time rehearsing. She'd studied scenes from the movie about Gypsy Rose Lee, until she could practically do every move in her sleep. Of course she could never perform that kind of sexy striptease at Covers, but that didn't matter in the least. She was going to do the dance for Michael, and she'd never perform it for anyone else . . . except maybe Kevin. And she'd only do it for Kevin if he bribed her with a bottle of champagne.

Mary Beth grinned in anticipation. She was going to knock Michael out of his socks with her dance. There was no way he'd be able to resist her. The other girls might think they had a chance, but they didn't. They were going to lose, and she would win the contest.

It was only ten-fifteen, too early to get into her costume. Mary Beth went back into the rec room and checked the stereo to make sure she'd programmed her music correctly. Then she switched on the lamps she'd positioned around the room. They all had peach-white bulbs to give her skin a rosy glow.

Mary Beth had been busy all afternoon, preparing for Michael's private show. She'd pushed the leather couches to the side of the room, and carried the ladder up from the garage. Even though she was afraid of heights, she'd climbed up to reposition the spots on the track lighting. The area in front of the window would be her stage. She'd use the dark blue drapes for a backdrop and the wicker peacock chair would be her prop.

A car door slammed, and Mary Beth raced to the window.

Was Michael here already? But his car wasn't in the driveway where he always parked. It must have been one of the neighbors coming home late. At least she hoped it was one of the neighbors!

Mary Beth shivered. She didn't like to admit it, but she was getting scared. The wind was howling even harder now, and every time the house creaked, she felt like screaming. She had to calm down or she wouldn't be able to do her dance. It was impossible to be sexy when you were scared out of your skin.

Suddenly, the neighborhood dogs started to bark. Mary Beth raced to the window again, but she couldn't see anything. Her father had wanted to buy a dog for protection, and Mary Beth wished her mother hadn't talked him out of it. Who cared if a dog chewed the furniture and left messes on the rug? Dogs were loyal and they defended you with their lives.

Mary Beth took a deep breath and let it out again. She was perfectly safe. There was nothing to worry about. But just as she'd managed to calm down, the lights flickered and there was a terrible crash. Thunder? In L.A.? They only had a couple of thunderstorms a year in Southern California!

Rain started to fall, a little patter at first, like tiny feet scampering on the roof. Then there was another loud clap of thunder and rain gusted against the windowpane. It sounded like a snare drum, growing louder and louder as rain pelted down from the sky. The sound made Mary Beth even more frightened. She'd never liked snare drums. They reminded her of executions.

Mary Beth screamed as the lights flickered again. She tried to tell herself she was being silly, but. every horror movie she'd ever seen flashed through her mind. There was always thunder and lightning whenever anyone got killed. Perhaps that was because the scriptwriters knew that thunderstorms made people nervous.

There was another loud crack, and the lights went out. Mary Beth raced across the rec room and stumbled against the couch. She'd forgotten that she'd moved it, and now she'd have a sore toe when she danced. This night wasn't turning out at all as she'd planned.

She was just feeling around for the box of matches that sat on the end table when the lights came back on. Sometimes a storm knocked out the power for hours. She had to prepare for an emergency. She grabbed the box of matches and hurried to the gas fireplace. At least the gas wouldn't go out, thank goodness. She'd light a fire and that would be very romantic. If she couldn't do her striptease for Michael tonight, she'd have to settle for cuddling in front of the fire.

It only took a moment to light the fireplace, and Mary Beth sighed in relief as she glanced at the clock again. It was ten-thirty. An hour and a half to go. The lights could go out now and she wouldn't care. The fireplace would provide plenty of light.

But how about the security system? Was it electric? Mary Beth wished she'd paid more attention when her father had explained it to her. Did she have to reset it, or would it go back on automatically?

It paid to be safe. Heart pounding, Mary Beth hurried down the stairs to the box in the entry way. The red light was flashing and that meant the system was armed. Or did it? She could check the instruction book, but she wasn't sure where her father kept it. She'd turn it off and re-arm it. Then she'd be safe.

Mary Beth turned off the system and punched in the code to re-arm it. But the red light kept flashing. What did it mean? She thought about calling her mother to ask, but there was no reason to worry her. Michael would be here soon, and he was better than any security system.

She was about to start back up the stairs to the rec room when the telephone rang. Mary Beth rushed to the kitchen and took the call there.

"Standby Security." The caller was a lady with a thick southern accent. "Code, please?"

For a moment Mary Beth was completely stymied. What code? Then she remembered what her father had told her to say if the security company called. "Uh . . . this is Mary Beth. And our code is seven forty-seven."

"We just got two alerts from your place. Is there a problem?"

"No, nothing's wrong. I just re-set the system because our lights went off, but the red light's still flashing."

"Okay, Mary Beth." The female voice sounded much friendlier. "The storm must have knocked something out on your system. We'll ignore all alarms, and send out someone to fix it."

"You're going to send someone out now?"

"Absolutely. It's part of our total protection package. We'll have our technician at your door within the next two hours."

Mary Beth was puzzled. "But what if someone breaks in? Will the alarm still go off?"

"No. We'll have to take you off-line. But don't worry, hon. If there's any problem, just hit the panic button, and we'll send an armed guard right out."

Mary Beth was frowning as she hung up the phone. This was just great! Her Dad had bought the best alarm system money could buy, and it had gone out already. What if someone broke in and killed her before she could hit the panic button? And even if she managed to press the button, would the armed guard get here in time? Perhaps she should have agreed to go to someone's house, or have a couple of the girls come here. Was winning the contest really more important than her safety?

There was nothing to do but wait, and Mary Beth scowled as she climbed up the stairs to the rec room. Her plans were ruined. There was no way she could do the dance for Michael, not when she was expecting the technician from the security company. This night was a total disaster.

She flopped down on the couch just as the lights flickered again. She tried to look on the bright side. At least she didn't have to go back down and reset the security system. It was off-line and it would remain off-line until it was fixed.

It was a scene straight out of a thriller, and Mary Beth shivered. The thunderstorm was bad enough, but now the security system was on the blink. The lights were flickering, the rain was pounding against the window like an enraged animal trying to gain entrance, and Michael would probably be late because everybody in L.A. drove like an idiot when it rained.

Gradually, Mary Beth began to calm down as she watched

the fire. She remembered her mother talking about the mystery of an open hearth, and how she used to sit in front of the fireplace as a girl, imagining fairy tale scenes in the flames. Maybe that was possible if you had a real fire with real wood, but it didn't work with a gas fireplace. All Mary Beth could see were little blue flames that turned into red and yellow as they curled around the fake logs. Still, there was something relaxing about the hiss of the gas and the constant pattern of the flickering flames. It was cozy and it was nice. Almost like Michael.

Mary Beth kicked off her shoes and leaned back against the couch pillows. Let the wind howl. Let the rain rattle against the windowpane. She didn't care. She was toasty warm and very tired. Maybe she would close her eyes and take a quick nap. Then she'd be alert when Michael came.

She was about to doze off when the doorbell rang. Mary Beth jumped up and slid her feet into her shoes. That was fast. The technician from the security company was here already. Maybe he'd be finished before Michael arrived, and she could do her dance after all.

But what if it wasn't the technician? It could be the killer. The police seemed to think he was out there somewhere, stalking his next victim. But that was ridiculous. Killers didn't ring doorbells. They just broke right in and murdered you, didn't they?

She'd never know who it was if she didn't look. Mary Beth hurried down the stairs and tiptoed to the front door. She didn't turn on the lights. She'd seen a movie where a lady had been shot when she put her eye to the peephole, and there was no way she'd take a chance like that.

Everything was distorted through the peephole, but the motion lights her father had installed made the front step as bright as daylight. The figure at the door was standing near the bushes, face tipped away from the peephole. All Mary Beth could see was the back of someone's head.

Mary Beth clicked the intercom on. "Who is it?"

"It's me. Are you okay, Mary Beth?"

Mary Beth gave a relieved sigh. It wasn't the technician, but it wasn't the killer, either. "I'm just fine. Wait a second, and I'll open the door."

She started to punch in the code to turn off the security system, but then she remembered. It wasn't working anyway. Mary Beth pulled back the dead bolt and twisted the doorknob so the other lock popped. Then she opened the door with a smile on her face.

"What's that?" Mary Beth's eyes widened as she caught sight of the tire iron. "Did you have car-? Oh, my God!"

The tire iron was whistling through the air, straight at her head. Mary Beth ducked and reached for the panic button. She'd almost managed to press it before everything went completely and permanently black.

Nine

"It was awful, Jude." Michael slumped down in a chair. "I listened to the traffic report on the radio. It said the freeway was impossible, so I took Sepulveda. And the pass was bumper to bumper all the way. By the time I got there, the police had the whole area roped off."

Judy slipped her arm around Michael's shoulders and gave him a sympathetic hug. "I know, Michael. It must have been horrible for you."

"Not just me. Mary Beth's mother was so hysterical that they had to sedate her. She kept blaming herself for not staying home from work to take care of Mary Beth."

"That's too bad." Judy shook her head. "I guess it's natural to blame yourself when something like this happens, but she had no way of knowing."

"That's what I tried to tell her. And then I started feeling guilty because I went to that student performance and I didn't take Mary Beth along."

"But you didn't know, either!" Judy hugged Michael again. "And you told me that Mary Beth was getting too serious about you. If you'd taken her with you, she might have gotten the wrong idea."

"But she'd still be alive! And I could have handled it. I was running away from my problems, and that's never a good thing to do."

The front door opened and Andy came in, followed by Ingrid and Carla. As they took their places around the table, Andy looked solemn, Carla was frowning, and Ingrid looked just plain scared.

"Where's Linda?" Ingrid sounded nervous. "She said she'd meet us here."

Judy nodded. "She just called in. Her father's bringing her."

"Thank goodness!" Ingrid looked relieved. "For a minute there, I thought maybe . . ."

Ingrid's voice trailed off, and Judy knew immediately what she'd been thinking. "Relax, Ingrid. Linda's father is going to drive her here every day, and her mother's picking her up after every performance. Her parents are totally freaked."

"Of course they are." Carla was still frowning as she took a chair next to Judy. "Linda's a performer, and only the performers have been killed."

A little color came back to Ingrid's face as she sat down next to Michael. "I never thought of that, but it's true. Deana, and Becky, and now Mary Beth. Do you think it's a pattern?"

"Maybe," Andy said. "My uncle thinks it is. And so does Detective Davis. They ruled out the random violence theory because the killer knew where Mary Beth lived, and she opened the door for him."

"Do they think it's someone she knew?" Carla shuddered slightly.

"Not necessarily. The storm knocked out the burglar alarm at Mary Beth's house. She reported it, and the company sent out a technician. Mary Beth may have thought the killer was a repair man from the security company."

The front door opened again, and Linda walked in. She looked as if she'd been crying and her face was very pale.

"Sit down, Linda." Carla patted the chair next to her. "Mr. Calloway's in the office with Detective Davis, and he wants to talk to us when we're all together. We're just waiting for Berto and Nita. They went to pick up Vera."

Linda nodded, and sat down. "This whole thing is awful! I just talked to Mary Beth yesterday, and now she's dead. Somebody's killing us off, one by one. It's just like that movie, *Ten Little Indians!*"

"Except we're not on an island," Andy reminded her. "And the killer in *Ten Little Indians* turns out to be a member of the group."

Ingrid's mouth dropped open. "They don't think any of *us* did it, do they? I mean . . . what reason could we have for . . . for . . ."

"Relax, Ingrid. We're not on their suspect list. They think the killer is someone who came in to watch the show."

"Someone in the audience?" Linda looked shocked. "But we know almost all the regulars. They're our friends!"

Carla shook her head. "Not all of them. We get tour groups once in awhile, and Mr. Calloway advertises in the paper. I'm at the ticket window every night, and there's always some new faces in the crowd. And don't forget, it could be somebody who just came here once to see the show."

"I didn't think we were *that* bad." Judy cracked a joke, and they burst into nervous laughter. But Linda didn't laugh. She just stared at them in disapproval.

"How can you laugh about something like this? It's horrible!"

Carla nodded. "You're right. It is horrible. But we weren't laughing at what happened. We were laughing to relieve the tension."

"That's right. And Judy's joke *was* pretty funny." Andy gave Judy a thumbs up sign.

"Think about it, Linda." Michael took up the argument. "If we can't laugh, we can't carry on. And if we can't carry on, we might as well give up and die right along with Deana, and Becky, and Mary Beth."

Linda looked thoughtful, and then she nodded. "I guess that's true. I'm sorry, Judy. What you said was funny. I just didn't think it was right to laugh."

Just then the front door opened again, and Berto, Vera and Nita came in. They looked solemn, too. This was almost like a funeral, and Judy hated funerals. Her mother had died when Judy was only two, and she hadn't gone to that one. But she still remembered her father's funeral. She'd been in fourth grade, and the neighbors had driven her to the church. Everyone had cried, especially her father's partner. Mr. Roberts had been so upset, he'd broken down in the middle of the service. Of course, that had been an act. Rob Roberts had claimed the business was bankrupt, but Judy had never believed it. She was sure he had cheated her out of her inheritance, and that was why Judy had ended up as a charity case at the church orphanage.

"You're right on time." Carla motioned to three empty chairs. "I'll go tell Mr. Calloway we're all here."

A few moments later, Mr. Calloway came out of the office with Detective Davis. They took chairs, and the detective flipped open his notebook.

"You've all heard what happened to Mary Beth Roberts?" Everyone nodded, and Detective Davis looked straight at Judy. "That theory of yours was good, young lady. But Mary Beth's parents haven't had any dealings with the courts. I'm afraid we're back to square one."

Judy sighed. "I'm sorry I even brought it up. Your men probably wasted a lot of time."

"Don't worry about that. Let's go over our list of connections and see what still applies. Then we'll all try to think of some new connections between the three girls."

Everyone nodded again, and Detective Davis glanced down at his notebook. "All three girls worked at Covers, they were approximately the same age, and they went to the same high school. Is that right?"

"No." Michael spoke up. "Mary Beth went to a private school. The other two girls went to Burbank High."

Detective Davis scribbled in his notebook. "Okay. Any other connections?"

"It's not exactly a connection." Andy frowned slightly. "But Carla mentioned a distinction that might be important. All three girls were performers."

Detective Davis looked pleased. "That's a good point, son. How many female performers work here?"

"There were four." Linda sounded very nervous. "I'm the . . . the only regular left."

Detective Davis turned to Mr. Calloway with a frown, and Mr. Calloway nodded. "That's right. We usually have eight acts a night. Five are regulars, and the other three are hired for limited, one-week engagements."

"I see. Did you hire any new talent to replace the acts you lost?"

Mr. Calloway turned to Carla, and she flipped open her stenographer's notebook. "We've got seven new acts signed up. There's a magician from North Hollywood, a three-piece band from Northridge, a singer from Canyon Country, two stand-up comics, one from Studio City and the other from Van Nuys, a honkytonk piano player from Simi Valley, and a juggling team from Burbank. We signed them for one week only, and we'll pick the replacements after we see how they do. They're all guys."

"Is that intentional?"

"Not really." Mr. Calloway sighed deeply. "We hold open auditions every Tuesday, but we haven't had a girl show up since Deana was killed."

Judy nodded. She wasn't really surprised. Underage performers needed parental permission, and after what had happened, most parents wouldn't let their daughters work at Covers.

"Excuse me." Berto spoke up. "Could you tell us, please . . . was there another arrow?"

Detective Davis nodded. "Yes. It was in the same location as the other two."

Judy looked around the table, and she saw several people shudder. They all knew the location Detective Davis was talking about. The arrow had been thrust into Mary Beth's chest.

Berto's face turned pale and he swallowed hard. "Nita and I asked around on the street, but nobody has heard of a gang using arrows. I think they would have told us. The gangs like to brag about things like that."

"I don't think it's a gang thing, either." Vera spoke up. "Mary Beth never would have opened the door to anyone wearing colors. She was so scared, she had Michael stay with her every night until her mother came home from work."

Detective Davis frowned slightly as he turned to Michael. "But you didn't arrive last night until almost one o'clock."

"That's right. I played at a student performance at U.C.L.A. I was supposed to be at Mary Beth's house by midnight, but I got stuck in traffic. There was an accident in the pass. It was stop and go all the way."

"Which pass?"

"Sepulveda."

Detective Davis scribbled a note, and Judy knew he'd check out Michael's story. "Where was the student performance?"

"At Royce Hall. I accompanied Sarah Belmont on the guitar. She sang original compositions."

"What time was the performance over?" Detective Davis made another note as he spoke.

"At ten. Then I went with Sarah and her boyfriend for a cup of coffee. We left the Westwood Hamburger Hamlet at eleven-thirty."

"Why didn't you take the freeway?"

"It was raining pretty hard, and the radio said the freeway was all backed up. I thought the pass would be less crowded."

Judy began to feel a little nervous as Detective Davis quizzed Michael. This was beginning to sound like an interrogation. Surely he didn't suspect Michael of playing a part in Mary Beth's death?!

"It took you an hour and a half to get to Studio City?" Detective Davis looked grim.

"Yes, sir. It was bumper to bumper because of the accident."

"What kind of car was involved in the accident?"

"I don't know." Michael sat up a little straighter. "Everything was cleared away by the time I got to the scene."

"If it was cleared away, how did you know there'd been an accident?"

"There was glass in the road at the corner of Valley Vista and Sepulveda. I don't actually *know* that there was an accident. But the traffic was so bad, I assumed there was. And I thought that was where it had happened."

Judy couldn't take anymore. Detective Davis was questioning Michael like he was some sort of criminal. "If you're finished interrogating Michael, could I please ask a question?"

"I'm not interrogating him, young lady. I'm just getting the facts. Now, what did you want to know?"

"I was just thinking about the arrow. What if it isn't a gang symbol?"

Detective Davis raised his eyebrows. "What do you mean?"

"Couldn't this be the work of a serial killer? I read a book about serial killers once, and it said they're just like painters because they like to sign their work. It's their . . . I've forgotten the phrase, but—"

"Calling card." Andy spoke up. "There was one serial killer called Sneakers, and he always took the shoes off his victims. And there was another one they called Bad Bart. He left a subway token in his victim's mouth. But I don't think this guy's a serial killer. They generally murder in cycles, and there's no cycle here."

Detective Davis frowned. "No cycle?"

"No, sir. In a textbook scenario, the killings are less frequent at the beginning. The first two may be a month or more apart. And then the murders start escalating. The third murder could be in three weeks. And then two, and then one. A serial killer's like a train, picking up speed. He goes faster and faster until he's out of control, and then he jumps the rails."

"What happens then?" Ingrid looked frightened, but she was also fascinated.

"When a serial killer loses control, there's generally a mass murder. But I told you before, I don't think this is the work of an ordinary serial killer."

"Why not?" Michael spoke up.

"Mary Beth was personally targeted. The killer may have wanted to kill her earlier, but he didn't. He waited until she was alone."

Detective Davis frowned. "You don't think that the victims of a serial killer are personally targeted?"

"Not usually. They may look like they are, at first. The victims may have common physical characteristics, like blonde hair, or glasses, or anything like that. Or they may all share a certain profession. Jack the Ripper was a serial killer who murdered only prostitutes. But the traditional serial killer isn't after anyone specific person. If his internal clock says it's time to kill, and the victim he's chosen isn't available, he finds another victim that fits his profile."

Detective Davis was clearly impressed. He stared at Andy and blinked. "How do you know all this?"

"I read a lot, sir. And I'd like to go into police work someday."

Judy glanced at Andy in surprise. Why didn't he tell Detective Davis that his uncle was on the police force? But Andy just smiled and didn't say anything at all about his uncle.

"All right." Detective Davis nodded, then closed his notebook and stood up. "Call me if you think of anything important. And let's all hope we don't have to meet like this again."

Judy waited until Mr. Calloway had left to walk Detective Davis to his car. Then she turned to Andy. "Why didn't you tell him about your uncle?"

"My uncle said not to mention him. He's going to keep an eye on things unofficially. And he said that so far, Detective Davis is doing a good job."

"Oh, sure." Linda gave a worried sigh. "He hasn't caught the killer yet, has he?"

Andy shrugged. "These things take time. Don't worry, Linda. They'll catch him eventually."

"It better be sooner than that!" Linda looked very frightened. "I'm the only one left!"

It was clear that Andy wanted to say something. He looked around at the group, and then he seemed to make up his mind. "Can I trust you all to keep your mouths shut? My uncle could get in big trouble if you tell anyone else, okay?"

"Sure." Michael nodded. "You can trust us, Andy."

"You're perfectly safe, Linda. They've got an undercover tail on you."

"They do?" Linda looked slightly relieved. "Can I tell my parents?"

"No. The killer might be someone you know. And if somebody slips up and mentions it to the wrong person, the killer might hear about it. They want to catch him if he follows you."

Linda nodded. "Thanks for telling me, Andy. I won't worry quite so much now. But I still won't go anywhere alone."

"That's fine. It might tip off the killer if you *weren't* scared, so keep right on acting nervous, okay?"

"That's easy."

Linda gave a little laugh, and everyone else joined in. Then Mr. Calloway walked back in, and they all fell silent. He looked very serious.

"Okay, guys. I've thought it over, and I think it would be safer if I closed down Covers until this whole thing is over."

"But . . . why?" Judy was puzzled.

"Three of my performers have been murdered, that's why!" Mr. Calloway looked very upset. "We can't keep giving performances every night. It's dangerous."

Carla sighed. "I think you're making a mistake, Mr. Calloway. It's like locking the barn door after the horse has been stolen. The killer already knows where we live. And he killed Mary Beth at home, on a night when we were dark. Closing down Covers won't change that."

"Carla's right." Andy spoke up. "Nobody's been murdered around here. If the killer's smart, he knows that Covers is staked out every night. This might be the only place where we're all safe."

"I don't know." Mr. Calloway looked very uneasy. "Is it fair to take a chance with your lives? I feel responsible for all of you."

Linda's face was still white, but she sat up a little straighter. "I'm the next target, Mr. Calloway. And I don't think you should close down. We'll just have to be extra careful, that's all."

That was the cue for everyone to chime in. No one wanted Covers to close down. Even though Mr. Calloway officially owned the club, they all thought of it as theirs. It was Michael and Linda's chance to be seen on stage, and Judy's opportunity to work as a stage manager. Covers was a place where Carla could practice running a small business, and where Andy could try out new recipes in the kitchen. Vera wanted to own a bar someday, and Covers was her opportunity to practice mixing drinks, ordering supplies, and getting along with the customers. Even Berto and Ingrid and Nita had a stake in the club. While it was true that they only took orders and served food, it was a lot more fun than working in an ordinary restaurant.

"Okay, okay." Mr. Calloway held up his hands for silence. "I'll keep Covers open for now. But nobody goes anywhere without a cell phone, and we'll continue the car pool."

There were smiles all around, and Mr. Calloway turned to Andy. "You're the expert here, Andy. Is there anything else we should be doing?"

"We could check the guest register and try to find someone who might have a motive. I realize that Detective Davis went over it already, but we know our audience. Maybe we can spot something he missed."

"Okay." Mr. Calloway motioned to Carla to get the register. Then he turned back to the rest of them. "Are you absolutely sure you want to give a performance tonight?"

One by one, they nodded. And then Michael spoke up. "The show goes on, Mr. Calloway. And it's going to be the best show we've ever done. There's no way some sicko is going to close us down!"

Judy gave a satisfied sigh as she brought up the lights for the last act. Michael was closing the show tonight, singing his newest song. She'd tried a new effect tonight, soft lighting on his guitar, and a full spot on his face. Since she'd used only two lights and the rest of the stage was dark, Michael seemed to be floating in space, anchored only by the stool and his guitar.

Judy sighed again. Michael was so handsome. His dark wavy hair gleamed under the lights and his deep, intense eyes glowed with inner strength. His skin was tanned almost bronze by the summer sun and he was dressed in a soft blue shirt and jeans. He had a strong body, and she could see the muscles in his arms ripple as he strummed his guitar. His fingers were sensitive, stroking and caressing the strings, and she knew they would be just as sensitive touching her neck, her face, and her . . .

Time to dim the spot. Judy reached out and brought the spot down gradually as Michael reached the last note of the song. There was a burst of thunderous applause and then a rhythmic clapping. An encore. They always wanted an encore. It would be another love song. Michael liked to end the evening on a mellow note.

Judy brought up the spot again, and the audience was instantly silent. Michael smiled at them, and Judy heard their collective gasp. Michael's smile was like sunlight on a cloudy day, glorious and radiant, stretching across his face. It turned the brooding, moody musician into a bright, shining beacon of radiant talent.

The song started, one of Judy's favorites, and another original. She wasn't sure, since Michael had never mentioned it, but she thought perhaps he'd written it for her. It was about his childhood friend, a girl who'd climbed trees and played ball with him. The last verse was wonderful, all about how he'd suddenly realized that she had grown up. And how foolish he'd been not to realize that she was right there all the while.

Judy slipped into her favorite daydream, the one she had every time Michael sang this song. Any moment now, Michael would turn to see her in the shadows. And he'd smile at her and tell everyone he'd written the song just for her.

"It's a full house tonight."

A soft voice brought Judy out of her reverie, and she turned to see Carla standing beside her. Even though she was upset at

having her daydream interrupted, Judy managed a nod. Carla
didn't know that she had intruded on her favorite fantasy.

"Did he write that song for Mary Beth?"

"No. He wrote it last summer. As far as I know, he didn't
write any songs for Mary Beth."

"Really?" Carla raised her eyebrows. "I thought Michael
wrote a song for every girl he dated."

Carla looked amused, and Judy couldn't help but laugh.
"You're right. He usually does. But Michael didn't really date
Mary Beth. They never went anywhere together."

"Mary Beth thought they were dating. She told me all those
nights at her house counted as dates. She even bragged that she
was going to win the contest."

"Mary Beth bragged to you, too?" Linda joined them just in
time to hear Carla's comment.

"She bragged to everyone. But she was just using Michael.
She wasn't really serious about him as a person."

"How do you know that?" Judy was puzzled.

"The first batch of cell phone bills came in this morning.
Mary Beth called her old boyfriend's apartment every night. I
checked it out."

"But her parents made her break up with him!" Linda ex-
claimed. "At least that's what she told us."

Carla nodded. "Maybe that's why she called him from her
cell phone. She didn't want his number to show up on her parents' phone bill."

"Pretty sneaky." Judy was clearly impressed. "Mary Beth
was playing both sides of the fence. She wanted Michael so
she'd win the contest, but she also wanted to hang onto her old
boyfriend. What a bitch!"

Both Carla and Linda looked shocked, and Judy quickly tried
to explain. "Maybe I shouldn't have said that, but it's true. She
was a bitch. And you'd say it, too, if she were still alive . . .
wouldn't you?"

"I would," Carla agreed. "She was taking advantage of
Michael."

Linda looked hesitant at first, but then she nodded. "You're right. She *was* a louse. Michael's a very nice guy, and I hope everybody's going to forget all about this contest thing."

"But they're not." Carla gave an unhappy sigh. "The next contestant's already in line and chomping at the bit."

"Who?" Judy and Linda both spoke at once as they turned to Carla in surprise.

"Ingrid. Michael's taking her home tonight."

"But why is he taking Ingrid home?" Linda looked puzzled. "She was supposed to ride with Andy. It's on the schedule."

Carla nodded. "I know, but she switched. Her church is sponsoring a twenty-four hour bowling tournament to raise funds for their new building. She's scheduled to bowl at midnight, and I heard her ask Michael to be a member of her team."

Judy asked the important question. "So it's not really a date?"

"I don't know what you'd call it, but Michael asked her out for breakfast after they're through bowling."

Judy frowned. "Oh-oh. That counts, according to the rules the girls made up."

"Oh, my God!" Linda gave a little shiver. "Isn't she afraid to go out with Michael? I mean . . . I probably shouldn't bring this up, but every girl he's dated this month has been murdered!"

Carla nodded. "I know. I asked her about that, and she says she's not worried. Deana, and Becky and Mary Beth were all performers. Ingrid just works here."

Judy looked very serious. "That's true . . . but what if it's all a coincidence, and the killer goes after a waitress next?"

Ten

"Miss Judy? You must promise to be very careful tonight. The moon is almost full, okay?"

"Sure, Marta." Judy turned to grin at their housekeeper. Marta was very superstitious. "Do you want me to wear a necklace of garlic to keep the vampires away?"

The heavy-set Mexican housekeeper frowned as she shook her head. "Please, Miss Judy. This is no time for joke. Three girls at your work, they lose their life."

"It's all right, Marta. I'm very careful. And you're not really worried about me, anyway. You're just afraid I'll turn up dead, and then my parents'll find out about that permission slip you signed so I could work at Covers."

"That is not true, Miss Judy!" Marta shook her head again. "I am very fearful of your safety. You go out into the night alone, and that is not good. Something very bad could happen to you."

"Relax, Marta. Nobody's going to hurt me. I'm perfectly safe."

Judy was slightly puzzled as she went out the door. Marta had looked genuinely concerned. Perhaps Marta really did care about her. Stranger things were possible, but Judy knew better than to count on that.

Things were beginning to settle into a routine at Covers. The new acts were working out, and Michael was back to smiling once in a while. Of course, most of those smiles were for Ingrid. Michael and Ingrid were getting to be an item. He'd taken her home every night, and he'd gone to her house for dinner twice. Judy had seen him leave in the afternoons, too, and she knew he was spending the time with Ingrid.

Judy backed her Volvo out of the garage and drove down the circular driveway. Michael had been so busy with Ingrid he'd barely noticed her lately, except for a couple of pats on the head, and one brief hug after she'd come up with the perfect way to light his new number. Judy wished she could think of some way to get Michael's full attention, but that was probably impossible. She'd just have to be patient, and wait. His romance with Ingrid was bound to play out, sooner or later. When Michael broke up with Ingrid, he'd turn to her. He always did. And she'd be right there to give him all the understanding and comfort she could.

What did Michael see in Ingrid, anyway? Judy shrugged as she stopped at a red light. Girls always ended up looking like their mothers, and Judy had met Ingrid's mother. She was a plump Swedish housewife who stayed at home every day, cooking and cleaning for her family. Was that what Michael wanted? A girlfriend who would devote her life to making him meatballs and Swedish pancakes with lingonberry sauce, waiting on him hand and foot? Or was he just passing the time with Ingrid until his true love came along?

As Judy turned on Olive Street, she saw the sign for Don's Place in the distance. Michael had introduced her to Don's Place last summer and Judy loved their burgers. The inside was decorated like a rustic bar, where all the regulars gathered to share tap beer and listen to fifties hits on the jukebox, but the patio in the back was pure hamburger heaven.

Don's patio reminded Judy of the pictures she'd seen of lakeside cabins in the Midwest. There were oilcloth covered tables with molded plastic chairs. Each table had a tupperware container of peppers that were so hot, it was a miracle they didn't melt the plastic. Don's wasn't fancy and it didn't have any pretensions, unlike most of the other hamburger places in the Burbank area. There was no menu, unless you counted the hand-painted sign that was tacked up on the wall advertising the three entrees produced by Don's kitchen.

Don's served burgers, B.L.T.s, and grilled cheese sandwiches, accompanied by either French fries or onion rings. The food was delivered in red plastic baskets lined with wax paper. It was all finger food and that meant no silverware was needed. There were no appetizers or desserts or fancy salads. Don's wasn't that kind of place. But once you bit into a crunchy onion ring or tasted a perfectly grilled burger dripping with mayo, catsup and mustard, you were addicted.

Michael had discovered that the studio people ate at Don's, and he called it the great equalizer. Executives shared picnic tables with grips, and it was the perfect place for would-be talent to rub shoulders with studio heads. Michael had taken Judy there almost every week last summer, and they'd munched double cheeseburgers with plenty of luminaries in the biz. Everyone who ate at Don's had the same problem. The burgers were so juicy and so thick, they were impossible to eat neatly. Judy had passed handfuls of paper napkins to producers and electricians alike, and she'd seen several big-name stars drip pickle juice on their clothes. She'd been looking forward to going to Don's this summer, but Michael had been much too busy to take her there. Judy just hoped he wasn't taking Ingrid to what she thought of as their special place.

Don's was just up the block, and Judy pulled over to the side of the street. Her eyes scanned the cars in the parking lot and she breathed a sigh of relief. Michael's car wasn't there. But just as she was about to leave, she saw a familiar car approaching. It was Michael's old white Lincoln, and he was pulling into the driveway.

As the car pulled in, Judy saw that Ingrid was with him. She was sitting so close, there was room for another two people in the front seat. Her blonde head was nestled against Michael's chest and his arm was around her shoulders.

Michael parked the Lincoln and opened his door. He got out

first, and then he helped Ingrid out of the car. They were laughing as they walked toward the patio, and Judy wished that she could join them.

But her better sense prevailed, and Judy pulled out into traffic again. While Michael might be glad to see her, Ingrid surely wouldn't. Judy couldn't really blame her. She knew that if their positions were reversed, she wouldn't be happy about sharing Michael with another girl. Suddenly, a funny picture popped into her mind, and Judy laughed out loud. She hoped that Ingrid would try a jalepeño pepper and turn as red as a tomato. But that was just wishful thinking. Ingrid would never eat anything that had been sitting on the table for hours in a tupperware container. And she probably wouldn't drip catsup and pickle juice on her clothes, either.

Judy knocked on the dressing room door. "Twenty minutes, Linda. You're doing the opening act, tonight."

"I know," Linda answered, sounding very upset. "Can you come in for a minute?"

Judy opened the door and stepped in. But she frowned when she saw Linda's pale face. There were dark smudges under her eyes that her makeup couldn't hide, and her hands were shaking as she brushed her hair. "What's the matter, Linda? Are you sick?"

"No. I'm just scared."

Judy nodded. Linda always had the jitters when she sang a new song. "Don't worry, Linda. That new song of yours is fantastic. They're going to love it."

"That's not it. I know the new song is good, but I'm scared to death to go on stage. What if *he's* out there?"

"Who? He who?" Judy grinned. "And I'm not trying to yodel."

Linda didn't smile back. "You know who. The killer."

"But they're staking out this place. Andy says they have at least three undercover cops in the audience every night."

"I know." Linda still looked worried. "But how about when

I'm not performing? He could kill me right here in the dressing room."

"Listen to me, Linda. You've got round-the-clock protection. Andy told you that. Nothing's going to happen to you. I know it isn't."

"That's easy for you to say. You don't have to get out on that stage every night. He's stalking me, Judy—I can feel it! He's just waiting for my round-the-clock cop to look the other way, and then he's going to kill me just like he killed Deana, and Becky, and Mary Beth!"

"Relax, Linda." Judy patted her hand. But Linda was so upset, she started sobbing. There was no way she could go on in this condition, and that meant Judy had to calm her down in a big hurry. "You know that victim profile that Detective Davis and Andy are always talking about? You don't fit."

"What the hell do you mean? I'm female and I perform at Covers. I fit that victim profile perfectly!"

Judy raised her eyebrows. Linda really *was* upset. Judy had never heard her swear before. "But you don't. You haven't dated Michael. Only the girls who dated Michael have been killed."

"But I *did* go out with Michael." Linda frowned deeply. "I just haven't told anybody about it!"

"You tried to win the contest?"

Judy was so shocked, she stepped back a pace. But Linda shook her head.

"That was before anybody ever mentioned that stupid contest. Michael took me to the movies three months ago. Remember when everybody was talking about Robert DeNiro's new picture? Well, Michael's girlfriend couldn't go, so he asked me if I wanted to see it."

Judy nodded. "So Michael took you to the movies?"

"Well . . . not exactly. He met me there. And I already had my own ticket. We sat together, though. And he did buy me popcorn."

"That's not exactly a date." Judy smiled at her friend. "I don't think you have anything to worry about."

"But the killer might think it was a date, even if it wasn't. And he might kill me!"

Judy's smile turned to a frown. Linda's terror was real. She had to think of some way to reassure her, or they wouldn't have a first act tonight.

"Look, Linda. There's something else you're forgetting. Deana, and Becky, and Mary Beth were all killed when they were alone. Just pretend you're my Siamese twin tonight. Stick close to me, and you'll be safe. Make sure you're never alone, not even for a second. Can you do that?"

Linda nodded. "Sure, if you don't mind. But I hate to bother you every time I have to go to the ladies' room."

"No problem." Judy smiled at her friend. "We'll stop by the office and ask Carla to help us. If I'm busy, she can keep you company."

Linda looked relieved. "I really appreciate this, Judy. You're a good friend. Now tell me the truth. Which outfit do you think I should wear for the first set?"

"Wear this." Judy chose a soft pink dress and tossed it to Linda. "I'll light you with a rose filter and that'll bring a little color back to your face. And hurry up, Linda. We start in ten minutes."

Judy dimmed the spot at the end of Linda's first number, but she didn't go to black as she usually did. Linda was still too nervous to handle a totally dark stage.

"Ready?" She turned to Michael who was waiting behind the screen. Linda was doing a duet with him for the second number.

Michael frowned. "I'm ready. But aren't you going to black like we did in rehearsal?"

"Not tonight." Judy didn't bother to explain. It would only embarrass Linda.

Michael nodded, and then he walked out to join Linda on stage. Judy brought the lights back up again, and they started to sing their duet. It was then that Judy realized she wasn't alone behind the screen. Ingrid was standing there watching.

Ingrid's eyes were shining as she gazed at Michael. She seemed totally oblivious to everything but him. Her hands were clasped tightly together and there was an expression of utter adoration on her face.

"Aren't you supposed to be waiting tables?" Judy frowned deeply.

"I'm on break. Don't worry, Judy. I'll stand right here in one place and I won't get in your way."

Judy nodded, and turned her back as she flicked another switch on the light box. She didn't feel very friendly toward Ingrid right now. Michael had taken her to Don's.

"Judy?" Ingrid touched her on the arm. "Isn't he the most handsome man you've ever seen?"

Judy couldn't bite back her sharp retort. "What do you care? You're just going out with him to win the contest."

"No, I'm not!" Ingrid looked crushed. "It started out that way. I won't deny it. But . . . something happened, Judy. I think I'm in love with Michael."

"But is Michael in love with you?" Judy's voice was hard. Ingrid was a fool if she thought that a couple of dates meant that Michael loved her.

A smile spread across Ingrid's pretty face. "I think he loves me, Judy. I'm almost sure of it. And I think he's going to tell me he loves me on Sunday night."

"What makes you think that?" Judy's heart was beating so hard, it was difficult to speak.

"He said he had a surprise for me. And he promised to give it to me on Sunday night. And he asked my mother if she knew my ring size."

Judy swallowed hard. Had things really gotten that serious between Michael and Ingrid this fast? "So you're expecting an engagement ring?"

"Oh, no. Nothing like that. But maybe . . ." Ingrid's cheeks turned so pink that Judy could see her blush in the dim light seeping back from the stage.

"Maybe what?"

"I thought that maybe he might be having his fraternity ring made smaller for me." Ingrid sighed deeply. "At least, that's what I hope."

Judy nodded. She didn't trust herself to comment. If Michael was giving Ingrid his frat ring, he was making a terrible mistake.

"He told me he was crazy about me. And he really likes my family. You don't think it's wrong for me to get my hopes up, do you, Judy?"

Judy sighed. "I don't know, Ingrid. Michael doesn't confide in me anymore. Maybe you're right . . . and maybe you're not. Is he taking you somewhere romantic on Sunday night?"

"He said he made ten o'clock reservations at Monty's Steakhouse."

Judy frowned slightly. Monty's Steakhouse was at the top of a high-rise building in Westwood, and it definitely had a romantic view. It was also terribly expensive. If Michael was taking Ingrid there for dinner, it must be a very special occasion. "Ten o'clock's pretty late for dinner. Why aren't you going earlier?"

"I'm working at the church carnival until eight. Michael's picking me up there. We're dropping by his frat house so he can introduce me to some of his college friends, and then we're going to Monty's."

Judy tried to keep the expression of dismay off her face. Michael had never introduced her to any of his frat brothers. And he'd certainly never taken her to Monty's! "Are you all going in a group?"

"No." Ingrid shook her head. "He said it would be just the two of us. Vera says she thinks he's going to propose, and I'm so excited, I can hardly stand it!"

Judy raised her eyebrows. "You told Vera about it?"

"Well . . . yes. But she promised not to tell anyone else. I just had to tell someone!"

Judy nodded. "Did you tell anyone else?"

"I mentioned it to Andy. He thinks Michael's going to give me a friendship ring. But Berto's sure it's going to be his frat ring."

"So the only ones you didn't tell are Carla, Mr. Calloway, and Linda?" Judy's frown deepened.

"I told Linda. She said she really didn't know Michael well enough to even guess. And I mentioned it to Carla, but she didn't have an opinion, either. Of course, that's not surprising. Carla doesn't know very much about men."

"You told *everyone?*" Judy could hardly believe that Ingrid had asked everyone what they thought Michael's intentions were.

"No. I didn't tell Mr. Calloway. They're very close, and I thought he might mention it to Michael. And I wouldn't want Michael to think I had a big mouth."

"Of course not." If Judy hadn't been so upset, she might have laughed out loud. She was about to tell Ingrid that she really ought to learn to keep a secret, when the audience burst into applause. The duet was over. Judy clamped her mouth shut, and turned back to the light box to dim the lights.

"I've got to get back to work." As Ingrid moved past, she reached out to touch Judy's arm. "I'll call and tell you what happened first thing Monday morning. Isn't it fantastic, Judy? I'm so excited, I could just die!"

"Fantastic." Judy tried to smile as Ingrid gave a little wave and went back out on the floor. Was Michael really going to propose to Ingrid? The girl who couldn't keep her mouth shut, and blabbed her hopes and dreams all over Covers? It seemed impossible, but Judy knew that Michael had always beena sucker for a pretty face. And Ingrid was certainly pretty.

The applause died down, and Judy brought up the spot again. Linda and Michael were doing another song together, something Michael had written two nights ago. They'd rehearsed it only once, and Judy had been so busy writing down lighting cues, she hadn't paid any attention to the song.

Then Michael started to sing, and Judy drew in her breath sharply. The song was about a girl with hair the color of sunshine. A sweet and gentle girl he loved. Linda's voice answered Michael's on the chorus, proclaiming the girl's love for him and promising how she'd always hold him close in her heart.

Judy turned to look at Ingrid. She stood transfixed, a tray of food in her hands, gazing up at Michael with a look of loving devotion. It was enough to make Judy weep.

It seemed to take forever, but at last the song was over. Judy's hand was shaking as she dimmed the lights and the audience burst into wild applause. The audience always loved sappy love songs, and this was the sappiest love song that Judy had ever heard.

But it wouldn't be sappy if Michael had written it for me, Judy's conscience reminded her. *Then it would be beautiful.*

Judy felt her eyes sting, and she blinked back bitter tears. The way things were going, Michael would never write a love song for her. And she wanted him to, desperately. When she went to bed every night, she gazed out at his window and prayed he'd notice her. She knew she could make Michael happy, if he'd only give her a chance.

She waited until the applause had died down, and then she brought up the lights again. Linda had one more number, a country western song she'd written about a girl who mourned for her lost lover. The melancholy refrain threatened to bring more tears to Judy's eyes, and she busied herself at the light board, playing with the spot until she had just the right amount of color in Linda's face. When she turned around, Michael was standing behind her, grinning.

"I guess they liked our last number." Michael looked pleased. "Linda's good, isn't she?"

Judy nodded. "She's very good. And you made her sound even better."

"Thanks, Jude." Michael reached out to give her a hug. "Are you still president of my nonexistent fan club?"

"Always. And it won't be nonexistent for long."

Michael grinned. "May your words be as true as bread and milk."

"What?!"

Michael's grin grew wider. "Search me. I don't know what it means, either. It's an old Swedish proverb that Ingrid taught me."

Judy took a deep breath. The time was right. Michael had

mentioned Ingrid and this was the perfect opportunity to tell him that she'd blabbed their plans to everyone at Covers. Would Michael be so upset by Ingrid's indiscretion, he'd break up with her?

"Michael? Can I talk to you about something very serious?"

"Of course, Jude."

Michael smiled, and the warmth in his eyes made Judy almost lose the ability to speak.

"It's . . . uh . . . it's about Ingrid."

"I saw her back here when I was singing. She's an inspiration, Judy. I've never met anyone so absolutely good. Do you know that she spends four hours every Saturday morning working as a volunteer with retarded kids?"

"Uh . . . no . . . I didn't know that."

"She's so loving." The expression in Michael's eyes was tender. "You wouldn't believe how patient she is. She's going to make a fantastic wife and mother one day."

"Yes. I'm sure she will." Judy felt suddenly cold, and she gave a small shiver. Michael really *was* crazy about Ingrid.

"So what is it?"

"What's what?" Judy was puzzled.

"You said you wanted to talk to me about Ingrid."

Judy took a deep breath. It was definitely time to change tactics. Michael had been totally taken in by Ingrid, and nothing she could say would change that. There was an old Roman custom of killing the messenger who'd brought bad news, and Judy knew it would be foolish to give Michael any bad news about Ingrid. Michael wouldn't kill her, but their friendship might die a painful death if she badmouthed the girl he thought he loved.

Michael was looking down at her, and Judy gave him a blinding smile, a smile she hoped looked totally genuine. "Oh, yes. About Ingrid. I was just going to tell you what a wonderful girl I think she is."

Eleven

It was almost seven o'clock on Sunday night, and Ingrid was so happy she was practically walking on air. She'd spent all afternoon working at the bake sale booth, and they'd sold everything except one loaf of Swedish rye.

"Ingrid, dear. Why don't you take this to your boyfriend's family." The plump Mrs. Bergstrom put the last loaf of bread in a white paper bag and handed it to Ingrid.

"Thank you, Mrs. Bergstrom." Ingrid smiled at her mother's friend. "How much did we sell?"

Mrs. Bergstrom glanced down at her tally sheet, and a satisfied smile spread across her broad face. "Twenty dozen rolls, sixty loaves of bread, and fifty dozen cookies. We made over five hundred dollars."

"That's wonderful!" Ingrid beamed at her.

"Putting the cookies in small packages was a good idea, Ingrid. We sold almost all of them at four for a dollar. And our original price was two-fifty a dozen. We made fifty cents extra on those smaller bags."

Mr. Bergstrom, a tall, middle-aged man with snow white hair, came up in time to hear his wife's comment. "My, my! It sounds like we have a retailing genius here. Maybe we should ask Ingrid to come down to the store and give us advice."

"I don't think you need my advice, Mr. Bergstrom." Ingrid smiled at him. The Bergstroms owned a very successful Scandinavian import store and they contributed generously to all of the church charities. "You can't sell lingonberries at four for a dollar."

There was a twinkle in Mr. Bergstrom's eyes as he nodded. "Yah, that's true."

"But, maybe you could . . ." Ingrid blushed and shook her head. "No. It was just a silly idea."

"What is it, Ingrid?" Mr. Bergstrom looked interested.

"Well . . . I was just thinking about those gift packs they sell at Christmas. I'm sure you've seen them. A bottle of wine, a couple of wine glasses, and some chocolates all wrapped up in a pretty basket."

Mrs. Bergstrom nodded. "Yah, I've seen them. They charge a fortune for something you could make yourself."

"That's just it." Ingrid blushed even harder as she told them her idea. "Why don't you make up Scandinavian gift packs? You could put a package of Swedish pancake mix and a jar of lingonberries in one of those wonderful griddles you sell. If you wrapped it all up and put a bow on top, people might buy the package for a gift."

Mrs. Bergstrom turned to her husband, and he began to beam. "I think that's a very good ideal We could do all kinds of packages, a little of this and a little of that, all wrapped up for Christmas."

"Everything except *lutefisk*." Ingrid shuddered as she thought of *lutefisk*. It was a slab of cod that had been dried as stiff as a board. The *lutefisk* was soaked in lye to reconstitute it, and then boiled or baked at Christmas. It was a Norwegian tradition, and Ingrid's father was Norwegian. He insisted that Ingrid's Swedish mother make *lutefisk* every Christmas.

Lutefisk smelled horrible when it was cooked, and it tasted the way it smelled. It had the texture of fish jello, and she'd begged her mother not to serve it when they had company at Christmas. But Ingrid's father, normally a reasonable and taciturn man, refused to sit down for Christmas dinner unless *lutefisk* was served as the first course.

"Don't worry, Ingrid. We won't include *lutefisk*." Mrs. Bergstrom laughed. "I always say that God gave us *lutefisk* to remind us of His suffering. And then He gave us *lefse* to prove that He had mercy."

"Ilka!" Mr. Bergstrom gently chastised his wife, but his eyes were twinkling.

Ingrid burst into laughter. "It's true. My father says *lutefisk* proves that God has a wicked sense of humor. And we must show our appreciation for His joke by pretending to enjoy it!"

The Bergstroms burst into laughter that lasted for a full minute. Finally, Mr. Bergstrom took out a handkerchief and wiped his eyes. "Oh, yah. That's good, Ingrid. My compliments to your father. I agree with his sentiments exactly. No *lutefisk*. But we will definitely have *lefse*. Ilka makes wonderful *lefse* from her grandmother's recipe."

"I know. My mother buys it every year." Ingrid nodded. Mrs. Bergstrom sold homemade *lefte* right before Christmas, and the thin pancake-like bread made of potato was one of Ingrid's favorite Norwegian foods. She liked to spread it with butter, sprinkle it with sugar, and fold it up like a tortilla. "Are you really going to make gift baskets, Mr. Bergstrom?"

Mr. Bergstrom nodded. "Yah. Your idea is good, Ingrid. And if you have any other ideas, I hope you'll tell me about them. I think you have a pretty good head for business."

"She certainly does!" Mrs. Bergstrom patted Ingrid on the shoulder. "Does your young man know how talented you are?"

Ingrid felt a blush rise to her cheeks. Her mother must have told Mrs. Bergstrom about Michael. "Oh, I'm not the talented one. Michael is."

"She's modest, too." Mr. Bergstrom smiled at his wife. "Come along, Ilka. Now that you've sold everything in the booth, we have time to see the rest of the carnival."

Ingrid lingered at the booth after the Bergstroms had left. There was really nothing to do now that they'd sold everything. The fair still had another hour to run, and Michael wouldn't be here to pick her up until eight. Perhaps she should walk around and see how the other booths and the rides were doing. She'd posted a notice at Covers advertising the carnival, and several people had promised to try to come. Since she'd been working at the bakery booth all day, she hadn't had time to see if any of her friends from Covers were here.

As she walked through the crowded fair grounds the church had rented, Ingrid could see that business was booming. Children and their parents were lined up to buy tickets on the merry-go-round, and everyone seemed to be carrying food.

"Hi, Ingrid!"

Ingrid turned and smiled as she recognized Lars Olafsen. Lars was tall and handsome, and she'd dated him a couple of times last year. Tonight he was taking tickets at the Tunnel of Love. "Hello, Lars. How are you?" she called out to him.

"Just fine. You want to take a spin for free? I could go with you."

"No thanks, Lars." Ingrid began to smile. Lars had probably been riding with girls on the Tunnel of Love all night. "I'm just getting ready to leave."

Lars looked disappointed, but he quickly recovered. "How about going to a movie with me next Sunday night? We haven't gone out in a long time."

"Sorry, Lars. I'm dating someone right now."

"That figures." Lars shrugged. "I knew I should have snapped you up when I had the chance. Is it serious?"

Ingrid hesitated, and then she nodded. "Yes, Lars. It's serious."

"Well . . . congratulations. My loss is his gain. Is it anybody I know?"

"I don't think so. He's a freshman at U.C.L.A."

Lars raised his eyebrows. "And that's where you're going next year, isn't it?"

"Yes." Ingrid smiled happily. She'd taken extra classes for the past three years, and she'd be graduating early, at Christmas. Six months from now she'd be on campus with Michael, and she could hardly wait. "How did you know my plans?"

"Your mother told my mother. And she also said you had a

new boyfriend, but she didn't tell me it was that serious. Are you going to marry him?"

"I don't know." Ingrid could feel herself blushing. Had her mother told the whole congregation about Michael?

"You still have my number, don't you?"

"Why . . . yes. I'm sure I do."

Lars grinned. "Invite me to the wedding. And if there isn't a wedding, call me right away."

"But . . . why?" Ingrid was confused.

"So I can console you. I'm really good at that."

Ingrid burst into laughter. "I'm sure you are. Bye, Lars."

"Bye, Ingrid. I'm going to be holding my breath, waiting to hear from you."

"Don't hold it too long. You'll turn blue." Ingrid was still laughing as she walked away. Lars was very popular and she knew he wouldn't be holding his breath waiting for her. But it made her feel wonderful to know that he thought she was attractive. If Michael hadn't come into her life, she might have considered going out with Lars again. He was handsome, and funny, and very sexy. But Lars Olafsen didn't make her knees turn weak when he kissed her, and he didn't turn her insides to soft, quivering jelly. Michael was the only one who did that.

Ingrid glanced at her watch. It was only seven-fifteen, and she still had forty-five minutes to wait before Michael would arrive. Since she'd been working in the booth all day, she really should check her makeup and hair to make sure she looked all right. But the ladies' room was near the entrance, and she didn't feel like walking all the way there and back. Perhaps there was something closer? Any reflective surface would do.

The House of Mirrors was right across the midway and Ingrid headed directly toward the brightly colored building. She could comb her hair and freshen her makeup inside, and she wouldn't have to walk all the way to the ladies' room.

As Ingrid approached, she noticed that there was no line. Mr. Swensen was manning the ticket booth, and he greeted Ingrid with a wave.

"We are closed, Ingrid. I am leaving now to meet my wife so there are no more tickets. I let you go for free."

"Thanks, Mr. Swensen." Ingrid smiled at the elderly man. "I just want to comb my hair."

Mr. Swensen laughed. "That might be pretty hard to do in there. Those mirrors are all wavy, you know?"

"I know." Ingrid laughed, too. "Is it scary inside?"

"No. I was in first to check it out. I wanted to tell the little ones to stay away if it would frighten them. But inside is not scary. The little children had fun in there all day. There are many mirrors, and it is a puzzle when you try to get out."

"Oh, great!" Ingrid frowned slightly. "If I go inside, will I be stuck in there all night?"

"There is a trick, Ingrid, and I will tell it to you. I also told it to the children. You must look at the floor. The building is old and you can see where many people walked in a path. Follow the path and you will come right out on the other side."

"Thanks, Mr. Swensen." Ingrid took one step toward the entrance, and then she turned back. "But you said you're leaving. Don't you have to turn out the lights?"

"The lights will stay on until everyone has gone home. Then the carnival people will pack up the rides, and turn them off."

Ingrid smiled as she climbed the steps to the entrance. She'd never been in a House of Mirrors before, and she had the whole place to herself. She'd always wanted to make funny faces at herself in a carnival mirror and now she could do it in privacy. It was too bad Michael wasn't here. He might enjoy walking through with her. They could have stopped in front of the mirrors and laughed at their reflections.

Today the temperature had been in the high eighties, and it hadn't cooled off that much when darkness had begun to fall. The inside of the House of Mirrors was air-conditioned, and Ingrid welcomed the blast of refrigerated air as she stepped through the doorway. Perhaps she should just stay here until it was time to meet Michael. It was the coolest place in the whole fairgrounds.

Ingrid began to smile as she stepped in a little further and caught sight of her reflection in one of the convex mirrors. Since the mirror curved out, it made her look as short and fat as a dumpling. She whirled around once, and watched her skirt billow out to expose legs that looked as solid and sturdy as tree trunks. Thank goodness she didn't really look like this! If she did, she'd be even heavier than her plump, jolly mother. She'd have to watch her weight, once she was married. Her mother had taught her to cook and appreciate good food, and that could be a definite liability.

Would Michael still love her if she got fat? Ingrid frowned and her chubby reflection frowned back at her. Of course he would, but his eyes might stray to the girls with slimmer figures. She owed it to Michael to keep in shape and continue to look attractive.

Ingrid moved deeper and deeper into the building, fascinated by the hundreds of different reflections. The mirrors were positioned to form a maze, and her distorted face greeted her from every angle. There were lights overhead that added to the illusion, high-lighting different parts of her body.

Ingrid gasped as she turned a corner and entered a room with green lights. This section was like being trapped in a giant terrarium, with pale green creatures, wearing her distorted face, staring at her from every corner. It wasn't exactly scary, but it did make her nervous. If she let her mind float free, she could imagine a giant hand lifting the cover to reach down and pluck her out, like a harmful bug on a prize fern. Ingrid hurried through the maze, following the path on the floor, and drew a deep sigh of relief when she came to the next corridor.

The next section had blinking red and yellow lights overhead, and Ingrid felt as if she were in the middle of the fires of Hell. To add to the illusion, it was warmer here. Her face looked suddenly demonic, and Ingrid almost screamed as she bumped straight into one of the mirrors and confronted her own giant reflection. It was fifteen feet high and terribly distorted, and it seemed to be accusing her of some horrible crime.

"Oh!" Ingrid stepped back and bumped into the mirror behind her. She turned to the left and bumped into another mirror. To her dismay, she found another mirror on her right. And still another, directly in front of her. Where was the path? Was she lost?

It was difficult to see the worn places on the floor. They didn't seem to show up under the red lights. Ingrid almost panicked until she realized that if she shut her eyes, the reflections would no longer confuse her. She banged into a couple of mirrors on the way, but at last she made it into the next corridor.

The last section was the worst of all, and Ingrid gasped as she stepped in. Strobe lights were flashing everywhere, and it was very disorienting. She stumbled as she lost her balance, and she reached out to steady herself on the surface of the nearest mirror. This section reminded her of the strobe effect that Judy had used, the night Mary Beth had performed her last dance.

Mary Beth's last dance. The dreadful finality of those words made Ingrid shudder. Mary Beth would never dance again. Mary Beth was dead, killed by a maniac she'd let into her own house. Why hadn't Mary Beth been more careful? She'd known that there was a killer on the loose.

But perhaps she'd known her killer, known him so well she'd trusted him completely. Perhaps she'd even been in love with him. Detective Davis had cleared Mary Beth's former boyfriend. He had come up with an air-tight alibi. Who else had Mary Beth trusted?

Michael. The answer popped into Ingrid's mind, and she winced. The thought was about as welcome as an invasion of ants at a picnic. Mary Beth trusted Michael completely, and she'd been expecting him that night. If Michael had knocked on Mary Beth's door, she would certainly have opened it. But of course, he hadn't. Michael hadn't arrived at Mary Beth's house until after she'd been killed. She'd heard him describe the scene of the accident that had slowed him down, and Detective Davis had confirmed that there had been a collision.

But he could have heard about it on the radio. Ingrid tried to push that thought from her mind, but she knew that several radio stations gave periodic updates on the freeways and surface streets. And Michael always listened to the traffic report. He'd done it the other night when they'd been stuck in traffic.

But she loved Michael. She had to trust him. That's what love was all about. Michael was sweet and kind and good. He'd never brutally murder a girl, and then thrust an arrow into her chest.

The arrow. Ingrid wrapped her arms around herself. The House of Mirrors was suddenly very cold. She could feel an icy draft seeping down, and she shivered violently. No one had been able to explain the significance of the arrows. The police were stymied because they hadn't been able to find any gang that used arrows for a symbol. But Michael had told her, just last night, that he'd been an archery coach at summer camp. And Judy had suggested that they might have something to do with Cupid

No. The whole idea was preposterous. Ingrid squared her shoulders and frowned at her flashing reflection. The strobe lights must be affecting her mind. There was no way Michael had killed the girls he'd been dating. What earthly reason could he have for doing a horrible thing like that?

Because he found out that they were dating him to win the contest. Ingrid gasped out loud as the thought occurred to her. Someone could have told Michael about the contest. Perhaps one of the girls had even admitted it. And Michael had been so incensed, he'd . . .

Ingrid did her best to push down that horrible suspicion. Michael might have been angry if he'd found out about the contest, but he certainly wouldn't have been mad enough to kill Deana, and Becky, and Mary Beth. Michael had agonized over their deaths. She knew that. He had told her. But had he really felt the agony he'd told her about? Or was he glad that the girls who'd led him on were dead?

There was no way she could think rationally with the strobe lights flashing. Her head was pounding and she had to get out. Ingrid hurried down what she thought was the path, but somehow her feet took a wrong turn, and she ended up in another circle of mirrors that seemed to provide no escape.

Relax. Don't panic. Just look for the path on the floor. Ingrid forced herself to take a deep breath and let it out again. Calm. She had to stay calm. These flashing strobe lights were driving her crazy!

And then she saw it. Another reflection in the mirror right behind her. A dark figure with one hand raised high in the air.

"Who's there?" Ingrid's voice was frantic as she cried out. But the other reflection didn't answer. Instead, the hand came down with deadly force, trying to crash into the top of her golden blonde head.

Ingrid moved sharply to the right. She banged into a mirror, but she managed to deflect the blow. She had to run. She had to hide! But she couldn't see the path on the floor with all these flashing lights.

"No! Stop!" Her voice was a terrified wail as the reflection raised its hand again. The killer was here in the House of Mirrors! She had to run away before the killer could strike again! But she couldn't tell which image was real and which belonged to the distorting mirrors. How could she run if she didn't know whether she'd bump straight into the killer?!

The killer's arm raised higher and higher, and Ingrid stared at the jerky motion reflected thousands of times in the myriad of shiny surfaces. The killer's multiple arms came down with blinding speed. And everything went completely black.

Twelve

Mr. Calloway sighed deeply as he looked around the table. There were only eight of his original crew left; Judy, Michael, Carla, Vera, Linda, Berto, Nita and Andy.

"Look, gang. There's no way we can ignore the truth any longer. Somebody's after the girls who work at Covers. And it's not just the talent."

"I'm afraid that's right," Detective Davis agreed. "You girls are all in danger."

Mr. Calloway looked determined as he faced them. "That's why I'm shutting down Covers. There's no way I'll put you girls in any more jeopardy."

"But it won't do any good!" Carla spoke up. "We're already in jeopardy, Mr. Calloway. Closing Covers won't help at all."

Linda nodded. "It's true, Mr. Calloway. Nothing you can do will make us any safer. We're all targets already."

"That's what I've been telling him." Detective Davis spoke up again. "If Covers stays open, we can screen the audience. There's a chance the killer may show up here, and then we've got him."

Vera looked very pale, and Judy noticed that she was blinking back tears. "I don't understand how you're going to spot him. He's not going to be dumb enough to sit in the front row with his bag of arrows."

"Quiver." Michael slipped an arm around her shoulders, as he gently corrected her, but Vera couldn't hold back her tears any longer. She began to cry.

"Don't cry, Vera." Judy reached out to pat her shoulder. "We'll take turns sticking close to you. You'll be fine as long as you're never alone."

But Vera only cried harder. "My parents want me to quit working here. They say it's too dangerous. They told me I have to quit tonight."

"Hey, Vera, I understand." Mr. Calloway patted her shoulder. "To tell the truth, I'm surprised you're the only one quitting."

Detective Davis nodded. "I understand your parents' concern, young lady. Would it help if I called them?"

"I don't think so." Vera frowned through her tears. "They said they'd made up their minds."

"All right, then. As far as the rest of you are concerned, I want you to assure your parents that we've got the situation under control. At least two of my men will be here every night to protect you. Just remember two things: never go anywhere alone, and call me if you see anything suspicious. Anything at all."

Everyone nodded, and Mr. Calloway walked Detective Davis to the door. When he came back, Vera looked up at him miserably.

"Are you mad at me?"

"Of course I'm not mad." Mr. Calloway patted her shoulder. "But I don't think you should quit. I think you should take a vacation."

"A vacation?"

"Right. I want you to take some time off at half pay. I'll keep your job open, and you can come back the minute Detective Davis catches the killer."

"But, Mr. Calloway . . . how will you get along without a bartender?"

Mr. Calloway turned to Nita. "Do you think you could take over the bar while Vera's gone?"

"Sure." Nita nodded. "I help Vera now when it's really busy, and I'm sure I could do it. I even know a guy you could hire to take over my job waiting on tables."

"It's all settled then. You're on vacation after tonight."

"But you'll lose money!" Vera looked worried. "I can't just stay home and collect half pay. That isn't fair."

"Sure it is. Especially if you do some work for me at home. Carla's been after me to hire somebody to mail out the flyers she designed. You can do that."

"Is that true?" Vera turned to Carla. "Do you really need somebody to stuff envelopes?"

Carla nodded. "It's true. I can't keep up with everything. Mr. Calloway promised I could have some help, but he hasn't gotten around to hiring anyone yet."

"But stuffing envelopes won't take me that long." Vera still looked concerned. "Is there anything else I could do?"

Judy nodded. "How about the cassettes, Mr. Calloway? We could move the equipment over to Vera's house and she could dupe the tapes for us."

"What tapes?" Linda was curious.

Mr. Calloway grinned at Judy. "Our show tapes. I've been taping every performance, and Judy thinks we should pick out the best numbers, and put them on a tape to sell at intermission. People are always asking if they can buy a cassette."

"That's a great idea, Jude!"

Michael looked pleased, and Judy felt a warm glow of pleasure as he smiled at her. But it wasn't fair to take credit for something that hadn't been her idea. "Carla's the one who told me that people were asking for cassettes. It was really her idea."

"Good for you, Carla!" Michael turned to smile at her. "Maybe you should go into the record business."

Carla blushed beet red. "Thanks, but ideas are a dime a dozen. Judy's the one who arranged to rent the equipment for high-speed duping. I just figured out the profit margin."

"Are we all going to be on the tape?" Linda was curious.

"You are." Carla grinned at her. "And Michael, of course. And there's one song of Deana's that we want on the tape, but we have to ask her parents."

Mr. Calloway nodded. "It's a go, Carla. I already asked them, and they gave us permission."

"Then the profits will be divided the way we originally planned?" Carla opened her notebook, and waited for Mr. Calloway's answer.

"Yes. We're splitting everything five ways. One share apiece for Michael, Linda, and Deana's parents. One for Covers, and one to be divided up among the rest of the regular staff."

"We get some of the profits?" Berto looked surprised.

"Absolutely," Carla nodded. "It's only fair."

Vera frowned slightly. "But we don't perform. Why should we share in the profits?"

"Because your jobs are important." Carla looked very serious. "We couldn't put on a show without you."

Nita stared at Carla in surprise, and then she grinned. "Thanks, Carla. It's nice to know we're appreciated. But how about you? This place couldn't run without you, either."

"But all I really do is take tickets. Anybody could do that."

"And keep the books." Judy pointed out. "You also do all the filing."

"And order the supplies," Andy chimed in.

"You do a lot, Carla, and we couldn't get along without you." Michael stood up and looked around the table. "I say Carla gets a share. Who agrees with me?"

Judy raised her hand. And so did Linda, and Andy, and Nita, and Berto, and Vera.

Mr. Calloway nodded. "Okay, Carla. You're in, by popular demand. Now is there anything else, or can we get to work? We've got time for a short rehearsal, if we hurry."

That was the cue for everyone to get up and start their preparations. Berto and Andy went to the kitchen, Carla headed for the office, Vera took Nita to the bar to fill her in on some last minute details, and Linda hurried off to photocopy some music. Judy was about to head backstage to check some props when Michael took her arm.

"Jude? I need to talk to you for a minute."

"Sure, Michael. What's up?" Judy smiled at him. She wished

he'd tell her that he'd finally realized that he loved her, but that was too much to hope for. Michael probably just wanted to change the order of his songs, or something like that.

"Who's taking you home tonight?"

Judy felt her heart beat faster. Was Michael asking her for a date? "I'm riding with Andy. Why?"

"Who else is he taking?"

"Just Carla. Linda's mother is picking her up."

Michael nodded. "Okay. I'm supposed to take Vera home, but I'll switch with Andy. Do you have anything to do after you get home?"

Judy shook her head. "Not really."

"Good. I need some time alone with you. We'll drop Carla off first, and then . . . do you think we could sit out by your pool and talk? It's important."

"Of course." Judy couldn't keep the smile from spreading across her face. At last! She wasn't sure what Michael wanted to talk about, but that didn't really matter. He'd said he wanted to be alone with her, and that was definitely a step in the right direction!

Carla was working in the office, when Judy stuck her head in the door. "Carla? Michael switched with Andy and he's taking us home tonight. We'll drop you off first, okay?"

"That's fine," Carla said as she looked up at Judy in surprise. "Wait a second—are you going out with Michael?"

Judy's heart pounded so hard, she was afraid Carla could hear it. But she managed to keep the smile off her face as she shook her head. "Of course not. You know how upset Michael is about Ingrid. He just needs someone to talk to."

"Are you sure?"

"I'm positive. We're just going out on my patio to talk. That doesn't even come close to a date."

"Okay." Carla nodded. "Just don't get too involved. You know what happens to the girls who date Michael."

Judy sighed. "They die. I know that, Carla. But you don't have to worry about me. I'm just Michael's buddy."

"Just keep it that way," Carla insisted. "Then you'll be safe."

"But who am I safe from? Do you think you know who the killer is?"

"Come in, Judy. And shut the door. We have to talk."

Judy's heart was pounding as she came in and shut the door behind her. "Tell me, Carla! What do you know?"

"Not as much as I'd like to." Carla motioned to a chair. "But I've noticed a few things around here. I haven't said anything, because I'm not sure, but . . . I think the killer is someone we know."

Judy's mouth dropped open. "You're kidding! Who?"

"That's just it. I don't know. But I'm sure the killer works at Covers."

"How do you know that?"

Carla sighed deeply. "Deana's car ran out of gas, but she stopped to fill it up before she came to Covers. I checked with the gas station she always uses, and they remember that she filled her tank that night. That means the gas was siphoned out right here in the parking lot."

"But anyone could have done that."

"That's true. But it could have been one of us, right?"

Judy nodded. "I guess so."

"Then Becky got killed, right after she left Laughs Galore. Who knew she was going to audition there?"

"We all did. She told us."

"Exactly." Carla nodded again. "And we all came to the show. Every single one of us knew she was staying late to talk to the owner. And we all had the opportunity to come back and punch a hole in her tire so it would leak air."

Judy's eyes widened. Carla had thought this all out. "And we all knew where Mary Beth lived. And we also knew that she'd be home alone. Is that what you're saying?"

"That's right. And Ingrid told us she'd be working at the church carnival. She even posted a notice on the bulletin board, giving us directions and asking us to come. We knew exactly when Michael was meeting her. She told us that, too."

"But . . . that's all circumstantial." Judy began to frown.

"That's true. I know it wouldn't stand up in court, but it all makes me think the killer is one of us."

"How about the arrows? What do they mean?"

"You told us, Judy. And I think you were right. They're Cupid's arrows, and the killer is warning us to stay away from Michael."

Judy shivered. "Do you really think one of us is killing the girls who date Michael?"

"I do. That's why I tried to warn you, Judy."

"Wow!" Judy drew a deep breath and let it out again. "Are you going to tell Detective Davis about this?"

"No. I don't have a shred of proof, and he'd just laugh at me. I wasn't going to tell you either, but . . . I wanted to warn you to be careful. I'm almost certain the killer is someone who works at Covers."

Judy nodded slowly. "It does make sense. Do you think the killer's one of the contestants?"

"Not necessarily. The killer could be anyone."

"But you think it's a girl?"

Carla shrugged. "Maybe. But maybe not. It could be Andy."

"Andy?!" Judy gasped.

"Sure." Carla nodded. "He's been trying to go out with almost all the girls at Covers. You know that. But the girls won't go out with him because they'd rather date Michael. Isn't that a motive for murder?"

"I guess so. How about Mr. Calloway? Do you suspect him?"

Carla nodded. "He's on my list. Don't forget that he's counting on Michael to bring in a crowd every night. And he's always complaining that Michael spends too much time dating, and not enough time writing music."

"But . . . Carla! You don't really think that Mr. Calloway would . . ."

"Not really." Carla gave a deep sigh. "But stranger things have happened. And then there's Berto."

"You suspect Berto?"

"Sure. Nita could have told him about the contest. They're very close. Maybe he's helping her win."

Judy shook her head. "That's pretty far-fetched. In fact, it's totally bizarre. It's almost as ridiculous as suspecting Michael!"

"But I *do* suspect Michael," Carla stated solemnly. "If he found out about the contest, he might be so angry, he's killing off the girls who try to win."

"But . . . why?"

"Maybe he thinks they're treating him like an object, and they're only dating him on a stupid bet. He could be taking revenge. And revenge is a motive for murder."

Judy shook her head, and shivered slightly. "Wait a minute, Carla. If I accept your crazy theory, *you* could be the killer!"

"Absolutely." Carla gave an approving nod. "I've got a motive. Everybody knows I don't date, and everyone suspects that I want to. I could be so insanely jealous of the other girls that I'm killing them off one by one."

"Are you?"

Carla began to smile. "What do you think?"

"I think you're cracking up. But I don't think you're a killer."

"Good." Carla's smile grew bigger. "But I hope I've proved my point. You really can't trust anyone."

"I . . . I guess not."

"I know you're not dating Michael, but the killer might think you are. And any one of us could be the killer. You will be careful, won't you, Judy?"

Judy nodded. "I'll be careful, Carla. I promise."

Thirteen

Judy unlocked the front door and led the way down the hallway. They'd dropped Carla off at home, and then they'd come straight here. When she got to the swinging door to the kitchen, Judy turned to face Michael. "Are you hungry, Michael? Marta always leaves something in the refrigerator for me when I get home from work."

"Sounds good." Michael nodded. "But did she leave enough for two?"

Judy laughed. "That's no problem. Marta leaves enough for an army. She's out to feed the world. And if I don't eat, she thinks I'm sick. Let's carry it out and sit on the patio."

Michael stood by while Judy opened the refrigerator. He took the tray Judy handed him and waited while she grabbed soft drinks. Then they carried everything out to the patio, and sat at one of the glass-topped tables around the pool.

"This is the life, Jude." Michael gazed longingly at the Olympic-sized swimming pool "I wish my parents had a pool."

"You can use ours any time you want to. I'm the only one who ever goes in."

"Really? Thanks, Jude. My parents thought about putting in a pool, but they decided to go for the tennis court instead. And you've even got a jacuzzi!"

Judy smiled into the darkness. The jacuzzi was a very romantic setting, especially at midnight on a warm summer evening. The air was cooling off a bit, and there were inviting wisps of steam floating up from the heated surface of the water. "I've got a great idea, Michael. Let's soak our worries away in the jacuzzi. Marta always turns it on for me so I can relax after work."

"That sounds like a blast!" Michael grinned at her. "I'll just run home and get my suit."

"Oh, don't bother. We keep extra suits in the cabana. I'm sure you can find one to fit you."

"Hey, that's even better. Do you think we should wait a few minutes? You're really not supposed to go in the water after you eat."

"I don't think it makes any difference." Judy grinned back. "If I get a cramp, you can save me. And if you get one, I'll save you. Go ahead and change into a suit. I'll run back to the house and get mine."

The moment Michael entered the cabana, Judy rushed into the house to get into her suit. As she came back down the stairs, wearing her best bikini, she hesitated at the wine cooler. Buddy had some very expensive bottles of wine, and sipping a fruity, chilled Beaujolais from a crystal wine glass was a great incentive to romance. Neither one of them had to drive any more tonight, since she was at home and Michael lived right next door.

Judy smiled as she took out a bottle and opened it. She hoped she'd chosen one of Buddy's best vintages. Of course there were no losers in Buddy's wine cooler. He only drank the best.

It took only a few moments to open the wine and put it on a tray with two glasses. She walked out to the patio, carrying the tray, confident that she looked very sexy in her new black string bikini.

Michael was already immersed in the steaming water, and he smiled as she approached. "That's a great suit, Jude. If you wear that in public, you'll have to beat the guys off with a stick."

"Really?" Judy leaned over and set down the tray. She knew she looked fantastic. One glance in the mirror had told her that. "I brought out a bottle of wine. Would you like a glass?"

Michael looked a little worried as he nodded. "But, Jude . . . you're really too young to drink."

"Oh, I know. I never do, unless Buddy and Pamela are giving a formal dinner. And then, it's only one glass. But we don't have to drive, and I thought maybe we needed to unwind after everything bad that's happened."

"Okay," Michael agreed. "A glass of wine would be nice, and you made your point. But I don't want to catch you drinking when you're out somewhere!"

Judy grinned. He sounded concerned about her. "You won't. I can't drink unless I'm home."

"Why is that?"

"Because Buddy and Pamela have given me expensive tastes. I don't like the taste of anything except fine, vintage wine. Anything else make me feel sick."

Michael laughed as he picked up a glass. "I think they did you a favor. At least you won't be swilling beer in the backseat of somebody's car."

"You'd care if I did something like that?" Judy held her breath, waiting for Michael's answer.

"Of course I'd care. You're my little sis. I feel very protective toward you, Jude."

Judy tried not to let her disappointment show as she filled Michael's glass. She was tired of hearing that she was his little sis or his good buddy. She wanted more than that, but she knew better than to push it. Little by little, step by step, she'd make him see that she was really the girl of his dreams.

"That's all you're having?" Michael stared at Judy's glass. She'd filled it barely to the half-way mark.

"It's enough. I just want a taste. You can have the rest."

"I don't think that's such a good idea." Michael chuckled. "You might have to carry me home, and you're not strong enough for that."

"You'd be surprised. I've been working out with Buddy's weights, and I'm a lot stronger than I look."

Michael leered at her, just like Arte Johnson had leered at

Goldie Hawn on the old *Laugh In* re-runs. "You want to arm wrestle, little girl?"

"Sure." Judy climbed in the jacuzzi across from Michael and propped her arm up on the ledge in the classic armwrestling pose. "But I don't want to hurt you."

"I don't think you have to worry about that."

Judy grinned as Michael propped his arm on the ledge and clasped hands with her. "Do you want to count, or shall I?"

"The lady counts." Michael chuckled again. "And the lady loses."

Judy tossed her head, and gave him a sultry smile. "The lady always wins, one way or the other. One . . . two . . . three . . . go!"

"You *are* strong." Michael's eyes widened as Judy began to push his arm down. He took a deep breath and brought his arm back up again. "But I'm stronger."

Judy kept smiling, even though she felt more like wincing. She knew Michael was stronger than she was, but there was no way she was going to back down without a fight. She moved a little closer to him, and her breast brushed his arm. If she could just distract him, she might be able to win.

"Foul!" Michael grinned down at her. He knew exactly what she was doing. "You're trying to get my mind off the contest."

"And it's working." Judy giggled as his arm dipped lower.

Michael laughed and forced his arm up again. "Not for long. I know what you're doing now, and I refuse to let it affect me."

"Oh, yeah?" Judy kicked out underwater, and slid her leg around Michael's knees.

Michael started to laugh. "No fair. Body contact is out!"

"That's not in my rule book." Judy reached out with her other leg, and tried to topple him off the molded seat. "Anything's fair, as long as we don't drown each other."

"Okay . . . if that's the way you want to play." Michael reached down with his free hand, and grabbed her ankle before Judy could react. Then he tugged, and Judy slid off her perch into the steaming water.

When Judy came up, she was sputtering and laughing at the

same time. Michael's arms were around her, and she knew she'd never felt so happy in her entire life.

"That's better." Michael looked very serious. "Don't you know you're always supposed to let me win? It's bad for my fragile male ego if you don't."

Judy managed to look contrite. "You're right, Michael. I just forgot in the heat of the moment. But then, on the other hand . . . I think you're . . ."

"I'm what?" Michael looked very smug. "You were about to say I'm stronger than you are?"

Judy pretended she was considering it. But then she moved so quickly, Michael didn't have a chance. She wrapped her arms around his neck, pulled him down into the water, and let out a peal of laughter as he came up, sputtering. "I was about to say, on the other hand, I think you're all wet!"

Michael's arms tightened around her, and Judy took a deep breath. Was he going to kiss her? At last? But then Michael shoved off with his legs and they both went tumbling into the middle of the jacuzzi.

Judy giggled as she came up. "You sure know how to treat a girl, Mr. Warden. No wonder you're so popular."

"Maybe I wish I wasn't quite so popular." Michael looked suddenly serious. "Can we be serious for a minute, Jude? I really need to talk to you."

Judy nodded, and Michael lifted her and plunked her down on the molded seat next to his. She'd hoped this pseudo-wrestling could have gone on a little longer, but Michael obviously had something on his mind. He'd said he wanted to talk to her, and she was prepared to listen. She'd do anything Michael wanted.

"It's about the murders, Jude. I think I'm in big trouble."

"You?" Judy handed him a towel and took one for herself. "What kind of trouble are you in?"

"Detective Davis is still looking for connections. He's missed a big one, but he's bound to latch onto it one of these days. Have you noticed that every girl I've dated has been killed?"

"Of course." Judy matched his serious expression. "But you've dated almost every girl at Covers, haven't you?"

"Well . . . yes."

"Then it's just a coincidence. I think Detective Davis is smart enough to realize that."

"It's a little more than that." Michael frowned. "Remember the arrows, Jude?"

Judy nodded. "Of course I remember. How could I forget something like that?"

"My arrows are missing."

"Your arrows?"

"Right." Michael sighed deeply. "I used to work at a summer camp, before Mr. Calloway opened Covers."

Judy nodded. "The boys' camp at Lookout Point?"

"Right. I was a camp counselor, and we each had to teach a couple of classes. I taught guitar and archery. I didn't make the connection before, but after Ingrid was killed, I went out to the storage shed to look for my arrows. I had a quiver and ten arrows hanging on a hook right next to the door. They were there for four years, Jude . . . but now they're gone."

"But that doesn't mean anything!" Judy reached out to touch Michael's shoulder. "Maybe somebody moved them. They could be in a box somewhere."

"That's what I thought, at first. But I cleaned out the entire storage shed, and I couldn't find them. It looks bad for me, Jude. If Detective Davis finds out about those missing arrows, he's going to arrest me."

Judy sat in silence for a moment, and then she looked up into Michael's worried face. "Was the storage shed locked?"

"No. We don't keep anything of value in there. Gardening tools, old paint, drop cloths, stuff like that. There's absolutely nothing anyone would want to steal."

"Except a quiver with ten arrows." Judy looked thoughtful. "I wish I could remember if they were missing the last time I was in there."

"You were in our storage shed?" Michael raised his eyebrows.

"Sure. Your mother lets us borrow her fruit picker for our lemon tree. I go over to the storage shed to get it every time Marta makes a lemon meringue pie. It's this long pole with a basket on top, and you just reach up in the tree and . . ."

"I remember it well." Michael interrupted her. "I used to use it to get my kite out of our olive tree. When was the last time you borrowed it, Jude?"

"Just last week. Marta makes a lemon meringue pie every time Pamela invites her bridge club to lunch. It's their favorite dessert. I wish I'd looked around more carefully when I ran over to get your fruit picker, but, I didn't."

"That's okay, Jude. Maybe it's not important. I asked Andy to check it out for me." Judy looked puzzled and Michael explained. "My arrows were the standard target kind with a red circle right above the feathering. Andy's going to ask his uncle if the arrows they found were that type."

Judy frowned. "Did you tell Andy about your arrows?"

"No. It's not that I don't trust Andy, but I figured the fewer people who know about my missing arrows, the better."

"Very smart." Judy nodded. "And actually . . . I'm not entirely sure you should trust Andy."

Michael turned to her in amazement. "Why not? Andy's my friend!"

"That's true, but . . ." Judy began to frown. "I really shouldn't say anything. It's probably not important."

Michael slipped his arm around her shoulders and gave her a squeeze. "Come on, Judy. Everything's important, especially when I'm worried that Detective Davis might think I'm a suspect."

"That's just it. We're all suspects. Every one of us." Judy snuggled a little closer. The combination of the warm water and Michael's muscular body were making it difficult to concentrate.

"What do you mean?" he asked.

"Well . . ." Judy hesitated slightly. What harm would it do to tell him? "We all have motives, especially if you believe that the killer's a member of our group."

Michael tipped her head up so he could look straight into her eyes. "Whoa! I think you'd better explain that."

Judy sighed, and then she began to explain. She only left out two things. She didn't tell Michael that the theory was Carla's brainchild, and she didn't mention the contest. When she was through, Michael nodded.

"Okay. That makes some sort of crazy sense. But you said everyone had a motive. What's Andy's motive?"

"Maybe he's jealous of you. After all, you're dating the girls he wants to date. And if he thinks they're getting too serious about you, he kills them."

Michael nodded. "Okay. I don't buy it for a minute, but Detective Davis might. How about Berto?"

"Uh . . ." Judy thought fast. She didn't want to tell Michael about the contest. "Berto could be jealous, too. And he could be upset that the girls picked you instead of him."

"Carla?"

"You didn't ask her for a date. So she's killing off the girls you go out with. The same motive could apply to me."

"You?!" Michael raised his eyebrows.

"Sure." Judy nodded, and forced a smile. "Detective Davis doesn't know that we're just buddies."

"Okay. How about Linda? Is her motive jealousy, too?"

Judy nodded. "Of course. And it's the same for Nita, and Vera. It's a little different for Mr. Calloway, though."

"Mr. Calloway has a motive?" Michael looked astonished.

"Definitely. He's always after you to pay more attention to your career. If he thought you were getting serious about one of the girls, he might break it up by killing her."

That was too much for Michael. He started to laugh. "I don't believe this, Jude! I'm the only one who's not on the suspect list."

"You are on it. After all, your arrows are missing."

"You're right." Michael winced, as he pulled her a little closer. "Jude? You really don't think that I . . . I could actually . . . I mean . . ."

Judy reached up to touch his face. "Of course not! I'm just

telling you what Detective Davis might believe, that's all. Of course, he won't believe it for long. You have alibis for the nights of the murders, don't you?"

"No, I don't. I came straight home the night Deana was killed, but my parents were already in bed, and they didn't hear me come in."

"But the night that Becky was killed, you were waiting for her at her sister's apartment. Didn't anyone see you there? A doorman, maybe? Or another neighbor?"

Michael shook his head. "There's no doorman. And no valet parking, either. I parked on the street and went straight in. There was no one in the lobby and I didn't see another soul in the hallway. I was there, but I can't prove it."

"How about the night that Mary Beth was killed? You said you were stuck in a traffic jam."

"I was. But I can't prove that, either. For all Detective Davis knows, I could have heard about the traffic jam on the radio!"

"Oh no!" Judy swallowed hard. "How about when Ingrid was killed? Did anyone see you at the carnival?"

"No. It was so late, they weren't taking tickets anymore. I just walked right in. I waited by the ticket booth, the way we'd agreed, but I didn't see anyone I knew. There's absolutely no way I can prove I *wasn't* inside the House of Mirrors."

Judy shivered. "It doesn't look good, does it?"

"Not at all. That's why I'm so worried about those missing arrows. If the markings on the arrows they found at the crime scenes match the ones on my arrows, I'm dead!"

Judy wrapped her arms around Michael's neck, and gave him a hug. "Don't worry, Michael. I know what to do."

"What?"

"I want you to make sure you're never alone, not even for a single minute. That way, if the killer strikes again, you'll have an alibi."

"Let's just hope he doesn't!"

"Wrong." Judy shook her head. "You'd better hope he does. If you've got an alibi, that'll clear you."

Michael looked absolutely shocked. "Judy! You can't mean

that! You're not thinking clearly. There's no way you could actually hope that someone else will die!"

"Of course I don't hope that," Judy back-pedaled quickly. "I just hope that the killer *attempts* to strike again. Even if the police fail to catch him, you'll have an alibi, and you'll be in the clear."

Michael nodded. "That's true. I wish the police would actually catch him, though. I feel really strange about dating Nita. I can't help but feel that I'm putting her life in danger."

"Dating Nita?" Judy shivered. The water was hot, but she had suddenly turned cold. "When are you dating Nita?"

"Tomorrow night. She asked me to take her to a midnight movie after the show, and I said yes. We're going to the drive-in. Berto's going, too."

"Oh." Judy began to feel a little better. It couldn't be much of a date if Nita was taking her brother along.

Michael looked suddenly thoughtful. "Say, Jude . . . you like Berto, don't you?"

"Sure. He's okay."

"Why don't you come along with us? We could do sort of a double date. And you could drive so you and Berto could be in the front seat. It's going to be damn awkward, snuggling up with Nita, if her brother isn't otherwise occupied. You know what I mean?"

Judy nodded. She knew exactly what Michael meant. If she distracted Berto, Michael and Nita could be free to do whatever they wanted in the back seat. She bit back her angry retort, and tried to think rationally. Perhaps it wasn't such a bad idea. If she went along, she could keep her eye on Michael and Nita. She might even snuggle up a little with Berto, and see if she could make Michael jealous. And if she drove, she could drop Nita and Berto off first, and then she'd have Michael all to herself on the long drive home.

"Why not?" Judy shrugged carelessly. "I'll go. It might even be fun."

"Great!"

Judy's heart pounded hard as Michael reached out and pulled

her close for a hug. But the next words he spoke made her feel like crying.

"You're a real pal, Jude. And you're saving my life. I sure wasn't looking forward to Berto staring at us all night. You're my absolute favorite kid sister, Jude—you know that?"

Michael hugged her again, and Judy hugged him back. She wasn't as depressed as she usually was when he called her a pal or a kid sister. Would tomorrow night work? Would Michael be upset if she came on to Berto? There was nothing to do but try it and see. Maybe, if he saw that another boy thought she was hot, he'd finally stop thinking of her as just a friend.

Fourteen

"You like this movie, Judy?" Berto leaned close to whisper in her ear.

"No. It's stupid," she whispered back.

"You don't like spy movies?"

"*I do* like spy movies. That's the problem." Judy turned to face Berto. "This is the worst spy movie I've ever seen. Six guys just opened fire on our hero with Uzis, and he outran the bullets. Can you explain that?"

"Fast feet. *Very* fast feet."

Berto was perfectly deadpan and Judy laughed. Going out on this double date might be fun if the other couple was someone other than Michael and Nita. Actually, Nita would be okay with a different guy. But knowing that Michael was only inches away, cuddling in the backseat with another girl, was enough to make Judy grind her teeth in frustration.

Berto leaned close again, and made a small gesture toward the back seat. "You like him, huh?"

"Who, Michael?" Berto nodded, and Judy sighed. "Sure. I like him. Everybody likes Michael, including your sister."

"I know. But I wish she wouldn't like him quite so much. And I wish she wouldn't go out with him."

"Why not? Don't you like him?"

Berto frowned. "It's not that—I like Michael. But I don't like the way Nita's treating Ramon."

"Ramon?"

"Ramon Morrales. Nita's been going steady with him for over a year. Ramon's uncle owns a roofing company in Phoenix, and he gave Ramon a job for the summer. Ramon's only been gone for a couple of weeks, and now Nita's going out with Michael."

Judy nodded. "Did Ramon and Nita break up?"

"No. They're still making wedding plans for when Nita graduates, and Ramon is making payments on the engagement ring they picked out. I don't think he knows there's another guy in the picture."

"But that's not right!" Judy shook her head. "Nita shouldn't be going out with Michael if she's practically engaged to Ramon."

"I know. I told her that last night, but she wouldn't listen to me. Nita says she's just having fun with Michael, and it's not serious between them. But it looks pretty serious to me."

Judy cast a quick glance into the back seat. Michael had his arm around Nita, and he was kissing her. When she turned back to face Berto she was frowning. "It looks pretty serious to me, too. Do you think she's going to dump Ramon?"

"I don't know. I hope not. Michael's not right for Nita. I don't think he's ready to get married and settle down. What do you think?"

"I think you're right. And I think it's a good thing that we're here. At least we can keep them from getting too . . . uh . . . serious."

Berto frowned. "How are we going to do that? I think they forgot that we're even in the car!"

"Well then, I guess we should remind them." Judy opened her purse and took out a twenty-dollar bill. "Does Nita like popcorn? I happen to know that it's Michel's favorite food."

Berta looked confused for a moment, and then he began to grin. "Nita likes popcorn, but she likes hamburgers even more. And they take longer to cook. You want me to take Michael with me when I make a run to the concession stand?"

Judy grinned back, and passed him another twenty. "You got it, Berto! Blow as much money as you can on food, especially the kind that takes a long time to eat. If we're gobbling food and passing things back and forth, Nita and Michael will forget all about romance."

"Maybe." Berto didn't look entirely convinced. "But you don't know my sister. Don't get me wrong, Judy. I love Nita . . . but she's got a one track mind."

Judy pulled up in front of Berto and Nita's house, but she didn't shut off the engine. Instead, she nudged Berto and called out cheerily, "We're here!"

"Come on, Nita." Berto grinned at Judy as he caught his cue. "I just saw Mom pull back the curtain. We'd better get inside before she thinks something is wrong."

Nita nodded. She didn't look happy, and Judy barely managed to keep from grinning. Berto had brought back the perfect food from the concession stand. A giant tub of buttered popcorn they'd passed back and forth, hamburgers dripping with mustard and ketchup and mayonnaise that were impossible to eat unless you used both hands, a large pizza that had to be doled out from a box, and ice cream in pointed cones that had to be held and eaten before they melted. The only time Nita had been able to snuggle in the backseat with Michael was on the drive home. And even then, Berto and Judy had kept them busy talking about the new song Michael was singing at Covers tomorrow night.

Michael got out of the car, and motioned to Nita. "I'll walk you to the door."

"That's okay. I'll take her." Berto grabbed Nita by the hand. "You shouldn't leave Judy alone in the car. This isn't exactly Beverly Hills."

"Oh. Right." Michael nodded, and opened the door to the front seat. "See you tomorrow, Nita."

Judy waited until Michael had slid into the passenger's seat, then she locked the doors and put the car in gear. "Berto told me that they have a lot of car-jackings in this neighborhood. And he warned me that they really go for expensive cars like this Volvo."

"It *is* a nice car, Jude. You're lucky to have it."

"I know." Judy drove down the deserted street, and turned at the entrance to the freeway. "It's not exactly my dream car, but it's very reliable."

Michael turned to look at her in surprise. "Well, it's *my* dream car! It's top of the line, Jude. They don't make them any better than this. You've got every option they offer, including a CD player. I like my old Lincoln, but I'd trade it for a brand new Volvo any day of the week."

"Okay." Judy nodded. "It's a deal. I'd much rather have your Lincoln. It's embarrassing, driving around in an expensive car like this."

"You're kidding! You really don't like your Volvo?"

Judy sighed. "It's not that I don't like it. It's just, well . . . it's hard to be one of the gang, when you're driving around in a car that cost fifty thousand dollars. Whatever you do, don't tell anyone that I actually own it. I always say that I borrowed it from Pamela."

"Don't worry. I won't rat on you." Michael reached out to pat her shoulder. "But everybody knows my parents have money. I don't see why you're so embarrassed about being a rich kid."

"It's okay for a guy to have money." Judy tried to explain. "But it's different for a girl. All the other girls at Covers are on a budget. They wouldn't like me if they knew I got a weekly allowance that was bigger than their whole paycheck. Of course, they don't really like me anyway, so I guess it doesn't really matter."

Michael looked concerned. "Hey, don't talk like that. The other girls like you, Jude. They think you're very good at your job."

"Sure. They think I'm a good stage manager, and I am, but that doesn't mean I'm a friend. And it doesn't mean that they like me. When girls like you, they invite you to go shopping with them, or meet them at the movies, or come to their houses for dinner. And nobody's ever invited me anywhere!"

"Maybe they just don't know you well enough to like you.

Why don't you invite them all to your house for a swim? It's a good way to get acquainted."

"Oh, sure." Judy tried not to sound bitter. "What do you think would happen if I invited Nita to my house? You've seen where she lives. Do you think Nita would enjoy meeting our Mexican housekeeper? Would she be happy that I had a suite of rooms with a big-screen color television, and tons of clothes in my walk-in closet? Do you honestly think that Nita would feel more friendly toward me if she saw Buddy's million-dollar Picasso, or Pamela's five carat diamond ring?"

Michael sighed. "Okay. You made your point. Maybe inviting the girls to your house isn't such a hot idea. But I don't think the girls dislike you, Jude. Linda's always saying how nice you are."

"Well . . . Linda's an exception. And she's also a saint. Linda loves everybody, and everybody loves her back. But you're right, Michael. Linda is as close to a friend as I've got."

"There's Carla, too." Michael nodded. "I know she likes you."

"That's true. But I'm not sure that counts. Carla's just as unpopular as I am. She's never had a date, either."

"You've never been out on a date?" Michael sounded shocked. "I don't believe it!"

"Believe it. It's true. Nobody's ever asked me out."

"How about tonight? It sure looked to me like Berto was having a good time."

Judy frowned. "Tonight wasn't exactly a date. Berto didn't ask me to come along—you did. And I wasn't *your* date. Nita was."

"Okay." Michael was silent until they got off the freeway and turned down their street. "I know it's not exactly a date, but will you do it again?"

"Do what?"

"Go out with Berto and Nita and me. I asked Nita to go to the zoo tomorrow afternoon, but she told me that she couldn't go out alone. Berto and her mother are worried about the killer. I really want you to come along, Jude. You and Berto had a good time tonight, didn't you?"

Judy turned in at her driveway, and stopped the car. "Nita can't go out with you unless she takes Berto along, right?"

"Well . . . yes." Michael had a grace to look a little uncomfortable. "But we'll all have a good time, I promise. We'll spend the afternoon at the zoo, and then we'll all drive to Covers together."

Judy was glad it was dark, so Michael couldn't see how disappointed she was. Michael was using her. He wanted time alone with Nita, and that wasn't possible if Berto came along as a chaperone. Michael needed a date for Berto, so she was elected. Still, it would give her more time with Michael. And any time she could spend with him was a plus.

"Who's driving?" Judy asked the important question.

"Me. You used your car tonight, so I'll take mine tomorrow."

The wheels in Judy's head began to spin, and she knew exactly why Michael wanted to drive. After they finished the show at Covers, he'd drop her off at her house, then he'd take Berto and Nita home. Berto wouldn't let Nita sit out in the car with Michael, but Nita might invite Michael in. Berto would have to go to bed eventually, and then . . .

"Okay, I'll go." Judy nodded. "But only on one condition."

"What's that?"

"I'll drive. Your backseat is a disaster area."

"Come on, Jude. It's not that bad. I know the upholstery's shot, but I'll put a blanket over the seat."

"That's not the problem. The last time I rode in your back seat, the springs stuck me every time you went over a bump. I don't exactly enjoy being goosed by a car."

Michael began to laugh. "Not even *my* car?"

"Not even yours."

"I could rent you a suit of armor."

"No, thanks. I'll go to the zoo if we take my car. But if I have to ride in your back seat, I'm passing."

"Okay. We'll take your car." Michael opened the door, and got out. He waited until Judy had locked up her car, and then he waved. "See you tomorrow, Jude."

"Good night, Michael." Judy watched as Michael headed for

the low hedge that separated his house from hers. He vaulted over, and then he turned to grin at her.

"Now that I think about it, I'm glad you're driving. Your backseat is *very* comfortable—Nita and I really enjoyed it."

Judy was thoughtful as she let herself into the house. Had she made a mistake by insisting that she drive? If she drove, Michael wouldn't have to pay attention to traffic. And that meant he could concentrate entirely on Nita.

Marta had left her usual tray of snacks, and Judy carried it out to the patio. She sat at the same table they'd used last night and stared at the jacuzzi, remembering how warm and strong Michael's arms had felt when he had held her. Of course, it hadn't really been an embrace. The only time Michael had really held her was right before he'd ducked her head under the water.

Judy bit into a rare roast beef sandwich, and sighed deeply. At least tonight hadn't been as bad as she'd imagined. Berto was fun, and he'd been very understanding. He probably suspected that she was in love with Michael, but Judy was sure he'd keep her secret.

It was really too bad she wasn't interested in Berto. He was handsome, and smart, and awfully nice. Judy hadn't had much experience at these sorts of things, but she was almost sure that Berto would jump at the chance to ask her out if she gave him the slightest bit of encouragement. But she wouldn't encourage him. Michael was the one she wanted, not Berto. Michael was the only man in the world for her.

What she wouldn't give to trade places with Nita! Judy felt her eyes fill with tears, and she blinked them back angrily. She couldn't give way to her emotions. Crying would do absolutely no good, and her eyes would be puffy and swollen in the morning.

Judy took a deep breath and squared her shoulders. She couldn't afford to waste time feeling sorry for herself. Only idiots had time for self-pity. She would concentrate on coming up with a plan. Somehow, she had to make Michael see Nita for what she really was. Nita was a flirt and a cheat. She was going out with Michael while she was practically engaged to another man.

Could she tell Michael that? Judy sighed, and shook her

head. If she told Michael about Nita and Ramon, she'd be risk-ing disaster. Judy knew that no matter how many times people said they wanted the truth, they really preferred not to face it. Michael might hate her for bringing him the truth. That was a chance she couldn't take.

So what could she do? She hated to wait, but there was no other choice. She'd just have to let nature run its course, and keep her fingers crossed that Michael would wise up before he really fell for Nita.

Judy frowned as she went back inside and climbed the steps to her suite. That remark Michael had made about her back seat still rankled. It was too bad it was so comfortable, so well suited for kissing and cuddling.

But was it? Judy began to grin as she thought of a perfect so-lution. The Volvo had a feature she'd never used. It was built es-pecially for owners who lived in cold climates so that they didn't have to get into a car with icy-cold seats. When she got up to-morrow morning, she'd read the owner's manual to find out how to activate the heater that warmed the back seat.

Judy laughed out loud. Berto would love her little plan. He'd help her keep an eye on Michael and Nita, and if things got a lit-tle too hot in the back seat, he would warn her. And then Judy would make sure that they got even hotter!

Fifteen

Judy's self-control slipped to a dangerously low level as she watched Michael perform the last set of the show. He'd written a new song, a ballad about a girl with laughing brown eyes and long, dark hair the color of midnight. It was a song for Nita. Judy knew that Michael was falling for Nita, and he had no idea that she was only out for a good time while her boyfriend was gone.

Michael looked very serious as he strummed his guitar. His eyes were shining, and his voice was rich with emotion. He was singing about the girl of his dreams. But Nita wasn't the girl of his dreams . . . unless Michael was having a nightmare!

Despite Judy and Berto's precautions, Nita and Michael had managed some time alone together. Those times had happened right here at Covers, where they both felt they were safe. Berto had told Judy he'd discovered them kissing, in back of a flat during rehearsal. And Judy had seen them hugging in the parking lot, and in the hall. Even Carla had seen them exchanging long, intensely passionate glances outside the office, and Andy had caught them embracing outside the kitchen door. Everyone at Covers had noticed that Nita was Michael's new girlfriend. Michael was very open about it, and so was Nita. They weren't bothering to keep their relationship a secret.

Judy and Berto had talked it over, and he'd decided to confront his sister tonight. He planned to give her a little lecture about how wrong it was to get involved with two men at the same time. He would say it wasn't fair to Ramon. Nita should either call things off with Ramon and go out with Michael, or break up with Michael to save her relationship with Ramon. Either way, Nita would have to make a choice. Berto and Judy agreed on one thing—they both hoped that Nita would choose Ramon. For different reasons, of course.

Judy thought about their date at the zoo. She might have had a good time if she'd gone only with Berto, but watching Nita and Michael walking around all afternoon holding hands had been a real bummer.

When they'd arrived at the zoo, they'd parked under a shade tree at the very back of the parking lot, and walked toward the entrance. On the way, they'd encountered the usual crowd of vendors in front of the entrance, selling trinkets. The vendors all said their proceeds went to charity, but Judy had been very skeptical, since she'd never heard of the charities they claimed to represent. When Judy had been approached by a woman in a white nurse's uniform, asking for donations to something called Human Relief, Judy had demanded to know exactly how her donation would be spent. The nurse, who Judy was sure wasn't really a nurse, had hemmed and hawed, then she'd rattled off a glib answer about Judy's global sisters and brothers in need. Judy had stared straight into the woman's eyes, all ready to reply that she was an only child and she didn't have any brothers and sisters, global or otherwise. But Michael had come up beside her to drop a dollar into the nurse's bucket. Since she hadn't wanted Michael to think that she was uncharitable, Judy had dropped in her dollar, too.

When they'd walked through the turnstiles, Michael had turned to Nita and asked her what she'd wanted to see first. Nita had told him that she simply adored birds. Judy hadn't been interested in birds at all, but she'd marched right along at Berto's side to spend a boring half-hour in the aviary. After that was over, Judy had suggested the reptile house, but Nita had shuddered and admitted that she couldn't stand snakes. They'd gone off to see the gorillas instead, and Judy had spent another half-hour on an uncomfortable bench, watching a grandfather gorilla pound his chest while two females groomed each other.

The big cats had been next, but the day had been too warm for any lively exhibitions. The leopards had been dozing in the sun, the jaguars had plodded around listlessly, and the lions had been napping inside their cave.

The whole afternoon had been a waste. Flamingo Island had smelled horrible, the koala hut had been so crowded they'd had to wait in line for twenty minutes, the polar bears had been too sleepy to swim, and the elephants had stood so motionless, they'd looked as if they were stuffed and mounted. To make matters worse, Nita and Michael had actually seemed to be enjoying themselves. They'd walked along, holding hands and carrying on a lively conversation, while Berto and Judy had plodded along behind them, looking glum.

After Covers had closed on Wednesday evening, Michael had suggested they all go out for a bite to eat. They'd ended up at a little Mexican place where everyone had spoken Spanish. Nita and Berto had cracked jokes with the waiter, and Michael had joined right in. He'd taken three years of Spanish in high school, and he'd done a great job of holding his own. Unfortunately, Judy had taken French, and she'd been totally left out of the conversation. She'd also been totally left out of the food. The menu had been written in Spanish and she'd ordered a tripe burrito by mistake.

On Thursday afternoon, they'd all gone to a preview house, a place Judy had never been before. Nita had received four tickets in the mail, and she'd explained that it was just like a movie, only better. They'd spent two hours watching pilot episodes of television situation comedies, or sit-coms as they were called in L.A. The theater seats had been equipped with recording devices, and the announcer had asked the audience to press various buttons to register what they liked or didn't like about the shows. The red button had indicated extreme dislike, and Judy had pressed it down for a solid two hours. Perhaps the pilots hadn't been that awful, but watching Michael and Nita laugh at the jokes and nudge one another had put her in a terrible mood.

And now it was Friday, the fifth date in a row for Nita and Michael. They were slated to go to another midnight movie, and Judy had read the reviews. The reviewer had said it was a touching, sensitive story of a love that survived despite terrible odds. It was the type of movie she might have wanted to see with Michael. There would be plenty of opportunities to hold hands and hug. But Michael would be with Nita.

At least Berto had promised to confront Nita tonight, and Judy hoped he could shame her into dropping her relationship with Michael. Berto had told her he hoped his sister would listen to reason, but that didn't guarantee success. Judy was so busy worrying about Berto's upcoming talk with Nita, she totally missed her light cue at the end of Michael's love song. The moment she realized it, she quickly dimmed the lights, but the old light box wasn't built to handle any sudden changes. There was a loud snap, the stage went completely dark, and Judy groaned. She'd blown a fuse!

Luckily, Judy was prepared. She grabbed the flashlight she always kept in her pocket and replaced the fuse. Then she brought the lights slowly up again. But when she glanced out on stage, she realized that Michael was nowhere to be seen.

"Damn!" Judy swore softly under her breath. She whirled around and gasped as she bumped straight into Michael. Thank goodness he didn't look mad, but she had no idea why he was grinning.

"Sorry, Michael." Judy started to apologize. "It's my fault. I guess I was thinking about something else, and . . ."

"It doesn't matter." Michael interrupted her. "I wanted to get off stage in a hurry anyway. Have you seen Nita?"

"No. I suppose she's out on the floor, waiting on . . ."

"I'm right here." Nita stepped out from behind the screen. "Are you ready, Michael?"

Michael nodded, and turned to Judy. "Okay, Jude. Wait for us to get out on stage, and then bring the lights up full."

"But . . . but, why?" Judy was confused. The show was over, except for Michael's encore.

"Nita's helping me with the encore tonight. Just light it the way you usually do. I'll take care of the rest."

Judy nodded. What else could she do? And then she watched with a sinking heart as Michael picked up another stool and carried it out on the stage for Nita.

Carla stepped behind the screen to join Judy, just as Michael got Nita settled on her stool. He sat down next to her, gave her a little hug, and grinned as the audience applauded. Judy knew why they were applauding. Nita had laughing brown eyes and hair the color of midnight. They knew that Nita was the girl he'd described in his ballad.

"What's going on?" Carla turned to Judy with a question in her eyes.

"I don't know. Michael just said that Nita was helping him with the encore tonight."

"But she's a waitress! She doesn't sing, does she?"

"Search me." Judy shrugged. "I really don't know her that well."

Michael began to strum his guitar. He was staring straight into Nita's eyes, and Nita was smiling.

"She's grinning like the cat that ate the canary," Carla sighed with disgust. "She probably thinks she won the contest."

Judy nodded. "Maybe she did. She certainly looks smug."

Then Michael started to sing to Nita. It was a new song he'd written about a man who'd found his one true love. Judy listened to the lyrics for a moment, and then she turned to Carla. "I wish I hadn't blown that fuse at the end of Michael's set."

"Why?"

"Because it would look deliberate if I blew another fuse right now. And I'd love to!"

Carla laughed. "I think you should do it anyway. You can always say the light board has a short."

"Should I?" Judy touched the switch with the tips of her fingers. "Really?"

"Go ahead, Judy. Live dangerously. Do it!"

"Michael's going to kill me." Judy winced a little. "He'll never believe it wasn't deliberate."

Carla picked up the· special carbon dioxide fire extinguisher that hung next to the light board. "Sure, he will . . . especially if I say there were flames shooting out of the box, and I sprayed it down with this thing."

Judy stared at Carla for a moment, and then she nodded. "Okay. But if you ever tell anybody . . ."

"I won't. I promise." Carla glanced out at the stage again, and clutched her stomach. "Hurry up, Judy. All this sappy love and devotion is making me sick."

Judy's fingers tightened on the switch. She hoped Carla was right. Michael would never forgive her if he suspected she'd blown a fuse on purpose. "Get ready with that fire extinguisher, Carla. Here she blows!"

With one shove, Judy pushed up the lever to its maximum position. There was a loud pop, and everything went black. Almost immediately, flames shot out from the light box. Carla gasped, and began to douse them with the spray from the fire extinguisher, but the flames kept right on coming.

"Oh, my God!" Judy grabbed the second fire extinguisher and pressed the release. The flames were still leaping from the center of the light board. They battled the blaze for a moment, and then Judy shouted at Carla.

"I'll take over here. You go out and trip the circuit breaker by the side of the building!"

"I'll do it, Jude! Just keep spraying that foam!"

Michael raced from the stage, and ran toward the emergency exit at the rear of the building. A moment later, the lights in the showroom clicked off, leaving them in absolute darkness. Several people in the audience screamed, and Judy heard Mr. Calloway's voice, telling everyone to stay calm. The powerful flashlight that Mr. Calloway always carried winked on, and he began to lead the audience toward the exit.

The flames were almost out now, and Judy turned to Carla. "I can't believe it, Carla. There really *was* a short!"

"And how!" Carla's voice was shaking. "It's a good thing it happened now, when we were prepared. I'd hate to think what would have happened if we hadn't been ready with those fire extinguishers."

The last flame fizzled out, and Judy gave a big sigh of relief. "We've got it, Carla. Everything's under control. We'd better go out and tell Mr. Calloway."

"Right. And first thing tomorrow morning, I'd better call an electrician. I think that old light board has had it."

Judy switched on her flashlight, and the two girls linked arms as they walked through the deserted showroom. They were almost at the door when Carla turned to Judy.

"I don't think that Nita will ever get up on stage with Michael again. I saw her running for the exit, and she looked completely freaked."

"Good." Judy began to smile. "I don't think Michael will ever sing that song again, either."

"Why not?"

Judy's smile widened until it stretched out happily across her face. "It's the title, Carla. It was just too appropriate."

"What is it?"

Carla looked curious, and Judy laughed out loud. "It's called *"The Flames Of Love."*

Sixteen

Nita sighed as she snuggled in Michael's arms in the back-seat of Judy's Volvo. Traffic was light on the Golden State Freeway. It was two o'clock on Sunday afternoon and it was unusually hot. Most people were probably staying inside the air-conditioned comfort of their homes, except for the more adventuresome who had gone off to picnic in shady parks, or enjoy the sea breeze at the beach. Nita did her best to look cheerful as Judy took the Exhibition Boulevard ramp off the freeway, and drove toward the Natural History Museum. Perhaps they wouldn't have to spend the whole afternoon inside. If they finished early, they'd still have time to do something that was fun.

Moments later, they were pulling into a parking space right in front of the museum. Judy shut off the engine, and turned around to face Michael with a frown. "Are you sure it's open today? I've never found a parking space this close to the entrance before."

"It's open. I called first to check. But they told me they didn't think they'd be crowded. They never are when it's this hot."

"This is great!" Berto looked excited. "We won't have to wait in line to see their new Egyptian exhibit. I heard they've got an incredibly preserved mummy."

Michael opened the door and helped Nita out. Then he put

his arm around her shoulder and gave her a little squeeze. "I'm glad we decided to come today, aren't you?"

"Definitely. It should be wonderful!" Nita smiled, even though she felt more like frowning. She hated museums. They were stuffy and boring, and they usually smelled like damp basements. She'd hoped they would go somewhere else, like the beach, where she could show off her new bathing suit, and Michael would rub suntan lotion on her back. Anywhere would have been better than this horrible old museum. It was impossible to be romantic when you had to look at a bunch of old, dead things.

As they climbed the steps to the ornate doors, Michael glanced down at her new red sandals. "Are you sure you'll be able to walk in those? We're going to be covering a lot of ground."

"I'm sure." Nita nodded. She wasn't about to admit that the thin straps on her sandals were beginning to chafe her ankles. The sandals went with her new red sundress. That was why she'd worn them. But Michael hadn't even commented on her appearance. Ramon's eyes would have practically popped out of his head if she'd worn her revealing halter top and short skirt for him.

"I guess no one else showed up." Judy flashed her museum membership card at the door, and led them into the two-story marble lobby. "Carla said she'd try to make it, and so did Andy. Even Mr. Calloway thought the museum would be fun on a Sunday."

Nita glared at Judy. Having Judy and Berto along was bad enough, but if Carla, and Andy, and Mr. Calloway showed up, she wouldn't have a chance for a moment alone with Michael. "You invited other people?"

Judy looked very proud of herself as she nodded. "Sure. I told everyone at Covers that we were coming here today, and I invited them all to join us."

"That was a good idea, Jude," Michael smiled at Judy. "Going through the museum is always more fun if you're with a group of friends. Maybe they'll show up later."

"Maybe. What shall we do first? The Egyptian Room?"

"Great idea!" Berto looked delighted.

"That's fine with me." Michael nodded. "What do you want to see, Jude?"

"The dioramas, but we can leave that for last. What's *your* favorite section?"

Michael frowned. "It used to be the antique cars in the basement, but they moved those. How about the American History section? There's lots of good stuff in there."

"Okay." Judy nodded. "We'll do the Egyptian exhibit first, and then we'll go through the American History section. What do you like best, Nita?"

Nita hesitated. She didn't want to admit that she'd never been to the Natural History Museum before. She'd been sick when they'd gone there for a field trip in fourth grade, and she'd never bothered to go on her own. But Michael would think she was a real idiot if she didn't come up with something. The safest thing was to agree with Judy. She sounded like she'd been here before. "I like the dioramas, too. They're wonderful."

"Okay." Michael nodded. "Two votes for the dioramas. What else do you like, Nita?"

Nita racked her brain to come up with an answer. What did they have in museums? Bugs? Birds? Rocks? She didn't want to say the wrong thing. Then, like a flash of lightning, she remembered a movie she'd seen where Cary Grant was putting together some dinosaur bones and Katharine Hepburn kept looking for a leopard. If they had a dinosaur in this museum, she'd be home free. "Actually . . . I'm very interested in dinosaurs."

"Great!" Michael gave her a hug. "So am I. But I hated it when they changed all the names. I memorized all the old ones when I was a kid, and I never got used to the new ones."

Nita nodded, and tried to look as if she knew what he was talking about. "Me, too. I think the old names were better."

"Listen up, gang." Michael took charge. "Here's the order of business. We'll do the Egyptian exhibit, take a little lunch break, and then we'll go on to the American History section. After that, we'll take in the prehistoric animals, and then we'll go to the dioramas. If we happen to get separated, everyone knows our agenda. And if that fails, we can always meet at the car."

"You remind me of my fifth grade teacher," Nita giggled as she slipped her arm around Michael's waist.

Judy frowned. "Did you like your fifth grade teacher?"

"Oh, I was crazy about him. He was kind, and smart, and very handsome. I wanted to marry him when I grew up."

"But you changed your mind?" Michael was curious.

"Not exactly." Nita gave a little laugh. "We had a class picnic on the last day of school, and everybody brought their families. That's when I found out that my fifth grade teacher was engaged to be married."

Judy saw her opportunity and grabbed it. "So you learned a valuable lesson, right?"

"What lesson?" Nita looked puzzled.

"You learned that people who are engaged, or about to be engaged, are off-limits."

Nita gave Judy a long, hard look. It was clear that Berto had told Judy about her relationship with Ramon, and that meant she had to shut Judy up before she mentioned it to Michael.

"I did learn a valuable lesson, but that wasn't it." Nita's dark eyes flashed a warning. "You see, my fifth grade teacher ended up marrying someone else. And that taught me that anyone can change their mind, right up until the day of the wedding."

Berto looked very uncomfortable as he grabbed Judy's arm. "Come on, Judy. Let's go see that mummy while we've still got the whole museum to ourselves."

"Good idea." Michael took Nita's arm, and steered her off toward the exhibit of Egyptian artifacts. Then he leaned close to ask an important question. "Were you terribly heartbroken?"

Nita shook her head. "I got over it by the end of the day. But every time I look at you, I remember how crazy I was about Mr. Scott. That's why I wish we could be alone. I'd like to show you exactly how wild I was about him."

Nita heard a little gasp behind her, and she knew that her voice had carried. It served Judy right. She shouldn't have interfered. Judy was probably upset about the contest, but Nita wasn't even trying to win anymore. The contest didn't matter, now that she'd really gotten to know Michael. She liked him. Very much. But should she dump Ramon and concentrate entirely on Michael?

As she walked down the marble hallway, Michael's arm around her shoulders, Nita thought of the life she would lead if she married Michael. Even if he didn't make it as a singer, they'd still have his family money to fall back on. Nita had seen where he lived. His parents' house was practically a mansion, and Michael was an only child. It would all be his someday. What she wouldn't give to live in a beautiful house like that!

"It's great, isn't it?" Michael pointed to a gruesome mummy in a glass case.

"Yes. It's wonderful!" Nita smiled up at him happily. It was a good thing Michael didn't know the reason why her eyes were sparkling, and her face was flushed with excitement. He might get totally freaked if he guessed that she'd just made a very important decision. She was going to be Mrs. Michael Warden, or die trying!

Seventeen

Judy took a savage bite of her tuna salad sandwich and chomped down so hard her teeth ground together. After they'd finished looking at the Egyptian artifacts, they'd decided to have something to eat before they tackled the American History exhibit. Now they were sitting out on the balcony adjacent to the food service area, eating their lunch.

Berto was munching on a cheese sandwich with catsup and dill pickles, a combination that made Judy shudder. And Nita and Michael, who were seated on a ledge overlooking the grounds, were sharing a plate of nachos. Nita and Michael were the reason Judy was grinding her teeth. Nita was feeding the crispy corn chips to Michael, one by one, while they stared soulfully into each other's eyes.

"It's a good thing I didn't order any sugar," Judy said to Berto, her eyes blazing. "There's so much sweet stuff around here, I'm practically in a diabetic coma."

Berto sighed. "Yeah. I know. It makes me sick, too. While you were at the counter, ordering your sandwich, Nita told me that she's very serious about Michael."

"Oh-oh." A frown spread across Judy's face. "How serious is she?"

"She's going to call Ramon tonight and tell him that things are over between them."

Judy felt her heart begin to pound in alarm. "Didn't you try to talk her out of it?"

"Of course. I told her it was a mistake to rush into such a big decision, but Nita said she'd made up her mind. She said she was going to marry Michael, and that was that."

"Michael asked her to marry him!?" Judy was shocked.

"No. Nothing like that. But he will."

"How do you know?" Judy's voice was shaking. Berto looked entirely convinced.

"Once Nita decides on something, that's it. And she always gets everything she wants. If she wants Michael to marry her, he'll do it."

Judy raised her eyebrows. She wanted to tell Berto that this might be one time Nita didn't get what she wanted, but she swallowed her words when she saw how upset Berto was. He'd told her how much he was looking forward to having Ramon in the family, and it was clear he was terribly disappointed.

"Thanks for telling me, Berto. I'm just sorry that poor Ramon will be hurt. From what you told me, he sounds like a really nice guy."

Berto nodded. "He is. Say, Judy . . . maybe I should . . . "

"No way." Judy interrupted what was sure to be an offer to set her up with Ramon. "I hate arranged dates. And I'm already interested in someone."

"Anybody I know?" Berto grinned at her.

"As a matter of fact, you know him quite well."

Judy didn't realize how that sounded until she saw the pleased expression on Berto's face. Oh, great! Berto thought she was talking about *him!* Judy tried to figure out some way to let him down easy, but everything she thought of sounded too cruel. She guessed it wouldn't hurt to let Berto think she was interested in him, at least for today. She'd straighten everything out later, when she wasn't so preoccupied with Nita and Michael.

"Here, Judy . . . I'll take your tray."

Judy barely noticed as Berto got up and carried their trays to the trash container against the wall. She was too busy trying to decide what to do about Michael and Nita. They really looked as though they were falling in love. Of course it wouldn't last. Judy knew that. Nita wasn't right for Michael at all. They didn't have a thing in common. Michael would be truly miserable if he married Nita, but he wasn't thinking clearly enough to realize it. It was up to her to save him from Nita's clutches. But how?

Suddenly Judy began to smile. She'd show Michael just how unsuitable Nita was, and the American History exhibit was a good place to start. Michael was a Civil War buff—that was why Judy had memorized the whole time line of Civil War battles in her encyclopedia. All that work was about to pay off. She'd get Michael talking about the Civil War, and ask him some pertinent questions. He'd realize that she could carry on an intelligent conversation, and Nita wouldn't be able to say a thing.

"Are you ready to go?" Berto came back to the table and held out his hand to her.

"I'm ready." Judy took his hand and stood up. "Do you know much about the Civil War, Berto?"

"Sure. That's my favorite time period."

"Really!" Judy smiled happily. Berto was bright, and she had no doubt that he could hold up his end of the conversation. They would have a three-way discussion which would leave Nita out in the cold . . . she hoped. Judy held her breath as she asked the question. "How about Nita? Is she a Civil War buff?"

"Nita?" Berto's mouth dropped open, and he began to laugh. "You've got to be kidding! Nita hates history. Remember that television miniseries about the Civil War?"

"The Blue and The Gray?"

"That's the one." Berto nodded. "Nita read the title in the T.V. Guide, and she asked me who was playing."

Judy was puzzled. "I don't get it."

"Neither did Nita. She thought blue and gray were the colors for a football team!"

"Isn't that fascinating, Nita?" Judy had the smile of a predator as she turned to face Nita. "I just love those colorful stories about Jefferson Davis, don't you?"

"They're very interesting." Nita smiled right back. She knew what Judy was trying to do and she was determined to turn the tables on her. Judy wanted Michael to think she was stupid because she knew nothing about Civil War History, but her little plan wouldn't work. Judy might not realize it, but she'd met her match.

"You're not bored?" Michael slipped his arm around Nita's shoulders and led her to the next exhibit.

"How could I be bored?" Nita gave him her best wide eyed look. "I just wish history class had been this interesting. Then maybe I wouldn't have slept through the lectures."

Michael nodded. "You must have had a bad teacher. That's too bad, Nita."

"I know." Nita sighed deeply, and played her ace in the hole. "You make history come alive for me, Michael. And now I realize how much I missed. I don't suppose you could . . . but, no, that would take so much of your time. It's too much to ask."

"What is it, Nita? Ask me."

Nita sighed again. "Oh, I was just wishing you'd tutor me in history. I feel like a real dummy, especially since the rest of you know so much about it. Do you suppose you could explain the exhibits to me? If you wouldn't mind, that is . . . "

"I'd love to!" Michael hugged her tightly. "And there's no reason for you to feel like a dummy. Now look over here . . . "

Nita smiled triumphantly as Michael led her over to a glass case where several uniforms were displayed. She knew she was in for a long, boring explanation, but it was worth it to beat Judy at her own game.

The dinosaur exhibit was great. Even Nita had to admit that. It had been built for kids and each model of prehistoric beast had a button you could press to make it move and hear the sounds it had made. Luckily, Nita's eyesight was excellent. She'd managed to read the descriptive plaques from all the way across the room and she'd used the information written on them to join in the conversation. But how many times could she say, "Oh, look! There's an ankylosaur. They think it's an ancient rel-

ative of the armadillo." Or, "The ornithischians look dangerous, but they were herbivorous. Do you think the early cave
dwellers kept them in cages like we do with parakeets?"

At last it was over, and Nita walked out of the dinosaur room
with her head held high. She'd managed to hold her own, but
she knew she couldn't fake it forever. Berto and Michael seemed
fascinated by a display of rocks and minerals against the wall. If
she could just get a couple of minutes alone in the hall of dioramas, she could cram for those exhibits just like she'd crammed
for her tests in school.

"Michael?" Nita tapped him on the shoulder. "I need to
make a trip to the ladies' room. Shall I meet you back here in a
couple of minutes?"

"That's fine with me." Michael grinned at her. "Take your
time, Nita. If we're not right here, we'll be in the pre-Columbian
room. It's right through that archway to your left. Judy says
they've built a model of an Aztec temple in there, and I'd like to
take a look. Then we'll go to the dioramas, okay?"

Nita nodded. "I'll join you at the Aztec temple. I'd like to see
it, too."

As she walked down the marble hallway, Nita gave a huge
sigh of relief. She'd been a little afraid that Judy would offer to
come to the ladies' room with her. But she hadn't. She was more
interested in staying with Michael and impressing him with how
much she knew about Aztec Indians. It was a lucky break for
Nita. She'd make a quick stop at the ladies' room, and then
she'd choose a couple of dioramas and study them carefully.
She'd memorize all the information on the plaques, and then
she'd be sure to make points with Michael.

The ladies' room was deserted. They seemed to be the only
ones left in the whole museum. They'd only seen one tour group
today, four adults and a bus load of Sunday school children, but
they had already left. Nita combed her hair, put on a bit more
lipstick, and walked out into the marble hallway again.

Her footsteps echoed hollowly, and Nita shivered. She'd
never liked stone buildings. They always felt cold and forbid-
ding. The museum might be fun on a day when it was crowded,

but she felt like the only person left alive as she entered the hall of dioramas.

Suddenly Nita thought of it. She was alone, completely alone. And all the other girls had been murdered when they were alone. She hesitated at the doorway. Should she rush straight back to the safety of their group?

No. Nita made up her mind. Even though it seemed like it, she wasn't really alone. There were docents wandering around, and a guard at the door. No one could get in without a ticket. Since the museum was almost deserted, the woman at the counter would be sure to remember anyone who'd come in today. The killer would be a fool to risk that kind of exposure. She was perfectly safe as long as she didn't leave the museum.

Nita shivered as she walked forward. Everything here was dead and stuffed. They tried to make the animals look alive by painting the background to resemble their habitat, and they'd filled the display cases with things that would have surrounded them in nature. It was a remarkable illusion, but the leopard's eyes were lifeless as he sat on his real tree branch, and the hyenas were frozen in place, laughing forever at a painted sky. And everything was behind glass, everything except one exhibit. And that exhibit was absolutely wonderful!

Nita gasped out loud as she reached the end of the long hallway and sat down on a bench which had been placed directly in front of the huge diorama. This exhibit was immense, covering the whole end of the wide hallway and extending back for what looked like at least forty feet. It was an African watering hole, with huge elephants and giraffes and even a lion. And it had sound effects. There were monkeys chattering in the trees, exotic birds singing their strange, throaty calls, the distant roar of a lion, and even the sound of water splashing as the animals waded and drank. Nita had never seen anything so lifelike before. The person who had designed this diorama could get a job making sets for the movies, no problem. There was only one thing that spoiled the illusion, and that certainly wasn't the designer's fault. A door at the side of the hallway was propped open, and Nita could see the delivery dock at the rear of the building, and beyond it, Judy's car in the distance. The sight of Judy's car made Nita frown. Michael had told her that Judy owned the expensive Volvo, free and clear. He'd also told her that a brand new Volvo, with all the options, sold for over fifty thousand dollars. Judy was rich, and she could buy anything she wanted. But Judy wanted Michael, and he was one thing she couldn't buy.

That thought made Nita feel much better. She was going to end up with Michael, and there wasn't a thing Judy could do to stop her. Nita got up and read the plaques at the side of the diorama. She'd prove that she was every bit as smart as that spoiled little rich girl!

As Nita read, she memorized the important facts. Elephants were the largest living land mammals, and they came in two species, *Loxodonta africana,* the African elephant, and *Elephas maximus,* the, Indian elephant. The elephants at the watering hole were African elephants and they could grow to twelve feet tall and weigh more than six tons. They lived in herds and fed on grass and foliage.

Another plaque described the giraffes. Nita learned that *Giraffa camelopardalis* was the tallest living land mammal. The males could reach eighteen feet, and over a third of their height was neck and head. They lived by grazing, often on trees, and they were speedy runners who were related to the deer.

It took only a few more moments for Nita to memorize everything on all of the plaques. She'd always been able to memorize rapidly, and her teachers had often chastised her for not applying herself in school. Nita guessed they were right. She knew that if she took the time to study, she could get excellent grades. Today, she wanted to memorize everything so that she could impress Michael. It was a great incentive. If she'd gone to school with Michael, she might have been a straight 'A' student.

A glance at her watch told Nita she'd been gone for only five minutes. They were probably in the pre-Columbian room by now, looking at the model of the Aztec temple. There was no need to hurry. Michael had told her to take her time. She could sit on the bench for a few minutes and rest her aching feet.

Nita walked over to the door, closing it firmly. That was better. Then she sat back down on the bench, slipped off her sandals, and smiled. Now that the traffic noise was gone, she could hear the sounds of the African jungle much more clearly. She was surrounded by monkey chatter, calling birds, and the trumpeting of an elephant in the distance.

Looking at all the exhibits had been exhausting, and Nita shut her eyes for a moment to concentrate on the bird calls. They were strange and exotic and wonderful, so different from the birds she heard in Los Angeles. She could hear the squawking of something that sounded like a parrot, but there was another call that was delightfully musical. The birds in the *barrio* weren't very musical. They screeched at the tops of their lungs from the high tension electrical wires, and the sounds they made weren't music. The *barrio* birds sounded as if they were protesting all the crime and violence on the streets. Maybe they were. There were times when Nita wished that she could sit up on a high tension wire, far away from the gangs with their knives and guns, and the young taggers that invaded her neighborhood to scrawl their names on fences, and walls, and mailboxes. She tried to avoid any contact, but that was almost impossible. There were dope deals going down on her corner, and she woke up to the sounds of gunshots almost every weekend. It was so dangerous that when the man next door had suffered a heart attack, the ambulance had refused to come without a police escort.

Nita heard the faint roar of a lion, and she shivered. The jungle seemed peaceful, but there was violence in its depths. Down in the barrio, she was living in a concrete jungle, but she wasn't stuck there like the giraffe or the elephant. She had a way out, and that way was Michael. He might not make it big in show business, but he would never have to live in a slum.

What time was it? Nita opened her eyes and glanced at her watch. Fifteen minutes had passed. It was time to get back to Michael and Berto, and that bitch, Judy. She didn't want to give Judy too much time with Michael. That would be asking for trouble.

Nita was just slipping on her sandals when she heard it, a small mewling sound from the depths of the diorama. At first she thought it was some kind of jungle noise, but it sounded very familiar. There it was again! Nita got up and moved forward, leaning over the velvet ropes. It was a kitten, she was sure of it, and it sounded real. The door had been open and kittens were naturally curious. It was possible the poor thing had wandered in and climbed into the diorama. It was probably frightened because it couldn't find its way out. Nita loved kittens. They were adorable little balls of soft, warm fur. She couldn't just leave it there.

Nita hesitated, wondering whether she should go and notify the guard. But the guard would probably toss the kitten out of the museum, and it sounded too young to get along on its own. It might try to run across the busy street, and get hit by a car. Or if it was lucky enough to stay out of the traffic, it could still starve to death!

A thought flashed through Nita's mind and she grinned as she stepped around the velvet ropes. She'd find the kitten and take it home with her. Her mother wouldn't mind. They still had the litter box they'd used with their old tomcat, and it would be nice to have a pet.

The kitten cried out again, and Nita held her breath as she walked straight into the diorama. She just hoped she could find the kitten before anyone caught her. She'd be very careful not to touch anything unless she absolutely had to. Walking into the diorama was bound to be against the rules.

"Here, kitty-kitty-kitty." Nita called out softly. If anyone spotted her, she'd probably be kicked out of the museum for life. But then she heard a scratching behind the trunk of the huge baobub tree. The kitten was back there, and it sounded even more desperate. She had to hurry. It could be tangled up in the vegetation, caught helplessly as it fought to get loose. She had to find it and free it quickly before it strangled itself.

The big bull elephant looked very real as Nita inched carefully around it. And the jungle noises were louder, now that she was actually inside the diorama. It was so real, Nita actually felt a prickle of fear as the lion roared, and she chided herself for being foolish. She wasn't really in a jungle. These were dead, stuffed animals and there was no way they could hurt her.

But the illusion was very compelling and Nita held her breath as she slipped past the giraffe, and headed for the trunk of the massive tree. It even smelled like a jungle in here, moist and green and sweaty. Of course she'd never been in a jungle, so she couldn't possibly know how it smelled. It just seemed as if it would have to smell like this, from the pictures she'd seen.

As Nita stepped deeper and deeper into the display, the shadows grew darker and more ominous. The vegetation was thicker, and she had to be careful not to trip over the tangle of vines. The lights didn't shine back here, but it was still very hot. Hot and airless, like being stuck in a boarded-up warehouse in the middle of a heat wave.

Nita paused to let her eyes adjust to the dark. It was scary back here, and she could feel cold drops of perspiration dripping down her back. What if she'd been wrong? What if the cry she'd heard was only part of the jungle sounds? It could have been a baby lion mewing, or a newborn leopard crying for its mother.

But there had been a scratching noise. She hadn't imagined that. Of course, they'd probably taped the jungle noises in a real jungle. And big cats sharpened their claws on tree trunks, didn't they?

No. There was something back here, something alive. Nita was sure she could hear it breathing. Animals panted when they were afraid, and this poor little kitten must be terrified. She had to find it and rescue it. She'd come too far to give up now.

Just as she approached the massive tree trunk, Nita heard that desperate cry again. She stopped and looked up, expecting to find the terrified little animal clinging to a tree branch, but there was nothing there. No kitten in any of the branches. No kitten caught in a hanging vine. But she could still hear the breathing and it seemed to be coming from behind the tree trunk.

Nita took a step forward and parted the vines. She saw a dark shape, massive and looming, so still it looked like part of the tree trunk. But even in this dim light, Nita could see that it had a human shape. Legs. Torso. Arms. And one arm was raised high in the air.

Time seemed to stand still as Nita's mind spun in horrified circles. The kitten had come in through the open door. And so had the shape, the human shape, with its arm raised in the air. But there was no kitten. It had all been a trap to lure her back here.

Nita stepped back just as the killer's arm came down, narrowly missing her head. She tried to run, but her foot was tangled in an electrical cable. She tugged, hard, and something snapped. The jungle noises stopped abruptly, and all she could hear was her own tortured breathing. And then she caught sight of the killer's face, grotesque with rage. Nita opened her mouth to scream, but the tire iron came down too fast for her to utter a single sound.

Eighteen

Judy took a sip of water. Her hands were trembling, and her mouth was dry. After the guard had found Nita's body, Detective Davis had asked them all to come down to the station to give statements.

"And what did you do when Miss Cordoza didn't come back to join you?"

Judy sighed deeply. "I said I'd go see if she was all right. I had heard her say that she was going to the ladies' room."

"What did you do when you discovered that she wasn't there?"

"I looked around in the halls. I thought maybe she'd stopped at some exhibit and lost track of the time."

"How long was it before you went back to get the boys?"

Judy sighed again. "I don't know for sure. I didn't look at my watch."

"What happened when you got back to pre-Columbian room?"

"I told the guys that I couldn't find Nita, and we split up to look for her." Judy took another sip of water. "We were all wearing watches so we agreed to look for twenty minutes, and meet back in the lobby.'

"You didn't think there was anything wrong?"

"No." Judy shook her head. "We just thought Nita was look-

ing at something on her own. I don't think any of us even
thought about . . . about the killer."

"And when you all met in the lobby after your search, you
notified the guard?"

Judy nodded. "That's right, sir. By then we were getting nervous. Nita had been missing for a long time. That's when I
thought about the killer. But I didn't say anything to Michael or
Berto."

"Why not?"

"I didn't want to say it because . . . well . . . I was afraid that
if I'd said it out loud, it might come true. I guess that's kind of
crazy, isn't it?"

"No, not really." Detective Davis looked very understanding.
"Now I want you to tell me what was running through your
mind when you all split up to look for Nita. Where did you go?"

"I looked in the restaurant first. I thought maybe she might
have gotten hungry and gone in there to buy a snack. And I
checked the patio area where we'd eaten our lunch. After that, I
retraced our footsteps, all the way back to the entrance."

"Why did you do that?"

Judy frowned slightly. "I thought maybe Nita had dropped
something, and she'd gone back to try to find it. I kept thinking
I'd run into her any second, standing in front of some display,
reading one of those little plaques. Nita always read the plaques."

"Did you look in the diorama section?"

Judy nodded. "Yes, I did. That's where we were going next,
and it occurred to me that Nita might be waiting for us there. I
went to the North American section first, the one with the polar
bears, and the penguins. I ran into an elderly couple standing in
front of the wolves. She was sketching the grey wolf, so I figured
they'd been there for awhile. I asked them if they'd seen Nita,
and they told me that no one else had come in for at least an
hour."

"And then you went across the hall to the other diorama section?"

"Yes." Judy's voice started to shake. "I walked through the
whole thing. And I noticed that the sound system wasn't work-

ing at the . . . the big diorama at the end of the hall. But I had no idea that Nina's foot was tangled in the speaker cords!"

Judy's voice quavered, and she took the tissue Detective Davis handed her to wipe her eyes. "I'll never forgive myself, Detective Davis. I should have told the guard that the sound system wasn't working!"

"That's all right, Miss Lampert." Detective Davis' voice was kind. "There's no way you could have known that your friend was inside the diorama."

"But I should have been smart enough to realize that something was wrong! If I'd just mentioned it to the guard, he would have found Nita right away. And then we could have called for an ambulance and . . ."

"Look, Miss Lampert . . ." Detective Davis interrupted her. "An ambulance wouldn't have helped. Your friend died instantly."

Judy shuddered, and took another sip of her water.

"I have only a few more questions, if you feel up to it."

"Of course." Judy drew a deep, shaking breath. "I'd like to help, but I don't know what else I can tell you."

"Let's go back to the last time you saw Miss Cordoza. You were in the pre-Columbian room?"

"No. We were looking at a display of rocks and minerals in the hallway. That's when Nita excused herself to go to the ladies' room."

"And Miss Cordoza's brother and Michael Warden were with you?"

Judy nodded. "Michael told Nita that she should take her time. We'd go on to the pre-Columbian room and she could meet us in there."

"What happened after Miss Cordoza left?"

"We looked at the rock exhibit for a while, and then we went into the pre-Columbian room. We looked at everything so it must have taken us at least fifteen minutes or so. I was showing Michael and Berto the scale model of the Aztec temple when I realized that Nita had been gone for quite a while."

"The two boys were with you all that time?"

"Yes." Judy nodded. "I left to look for Nita in the ladies' room and they stayed right there in front of the temple. When I came back to tell them that I couldn't find Nita, we split up to search for her. I already told you where I went."

Detective Davis looked down at his notes. "You went to the restaurant first. And then you went back to all the exhibits you'd seen before. Is that right?"

"That's right. And then I went to the diorama, and—oh! I almost forgot to tell you. I went out to the parking lot again, to see if I recognized any of the cars."

"Why did you do that?"

"I told everybody at Covers that we were coming to the museum. I thought maybe Nita had run into somebody she knew, and was sitting out in the car with them. I know that doesn't make a lot of sense, I guess I was starting to panic."

Detective Davis jotted down a note. "You say you told everyone at Covers that you were going to the museum?"

"That's right. I asked them to join us if they could. But nobody showed up."

"Thank you, Miss Lampert." Detective Davis stood up. "You've been very helpful. If you remember anything else, I want you to call me."

Judy stood up. The interview was over. "Yes, sir. Was there . . . uh . . . did you find another arrow?"

Detective Davis looked grim as he nodded. "You're free to go, Miss Lampert. Thank you for your cooperation. I'll have someone transcribe your statement, and I'd like you to drop by tomorrow to sign it."

"I'll be glad to do that." Judy started for the door. "Is Berto through yet?"

"He left with his family, right after we finished taking his statement."

"Oh. Of course." Judy winced slightly. "Poor Berto. Is he all right?"

Detective Davis nodded. "He's doing fine, under the circumstances. We told him he could wait until tomorrow to be interviewed, but he said he'd rather do it tonight, when things were fresh in his mind."

"How about Michael? He rode with me."

"I think you'd better go on without him. He'll be here for a while."

Judy began to frown. That sounded very ominous. Surely they didn't think Michael had anything to do with Nita's death? "Will it be long? I could wait," she said.

"That's not necessary, Miss Lampert. We'll give him a ride home when we're through questioning him."

Judy walked out to the parking lot, her heart pounding hard in her chest. Detective Davis said they were "questioning" Michael, and he'd referred to the statements they'd taken from her and from Berto as "interviews." They *did* suspect Michael!

Judy's hands were shaking as she took out her keys and opened the door to her Volvo. She was going to drive straight home, and wait for the police to bring Michael back. She'd catch him before he went into his house, and find out exactly what Detective Davis had asked him. Michael hadn't killed Nita. That was one thing she knew for certain!

It took only a few minutes to get home. It was seven o'clock on a Sunday night, and there was very little traffic. Judy pulled into the garage, shut off the engine, and leaned back in the seat with a sigh. Michael would be very upset when he came home from the police station, and he'd mentioned that his parents were gone for the weekend. There was no way she was going to let him go home to an empty house with no one to talk to.

Judy got out of her car, and headed for the house with a smile on her face. She'd tell Marta to make some of her special sandwiches, and she'd watch for Michael to come home. Then she'd invite him to come over and have a bite to eat. They'd sit out on the patio, and Judy would be sure to turn on the jacuzzi so that they could relax in the hot, steamy water. Michael would need a friend tonight . . . a very special friend who could love and comfort him. Tonight was the night. Tonight Michael would finally realize that Judy was the one girl in the world who would always be there for him.

Nineteen

It was almost midnight, and Judy and Michael were in the jacuzzi, sipping wine. Judy had set a tray of snacks right next to the jacuzzi, but Michael had barely touched his favorite aged cheddar or the hard salami Judy knew he loved. He'd told her he was too upset to eat, and Judy couldn't blame him. He'd looked awful when the police had brought him home around eleven. There had been dark circles under his eyes, and his hands had been shaking. Judy knew he'd had a terrible experience at police headquarters, but he hadn't wanted to talk about it then. He'd told her that they would discuss it later, and Judy was patiently waiting for Michael to bring it up.

"Thanks, Jude." Michael leaned back in the steamy water, and sighed deeply. "I don't know what I'd do without you. You always seem to be there when I'm feeling awful."

"That's what friends are for." Judy's voice was soft. "I love you, Michael."

Michael draped a friendly arm around her shoulders. "And I love you, too. You're one in a million, little sis."

Judy could feel her frustration grow. Michael was so near and yet so far. His arm was warm around her shoulder, and he'd told her that he loved her. The action was right. The words were perfect. But she knew he still thought of her as his little sister.

"I'm not your sister, Michael." Judy kept her voice soft, but she could hear the tension behind her words. "We're not even related."

Michael grinned. It came out lopsided, but Judy didn't mind. "Don't tell that to Detective Davis. I'm trying to pass you off as my sister so he'll let you visit me in jail."

It was a lame joke, but Judy laughed. At least Michael was trying. And hearing him try to joke was better than watching him stare at the surface of the water with troubled eyes. Then the full implication of what he'd said hit her like a blow to the stomach. "Jail? What do you mean?"

"They asked me about the arrows, Jude." Michael pulled her a little closer until she was snuggled up against his side. "I had to tell them. They would have found out from my parents, anyway."

Judy nodded. "Did you tell them the shed wasn't locked?"

"I told them, but I don't think it made any difference. They think I'm the serial killer."

Judy stared up at Michael's face. He looked very anxious. "Don't worry, Michael. They can't arrest you unless they have proof. And they can't prove you killed anybody!"

"I know. But innocent people have been convicted before."

Judy shivered. Michael had a point. She'd read about people convicted for murder who weren't released until years later, after the real killer confessed. "I don't understand, Michael. You had no reason to kill those girls. Why do they think you did it?"

"They've got this crazy theory. They think I was angry with the girls because they wouldn't sleep with me. And so I . . . I killed them."

"That *is* crazy!" Judy wrapped her arms around Michael's waist and held him tightly. "You have to prove them wrong."

"That's easy for you to say. How am I going to do that?"

Judy almost laughed out loud as an idea popped into her head. It was brilliant and it accomplished exactly what she'd set out to do tonight. "It's simple, Michael. You sleep with a girl, and you *don't* kill her. That'll prove their theory is wrong."

Michael threw back his head and laughed. "Very funny, Jude.

I'm sure there are millions of girls out there who would love to sleep with me, just so I can prove I won't kill them. All I have to do is ask, right?"

"That's right." Judy gave him a big smile. "Ask me. I'll do it."

Michael's mouth dropped open. "What?!"

"I'll sleep with you. And then I'll go down to police headquarters in the morning, and I'll tell them exactly what happened. That ought to shoot their silly theory all to hell."

Michael blinked, and stared at her hard. "You'd actually—I mean, you really would—Jude!"

"I shocked you." Judy managed to sound contrite. "I'm sorry, Michael. But I do love you. And it would solve all your problems."

"That's insane. That's utterly, completely insane!"

"Why?" Judy put on her sexiest smile, and ran her fingertips over his chest. "Don't you want to sleep with me?"

"I . . . look, Jude. I never really thought about it before. I mean, you're like a little sister to me. It would be like—like incest!"

"I told you before, we're not related. So it couldn't possibly be incest. Don't you find me attractive, Michael?"

Michael swallowed hard. "Sure. I mean, you're very pretty, and you're my best friend and all, but . . . look, Jude. This whole thing is crazy. It won't work."

Judy knew it was time to take charge. Michael obviously wasn't thinking clearly. But she was. Since he'd never considered her as a possible lover, it would take him awhile to get used to the idea. In the meantime, she'd help him out a little by proving to him that she was sexy and desirable.

"It *will* work, Michael. I'll show you." Judy slipped her arms around Michael's shoulders and brushed her lips against his neck. She heard him gasp, and she smiled. Michael might not realize it, but it was working just fine. His heart was racing and she'd heard him groan, low in his throat. "See? I told you it would work. Just relax, Michael. I'll take care of everything."

Before Michael could react, Judy pulled his face to hers and kissed him. She had to be careful. She didn't want to scare him with the depth of her passion. She kissed him softly at first, just brushing her lips against his. But then her self-control began to slip. The man of her dreams was in her arms. She'd waited so long for this moment!

Michael groaned again as her tongue began to probe his mouth. He was fighting to keep from kissing her back. But he couldn't resist for long, Judy knew that. And he didn't. He grabbed her roughly and pulled her tightly against him, almost bruising her lips with the intensity of his kiss.

"Oh, yes!" Judy rubbed her body against his, her breasts pressing tightly against his chest. Michael wasn't resisting now. His hands moved swiftly over her back, rubbing, caressing her satiny skin, releasing the hook on the top of her bikini.

Together, they moved into deeper water, feeling the hot, rushing water flow past their joined bodies. Judy felt as if she were floating on a sea of pure, heavenly heat. She ground her body against his, and he pulled her even more tightly against him. There was no stopping now. She would be one with the man she'd loved in secret for so long.

And then, abruptly, he thrust her from him so fiercely that she almost fell. There was anguish in his eyes as he stood and faced her. And then he spoke the words that drove arrows of pain straight into her heart.

"No, Jude. It's not right. I'd never forgive myself if I took advantage of you."

"But you *aren't* taking advantage of me!" Judy rose from the water like a modern Venus, her breasts marble white in the moonlight. The night was cool, and the sudden chill in the air matched the bleak void that had suddenly invaded her heart. "I want you, Michael. I want you so much!"

"I told you, Jude. This isn't right. Don't you see? We're friends. We're good friends. I don't want to be more than that."

Judy felt a flash of pure rage. It rushed through her body like a raging fire, and suddenly she wasn't cold any longer. Michael had kissed all those other girls. He'd hugged them and caressed them and made love to them. Why was he was playing hard to get with her?

Because she was the one who mattered to him. The moment it occurred to her, Judy began to smile. Of course! Michael hadn't really cared what the other girls thought of him. He hadn't wanted a lasting relationship with any of them. But he did with her. And that was the reason he didn't want to spoil things between them by rushing into bed with her.

"Oh, Michael!" Judy threw her arms around his neck again, and rubbed her breasts against his warm chest "I understand. Really, I do. But you don't have to worry that you're rushing me. I'm ready, Michael. I know that we were born to be together."

Michael stood there like a statue, but that didn't matter. Judy pulled his head down and forced his lips against hers. She'd *make* him respond to her! One taste of her willing lips, and he'd forget all about his worries.

"Jude . . . please."

Michael stepped back so quickly, Judy almost fell. But she wasn't discouraged. She'd felt his lips warm against hers, right before he'd pulled away. And he was trembling, another sign that he wanted her. Michael wasn't immune to her charms. Far from it. All she had to do was give him no choice.

"Don't be a fool, Michael." Judy smiled her most engaging smile. "I know you want me. You're just afraid to admit it. Well . . . you don't have to admit it. I'll do everything for you."

"Jude . . ."

Michael began to protest, but Judy silenced him with another kiss. This was better. She could feel him beginning to respond. But just as she thought she'd driven away the last of his foolish inhibitions, Michael thrust her from him so roughly, she stumbled and fell to her knees in the bubbling water.

"Michael . . . wait!" He was trying to climb out of the water, and Judy clung desperately to his arm. "You can't leave! Not now! Not ever!"

But Michael didn't even look at her as he tried to shake off her embrace. Judy felt the beginnings of despair, but she couldn't abandon all her plans now. Michael had to see that she loved him. He had to believe her! "Is it *them,* Michael? Do you love the other girls more than you love me?"

Michael turned to stare at her. "What other girls? What are you talking about?"

"They weren't right for you, Michael. You know they weren't. They all had a contest, and you were first prize. Ask Carla. She walked out. And I wasn't part of it, either."

Michael hesitated. He was clearly confused. But he was also intrigued. "What contest? What are you talking about?"

"They had to date you for two solid weeks. And the first one to do that won the contest. Deana started it. But she didn't really want you. She was just using you to win the contest. Did you ever really love Deana?"

Michael didn't answer, and Judy smiled. Suddenly she felt very happy. "I was right! I was sure you didn't love her. But how about Becky? Did you love Becky?"

Michael was still silent, and Judy's smile grew wider. "Just as I thought! You're no fool, Michael. You knew that Becky was only using you. And Mary Beth was even worse. She let you think she was serious about you. And all the time, she was seeing her old boyfriend behind your back! Ingrid was different. There was nothing wrong with the way she treated you, but Ingrid wanted to marry you! And so did Nita. All Nita wanted was your money so she could get out of the *barrio.*"

Michael's face was very white. It was probably just the effect of the moonlight. Judy ignored it as she wrapped her arms around him again, and snuggled her bare breasts against his chest. "Are they the reason you can't let yourself love me? Do you still love any of them?"

"How could I love them? They're dead!"

Judy felt the laughter bubble up out of her throat. "Of course they're dead. I killed them!"

"You . . . killed . . . them?"

Michael looked as if he'd been hit by a baseball bat, and Judy laughed harder. He looked so shocked. "Of course I killed them! See what I've done for you, Michael? I killed them all because I love you! The arrows of love, don't you see? Love kills. It was a message, a warning to stay away from you. But they were too stupid to catch on. And now you're mine! All mine!"

"My God! You're . . . you're sick!" Michael shoved her away so hard, Judy stumbled and almost fell. "You're drunk, or stoned, or something, Jude. If I didn't know you better, I might even believe you. You'd better get in the house and sleep it off. You're acting totally insane!"

Michael started to get out of the jacuzzi again, but Judy pulled him back. She clung to his arm and began to sob. "But I love you! Can't you see? I love you, Michael! Why won't you make love to me when I want you so much?"

Michael looked disgusted as he pried her fingers loose and stepped out of the water. But Judy was right behind him. There was no way she was going to let him get away now!

The platter of snacks was still on the lip of the jacuzzi, and Judy grabbed the sharp knife she'd used to cut the salami. "If I can't have you, nobody can! I'll kill you! Then you can rot in hell with all of them!"

Judy lunged, but Michael was too quick for her. He side-stepped neatly, sent the knife clattering from her fingers, and pushed her back into the steaming water. Judy thrashed around for precious moments, trying to regain her footing. When she climbed from the jacuzzi at last, sputtering angrily at the man who had betrayed her, Michael was gone.

She stared at hedge for a moment. The branches were still waving gently where Michael had passed through. Then she picked up the knife with a corner of a towel and carried it into the house. Michael was probably sitting in his room right now, grateful that he'd escaped with his life. But he hadn't. Not yet.

Michael's fingers were shaking as he dialed the phone. What a night for his parents to be gone! He had to tell someone what had happened. Of course he didn't believe Judy's story for a moment, but there was no doubt in his mind that she had tried to kill him.

Michael breathed a sigh of relief as Andy answered the phone. "I'm really glad you're home! Do you think you could drive over here? Judy's acting really weird and I think she's flipped out."

"Sure." Andy agreed instantly, but he sounded puzzled. "What did she do?"

"She says she's the killer. Of course I know that's ridiculous, but when I said I didn't believe her, she picked up a knife and lunged at me. Maybe you can talk some sense into her, Andy. She likes you."

"Okay. Hold on a second, will you?" Michael waited while Andy talked to someone in the background. When he came back on the line he sounded very serious. "Carla's here and she wants to come, too. Is that all right?"

Michael nodded. "That's great! Maybe another girl will help. Come over here first and we'll all walk over to Judy's house together."

As Michael hung up, he glanced at his watch. It was almost one o'clock in the morning, and Carla was with Andy. He hoped a little romance was developing between Carla and Andy. Carla was a nice girl, and Andy had been a loner for too long. It would be a good match for both of them.

Five minutes passed while Michael paced the floor. Andy lived about twenty minutes away, so he had some time. He wondered if he should call Judy on the phone to try to calm her down, but that might upset her even more. He stared at the phone, debating the pros and cons, and finally he decided to leave well enough alone. Judy had looked very determined when she'd lunged at him with that knife.

Another five minutes passed, and Michael pulled back the curtains to look out the window. There was a light on in Judy's bedroom. Perhaps she'd passed out. Then the phone rang, and he raced to answer it.

"Michael?"

"Yeah?" Michael gripped the receiver tightly as he recognized Judy's voice.

"I feel terrible, Michael, and I'm sorry I was so weird. It's just I was so nervous over Nita and all, I drank a whole bottle of wine all by myself. Did I do anything awful?"

Michael frowned. What should he say? He didn't want to push her over the edge. "Uh . . . well . . . you were a little strange."

There was a long silence and Michael wondered if he'd made things worse. But then Judy spoke again.

"I'm sorry, Michael. I was really upset when you left, but I'm much better now. I took some of Pamela's sleeping pills and they're making me feel nice and woozy. I think I'm going to go to sleep now."

"No!" Michael felt his pulse race. "Don't go to sleep, Jude. Talk to me. How many pills did you take?"

There was another long silence and then Judy yawned. "I think I took them all, the whole bottle. I kept thinking that if one made me feel good, two would be better and then three and I . . . I guess I lost count."

"Jude. Hang on." Michael made a lightning decision. "Can you unlock the front door for me?"

"I would, but I'm sooo sleepy, I just can't keep my eyes . . ."

There was another lengthy silence and Michael shouted into the receiver "Jude? Judy! Wake up!"

"No. I want to go to sleep forever. I don't deserve to be your friend. But I love you, Michael . . . and . . . goodbye."

Michael frowned as he heard a dial tone. Judy had hung up. And she'd taken a whole bottle of sleeping pills. He had to go over and wake her up, keep her moving until he could call an ambulance. But the front door was locked.

What could he do?

The moment he thought of it, Michael went into action. He grabbed a hammer from the rack of tools in the garage and raced for Judy's house. The Lamperts would have to replace a window, but that was a small price to pay for their daughter's life.

Detective Davis put down the phone and grabbed his partner's shirt sleeve. "Come on. Let's roll. We've got an attempted homicide!"

Less than thirty seconds later, they were in the car, heading for the Lampert resident. Detective Davis sounded grim as he explained the call. "That was Judy Lampert. She was practically hysterical. She said her next-door neighbor is breaking into the house and she thinks he's going to kill her."

"Judy Lampert? Wasn't she at the museum when Nita Cordoza was killed?"

"That's right." Detective Davis nodded. "And her next door neighbor is Michael Warden."

"The suspect?"

"Right again. Her house is just up the block. Kill the lights and let's go in nice and quiet. And pray we're in time to save her!"

"Jude! No!" Michael really wanted to call for help, but Judy had gone positively ballistic, and he knew he didn't dare leave her for a second. He'd found her in her bedroom pacing the floor with a knife clutched in her hand. She'd already stabbed herself once. He'd seen the cut on her arm, but she hadn't let him bandage it. Naturally, he'd grabbed the knife and tossed it to the floor and now he was struggling with her, trying to keep her from grabbing it again. He'd been so busy, trying to keep Judy from hurting herself, he hadn't even heard the footsteps on the stairs.

"Hold it right there!"

Michael whirled to see Detective Davis and his partner, guns drawn, standing in the doorway. And two more policemen were right behind them. Help was here! But before Michael could explain what had happened, Detective Davis had slapped handcuffs on him!

"Hey! I'm just trying to help her!" Michael's voice was shaking. "She took some pills and she's trying to kill herself!"

Detective Davis nodded to one of the other policemen. "Take him down to the station and book him. We'll take Miss Lampert to the hospital, and get her statement."

Michael was still trying to explain as he was unceremoniously escorted down the stairs and out to the squad car. As they were about to pull out from the curb, Andy and Carla ran up to the car.

"What's going on?" Andy sounded frantic. "Is Judy all right?"

"She's fine. Just a cut on the arm." The officer's voice was grim. "We caught him just in time."

"Caught who? What happened?" Andy looked shocked as he caught a glimpse of Michael in the back seat. "What's Michael doing in there?"

"He attacked Miss Lampert, and we caught him redhanded. They're taking her to the hospital right now."

"But Michael wouldn't hurt Judy!" Carla spoke up. "He called us and told us to come right over. He said Judy'd been drinking and she was acting very weird. She even tried to stab him with a knife. Really, officer . . . this is all some kind of misunderstanding."

The officer didn't look convinced. "We'll see about that. Follow us down to the station. We'll need statements from you, too."

Just then Judy came out of the house. A towel was wrapped around her arm and blood was already seeping through it. Detective Davis walked on one side of her, his partner on the other.

"Judy!" Carla rushed up to her. "Are you all right?"

Judy looked very pale as she nodded. "I'm okay. Thanks for coming, Carla. Did the police call you?"

"No. Michael did. He said you'd been drinking and you were . . . uh . . . very upset."

Judy nodded. "It's true. I was upset. But I only had a sip of wine. My glass is still out at the jacuzzi. Michael drank all the rest."

"What happened?" Andy rushed up to join them.

"Hi, Andy." Judy gave him a wan smile. "Michael and I were in the jacuzzi. It was nice at first. We had some snacks, and then he got serious. He was mad at me because I wouldn't sleep with him, and he started shouting things about Nita and Ingrid and what happened to all the other girls who'd turned him down."

"Are you sure?" Carla didn't look convinced.

"Oh, yes. I was so shocked I remember every word. When Michael reached for the knife on the cheese tray, I dashed into the house and locked the door. I know he didn't mean it, but he really looked like he was going to kill me!"

Andy frowned. "But he called us and said *you* tried to stab *him* with the knife."

"What?!" Judy looked shocked. "But that's not what happened at all!"

Carla gave a deep sigh. "Think carefully, Judy. When Michael broke into your house, are you sure he wasn't just trying to help you?"

"With a knife in his hand?" Judy's voice faltered, and she started to cry. "I don't know what to believe! Michael told me he killed all those girls. And I got so scared when I saw him breaking into the house with that knife, that I . . . I called Detective Davis and asked for help."

Detective Davis put his hand on Carla's arm. "You can talk to Miss Lampert later. You two go down to the station and give your statements. I want to know everything the suspect said to you on the phone."

"The suspect?" Andy looked very concerned. "You don't believe her, do you? Michael didn't kill those girls!"

Detective Davis was grim as he turned to face Andy. "He doesn't have an alibi. He told us that earlier tonight."

"But . . ." Andy swallowed hard. "That doesn't mean Michael did it!"

"Of course not." Detective Davis patted Andy on the shoulder. "If there's no proof, he'll be released. But there's still the attempted murder charge. Miss Lampert and Mr. Warden were struggling over the knife when we arrived at the scene. If Miss Lampert wants to press charges, he'll go to trial."

Judy looked frightened. "Oh, no! I don't want to press charges, Detective Davis. Michael just . . . he just flipped out, that's all. I don't want him to go to jail! I just want him to get some help."

"That could be arranged. The court will order a period of observation in a mental facility if you request it."

Judy looked hopeful. "If I did that, would Michael get some counseling for his problems?"

"Of course. Make up your mind in the morning. There's no rush. He can cool off in a cell tonight."

"Well . . . all right." Judy gave Detective Davis a shaky smile, and then she turned to Andy and Carla. "If you see Michael, tell him that I'll wait for him, and I'll be right there when he gets out. That should make him feel much, much better!"

Twenty

Judy parked her Volvo in one of the tree-shaded spaces marked for visitors, and walked up the flagstone path to the lovely white house that was set on the crest of the hill. It was almost September, and here in the countryside, the trees were beginning to change color. A grove of maples created a riotous spot of bright red and orange against the rolling green hills, and the ash trees provided a lovely golden shade. There were spruce trees, too, their dark green branches reaching skyward, weaving gently in the autumn breeze. Even the sky was a perfect crystal blue, dotted by puffy white clouds.

The day was lovely, the scene pastoral. Judy felt her spirits lift as she approached the entrance. The heavy mesh screens on the windows were almost invisible in the bright noon sun, and it all looked quite ordinary and quite beautiful. Of course, not all things were as they appeared. Judy knew that. She'd been here many times before.

A discreet wooden plaque near the door identified the home as Brookhaven, and it could have been the setting for a romantic film. The peaceful grounds were deserted, and Judy felt as if she had stepped into a painted landscape. No one was out walking, although it was a lovely fall day. Perhaps they were waiting until after lunch to enjoy the warm fall air.

There was a small brass buzzer by the side of the door, and

Judy pressed it. Then she waited, tapping her foot on the floor-boards of the old-fashioned porch.

"Yes?" A tinny voice came out of the speaker box near the buzzer.

"It's Judy Lampert. I'm here to visit."

"Come in, dear."

The voice sounded friendlier now, and the door gave an audible click. Judy pushed it open, and waited in the vestibule in front of another door, until the outside door had clicked shut behind her. Then an older woman wearing a white nurse's uniform hurried toward her to unlock the second door.

"Hi, Miss Danver." Judy smiled as the nurse let her in. "How is he today?"

"Much better. The shock treatments seem to be helping. His parents were here yesterday, and they were sure he recognized them. He even made an effort to speak."

"That's good news." Judy nodded. "Do you think I could see him?"

"I'm afraid not, dear. He had quite a setback the last time you were here, and the doctor thinks it would be wise to wait for another few weeks."

"Oh. Of course."

Miss Danver felt her heart go out to the pretty blonde girl who came to visit every week. Judy was a dear, and it was a pity her presence made the patient react so violently. Still, there was no use denying reality. Michael Warden suffered a setback every time she visited.

"I brought him these." Judy handed the nurse a pretty box, wrapped in gold paper. "They're chocolate chip cookies, and they used to be his favorites. I made them myself."

Miss Danver smiled as she took the box. "That's very sweet, dear. I'll make sure that he gets them."

"Do you think he might be able to see me next week?"

"Perhaps." Miss Danver smiled as she told what she referred to as a little white lie. The doctor had left strict orders, and this poor, sweet girl was no longer on the visitor's list. "Just give me a call before you drive all the way out here. It's a long trip."

"Oh, I don't mind. It's so pretty here. And I always bring something for him, even if I can't see him. I know this sounds crazy, but it makes me feel better to be even this close to him."

"I understand." Miss Danver gave her a sympathetic smile. "I'm sorry, dear. But he's getting better every day. I'm sure you'll be able to see him before long."

Miss Danver put her arm around Judy's shoulders and walked her to the door. As soon as the inner door had closed behind her, she locked it and pressed the buzzer to open the outer door. She gave a deep sigh as she watched Judy walk down the path. Her shoulders were drooping, and her pretty blonde head was bowed. It was clear that she was very disappointed, and Nurse Danver imagined her sorrowful face, blinking back tears, as she walked all alone toward the parking lot.

Nurse Danver sighed again, as Judy rounded the bend and disappeared out of sight. She would have been very surprised indeed, if she'd been able to see the satisfied smile on Judy Lampert's face.

Judy was smiling as she pulled out of her parking space. It gave her great pleasure to visit Michael, even if she wasn't allowed to see him. It was good to know that he was here, behind locked doors. And he'd be here forever, if she had her way. After all, he'd almost ruined her life.

There was a country-western station on the radio, and Judy sang along as she drove down the road to the freeway entrance. The song was about how painful love could be. Judy smiled wryly. Michael had caused her plenty of pain, but now it was time to put all that grief behind her, and find someone new. Of course she'd have to be very careful to choose someone who would truly appreciate her.

Judy felt a sudden burst of excitement. She knew her new love was out there somewhere; all she had to do was find him. If he turned out to be unworthy of her affections, she'd simply get rid of him. Just like she'd done with Michael.

* * *

The next visitors arrived within the hour. Miss Danver let them in, and checked them off on the visitor's list. They were allowed. Carla Fields and Andy Miller didn't upset her patient at all.

"Carla, dear?" Nurse Danver held out the gold-wrapped box. "Would you take these in with you? They're cookies that Miss Lampert baked for Michael."

Carla nodded, and took the box. "Of course. Should we let him have one?"

"He can have as many as he wants," Nurse Danver told her with a smile. Carla wasn't as pretty as Judy Lampert, but she was a very nice girl.

Carla held the box in front of her as they walked down the long hallway, and turned the corner. Then she handed it to Andy. "Do you want to do the honors this time?"

"Sure." Andy stopped next to a wastebasket, and, tore the wrapping from the box. He lifted the lid carefully, and frowned when he saw what was inside.

"She sent another note." Andy unfolded the piece of blue stationery that had been placed on top of the cookies. "It says, *They haven't caught the killer yet, but I know you didn't do it. Maybe someone else will get killed while you're locked up, and then they'll know that you're innocent.*"

"What do you think? Is it enough?"

"No. It's in bad taste, but it doesn't prove anything. She's smart, Carla."

Carla nodded. "It's a good thing Michael didn't get it. Her last note almost did him in. I'm glad the doctor stopped all his mail, except for the cards his parents send him. Do you think we'll ever catch her, Andy?"

"Sure. She's bound to mess up sooner or later, and we'll be right there when she does. All we have to do is watch, and wait for her to make a mistake."

"And meanwhile, poor Michael is locked up in here." Carla took the note, and placed it carefully in the pocket of her purse. "Let's go see him, Andy. Maybe he's better today."

They found Michael in the crafts room, staring down at a tray of paints. There was an easel propped up in front of his chair, but the canvas on it was completely blank.

"Hi, Michael," Carla said.

Carla took the chair next to him, but Michael didn't seem to notice that she was there. He didn't even react when Andy took the paintbrush out of his hand.

"I want you to watch me very carefully, Michael." Andy dipped the brush in a pot of brown paint. "I know you don't want to talk, but there are other ways to communicate."

Carla frowned slightly as Andy drew some lines on the canvas. Then she gasped as she recognized the design. It was a quiver with five arrows.

"Look, Michael." Andy was very serious. "We know the arrows didn't kill them. We need to know what kind of weapon she used. It's very important."

Carla held her breath as Andy held out the brush to Michael. Was he well enough to tell them? Or were they pushing him too hard? It was a big gamble. If Michael retreated back into his shell, it would take months to bring him back.

"Please help us, Michael." Carla patted him on the shoulder. "We can't do it alone."

Michael's hand began to tremble. And then he reached out to grasp the brush. He dipped it into the black paint and drew a stick that was shaped like an "L."

"What is it?" Carla turned to Michael with a frown. "Can you tell us, Michael?"

Andy drew in his breath sharply, as Michael's head dipped in a nod. Michael's hand moved again, dipping the brush into the pot.

His hand raised slowly and he chose a blank spot on the canvas. And then he started to print, in bold block letters. TIRE IRON.

"She killed them with a tire iron?" Andy looked excited. This was a real breakthrough. "The tire iron was the blunt instrument?"

Michael nodded. He raised the brush to the canvas again. MINE MISSING. CHECK HER CA . . .

The word trailed off in a smear, and Carla reached out to take the brush from Michael's trembling fingers. He was clearly exhausted. But Michael waved her away, dipping the brush in the paint once more. This time he used bright red, and the drops that fell from the brush looked like a trail of blood.

They held their breaths as the tip of the brush touched the canvas again. The brush strokes wavered, but Andy and Carla could clearly make out the words that Michael laboriously painted. STOP HER BEFORE SHE KILLS AGAIN!

The Crush II

This book is for "Dollar Bill."

*With special thanks to: John, Lois, & Neal,
the good people from V.N.A., Marian, Iris & Trudi,
Danny & the laptop, and Ruel.*

Prologue

Judy Lampert had never been so mad in her life. Her face was red, her heart was pounding, and she felt like screaming in pure frustration as she knelt down on her adoptive parents' immaculately kept lawn and peered through a gap in the hedge. There was a party going on next door. She'd seen her friends pull into the driveway and get out of the car, carrying platters of food. But she hadn't been invited!

It was August in Southern California, and the afternoons were bright and sunny. The broiling heat of July had passed, and it was no longer necessary to run the air conditioning twenty-four hours a day. It was perfect weather for a party, and that seemed to be what was happening next door. Cars had been arriving for the past thirty minutes, pulling into Mr. and Mrs. Warden's driveway and parking in front of the house.

Judy had been in her bedroom suite when she'd heard music coming from the patio next door. It wasn't the type of music that Michael's parents would enjoy. This was rock music, excellent rock with a driving beat that made Judy's feet tap and wiggle with the desire to dance. But why were Michael's parents hosting a teenage party when their only son, Michael, was locked away at Brookhaven Sanitarium? It just didn't make sense.

The gardener had just watered the lawn, and Judy felt moisture seep through the knees of her jeans. That didn't matter. She had several new pairs hanging in her closet, and she had plenty of time to change clothes before she went to her night job at Covers, the teenage nightclub in Burbank. Getting her clothes wet didn't bother Judy in the least. Her primary concern was finding out exactly what was happening next door.

Judy parted the scratchy branches of the boxwood hedge so she could see most of the patio. Her drama teacher at Burbank High was sitting on a tall director's chair, surrounded by several people from Covers. Mr. Calloway owned Covers, and most of his staff were students. As Judy watched, Linda O'Keefe, one of the singers at Covers, grabbed Mr. Calloway's hand and pulled him up to dance with her. Linda had sung several duets with Michael before all the trouble had started.

As Judy watched, Andy Miller, the short-order cook at Covers, whirled into view. Andy was dancing with Carla Fields, and they looked so funny, Judy almost giggled out loud. With his carrot-red hair and the extra inches around his waist, Andy wasn't any girl's dream guy. But he could certainly do better than Carla!

Carla was the assistant manager at Covers, a nice girl, but not the type that any boy would look at twice. Carla had non-descript brown hair pulled up into a bun, and she wore horned-rimmed glasses. Today she was dressed in her usual outfit, a baggy skirt and an over-sized blouse. Carla came from a poor family and her clothes were all thrift store bargains. She didn't own anything that fit her properly.

Judy watched for a moment, and then she shrugged. Carla and Andy looked as if they were having fun. Perhaps it was a good match, after all. They were both born losers, and no one else would even think of dating them.

Alberto Cordoza, one of the waiters at Covers, came out of the house carrying a platter of snacks. Judy had gone out with Berto while Michael was dating his sister, Nita. Berto hadn't ap-proved of Nita's romance with Michael, and neither had Judy. She'd wanted Michael for herself. But then Nita had become the fifth victim of the "Cupid Killer," the name the police had given to the serial killer who'd left arrows at the scene of the murders, thrust into the dead victims' chests.

Since all the murdered girls had dated Michael, he was the prime suspect. But the police couldn't arrest him now, not while he was at Brookhaven Sanitarium for psychiatric evaluation.

Judy's eyes were drawn to the red and white banner that was strung over the patio. It said "WELCOME HOME" in big block letters. Could this mean that Michael had been released? No, that was impossible. Surely someone would have told her. The banner must be for someone else. But who?

Just then, Judy spotted Vera Rozhinski, the bartender at Covers, mixing her special non-alcoholic fruit drinks behind the patio bar. Vera's parents had sent her off to visit her grandmother in New Mexico, right after the Cupid Killer had struck for the fourth time. Of course Vera hadn't been in any danger. She'd never dated Michael, and she hadn't been serious about the contest the other girls had started.

Judy frowned as she thought about the contest and how much grief it had caused. Michael had just broken up with Liz Applegate, his girlfriend at U.C.L.A., and the contest had started as an effort to cheer him up. All the Covers' girls, with the exception of Judy and Carla, had decided to make a play for Michael. The object had been to date him for two solid weeks, and Deana Burroughs, a singer at Covers, had almost won. But the Cupid Killer had murdered her the night before she could be declared the winner.

That should have been enough to warn the other girls away, but no one had believed that Deana had been murdered just because she'd been dating Michael. Judy had tried to convince them that the contest was dangerous, but no one had listened. They'd all assumed it was a random killing, until it had happened again.

Becky Fischer, the club comedienne, had picked right up where Deana had left off. She'd dated Michael for over a week before she'd been killed. Mary Beth Roberts, their featured dancer, had been the third victim. And that was when everyone at Covers had started to panic.

Judy had told everyone her theory, that the arrows the killer left behind were a warning about the dangers of love. But no one had paid any attention to her. Despite Judy's warning, Ingrid Sunquist, a waitress at Covers, had dated Michael next, and she had been the next victim. Finally, Berto's sister, Nita, had fallen prey to the Cupid Killer.

Over a month had passed since the last murder. The police still suspected Michael. It was true that there had been no more killings while he'd been behind locked bars, but that didn't prove that he was the killer.

Judy had gone out to Brookhaven every week, even though Michael's doctor wouldn't let her in to visit. It was a terrible misunderstanding, and she needed to talk to Michael to straighten it out. She'd signed the complaint that had sent him to Brookhaven, but she'd only done it to save him. The police had been ready to arrest him, and Judy had known that he wasn't the Cupid Killer.

She'd thought the whole thing out very carefully. Michael had no alibis for the times of the murders, and he might have been convicted if he'd gone to trial. Since California had the death penalty, Michael might have even been executed. Judy had saved his life by signing that complaint, and once she'd explained it, she was sure that Michael would agree. Sitting behind locked doors at Brookhaven was a lot better than pacing the floor on Death Row!

Judy drew in her breath sharply, as she caught sight of Michael's parents. Mrs. Warden was much thinner, and her hair was almost completely gray. Mr. Warden hadn't changed all that much, but Judy knew he was probably suffering just as much as his wife. It must be terrible to have a son accused of murder, a son who was locked up in a mental institution.

As Judy watched, Vera smiled at Michael's mother and handed her a drink. And Mrs. Warden put her arm around Vera's shoulder. So this *was* a welcome home party for Vera. But why were Michael's parents hosting the party?

Judy reached out and pushed the rest of the branches aside. Now she had a full view of the patio. Someone was sitting on a stool by the doorway, and she gave a little cry of surprise as he turned her way. It was Michael! Michael was out, and no one had told her! She had a right to be at his welcome home party. After all, she had saved his life.

It was agony to watch all her friends having fun, and to know that Michael was with them. Judy knelt on the damp ground for what seemed like hours, feeling terribly sorry for herself.

At last, the party began to break up, and Judy watched as the guests left, one by one. Now it was just the Warden family, and Judy leaned closer so she could listen. Michael's parents didn't say anything important, just how glad they were to have Michael home. Judy was almost ready to go back to her house, when she heard something that made her heart race in her chest. Michael's parents were talking about a dinner invitation. If they left Michael alone, she'd have a chance to talk to him!

"Are you sure you don't want to join us for dinner?" Mrs. Warden reached out to take Michael's hand. "The Jacobsons invited you, too."

"No, thanks. And don't worry about me. I'm going to take a drive up Laurel Canyon and spend some time at the lookout. I promised Dr. Tunney I'd start working on my music again, and I'd like to have one song finished before I go back."

"Well . . . all right." Michael's mother looked disappointed, but she smiled anyway. "Whatever you think is best, dear."

Michael glanced at his watch. "Hey . . . it's almost six-thirty. Don't you have to be there at seven?"

"You're right." Michael's father stood up. "We'll see you when we get back, son. And if you need us, just call."

"Are you going to stop at Covers for the show?" Michael's mother looked concerned.

"No, Mom. Dr. Tunney doesn't think I'm quite ready for that. He doesn't want me to run into . . . well, you know who. I talked to Mr. Calloway, and I told him I want to perform again. But he understands why I can't do that right now."

Judy's hands were trembling as she released her hold on the branches. Now she knew why she hadn't been invited to the party. It was the same reason Michael wouldn't be going to Covers to see the show. Michael didn't want to run into her!

It was terribly unfair, and there were tears in Judy's eyes as she walked back to the house and changed into clean jeans. She could see the driveway from her window, and she watched as Michael's parents got into their car and drove off. There was only one thing to do. It would take courage, but she'd never been afraid of a challenge. Now that Michael was alone, she'd march right over there and confront him directly.

Judy squared her shoulders and hurried down the stairs. She walked resolutely across the lawn again, and stepped through the gap in the hedge.

"Hi, Michael." Judy put on her best smile, but Michael didn't look very happy to see her.

"Judy." There was a frown on Michael's handsome face. "What are you doing here?"

Judy's smile wavered, but she managed to keep it in place. "I came to say welcome home. And I understand why you didn't invite me to your party. You don't realize that I saved your life."

"You what!?"

There was a shocked expression on Michael's face, but Judy ignored it as she rushed over to hug him. "I'll explain it all in a minute. But first I want to know about you. How long will you be home?"

"I'm on a weekend pass." Michael stepped back, out of her embrace. "And I was about to leave. I have to ... uh ... be somewhere in less than an hour."

Judy knew that was a lie, but she didn't let on that she'd eavesdropped on Michael's conversation with his parents. She just smiled and moved toward Michael again. "That's okay. This won't take long, and I have to leave soon, too. The show starts at eight, and I have to set up for the new singer."

Michael looked very uncomfortable, and he took another step back. "Sorry, Judy. I really don't have time to talk."

"I just wanted to explain why I signed that complaint to get you locked up at Brookhaven. You see, I knew the police were going to arrest you for the murders, and it was the only way I could keep them from doing it. You're safe at Brookhaven,

Michael. They can't put you on trial if the doctors say you're crazy. Now you can understand why I had to do it, can't you?"

"Judy . . . I . . . I really have to leave now."

Michael took a step toward the house. Judy managed to cut him off by grabbing his arm, but it was clear he didn't want to be close to her. "Come on, Michael. I only did what was best for you, and you ought to be grateful. And I'm so glad to see you again! How about a kiss for old times' sake?"

Michael gave a bitter laugh. "What 'old times' are you talking about? The last time I saw you, you told Detective Davis that I tried to kill you!"

"Please, Michael. I already explained why I had to do that." Judy got a good grip on his arm and pulled him closer. "Let's be friends again. It used to be so nice."

"You're deluding yourself, Judy. It was never nice. The past few weeks have been a nightmare!"

"I know." Judy slipped her other arm around Michael's shoulders, and hugged him tightly. "I'm really sorry about that, but everything's okay now. Don't you see, Michael? If you have to go to trial, you can get off by claiming temporary insanity."

"I'm not the one who's insane. You are. *You* killed them all. Not me!"

Judy shuddered at the cold expression in Michael's eyes, but she took a deep breath and went on. "I'll wait for you, Michael. I promise. And then we can pick up the pieces and start over. I know we can!"

Michael tried to break away, but Judy just hugged him tighter. She rubbed her breasts up against his chest, and snuggled her body against his. "I don't care what people say, Michael. I'll always love you. Forever and ever. Don't you believe me?"

"Oh, I believe you!" Michael stared down at her, his eyes as cold as glaciers. "Listen to me, Judy. I don't want your love. I never did, and I never will. All I want is for you to leave me completely alone!"

"You don't really mean that." Judy wrapped her arms around Michael's neck and forced his lips down to hers. A kiss would do it. There was no way Michael could resist her kisses.

But Michael's lips were like granite, cold and firm with no hint of passion. Even though Judy tried to make him respond, kissing Michael was like kissing a stone statue.

And then Michael thrust her back so hard, she almost fell. Judy stumbled and looked up at him, tears in her eyes. "I . . . I don't understand! You used to like to kiss me! We were such good friends!"

Michael turned on his heel, and walked toward his house. He opened the door, and then he turned back to look at her. "Forget it, Judy. Crawl back in the same hole you crawled out of, and don't bother me again. I'll never forgive you for what you did to me!"

Judy gave a deep sigh of resignation as he strode into the house and slammed the patio door behind him. It wouldn't do any good to pound on the door. Michael wouldn't let her in. He was still so angry about being locked up in Brookhaven, he wasn't thinking straight.

There was nothing to do but go home. Judy stepped back through the gap in the hedge, and hurried into her house. When she got to the privacy of her bedroom, she sat down on the bed and stared at her reflection in the mirror. She was prettier than any of Michael's dead girlfriends. With her light blond hair, deep green eyes, and perfect figure, she could attract any other boy she wanted. But Judy wanted Michael. He was the only one who could make her truly happy. And Michael had rejected her. Again.

Tears rolled down Judy's cheeks, and she didn't even bother to blink them back. She couldn't really blame Michael for being upset. He was still a suspect in the murders, and he'd never forgive her for that.

Judy's mind spun in crazy circles. There just had to be some way to get Michael to forgive her. Life wasn't worth living without his love. She had to prove to Michael that she loved him more than life itself.

The moment Judy thought of it, she raced to the desk for a pen and some paper. There was only one way to make Michael forgive her. It was drastic, but she would do it. Michael had loved her before. Judy was sure of it. And after tonight, he'd love her again, throughout eternity.

One

Carla Fields surveyed the audience with a smile. Every table was taken and there was a party of six, standing in the back near the entrance, waiting for stools at the non-alcoholic fruit juice bar. The flyer Carla had posted on the bulletin boards of six area high schools had done the trick. Covers was doing booming business.

"Carla?" Mr. Calloway rushed up to grab Carla's arm. "Has Judy Lampert called in?"

Carla's smile faded abruptly at the mention of Judy's name. "No, Mr. Calloway. Isn't she here?"

"Not yet. And no one's seen her. Call her house right away. If she's still there, tell her to get over here on the double!"

"Yes, Mr. Calloway." Carla turned and went toward the phone in the office. She'd hoped that Mr. Calloway would fire Judy, but he hadn't. And when Carla had asked him why he'd kept Judy on, after all the awful things she'd done, Mr. Calloway had told her that he couldn't fire someone on suspicion alone. There was no proof that Judy was the Cupid Killer, and until there was, it wouldn't be fair to fire her. Mr. Calloway always gave everyone the benefit of the doubt, even if they didn't deserve it.

Carla sat down behind her desk, and flipped through her file cards to find Judy's number. Even if Judy wasn't the Cupid

Killer, Carla still had reason to hate her. Judy had lied to the police and that was why Michael had been locked up in Brookhaven.

Working with Judy, feeling as she did, was one of the hardest things that Carla had ever been forced to do. But she certainly wasn't about to quit the best job she'd ever had. She'd managed to avoid Judy quite successfully in the past few months and so had Andy. Both of them believed that Judy had framed Michael for the murders she, herself, had committed. Proof, or no proof. That really didn't matter. Carla and Andy were sure they were right.

The phone was answered on the third ring, and Carla recognized the housekeeper's heavily accented voice. "Hi, Marta. This is Carla Fields from Covers. Is Judy there?"

"No, Miss Carla. She's gone to work."

Carla frowned. Judy was probably walking in the door right now, giving Mr. Calloway some excuse he couldn't refuse to accept. "What time did she leave, Marta?"

"It's been a long time. I heard her car drive away before *Jeopardy* started. That was at seven. And now *Wheel of Fortune* is over."

Carla glanced at her watch and frowned as she saw it was a few minutes past eight. Had Judy stopped somewhere on the way? She lived less than ten minutes away from Covers.

"Is there a problem?"

Marta sounded worried, and Carla tried to reassure her. After all, she had no quarrel with Judy's housekeeper. "It's all right, Marta. I'm sure she'll be here soon."

But Carla wasn't as confident as she sounded, and when she hung up the phone she gave an exasperated sigh. Judy knew the show started promptly at eight-fifteen.

"Did you reach her?"

Carla looked up from her desk to see Mr. Calloway standing in the doorway. He looked very worried and Carla knew why. There was no way they could do a show without a stage manager.

"No, Mr. Calloway. Marta said she left over an hour ago. Are we going to cancel if she doesn't show up?"

"We can't do that. We've got a full house out there. Can you fill in for Judy?"

"Me?" Carla was shocked. "But, Mr. Calloway . . . I don't know anything about the light board!"

"Neither does anybody else. What do you say, Carla? Will you give it a try? We'll all help you."

Carla took one look at Mr. Calloway's anxious face, and she nodded. "Okay. I'll try. But don't blame me if I blow out every circuit in the building."

"I'm here, Carla." Andy came up behind Carla, and sat down on a stool. "When Phil comes on stage, you bring up the baby spots. Got it?"

"I think so."

Carla waited until Phil MacMahon, the club magician, had positioned himself on stage. Then she brought up the spotlights and crossed her fingers for luck.

"Relax, Carla." Andy grinned at her. "Just leave the spots on until Phil asks for volunteers from the audience. Then turn on the houselights and wait until they get up on stage."

Carla followed Andy's instructions carefully. When the three volunteers took their places on the stage, she looked to him for her next cue.

"Go back to the spots now. When Phil pulls the flowers out of his hat, hit them with the magenta filter."

"Okay." Carla nodded, and then she turned to Andy. "You should be doing this. You know much more about it than I do."

"Wrong. I just know about Phil's act. I watch it every night from the kitchen. Get ready, Carla . . . he's going to pull out the flowers . . . now!"

Carla flicked the proper switch, and the flowers gleamed with a rosy light. She began to smile as the audience applauded. So far, so good.

"Okay . . . cut the magenta and go back to the spots. He's going to do a card trick next."

"Got it." Carla nodded, and breathed a deep sigh of relief. Everyone had been very cooperative when Mr. Calloway had explained their problem. Almost all of the performers watched the other acts, and they'd all agreed to help. Phil had helped her when Linda O'Keefe had sung her ballads, and Linda had helped with Rob Crawford's comedy routine. Berto had put down his apron and tray, and rushed behind the curtain to help with Tim Bradley's act, and The Alway Brothers, all three of them, had prompted her on Jerry Maxwell's jazz set. Vera Rozhinski had cued her for The Alway Brothers' juggling act, and Mr. Calloway had given her instructions for Greg and Gina Carlson's dance routine.

With Andy's help, Carla managed to light Phil's magic act without any major mistakes. She brought up the houselights for the intermission, and grabbed the handkerchief Andy provided to wipe the nervous perspiration from her forehead.

"I never knew this job was so hard. And I've still got three acts to go!"

"Relax, kid." Andy gave her a little hug. "Everybody's getting their own props, and that helps a lot. The Hot Rocks are up next, and you only have to change their lighting between numbers. And then there's Nicole Powell. All she needs is a spot on her guitar. The finale's easy. Just fade to black when Tim sings the last line of 'Sweet Night,' and you're through."

Carla nodded, but she wasn't convinced. She kept thinking of all the things that could go wrong. She could hit the wrong switch and plunge the stage into darkness, or the finicky old light board could burst into flames if she brought the lights up too fast.

Thankfully, none of the disasters that Carla had imagined actually happened, and she got through the whole show without doing anything drastically wrong. As she listened to the thunderous applause at the end of the show, Carla felt a swell of pride. She'd never realized that she had any talent at all, and with the help of her friends, she'd managed to light the show!

After the audience had left, the cast and crew gathered

around the big round table in the center of the room. It was a Covers' tradition. Vera mixed drinks, Andy prepared a big tray of leftover food, and they all got together after every performance so Mr. Calloway could critique the show.

Carla took the seat next to Mr. Calloway and opened her notebook. As the assistant manager, it was her job to take notes.

"Forget the critique tonight, gang." Mr. Calloway smiled at all of them. "I'm very proud of the way you all pulled together to make tonight's show a success. You're all troopers. Especially you, Carla. We couldn't have done it without you."

Carla blushed as everyone applauded. She really wasn't used to being in the limelight. Her usual job was to take tickets, usher people in, and run the office. She knew that Mr. Calloway appreciated the work she did, but it was very unusual for anyone else to pay attention to her.

"Thank you." Carla smiled at everyone. "I just hope I never have to do this again. I was so nervous, I almost lit Linda's hair with a bright green spot."

Everyone laughed, including Linda. And then Mr. Calloway spoke up again. "I've been thinking . . . the problem tonight could happen again. I think we need an understudy for the critical jobs. What if Andy calls in sick? Do any of you know how to run the kitchen?"

"I might be able to do it." Berto nodded. "Andy's been teaching me."

"Good. How about the bar? Could anyone fill in for Vera?"

"I think I could." Tammy Burns, one of the waitresses, raised her hand. "Vera showed me how to mix the drinks."

"But how about Carla's job? Does anyone know the ticket prices, and how many seats we have in the house?"

There was absolute silence, and Mr. Calloway nodded. "Just as I thought. I think it's time we hire someone who can fill in for any crew or staff position. Run an ad, Carla, and we'll start interviewing applicants."

"Did you find out what happened to Judy?" Andy looked very disgruntled. "She really left us in the lurch!"

Mr. Calloway shook his head. "She hasn't called in. I called her house again, but the housekeeper hasn't heard from her, either."

Carla frowned. She really didn't care what had happened to Judy, but she couldn't help being a bit curious. Judy had never failed to show up for a performance before.

"Do you think we should call the police?" Linda looked anxious. "I mean . . . it's our duty to report her missing, isn't it?"

"I called them at intermission, but they weren't very helpful." Mr. Calloway sighed. "They told me that she has to be missing for twenty-four hours before they can file a missing person's report."

"But can't they do anything?" Linda looked shocked. "I mean . . . what if she got carjacked or something?"

"I talked to Detective Davis, and he said they'd look for her unofficially. I described her car, and he promised to call if . . . "

The office phone rang, interrupting Mr. Calloway's explanation, and he rushed off to answer it. All conversation immediately ceased, as everyone listened in on his side of the conversation.

"Yes . . . that's right. A late model Volvo, dark gray."

Carla held her breath. She hoped they'd found Judy in the act of committing a crime. At least she couldn't sweet talk her way out of that! But the next thing Mr. Calloway said made her frown.

"Completely burned? I see. Did Judy . . . oh, no! And you're sure that it's Judy's car?"

Carla exchanged anxious looks with Andy. This sounded serious! And then Mr. Calloway started to speak again.

"Of course I will. The lookout on Laurel Canyon? Yes, I know where it is. I'll close up right now. If the traffic's light, I can be there in twenty minutes."

Mr. Calloway's face was gray when he came back to the table. He sat down, and swallowed hard. "They found Judy's car. She went through the guardrail at the Laurel Canyon lookout."

"But is she all right?" Linda drew in her breath sharply when Mr. Calloway shook his head. "You mean she's . . . "

Linda's voice faltered, and there was absolute silence. The seconds ticked by, and then Mr. Calloway cleared his throat.

"Her car burst into flames when it hit the bottom of the ravine. I'm sorry to have to tell you this, but . . . Judy Lampert is dead."

Two

They all stood in a tight little group by the side of the road, Andy, Carla, Mr. Calloway, and Michael. Andy had called to tell Michael the news, and Michael had insisted on meeting them here. Now they were waiting for the winch to haul Judy's car out of the ravine.

Carla glanced down, into the canyon, and shuddered. Judy's body was still inside the burned-out wreckage of her car. When a passing motorist had spotted the smoldering vehicle, a rescue team had been called. They'd climbed down and pronounced Judy dead. Then another team had hooked a steel cable to the wreckage, and a huge tow truck had arrived to pull the car up the side of the ravine.

"Are you all right, Michael?" Mr. Calloway sounded concerned.

Michael nodded. "Don't worry about me. I'm okay. I'm just having some regrets, that's all. Now I wish I'd been nicer to Judy when she came over to see me tonight."

"Judy came to see you?" Carla was instantly suspicious. She was sure that Judy had been up to no good. "What did she want?"

"She had some crazy theory about how she'd saved my life by getting me locked up at Brookhaven. I didn't really listen. I just wanted to get away from her. You guys know how hard it is for me to deal with Judy."

"Of course." Carla nodded. She understood perfectly. After all the grief Judy had caused Michael, she didn't see how he could deal with her at all!

"I think Judy wanted reassurance. She kept telling me how much she still loved me, and she tried to kiss me. But all I could think of was getting rid of her. I . . . I told her to get lost. And I said I never wanted to see her again. Of course I didn't know that she'd wind up . . . " Michael took a deep breath and shivered, ". . . like this!"

There was an ear-splitting squeal as the steel cable tightened. Carla knew it was only the squeal of metal, but it sounded like the howl of some sort of huge, prehistoric animal. She glanced down into the ravine again, and watched as the wreckage started to move. It was burned so badly, it was unrecognizable. "Are they sure that's Judy's car?"

"They're sure." Mr. Calloway nodded. "Detective Davis said his men managed to read the license plate. They ran it through their computers, and it's registered to Judy."

Andy was frowning as he walked over to the shattered guardrail and saw the path that Judy's car had taken. "I don't understand how Judy could have crashed through this guardrail. She had to slow for the curve. And that means she couldn't have been going that fast."

"Her brakes went out?" Carla posed the question, but Andy shook his head.

"That doesn't make any sense. If her brakes had failed, she would have gone off the edge over there." Andy pointed to an area over fifty yards away. "It looks like she came out of the curve, stomped on the accelerator, and deliberately crashed through the guardrail."

"You're right, son." Detective Davis walked up, just in time to hear Andy's comment. "This is no ordinary traffic accident, and that's why we're bringing up the car. Normally, we'd leave it down there, but in this case, we have a definite possibility of foul play."

Carla turned to Detective Davis in surprise. "Do you think someone ran Judy off the road?"

"Not necessarily. We could be looking at a suicide. And we won't know for sure until we gather all the facts."

Just then there was a shout from below, and they all peered down to see one of the crew scrambling up the side of the ravine. He was carrying a red purse, and Carla nodded as she recognized it. "That's Judy's purse. It's got her initials on the strap."

It took several minutes for the officer to climb up the steep bank. When he arrived at Detective Davis's side, he was puffing. "This was thrown clear, sir."

Detective Davis took the purse and opened it. They all waited while he went through the wallet inside. "Here's Miss Lampert's identification. And here's a letter addressed to Michael Warden."

"To me?" Michael looked shocked as he reached for the letter. "But why would Judy . . ."

"Not so fast." Detective Davis jerked the letter away. "This may be evidence. I'll have to open it."

They all followed Detective Davis as he walked over to his squad car. He opened the letter in the beam of headlights, and began to frown as he read it.

"What does it say?" Carla was so nervous, her voice was shaking. If Judy had been upset with Michael, she might have written something to implicate him in the Cupid murders.

Detective Davis looked shocked as he finished reading the letter. Then he sighed, and turned to Michael. "I guess it won't hurt to read it aloud. I'll need your permission, though. It's personal."

Michael nodded and Detective Davis cleared his throat. "It says,

> "*I'm sorry, Michael. I just can't live with my guilt any longer. You were right all along. I'm the Cupid Killer. I murdered Deana, and Becky, and Mary Beth, and Ingrid, and Nita. I killed them all because I was afraid you were falling in love with them. And I couldn't bear that because I love you so much.*

"I told Detective Davis that Marta would give me an alibi, and she lied for me. She had to. Her boyfriend doesn't have a green card, and I threatened to call Immigration if she didn't do exactly as I said.

"I'm sorry, Michael. I shouldn't have let them lock you up at Brookhaven. You told Detective Davis the truth, but he believed me, instead. Now I want to set the record straight. I threatened suicide and you broke into my house, trying to save me. But I called Detective Davis and told him that you were breaking in to kill me. I know I shouldn't have lied to Detective Davis, and now I'm so very sorry. I'm sorry for what I did to you, and I'm sorry for killing all those girls. When I saw you tonight, I finally realized that you would never love me. And I can't face the thought of living without your love.

"There's only one thing to do. I'm going to drive my car through the guardrail and kill myself. But I can't go to my death without clearing your name. Give this to Detective Davis. He'll know what to do.

"Goodbye, Michael. Someday, I hope you can find it in your heart to forgive me. My love for you is forever, and that love will never die. I'll always be right here at your side, watching over you."

Detective Davis gave a deep sigh as he turned to Michael. "It looks like this clears you. I'm sorry, Michael. She really had me fooled. No hard feelings?"

"Of course not. You were just doing your job." Michael reached out to shake the detective's hand. "Judy had almost everyone fooled. She was very convincing and manipulative."

Carla nodded. It was true. Judy had tried to convince everyone that Michael had attempted to kill her, and she'd almost succeeded. Of course Carla had never been fooled, and neither had Andy. But it had taken them several weeks to persuade all their friends that Michael was innocent.

Just then the winch gave another squeal, and Judy's car was pulled up, over the lip of the ravine. Michael stared at it and shuddered.

"Are you all right, Michael?" Mr. Calloway put his arm around Michael's shoulders.

"I'm okay." Michael turned away from the charred wreckage and faced Detective Davis. "Is she . . . inside?"

Detective Davis nodded, and then he turned to Carla. "You kids are free to go now. Why don't you ride home with Michael? Andy can follow you and pick you up there. This has been a shock, and I don't want him driving alone."

"No." Michael shook his head. "The least I can do is stay to identify her. I'm okay, Detective Davis . . . really I am."

Detective Davis frowned, but then he nodded. "All right, if that's what you want. Just wait by the ambulance while they get her out."

"You don't have to stay, Michael." Carla held Michael's arm as he walked over to the ambulance. "There's really no need."

Michael's face was white, but he looked very determined. "I have to look at her."

"I understand." Andy patted Michael on the shoulder. "Just wait right here with Carla, and I'll see if there's anything I can do to help."

Carla saw the resolved look on Andy's face, and she gave an approving nod. Andy was going to watch as they pulled Judy's body from the car. If she looked really awful, he'd think of some reason to keep Michael away.

They waited for several long, tense minutes, Carla holding tightly to Michael's arm. Then Andy came back with the attendants who were pushing the stretcher.

"Are you sure you want to see her?" Andy stared hard at Michael. "It's not a pretty sight."

Michael nodded. "I'm sure."

Andy nodded to the attendants, and one of them pulled back the sheet. Carla gasped as she saw Judy's face. Her light blond hair was covered with blood, and part of her face was burned.

"That's Judy." Michael swayed slightly on his feet.

Carla shivered. The sight was gruesome. "How can you be so sure?"

"She's wearing the ponytail holder I gave her for her birthday. And that's her gold chain. I'd recognize it anywhere."

Andy nodded to the attendant again, and he pulled up the sheet. Then he turned to Michael. "You're convinced?"

"Yes."

Michael started toward his car, and Carla hurried to keep up with him. "I don't understand, Michael. Why did you insist on seeing her? It was horrible!"

"I know." Michael sighed deeply. "But I had to make sure the nightmare was really over. It's all behind us, Carla. Judy Lampert is really dead."

Three

It was a bright, sunny, August afternoon, and Carla and Michael were at Brookhaven Sanitarium. Michael's release was official, and Carla had ridden along with him to pick up his things. Now they were standing in the center of the day room, saying goodbye to Dr. Tunney and Nurse Danver.

Carla almost giggled out loud as the doctor reached up to hug Michael. Michael was a couple of inches past the six foot mark, and Dr. Tunney was a very short, heavy-set man in his late forties. He reminded Carla of a koala bear, attempting to hug a giraffe.

"Take care of yourself, Michael." Dr. Tunney's eyes were glistening behind the thick lenses of his glasses. "We're all going to miss you."

Nurse Danver rushed up to hug Michael, too. And then she pressed a round, gift-wrapped package into his hands.

"What's this?" Michael glanced down at the package.

"It's just a little something from the staff. We didn't want you to forget us."

"There's no way I could ever forget you." Michael grinned at the gray-haired nurse. "You're the only ones who believed in me. Except for Carla, of course."

Carla beamed as Michael opened the package. And then she bit her lip to keep from laughing as she saw what was inside. It was a shiny metal bedpan which had been turned into a planter. The flowers inside were the same type that were planted next to the sidewalk outside.

"Uh . . . thank you!" Michael almost lost it as his eyes met Carla's, but he managed to control himself. "I'll keep this out on the patio at home."

Nurse Danver looked pleased. "The gardener fixed it up for us. He had a few plants left. Don't forget to water it three times a week, and fertilize it once a month."

"I'll remember." Michael gave Nurse Danver another hug. "Thanks for everything."

It took only a moment to collect Michael's belongings. Nurse Danver had already stuffed them into two large shopping bags. She buzzed them out, and Carla and Michael found themselves walking down the sidewalk, the doors of Brookhaven Sanitarium locked securely behind them. They didn't speak until they reached Michael's car.

"How does it feel to be free again?" Carla turned to him with a smile.

"Good." Michael grinned at her. "But it's also scary. I guess I got used to the routine in there. It's going to be weird, opening a door without waiting to be buzzed through."

Carla nodded. "You'll get used to it. And you've got a job, waiting for you. Mr. Calloway wants you back at Covers. It hasn't been the same since you left."

"I know." Michael opened the passenger door for Carla, and then he walked around to slide into the driver's seat. "I promised I'd start tonight. I'm a little nervous, though. I haven't performed for over six weeks."

"You can handle it. We'll all help you. And you've got all your old material."

"I've got some new material, too." Michael gave her a grin as he started the car and pulled out of the parking lot. "I wrote a song last night, and I think it's better than anything I've ever done before."

"That's great! What's it about?"

Michael looked at her, and Carla's breath caught in her throat. There was a wistful expression on his face, a look Carla had never seen before.

"You'll find out tonight. I'd tell you, but it's a surprise."

"Okay." Carla nodded, and leaned back in her seat as Michael pulled out on the highway. She supposed the song was about Judy, and how she'd died for love. Now that Judy was dead, Michael had no reason to hate her. Perhaps he was even grateful that she'd confessed to the murders and cleared him.

"Do you want to stop for a burger?" Michael glanced over at her. "I'm getting hungry."

"Uh . . . sure. If you want to. But I thought you were dropping me off at Covers and going straight home."

"I don't have to go home. My parents are coming to Covers tonight, and I'll see them then."

Carla raised her eyebrows. "But don't you have to change?"

"No. I brought along the clothes I'm wearing tonight. They're in the trunk. Since we don't have to be at work until seven, I thought I'd treat you to a hamburger at Don's Place."

Carla's heart beat a little faster. This was practically a date! But, of course, it wasn't. Michael was probably grateful she'd gone along with him to Brookhaven, and this was his way of paying her back.

"Is that a yes? Or a no?"

Michael was grinning and Carla grinned back. "It's a yes. I've heard a lot about Don's and I've always wanted to go there. Is anyone else meeting us there?"

"No one I know. What's the matter, Carla? Are you afraid to go out for a hamburger with a former mental patient?"

"Of course not!" Carla was almost offended until she realized that Michael was teasing her. She'd prove that she could tease him right back.

"You're sure?"

Michael's eyes were twinkling, and Carla put on her best worried expression. "I trust you, Michael. After all, Dr. Tunney said you were fully recovered. And by the way . . . they use plastic knives at Don's Place, don't they?"

* * *

Carla grinned as she took her place on the stool by the light board. The hamburgers at Don's had been great, and she didn't even care that she'd dripped mustard all over her blouse. Michael had been in a wonderful mood, and he'd told her funny stories about Dr. Tunney and Nurse Danver. They'd munched their way through two burgers apiece, and shared a huge order of onion rings. The time had passed so quickly, they'd almost been late for work.

When they'd come in the door at Covers, laughing and eating the rest of their onion rings, everyone else had been there. Michael had been greeted by warm handshakes from everyone on the staff, and Carla had rushed off to get her roll of tickets. But when she'd emerged from the office, Mr. Calloway had told her that one of the new waitresses would be selling tickets and seating the audience. It was a good thing she'd written down all the light cues, because he wanted her to fill in as the stage manager until they found a replacement for Judy.

"Are you ready, Carla?" Michael came up, behind the screen, and set down the stool he was carrying. "I'm doing the intro, tonight."

Carla looked down at her notes. "But what about the light cues?"

"Don't worry. Just light me the way you lit Mr. Calloway."

"Oh, sure!" Carla giggled. "If I do that, the spot's going to be four feet over your head. Mr. Calloway stands, and you're using a stool."

Michael grinned. "You're right. And I never thought of that. Do you want me to stand?"

"That's not necessary." Carla shook her head. "I'll adjust, once you get in position. Go ahead, Michael. I've got you."

"I wish." Michael sighed, and gave her a brief hug. "Okay, Carla. I'm ready."

Carla frowned slightly as Michael walked out on the stage and positioned himself on the stool. She was trying to remember their conversation. She'd said, *I've got you*. And he'd replied, *I wish*. What was that supposed to mean? If some ordinary guy had said those same words to an ordinary girl, it would be flirting. But she was Carla, the plainest girl at Covers. It was totally inconceivable that Michael Warden, the handsome star, had been flirting with her!

Somehow Carla managed to light Michael's introduction. She even succeeded in her attempt to change colors on the Covers logo in the background, just as Judy had done. But all the while she was pushing and pulling levers, and flicking switches on and off, Carla was thinking about what Michael had said. And then it was time for Michael's first song.

Carla dimmed to black, and brought up the spot very gradually. She'd experimented a bit with the lighting at rehearsal, and all of her changes were a huge success. A soft amber light was focused directly on Michael's guitar. That threw his face into shadow, and made him look a bit like the famous posters of James Dean. It was sexy without being blatant, and romantic without being sappy. Her lighting made Michael look unbelievably handsome, and Carla felt her heart beat a rapid tattoo in her chest.

"I've got a new song for you, tonight." Michael's voice was low and friendly, and Carla felt a flutter of anticipation. Michael had been very secretive about his new song. He'd told her how to light it, but he hadn't sung it for anyone at rehearsal.

"This song is the story of a remarkable girl. She's always right there to try to help her friend, but he doesn't realize she even exists. He's busy dating other girls and having fun, but this girl is loyal to the end. I call it 'Angel' because that's what she is. She's always there for him, just like a guardian angel looking over his shoulder."

Carla almost groaned out loud. Just as she'd suspected, Michael had written a song for Judy. Even though she was dead, Judy still had a hold on him. Carla couldn't blame Michael. He was an incurable romantic. But what Michael was doing was wrong. He was out on stage, paying tribute to the girl who'd almost ruined his life.

Michael started to strum his guitar, and Carla brought up the spot until Michael's face was surrounded by a rosy glow. Since he'd told her to leave the lighting just as it was until the song was finished, she sat back down on her stool, and sighed. She didn't want to listen, but that was impossible. Michael's mellow voice was impossible to resist. He had a way with a song that was almost magical.

As Michael sang his song, Carla felt her spirits take a nose dive. Even though Judy was dead, she had accomplished what she'd set out to do. Michael was hers. The words of his song proved that. And then the song ended on a plaintive note, and the audience began to applaud. They were glad that Michael was back. He was better than ever.

"Thank you." Michael stood up and bowed to the audience. "And now I think you should meet the girl who was the inspiration for this song. What do you think?

"Carla? Come out here, and take a bow. I think all of you know about the hassles I've been going through, and Carla's stuck with me through it all. She's my best friend, and I just wanted to show my appreciation by writing this song and singing it for her tonight."

Carla's mouth dropped open. Michael had written that song for her? But . . . that was impossible! No one had ever written a song for her before!

"I guess she's too shy." Michael turned toward the wings to give Carla a big smile. Then he faced the audience again. "You've all met Carla. She's filling in as stage manager tonight, but she's usually the girl who takes your tickets and seats you at a table. Let's have a big round of applause for Carla Fields, the nicest girl I've ever known."

Just then Linda O'Keefe came up behind the black screen that separated the stage wings from the audience. Her act was next. "Congratulations, Carla. You really made a big hit with Michael."

"But . . . I don't know how. I didn't do anything special." Carla knew she sounded puzzled.

"Oh, yes you did." Linda smiled as she patted Carla on the back. "Michael really appreciated the way you stood by him, when all the rest of us started to fall for Judy's lies. You were the only one who really believed that he was innocent."

"Andy believed in him, too."

"That's true." Linda nodded. "But it would look a little strange if Michael wrote a song for Andy."

Carla was grinning as Linda went out on stage to join Michael. They were doing a duet. She was still smiling happily as she brought up the lights and focused the spot on the two of them. Michael had written a song for her. And he seemed to like her a lot. But she warned herself not to get too excited about Michael's apparent interest in her. She was just his friend, nothing more. Michael Warden had no idea that she wished she could be much more than his friend.

"Great job, Carla!" Mr. Calloway was smiling as he came up to her at intermission. "Have you seen Michael? He's got a visitor."

"He just went to the dressing room, Mr. Calloway. Do you want me to get him?"

"I'll go." Mr. Calloway smiled at her. "You stay here and get your light cues ready for the second half."

Carla took a few moments to study her cue sheet. Phil's magic act was going to be complicated tonight, because he had a new trick. He was going to saw Gina Carlson in half, and Carla needed two spotlights, one on the saw, and the other on Gina's face. Of course Phil wasn't actually going to cut Gina in half. The whole illusion was done with mirrors. That meant Carla had to be very careful not to let the spots glint off the mirrors and expose the trick.

"Have you got it all figured out?" Phil rushed up, looking anxious.

"No problem." Carla nodded. "Just do the sawing part right, Phil. I like Gina."

Phil grinned. "Me, too. Don't worry, Carla. Everything went just fine in rehearsal."

As Phil rushed off to prepare his props, Carla glanced out at the audience. She smiled as she saw Michael heading down the steps. She still couldn't believe he'd written a song just for her. Was it possible he was beginning to think of her the way she thought of him?

Carla's heart raced as she considered that delightful prospect. But her smile changed quickly to a frown as she saw where Michael was headed. He was rushing straight toward table number four where a very familiar-looking girl was sitting. The girl rose to her feet as Michael approached. And she threw her arms around his neck and hugged him.

"Oh, no!" Carla winced as she recognized the girl. It was Liz Applegate, Michael's former girlfriend. And the hug she was giving Michael wasn't the hug of a *former* girlfriend. To make matters worse, Michael was grinning and hugging her back!

Carla sighed. So much for her rosy dreams of romance. Michael had mentioned that he was going to a party tonight, at the home of an old college friend. Now Carla knew who the old college friend was. It was Liz Applegate, the girl who had dumped Michael a couple of months ago.

Michael bent down to kiss Liz, and she wrapped her arms around his neck. It was clear that Liz wanted Michael, and Michael wasn't exactly resisting. Carla sighed as she read the writing on the wall. Michael and Liz would get back together, and she'd be left out in the cold!

"Hey, Carla." Andy stuck his head behind the screen and gave her the high sign. "What did you think of Michael's new song?"

"I thought it was wonderful. It's the most beautiful song I've ever heard." Carla's voice was very soft.

"Were you surprised?"

"And how!" Carla adjusted the spot, and then she turned to face Andy. "At first, I thought it was a song for Judy. I had no idea that Michael had written it for me until he told the audience."

"I know. I told Michael you'd be surprised. You should have gone out on the stage, Carla. Michael wanted you to."

"But . . . I just couldn't!" Carla was glad it was dark behind the screen so Andy couldn't see the blush that rose to her cheeks. "I've never been on the stage before, and I would have been terribly embarrassed. Look at me, Andy. I'm not pretty, or talented, or anything like that. The audience would have laughed at me."

Andy walked closer, and spoke very softly so no one else could hear him. "You're selling yourself short, Carla. You just have a low self-image, that's all. If you fixed yourself up a little, you'd be a knockout."

"Me?" Carla was so shocked, she almost missed the next light cue. "Don't be ridiculous, Andy."

"Michael told me he thinks you're pretty. And I wouldn't be one bit surprised if he asked you out. As a matter of fact, I'll bet you five bucks he does."

"Don't be silly." Carla shook her head. "Michael's not interested in me. Didn't you notice who's in the audience tonight?"

Andy looked puzzled. "Who?"

"Liz Applegate. Michael asked her to come. And I happen to know that he's going to a party at her house, after the show."

"Michael's back with his ex-girlfriend?" Andy raised his eyebrows.

"It looks that way. They were pretty tight, during intermission."

Andy frowned slightly. "Maybe they're just friends?"

"Oh, sure." Carla gave a bitter, little laugh. "Dream on, Andy. Liz is coming on to Michael. Believe me, I know."

"Are you jealous?"

Carla gave a little laugh. "Of course not. It just makes me mad, that's all. Liz made herself scarce all the while Michael was at Brookhaven. Nurse Danver told me she never came out to visit. She didn't even call, or send a card."

"So why is she back with him now?"

"I think she's bored. Remember that guy she dropped Michael for?"

Andy nodded. "Sure. He's rich and he's got a Ferrari. Michael told me all about him. Did they break up?"

"No, but he's gone for the summer, touring Europe or something like that. And now Liz is making a big play for Michael. Michael's going to end up getting dumped by her again. I just know it."

Andy didn't look convinced. "Michael's smart enough to see right through her. He knows you were the only girl who was really loyal to him, and I still think he's going to ask you out. Does our bet stand?"

"You're on." Carla reached out to shake Andy's hand. "But keep your wallet handy. I'm not entirely happy about saying this, but this is going to be the easiest five bucks I ever made."

Four

Liz Applegate plopped down on a chaise lounge and eyed the patio with disgust. There were empty glasses on every table and the leftovers from the Mexican bean dip looked gross. Someone had spilled a bowl of chips on the flagstone path that led through the rose garden, and the trash can was overflowing with paper plates and empty beer cans.

Normally, the mess wouldn't have bothered Liz at all. She simply would have ignored it, and jotted a note for the maid to clean it up in the morning. But Liz was in a very bad mood, and it was all Michael's fault.

She'd spent a lot of time preparing for tonight. Since her parents were gone, vacationing in Italy, she'd dismissed the staff before the party had started. Then she'd put new satin sheets on her waterbed, and programmed the CD player for her favorite type of romantic music. She'd even turned on the Jacuzzi. It was ready and waiting for two. And a bottle of champagne was chilling in a silver ice bucket, hidden away in the cabana. Liz had planned for a wonderfully romantic evening, *after* the party was over. And now the party was over, but there was one critical element missing. Michael.

Liz sighed as she remembered the last time she'd slept with Michael. Of course "slept" wasn't really the correct word. They'd been awake all night, kissing and cuddling.

That night had started with a party, too. And Michael had stayed after all the rest of her guests had left. She'd been counting on a re-play tonight, but Michael had volunteered to drive Bill home. Michael had grabbed Bill's truck keys when Bill had popped the tab on his fourth beer, and he'd declared himself Bill's designated driver.

Liz hadn't really cared if Bill drove himself into a ditch or not, but she had pretended to be just as concerned as Michael. She'd even hugged Michael and told him how wonderful he was for being such a good friend to Bill. She'd smiled as she'd agreed that Bill could leave his truck in her driveway for the night and come to pick it up in the morning, when he was sober. But all the while, Liz had been seething inside. She'd barely managed to control her anger as Michael had herded Bill into his car and driven off. Damn Bill for ruining her plans! She'd never invite him to another party! And damn Michael for volunteering to drive him home! Now she was stuck here, surrounded by the clutter of a successful party, completely alone.

Her stomach was growling, and Liz opened a fresh bag of chips. She hadn't eaten anything during the party. She'd been too excited, waiting for the time when everyone would leave and she'd be alone with Michael. And then, when Michael had told her that he was going to drive Bill home, she'd been too mad to be hungry. Liz was sure that Michael would be back. She just resented having to wait. Of course she hadn't told him that. She'd just smiled and promised she'd leave the gates open for him.

One glance at the clock over the wall by the bar, and Liz jumped up. Twenty minutes had passed since Michael had left. He was probably dropping off Bill right now, and it would take him at least another twenty minutes to drive back to her. There was no way she wanted him to find her moping around, waiting for him like some lovesick teenager. She'd get into her very best bathing suit and swim some laps in the pool.

Her white satin bikini was hanging right where she'd left it, on the hook inside the cabana. Liz peeled off her clothes and slipped into it, studying her reflection in the mirror. She knew she looked sensational in the white bikini. She'd been working on her tan all summer. Michael's eyes would pop right out of his head when he saw her wearing it.

Liz retrieved the champagne bucket and carried it out to a table. Then she walked to the pool, feeling better already, and dipped her toe in the water. The pool was warm, exactly the way she liked it, and she slid into the water without a ripple. The stars were bright overhead, and the palm trees waved gently in the warm night breeze. It was the perfect night for romance, and she was ready.

The water caressed her like an old friend as she glided the length of the pool. No sense working up a sweat. She was only killing time until she heard Michael's car pull into the driveway. He'd be back. She was sure of it. He wouldn't be able to resist the chance to repeat their last night together.

After three laps, Liz was tired. It had been a long day. She pulled herself out of the water and sat on the lip of the pool, enjoying the gentle breeze. The scent of night-blooming jasmine was a heady perfume, and she was glad her mother had taken an interest in gardening, and planted a border around the patio. Coupled with the lovely aroma of the roses that were blooming in the garden, it was almost an aphrodisiac.

Only five minutes had passed, and Liz was bored. She hated to wait. Waiting made her nervous. She found a clean wine glass and opened the bottle of champagne she'd saved for Michael. One glass should do the trick. It would relax her, and the time would pass more quickly. Of course she knew that it was dangerous to swim when she'd been drinking, but she didn't have to get back in the pool until she heard Michael open the gate.

The bottle was almost empty when Liz heard footsteps crunch on the gravel in the driveway. She set her glass on the nearest table, and got back into the water again. She wouldn't admit that she'd been drinking alone. Michael wouldn't approve of that. He was very old-fashioned in a lot of ways, and that was one reason why she'd dumped him.

Liz turned on her back in the warm water, and did a lazy backstroke. Michael might have reservations about spending the night with her, but those reservations would be quickly erased when he saw how sexy she looked in her bikini.

As she waited for Michael to join her, Liz began to smile. Michael might get even more turned on if he found her swimming without her top. He'd get so excited, he'd probably shed his clothes and jump right in to join her.

Liz unhooked her bikini top and tossed it out of the pool. It landed on one of her mother's hybrid tea roses, and Liz giggled. Her mother would have a coronary if she saw the bikini top draped over her prize rose bush. But her mother wasn't here, and there was no one to object.

A smile spread across Liz's face as she thought about Michael's reaction. She knew she looked sexy. She had a gorgeous tan all over, thanks to her mother's tanning bed. Why wear any suit at all?

It took only a second to slide out of her bikini bottom and toss it away. Liz gave a sexy giggle as she felt the water caress her bare skin. This was fun. No wonder everyone was always talking about skinny-dipping!

Liz treaded water for a moment, and listened. Had she imagined those footsteps on the gravel? No. There they were again, approaching the gate. Michael would be here any moment.

She gave a little shiver of anticipation and smiled again. She'd turned off the rest of the lights so the patio was in darkness. The only illumination came from the underwater pool lights. When Michael came around the corner and stepped onto the patio, his eyes would be drawn directly to her.

Liz debated for a second, and then she started swimming laps again. She didn't want Michael to think she'd arranged this whole scene, just for him. It was better to let him stumble upon her by accident. She'd say she hadn't heard him, and she'd pretend to be a little startled. Then she'd tell him that she swam like this often. That should be enough to get him to come over every night. Her parents would be gone for another ten days, and they could have a blast.

As she swam, Liz listened. Quiet footsteps crossed the patio, nearing the deep end of the pool. She turned her face away to hide a smile as she realized that Michael was planning to surprise her. When she finished her lap, at the deep end of the pool, he'd reach out for her. The thought of being in Michael's arms again made her heart race and her breathing quicken.

Liz took her time as she approached the shallow end of the pool. She'd give Michael plenty to look at when she swam her return lap. She'd do a backstroke so he could see her breasts, and then she'd switch to a side stroke with a scissors kick. That was bound to drive him wild.

Knowing that Michael was watching made Liz feel incredibly sexy. It was almost like doing a striptease. She arched her back, and floated for a moment, enjoying the night air as it caressed her body. Then she lifted one, perfectly tanned leg and trailed her fingers down her thigh.

When she was halfway across the pool, Liz turned to peer at the deep shadows by the diving board. She could almost make out Michael's shape in the darkness. She smiled and licked her lips. The night was so still, she could hear him breathing. He was turned on, she was sure of it. And by the time she reached the end of the pool, he'd be climbing the walls.

Only a few feet to go. Liz slowed, and treaded water, rising up from the pool like a modern-day Venus. She was almost close enough for Michael to touch her now. Almost . . . but not quite. Liz turned languidly on her back and gazed up at the twinkling stars above, floating very slowly toward the end of the pool.

There was a brief moment of suspense. And then she felt his strong hands grab her shoulders. She gave a playful little shriek, pretending fright. The neighbors were gone on vacation and she could make as much noise as she wanted.

And then Michael's hands pushed her down, hard. Liz sputtered and tried to protest as her head went under the water. This wasn't fair! And it certainly wasn't sexy! She'd been to the beauty salon this afternoon and now her new perm was ruined!

She tried to reach up to pry his hands loose, but her fingers encountered something strange. Michael was wearing gardening gloves. Why in the world was he wearing gloves? And why wasn't he lifting her out of the water to kiss her? If this was a playful game in the water, it had gone much too far!

The beginnings of fear made Liz kick out even harder. She tried to dig her fingernails into the heavy canvas gloves, but his grip was too strong to pry loose. If she didn't do something fast, Michael was going to drown her!

Liz thrashed and struggled under the water as precious seconds ticked by. Her lungs were screaming for air, and she could feel her strength ebbing. Her frantic struggles became weaker and weaker, and then, finally, her muscles failed her completely.

Her consciousness began to dim and her eyes fluttered open to stare up through the water that separated her from the life-giving air. Michael's face was a wavy, pale oval above the surface of the water, too far away to see clearly. But she could see the object he held half-submerged, only inches from her chest. It was an arrow!

Liz's last conscious thought, before the eternal blackness closed in, was clear and concise. The police had made a terrible mistake. Judy Lampert hadn't killed all those girls at Covers. Michael was the real Cupid Killer!

Five

Carla parked her car in the Covers lot, and got out with a sigh. The bank had been crowded and she'd spent over forty minutes waiting in line to do a routine transaction. She tucked the soft leather briefcase she used for banking business under her arm, and headed for the kitchen door. No sense walking all the way around to the front. It was after four, and Andy and his staff would be here, preparing the food for tonight's show.

Two weeks had passed since Liz Applegate's horrible murder, and the police weren't even close to solving the crime. Of course there were rumors, especially since Liz had been found with an arrow thrust into her chest. It was the same kind of arrow that had been used in the Cupid murders, the murders the police had considered solved when they'd read Judy's confession in her suicide note.

As Carla approached the open kitchen door, she heard voices inside. Berto was there, and he sounded very upset.

"You girls are crazy! Michael didn't have anything to do with Liz's murder!"

"Maybe that's true." Tammy Burns had a very high voice, and Carla recognized it immediately. "But I think it's very strange that Michael was there that night."

"It's not strange." Berto gave an exasperated sigh. "Michael used to date her, and she invited him to her party. It's just a co-incidence, that's all."

"Some coincidence!" Carla winced as she recognized Winona Evans's voice. She was the biggest gossip at Burbank High. "How about all the other coincidences, Berto? Michael used to date Deana, and Becky, and Mary Beth, and Ingrid, and even your sister, Nita. And they're all dead, too!"

"That's true, but Michael didn't kill them. Judy Lampert did. She confessed everything in her suicide note."

"If it *was* a suicide." Tammy was so excited, her voice almost squeaked. "Phil thinks Judy was innocent. He's sure that Michael murdered all those girls."

"What does Phil know? He wasn't even working here during the murders! And he doesn't even *know* Michael."

"That doesn't matter." Winona jumped in to defend Phil. "It doesn't take a genius to put two and two together. Phil and Tammy and I are positive that Judy didn't commit suicide. She was murdered, and Michael did it!"

Berto snorted. "No way! You guys are all wet!"

"No, we're not. It all makes perfect sense." Winona sounded very serious. "Michael admitted that Judy came to see him. And he also admitted that he was mad at her. What if Michael drove up to the lookout that night, and Judy followed him? He could have forced her to write that suicide note before he killed her."

"Oh, sure." Berto began to laugh. "Just how is Michael sup-posed to have done that?"

Tammy spoke up. "Maybe he could have held a gun to her head. That's the way they do it in the movies."

"Tammy's right." Winona took up the story. "Michael could have dictated the whole letter, and made Judy write it down. Poor Judy! I bet she was scared to death. And then Michael murdered her, and pushed her car over the cliff so it'd look like a suicide."

"You're not really serious, are you?" Berto sounded shocked. "Michael would never do anything like that!"

"How do you know?" Tammy was obviously in the mood for an argument. "The police thought he killed all those girls, and there had to be some reason why they locked him up in that nut house."

Carla felt her temper rise to the surface. How dare they discuss Michael like this? She pulled open the door, and pointed her finger at Winona.

"You've got a big mouth, Winona! And Tammy . . . I can't believe you! If I hear one more word of gossip about Michael, I'll . . . I'll see that you're both fired!"

Winona didn't look intimidated. "You can't do that. You're not the boss. Mr. Calloway is."

"Oh, can't I?" Carla faced her squarely. "I'm the assistant manager, and Mr. Calloway just made me responsible for the hiring and firing of personnel. Just try me, and see how long you last here!"

"Oh . . . sorry, Carla. We really didn't mean any harm." Tammy grabbed Winona's hand and hauled her to the swinging door so quickly, she stumbled. "You won't hear another word from us. I promise."

When the door swung shut behind the two waitresses, Berto raised his eyebrows. "Were you really going to fire them?"

"I lied. I can't fire them. Only Mr. Calloway can. But that whole thing made me so mad . . ."

"Come on, Carla." Berto led her over to a stool by the grill. "They were just talking, you know? Everybody's talking. Winona and Tammy aren't the only ones."

"Who's talking? Tell me!"

"Everyone. Think of it from their point of view, Carla. Liz used to go out with Michael, and now she's dead. They can't blame Judy. She's dead, too. So they started thinking that maybe she wasn't really the Cupid Killer, after all."

"But Judy confessed!" Carla shook her head. "We were right there when Detective Davis read the letter. Judy couldn't stand to live with her guilty conscience, so she killed herself."

Berto nodded. "Maybe. But maybe not. You knew Judy better than anyone. Did she seem to be the suicidal type?"

"Well . . . no." Carla frowned deeply "Not really."

"That's just it. It wasn't in character for her to commit suicide. And when Detective Davis came by yesterday, asking all those questions about her . . ."

"Hold it!" Carla interrupted him. "I was here yesterday, and I didn't see Detective Davis."

"That's because Michael took you to the printers to pick up the flyers. Detective Davis walked in, right after you left."

"Oh." Carla frowned. "What sort of questions did Detective Davis ask?"

"Well . . . he asked if Judy had ever threatened to kill herself. And then he asked us if we thought she was capable of killing all those girls."

"What did you say?"

"I told him that Judy had never said anything about suicide to me. But I also said I thought that she was capable of murder, especially since she was so jealous of the girls Michael dated."

"That's exactly what I would have said." Carla nodded. "Did he ask anything else?"

Berto looked very uncomfortable. "Yes. He asked me if I thought Michael was capable of murder."

"Michael?" Carla felt her temper rise. "But Judy cleared him!"

"I know. But Detective Davis seemed to think that Judy might have confessed to the murders, just to get Michael off the hook. She might have done it because she loved him so much. People do crazy things when they're in love, you know?"

"I guess they do." Carla sighed deeply. "What do you think, Berto? Do you actually believe that Michael is guilty of murder?"

"How can anyone know a thing like that? But I told Detective Davis that I didn't think Michael was guilty."

"That's good!" Carla took a deep breath. "How about everyone else? What did they say?"

Berto shrugged. "There's no way to tell. Detective Davis talked to all of us separately. Do you want me to ask around?"

"No. Don't do that. There's enough gossip as it is."

"Are you all right, Carla?" Berto looked concerned. "You look a little sick. I could bring you a glass of water."

Carla shook her head, and got up from the stool. "Thanks, but I'm okay. Go on back to work. I have to get the paychecks ready."

But she wasn't okay. Carla's legs were shaking as she walked to the office and sat down behind her desk. She was terribly worried about Michael. He'd been so relieved that he wasn't a suspect any longer. And now Detective Davis was starting the whole thing up again.

It took Carla much longer to get the paychecks ready than usual, but at last they were stacked in a neat pile on the corner of her desk. She was just starting to put address labels on the flyers that had to be mailed by the end of the day, when Michael stuck his head in the office door.

"Hi, Carla."

"Hi, Michael." Carla looked up with a smile. She didn't want Michael to know she was worried.

Michael sat down in a chair, and began to read one of the flyers she was mailing. He'd been very quiet for the past two weeks, and Carla suspected he was still in shock over what had happened to Liz. Naturally, the police had questioned him. He'd been one of the last people to see her alive.

"This is a good flyer, Carla."

"Thank you." Carla frowned slightly. Michael had seen the flyer before. He'd even helped her come up with some of the wording. It was clear that he was trying to start a conversation, and Carla put down her address labels to give him her full attention. "Is there something wrong, Michael?"

"No. Not really. But the police asked me to come in for questioning again."

"Again?" Carla was shocked. This made the third time that Detective Davis had asked Michael to come down to the police station. "What did they want this time?"

Michael swallowed hard. "They said they just wanted to double check the times I put in my statement, and they told me that I wasn't a suspect, but . . . I don't know, Carla. I hope this whole nightmare isn't starting up again."

Carla reached out to take Michael's hand. He looked sick. "Relax, Michael. Just answer all their questions honestly, and you'll be just fine."

"That's what I'm trying to do. But it doesn't look good, Carla. Everybody at the party heard Liz ask me to come back. She even said she'd leave the gates open for me. I wish you'd gone to that party with me. Then I'd have an alibi."

Carla nodded, but she didn't say what was on her mind. She wished he'd invited her, too. And not just for an alibi. She wished he'd invited her because he'd wanted to be with her instead of with Liz.

"I guess I'd better go." Michael gave a deep sigh, and got up from the chair. "Catch you later, Carla. I have to rehearse my duet with Linda."

As soon as Michael left, Carla started to paste labels on the flyers again, but her mind wasn't on her work. She was so busy worrying about Michael, she didn't even notice when Andy stuck his head in the door.

"Carla? Earth calling Carla!"

"Hi, Andy." Carla looked up, and gestured to a chair. Andy was the perfect person to ask about whether Michael was a suspect or not. His uncle had recently been promoted to chief of detectives.

"You need something, Carla?"

"I need information." Carla took a deep breath. "Is Michael a suspect in Liz Applegate's murder?"

Andy shrugged. "Everybody at the party's a suspect, and Michael doesn't have an alibi."

"But is Michael a *prime* suspect?"

"Very good, Carla." Andy grinned at her. "You're learning some authentic detective jargon."

"And you're learning how to beat around the bush. Is he, Andy? Yes, or no."

"Yes *and* no. You're right, Carla. Michael's a prime suspect, but so are five other people who went to the party. They don't have alibis, either. And they all heard Liz say she'd leave the gates open."

Carla watched as Andy got up to close the door. When he sat down again, he looked very serious.

"I'm going to tell you something, Carla, but you can't mention it to anyone. Deal?"

"Deal." Carla nodded.

"At first the police thought that they were dealing with a copycat, but now they're not so sure."

"A copycat?" Carla frowned slightly. "What's that?"

"It's some nut who copies another killer's M.O. The Cupid Killer story was splashed all over the media, and they made a big deal out of the arrows."

"I see." Carla nodded. "But they don't think it's a copycat murder anymore?"

"No, not since they found out that Liz was Michael's former girlfriend. You see, there's no way for a copycat killer to know that. They think Liz was targeted, just like all the other girls."

"But Judy killed the other girls! She confessed in her suicide note!"

"I know, but they think she might have been lying to take the heat off Michael."

Carla winced. Now she knew where Tammy and Winona had gotten their crazy theory. "But Michael didn't kill anybody, Andy! You know he didn't!"

"I know that, Carla. But the police are seriously considering re-opening their investigation."

Carla frowned. "That's awful! Michael was so relieved this whole thing was over, and now it's starting up again!"

"Hey . . . don't get so upset." Andy reached out to pat Carla's shoulder. "My uncle said they were just considering it. Maybe they'll decide not to reopen the investigation."

Carla was silent for a moment. This really was bad news. "I think you should tell Michael. He ought to know."

"Not me." Andy shook his head. "If you think he should know, you do it. But you have to warn him not to say anything to anybody. If my uncle ever suspects I'm talking about police business, he'll never tell me anything again."

"Okay . . . I'll tell him. But not until the time is right. He's going to be really upset."

"That's why I think you should be the one to tell him. And watch your back, Carla. Now that you're going out with Michael, you could be in danger."

"Me?" Carla blinked. What was Andy talking about? "I'm not going out with Michael."

"That's not what I heard." Andy picked up the pile of paychecks and rifled through them to pull out his. "Did you cash your check yet?"

"Of course I did. I just came back from the bank."

"Good. Then you can pay me that five dollars you owe me. Michael said he took you out last night."

"Oh, no he didn't!" Carla shook her head. "Mr. Calloway and Michael picked me up, and we went to a talent show at Sherman Oaks High School. It wasn't a date. We just went to hear Heidi Robinson sing."

"Mr. Calloway was with you?" Andy looked disappointed.

"That's right. And he hired Heidi to perform at Covers tonight."

Andy sighed. "Okay. I guess it wasn't a date if Mr. Calloway was along. But didn't you go out afterwards?"

"Yes, we did. We went to Hamburger Hamlet for chocolate cake."

"Ah ha!" Andy began to grin again. "Fork over, Carla. You owe me five bucks. If Michael took you to Hamburger Hamlet, it was a date."

"No, it wasn't. All four of us went."

Andy looked very disappointed. "Okay, okay. Keep your money for now. Say . . . what does Heidi Robinson look like?"

Before Carla could answer, they heard the clicking of high heels in the hallway, and a beautiful red haired girl came into the office. She gave Andy a friendly smile, and then she turned to Carla.

"Hi, Carla. Is this where I check in?"

"That's right." Carla glanced at Andy. He looked positively

bowled over. "This is, Andy Miller, our chef. Andy? Meet Heidi Robinson. She's performing tonight."

"Andy Miller?" Heidi's eyes widened. "Excuse me for staring, but aren't you the place kicker on the Burbank High football team?"

"Oh . . . yeah. That's me." Andy tried to appear casual, but Carla could tell he was rattled.

"I just *love* football! And I almost died, when you kicked that forty-two yard field goal last year. Do you think you'll go pro when you graduate?"

Andy shrugged, but he looked pleased. "Oh, I don't know. I might play in college, but my real goal in life has nothing to do with football."

"What's your real goal?"

Heidi sat down next to Andy, and blinked her incredibly long lashes. Carla could see that Andy was dazed, and she almost giggled. Poor Andy wasn't used to talking to gorgeous girls with sea green eyes, and perfect figures.

"Uh . . . I'd like to go into law enforcement. I'm particularly interested in crime solving, and I'm hoping to become a detective."

"That's fascinating!" Heidi batted her eyelashes again. "I think men in uniforms are so sexy."

Carla almost laughed out loud. Andy had told her he wanted to be an undercover detective, and undercover detectives didn't wear uniforms. But Andy just gulped, and didn't say a word about that.

"Do you think you could show me where the dressing rooms are, Andy?" Heidi stood up, and smiled again. "I have to change before rehearsal."

Andy stood up so fast, he almost knocked Heidi off her feet. "Sure thing. I'll do that right now."

"Oh, good!" Heidi took Andy's arm and gave it a little squeeze. "And maybe you can help me pick out which outfit to wear. I brought three, but one might be just a little too lowcut in the neckline, if you know what I mean. How about if I model them for you, and let you decide."

"Uh . . . sure. Anything I can do to help the new talent. Heidi's in dressing room three, right, Carla?"

Carla nodded, and made a supreme effort to hide her amusement. But the moment Andy had closed the office door behind them, she burst into giggles. Poor Andy. Heidi had knocked him off his feet, and then some!

"What's so funny?" The door opened, and Michael came in. "I heard you laughing way out in the hall."

"It's Heidi. Andy was here when she came in, and she's got him so flustered, he doesn't know which end is up."

Michael grinned. "I can understand that. Heidi's really gorgeous."

"Yes, she is. Let's just hope the audience thinks so, too." Carla knew she was being ridiculous, but she couldn't help feeling a little jealous. She wished that Michael hadn't said that Heidi was gorgeous. But Heidi *was* gorgeous, and there was no reason for Michael to think otherwise. Some girls were more gorgeous than others. It was a fact of life that Carla had learned to accept.

"Do you want to go to Club Fab tomorrow night?" Michael leaned over the desk to smile at her. "Their regular emcee is on vacation, and Mr. Calloway's thinking about hiring the guy who's filling in."

"Is Mr. Calloway coming with us?"

"No. He caught their show last night. How about it, Carla? Do you want to go?"

Carla's heart pounded so hard, she was afraid Michael could hear it. Was Andy right? Was Michael actually asking her for a date? She took a deep breath, and smiled back at him. "That sounds like fun. I'd love to go to Club Fab with you."

"Great! I'll tell Heidi we're all set then."

"Heidi?" Carla's spirits plummeted down to her toes. "I . . . I didn't realize you'd already invited Heidi."

Michael shrugged. "I didn't exactly invite her. She heard me tell Mr. Calloway that I was going, and she asked if she could come along."

"Oh. I see." Carla did her best to smile, but it didn't fool Michael.

"I'm sorry, Carla. I didn't realize you had a problem with Heidi. Do you want me to tell her that she can't come with us?"

"No. Of course not." Carla thought fast. She didn't want Michael to know that she'd actually thought he was asking her out on a date. "I don't have any problem with Heidi. I was just . . . uh . . . concerned about Andy. I mean, it's clear he's interested in Heidi. And I think he was planning to ask her out tomorrow night. If she's going with us, she'll have to refuse, and then Andy might never get the nerve to ask her out again."

Michael nodded. "I see what you mean. Why don't I ask Andy to come along with us, too? That should give Andy plenty of time to get to know Heidi."

"That's just fine with me." Carla did her best to look pleased, but she knew that tomorrow night would be a disaster. Heidi was gorgeous. Andy would hang on her every word. And even worse, so would Michael. Why should Michael pay attention to her? She was Carla Fields, his ugly duckling friend. If the evening turned out the way that she expected, Heidi would have two men competing for her attention. Michael and Andy would be so busy trying to impress Heidi, that they wouldn't even realize that Carla had come along for the ride!

Marc Allen was just bringing up the spot when Carla joined him behind the screen. She was very glad she didn't have to fill in as stage manager anymore. Office work wasn't as exciting, but it was a lot less nerve-racking. She'd spent the past hour to-taling the ticket sales, filling out the time cards, and finishing next week's schedule of rehearsals. Now it was time for Heidi's debut, and she hadn't been able to resist coming out to watch.

Heidi sat on a tall stool, near the apron of the stage. Her hair looked like burnished copper in the light, and she was wearing a skin-tight black leotard, with a patterned black and white skirt. The neckline on the leotard was low. Very low. Several of the guys at the front row of tables were staring at Heidi with their mouths gaping open, and Carla wondered whether Covers could be busted for allowing indecent exposure.

Marc Allen sighed, and reached for a tissue to wipe his forehead. The air conditioning was working perfectly, and Carla knew the beads of sweat that had popped out on Marc's forehead had nothing to do with the temperature. It was a reaction to Heidi, and every guy in the audience seemed to be having the exact same reaction. Heidi was hot.

Heidi started to sing in her low, husky voice, and there was a collective sigh from the audience. She was singing an old, blues ballad, the same song they'd heard her sing at the Sherman Oaks High School talent show. Carla watched her for a moment. She really was good. Everyone was spellbound, guys and girls alike, as Heidi crooned her song.

"She's a winner, huh?"

Carla jumped, as Marc leaned close to whisper in her ear. And then she nodded. Heidi was an excellent performer. Even though she'd heard Heidi sing this same song before, Carla felt tears come to her eyes, as Heidi sang the sad lyrics of a woman in love with a heartless man.

When Heidi's last note had died away, the audience burst into applause. But it wasn't just polite applause for a new performer. The applause swelled and grew until it was a deafening roar. The guys were whistling and stamping their feet, and their dates were clapping so hard, their hands were turning red. It was very clear that everyone thought Heidi was a wonderful performer. And even though she didn't like to admit it, so did Carla.

Heidi's second number received the same huge ovation, and so did the third. The audience applauded so long after Heidi's set was finished, that she had to come back to do an encore.

She was halfway through her encore, when Michael came up to stand by Carla. He slipped his arm around Carla's shoulders, but Carla knew he was barely aware of her existence. All Michael's attention was focused on Heidi as she finished her song.

Then Heidi left the stage, and joined them behind the screen.

Carla took a deep breath, and said the words she really didn't want to say. "That was wonderful, Heidi. You're really fantastic."

"Thank you." Heidi smiled, but her eyes were drawn to Michael. "What did you think? Am I good enough to be a regular at Covers?"

Michael's grin stretched to the limits, as he nodded. "You bet! That was incredible, Heidi. They loved you out there."

"Thanks. That means a lot, coming from you." Now Heidi's smile was for Michael, alone. "But I'm going to have to work very hard if I'm a regular here. I really don't have that many songs, and I can't sing the same things over and over. I need new material, but I'm not sure where to find it."

"I might be able to write something for you. How do you feel about doing originals?"

"I'd love to do an original! Do you think you could write something bluesy? My singing coach says I've got the right voice for singing the blues."

"Oh, you do! Maybe we should listen to some old Bessie Smith records, and see what we can come up with. But first, we'll have to find out your range. Do you know your best key?"

Michael was so busy talking, he didn't even give Carla a glance. He just followed Heidi down the hall and ducked into her dressing room. Carla sighed as she walked back to the office. She couldn't blame Michael for being excited. Mr. Calloway had friends in show business, and they often appeared in the audience at Covers. If Michael wrote a song for Heidi, and a record producer heard her sing it, Michael might be on the way to establishing himself as a songwriter.

Carla was frowning as she walked back down the hall to the office. She'd been on top of the world when Michael had sung the song he'd written for her, but now she was completely down in the dumps. She wanted Michael's attention, but how could she ever hope to compete with Heidi Robinson? Heidi was a gorgeous, talented girl, and Carla was . . . just plain Carla. Tomorrow night was going to be awful. If Heidi set her sights on Michael, Carla knew she wouldn't have the chance of a snowball in hell!

Six

Michael rang her doorbell promptly at seven, and Carla opened the door with a smile on her face. But her smile faltered when she saw that Michael was alone. If Andy wasn't coming along with them, they'd be stuck with Heidi all night.

Carla tried not to look worried as she asked the obvious question. "Where's Andy?"

"I'm picking him up next. Heidi called and said she'd meet us at the club. Her father's dropping her off."

Carla was still puzzled as she climbed into the passenger seat, and Michael drove off toward Andy's house. Michael had obviously gone out of his way to pick her up first. But why?

Michael stopped at a red light, and turned to look at Carla. "I suppose you're wondering why I didn't pick up Andy on the way."

"You read my mind." Carla smiled at him. "That's exactly what I was thinking."

"I really wanted some time alone with you. And this might be our only chance tonight."

Carla felt her heart start to pound. Michael looked very serious.

"I need to ask you for what Dr. Tunney calls a 'reality check.' And you're the only one I can trust. Have you noticed anything unusual about the way people are treating me at Covers? Maybe I'm just imagining things, but I get the impression that everyone's very jumpy when they're around me."

"You're right, Michael." Carla took a deep breath. She didn't want to be the one to explain why everyone was so nervous, but Michael had to know. "Pull over to the curb. We need to talk."

Michael pulled over to the side of the street, and shut off the engine. Then he turned to face her. "Bad news?"

"I'm afraid so." Carla nodded. "You were right, Michael. Detective Davis has been asking questions, and it appears that you're still a suspect in the Cupid Killings."

Michael frowned. "But . . . how? Judy confessed to the murders in her suicide note."

"I know, but Detective Davis has this crazy theory. He thinks that Judy might have been lying to clear your name."

"Oh, great!" Michael gave a deep sigh. "I don't know how much more of this I can take. First I'm a suspect, and then I'm not, and now I am again."

Carla nodded, and gave his arm a sympathetic squeeze. "I'm afraid there's even more. Detective Davis thinks that Judy might not have committed suicide."

"Let me guess." Michael sounded bitter. "Detective Davis thinks I forced Judy to write that note, and then I killed her so she couldn't talk. Is that right?"

"That's one of his theories. But don't worry, Michael. There's no way the police can prove something that never happened."

"Let's hope not." Michael didn't seem convinced. "I knew something was up when Andy started asking me all sorts of questions about the night that Judy killed herself. He wanted to know exactly where I was, and what I was doing. Andy always thought I was innocent before, but now he seems to think that I'm the Cupid Killer."

Carla thought about it for a moment, and then she shook her head. "You're wrong, Michael. Andy doesn't suspect you. He's just playing detective. You know Andy. He's storing up facts in that brain of his, and adding them all up together. Once he gets the whole story, he'll know that you're innocent."

"I hope so. I really like Andy and it makes me feel bad when he doubts me. How about you, Carla? Do you still believe I'm telling the truth?"

"Of course I do!" Carla nodded firmly.

"But what if Detective Davis proves that Judy didn't murder all those girls? Will you still believe that I'm innocent?"

"Absolutely. If Judy didn't do it, then the Cupid Killer is somebody else. But it's not you, Michael. I know that."

"Thanks, Carla." Michael began to smile. His eyes had lost that haunted look, and he actually laughed. "I guess you're the only friend I have left. Everyone else has deserted me."

"No, they haven't. Detective Davis just scared them, that's all. If the Cupid Killer's still out there, they could be in danger. They feel threatened, and that makes them jumpy."

Michael was silent for a long moment, and then he nodded. "You're right, Carla. I just never thought of it that way. You're really something, you know?"

Carla sighed as Michael reached out to hug her. She hugged him back, and found herself wishing that his friendly hug could turn into a passionate embrace. Of course, it never would. Someone as handsome as Michael would never get romantically involved with someone like her.

Michael started his car and pulled out into traffic again. He was grinning, and he seemed much happier. "Thanks, Carla. Talking to you always makes me feel better. We're really going to enjoy ourselves tonight . . . right?"

"Right." Carla nodded, but she wasn't convinced. Maybe Michael would enjoy himself, but she doubted she would. Not unless Heidi Robinson broke her leg and couldn't horn in on their evening!

"Oh, Michael! Isn't this fun?" Heidi reached out to squeeze Michael's hand. "That last comic was really super! Who's on next?"

Michael pulled his hand away and glanced down at his program. "Nancy Dell. She's a torch singer."

"Oh." Heidi sighed deeply. "I've heard her before. She's not very good. I sang one of her songs once, and everybody said I was much better."

Carla glanced at Michael. He was frowning, and she hid a

smile. Michael only approved of constructive criticism, and Heidi's comment had been just plain mean.

But Michael didn't say anything to Heidi. He just turned to Carla. "Come on, Carla. The waiters are busy. Let's get a round of drinks at the bar, and bring them back here."

"Oh, I'll go with you." Heidi jumped to her feet. "Carla has to work. She's supposed to check out the M.C. for Mr. Calloway."

Michael nodded, and pushed some money across the table toward Andy. "Thanks for reminding me. I'm supposed to check him out, too. "You and Andy go for the drinks. Carla and I'll stay here."

"Hurry back." Carla managed to keep a straight face as Michael moved his chair closer to hers. She waited until Heidi and Andy had left, and then she grinned at Michael. "I don't think that's exactly what Heidi had in mind."

Michael nodded. "I know it's not. She's been trying to pick me up all night. I wish Andy had driven, too."

"Why?" Carla held her breath. She was hoping for the right answer.

"If they had Andy's car, we could ditch them."

Carla pretended to be shocked, even though Michael had said exactly what she'd hoped he would. "That's not very nice, Michael. Don't you like Heidi?"

"Oh, she's all right, I guess. But I wish she'd start paying more attention to Andy. He was supposed to be her date."

"I know. But Heidi seems to be more interested in you."

"Yeah." Michael sighed deeply. "And she doesn't seem to realize that I'm not interested in her."

"But she's very pretty. Heidi's exactly the type of girl you always used to date."

"I guess I've changed. A pretty face just isn't as important as it used to be. Now I'm much more interested in personality. And a good heart. And a sense of loyalty. What do you think, Carla? Am I growing up?"

Carla didn't say a word. She just smiled. And then the M.C. came on, and both of them turned their attention to the stage, again.

* * *

It was almost midnight when they pulled up Heidi's circular driveway. Carla gasped as she saw the house. It was modeled after the Taj Mahal, complete with domes on the roof and colorful mosaic tiles.

"Thank you for a lovely evening." Heidi smiled her stunning smile. "Would you like to come in? Cook prepared a tray of snacks and we could go out by the pool."

Heidi was looking at Michael, but Andy answered. "Sure. We'd love to. Right, guys?"

"How about it, Carla?" Michael turned to her. "Do you have time?"

Carla saw Andy's hopeful expression, and she nodded. "It's fine with me. But I didn't bring my passport."

Michael and Andy laughed so hard they could barely get out of the car. But Heidi looked very puzzled.

"Your passport? Why would you need that?"

"Because your house looks just like the Taj Mahal."

"Oh, really?" Heidi looked pleased. "I've heard of the Taj Mahal. It's a famous French landmark, isn't it?"

Carla was struck speechless for a moment. Then she shook her head. "Not exactly. It's in India. But I was just teasing, Heidi. Your house is very beautiful."

"I know. Daddy got it for only three point four, and that's a steal."

"Three point four." Andy repeated the numbers. "Is that . . . uh . . . three point four *million?*"

Heidi nodded. "I know that doesn't seem like much, but the seller was desperate. He got busted for insider trading or something like that, and he had to liquidate all his assets. He wanted a lot more, but Daddy offered cash."

"Very impressive." Michael squeezed Carla's hand as he gazed up at the domes. "I'm surprised you're singing blues, Heidi. With a house like this, you should be doing Indian music."

Heidi giggled. "Maybe that's true, but I hate all that tom-tom stuff!"

Carla exchanged glances with Andy and Michael. Was it a

joke? Or was Heidi serious? But Heidi was so intent on ringing the doorbell, she didn't seem to notice their puzzled expressions.

The door was opened by a butler, who bowed low and ushered them in. "Good evening, Miss Heidi."

"Hi, Sidney." Heidi gave a casual wave. "Tell Susan to set up the patio. We'll need snacks, and a tray of drinks. I'm going to show my friends Daddy's posters."

"Yes, Miss Heidi. Right away."

The butler hurried down the hall in one direction, and Heidi led them to a wood paneled door at the other end of the massive hallway.

"This is Daddy's den." Heidi opened the door, and flicked on the lights. "He's got posters from every picture he's ever produced."

Carla was amazed as she stepped into the huge room and saw the posters. There were dozens of them, all framed behind glass, and some were actually from movies she'd seen.

"Tender Moments?" Michael stepped up to one poster, and read the name of the producer. Then he turned to Heidi with a shocked look on his face. "Your father is Ralph Robinson?"

Heidi nodded. "That's right. And my mother was Patsy Coleman."

"The Patsy Coleman?" Michael looked awed as he repeated the name of the famous blues singer. "No wonder you have such a dynamite voice!"

"Yes, Mother was good. But I'm even better. That's what she used to tell me before she died."

There was an uncomfortable silence. They all knew that the famous Patsy Coleman had died of a drug overdose six years ago. It had been in all the papers.

Andy cleared his throat, and changed the subject. "Your father's my favorite producer. Is he working on a new movie?"

"Of course." Heidi looked bored. "He's always working on a new movie. This one's a little different. It's all about an aging mega-superstar who takes young singers under his wing and . . . Michael!"

Michael turned to look at her, and Heidi gave him her best smile. "How would you like to audition for Daddy?"

"Me?"

"Yes, you." Heidi reached out to take his arm. "You want to get into the biz, don't you?"

"Well . . . sure. But I don't think that your father would be interested in someone without any film experience."

"Don't be silly." Heidi smiled up at him. "Daddy'll do anything I want him to. And he told me he needs a lot of teenage extras. I'll invite the whole Covers crowd. Even you, Carla."

Carla felt her face turn red. She knew exactly what Heidi was implying. Extras were supposed to look like ordinary people. They could even be plain like her.

"Come on. Let's go out to the patio and discuss it."

Heidi tightened her grip on Michael's arm and propelled him out of the room. She turned to look back at Andy and Carla, who weren't really sure whether they were invited or not. "Come on, you two. We have to work out a schedule. I'll take in groups of ten at a time. Any more than that would freak out Daddy. And once we get on the set, we'll just hang around until Daddy notices us."

Michael looked puzzled. "But wouldn't it be easier just to ask your father if we could audition?"

"No way!" Heidi rolled her eyes. "That's not the way things are done. You have to be discovered. It's part of the game. Just leave everything up to me, Michael. I know exactly what I'm doing."

Seven

"Oh-my-God! I'm so scared, I'm a nervous wreck!" Tammy Burns pulled out a mirror to check her curly brown hair as they approached the studio gates. Then she turned to Carla. "Aren't you scared, Carla? This could be your big break!"

"That's exactly what I'm afraid of." Carla glanced down at her high-heeled sandals. "I'm afraid I'm going to break my ankle when I try to walk in these things."

"But Heidi especially told you to wear those shoes. She said it would help you make a good impression."

Carla shrugged. "Well, I'm not going to make one if I fall flat on my face. I'm switching to my tennies."

"I think you're making a big mistake." Winona Evans capped her lipstick, and dropped it back in her over-sized purse. Both Winona and Tammy had been primping for the past two miles. "What do you think, Linda?"

Linda O'Keefe leaned forward. She was riding in the third seat with Berto and Vera. "I agree with Carla. If she can't walk in those shoes, she shouldn't wear them."

"Right." Vera joined in. "I think Carla should wear whatever's comfortable."

Michael was riding in the front seat with Andy, and he turned around to talk to Carla. "Wear whatever you want, Carla. Heidi told me her father needs over a hundred extras. There's no reason why one of them can't be wearing tennis shoes."

Carla gave him a quick smile, and took off her high-heeled sandals. Then she slipped her feet into her worn tennis shoes, and wiggled her toes gratefully. How could anyone walk in those ridiculously high heels? Heidi had taken her shopping and insisted she buy high-heeled strap sandals, and Carla had gone along with her suggestion. But when she'd practiced walking in them last night, in front of the mirror, she'd felt like a baby colt taking its first, tottery steps.

Andy pulled through the open gate of the studio, and stopped at the security booth. The guard, inside, was an older, gray-haired man who looked extremely bored as he pushed opened the small, sliding glass window. "Do you kids have a pass?"

"Not exactly." Andy shook his head. "Heidi Robinson said she'd leave a pass at the gate for us. We're meeting her at sound stage fifteen."

"Andrew Miller?" The guard got off his stool as Andy nodded. He walked to the front of Andy's van and taped a rectangular piece of paper on the corner of his windshield. Then he stepped back and smiled as he noticed their eager faces. "Are you kids going to an audition?"

"No, sir." Andy answered his question. "Heidi's just letting us watch while they shoot her father's movie."

The guard nodded, but his smile grew. "Do you know they're looking for extras?"

"Yes, sir. She said something about that." Andy blushed bright red. "The truth is, we're sort of hoping to be noticed."

The guard nodded. "Miss Robinson always brings her friends to the set when they're casting for extras. And it usually works. Do you need directions?"

"Yes, sir."

"Go straight past the courthouse, and turn to the right. That'll put you on New York Street. Follow it until you come to the stop sign by the big cannon. Turn left, and you'll see Lot B directly in front of you on your right. You can park in any space that's marked for visitors. Sound stage fifteen's the third big metal warehouse building on your left."

As Andy thanked the guard and drove forward, Carla stared out the window with fascination. Even though she'd lived in the area all her life, she'd never been inside a studio before. They passed a series of low bungalows, and Carla saw several glamorous women walking down the sidewalk. She'd never paid much attention to movie stars and she turned to Tammy. "Those women are beautiful. Are they stars?"

"I don't know." Tammy shrugged. "They could be. They're very glamorous."

Michael turned around to grin at them. "Then they're probably secretaries. Heidi told me that the stars all run around in turbans and casual clothes. They don't get their make-up on or their hair done until it's time to shoot a scene."

They drove past a tall barracks-type building, and Carla drew in her breath sharply. The man walking down the steps looked just like Robert Redford, but she didn't say anything. He was probably a production assistant who just happened to look like the famous star.

"That must be the courthouse." Andy pointed to a tall, imposing building with massive columns and a flight of steps.

"You're right." Carla nodded. There was a big sign on the front identifying it as the County Courthouse.

"Why do they need a court house at a studio?" Winona sounded puzzled.

"It's not a real court house." Michael explained as they drove past. "Look at the back. It's only a couple of feet deep. There's just enough room to put a camera inside."

Winona was embarrassed, but she brazened it out. "I knew that. I just wanted to find out if anybody else did, that's all."

"This must be New York Street." Carla smiled as she saw a row of brownstones with wrought-iron fences and steps leading up to their front doors. "But the next block is totally different. It looks like a small town in the Midwest."

Michael nodded. "They face this block for whatever movie

they're shooting. It could be Chicago, or Tokyo, or even Saigon. They just redo the fronts so it looks like another place. Heidi says they can do it fast, and sometimes this block changes overnight."

"Oh, great!" Carla laughed. "Maybe we'd better leave a trail of bread crumbs like they did in *Hansel and Gretel*. This might look like Paris when we come out."

Michael turned to grin at her. "Not a bad idea. Turn left, Andy . . . there's the cannon."

"Is it real?" Tammy wanted to know.

"I don't know." Michael answered her. "We can touch it when we walk past. Sometimes they make props that look real. And other times, they use the real things. Heidi warned me not to mail any letters in any of the mail boxes. They're real, but they're props. Tourists make that mistake all the time, and then they wonder why their postcards never arrive."

Andy parked between a silver Mercedes and a gold Ferrari, and they all climbed out of his van. As they began to walk across the parking lot, Carla spotted Phil MacMahon's Oldsmobile and the panel truck that belonged to the Alway Brothers. "Everybody's here already. Are we late?"

"No. They're early." Michael dropped back to take Carla's arm. "Heidi said she'd meet us outside the sound stage, and we'll all go in together."

"There she is!" Vera began to walk faster as she spotted Heidi's shining red hair. Heidi was standing next to a small group of Covers people.

"Oh, good! You're just in time!" Heidi hurried to Michael's side and took his arm. "I told Daddy some of my friends were dropping by."

Michael frowned slightly. "Are you sure he won't be mad when he sees so many of us?"

"Of course not!" Heidi pulled Michael to the front of the group. "Daddy won't mind a bit. Trust me."

Carla was ready to hang back. Heidi obviously wanted Michael to herself, and she wasn't about to jeopardize his chances by hanging onto his arm. But Michael seemed to want her with him because he squeezed her hand, and kept her firmly at his side. When they approached the sound stage door, everyone was completely silent. This was a big moment for all of them.

Heidi pointed to the light mounted above the door. "That light flashes red when they're shooting. It means you can't open the door until it goes out."

"Is there anything special we should do?" Michael looked a little nervous.

"Yes. Keep quiet, stay in a group, and don't trip over any cables. I had Daddy's assistant set up some chairs for us. Just sit and watch and don't ask any questions. Are you ready?"

Everyone nodded and Heidi pulled open the door. The huge metal building was shadowy inside, and they were completely silent as they trooped inside.

"This is the patio they're using for one of the sets." Heidi spoke in a low voice and they all nodded. "The exterior's on Mandeville Canyon, but they can't use the actual house. They'd have to take out all the windows, and do a bunch of remodeling for the cameras. It's a lot cheaper to duplicate it here."

Carla was surprised as they walked past. The patio looked a lot smaller than the actual patio at the back of a real house. There were four lounge chairs with colorful towels draped over their backs, and some glasses on the tables. But there was only the edge of a pool, and a ladder that led to a non-existent diving board. The place where the actual diving board and pool would have been, was walled off.

"You're probably wondering why there's no pool." Heidi smiled at them. "It's because they only need this particular part of the patio. There aren't any scenes in the pool so they didn't bother to build it. When one of the actors says he's going for a swim, he just races off and disappears behind that wall. When he comes back, he's dripping wet, and everyone in the audience thinks he was in the pool."

"Can I ask you a question?" Michael's voice was low.

Heidi nodded, and gave him a smile. "Sure, Michael. What is it?"

"Why is the patio roped off? And what does that sign, *Hot Set*, mean?"

"It means nobody can touch it. They started shooting a scene on the patio, and then they broke for lunch. Everything has to stay exactly as it is, so they can pick up where they left off. It's called continuity. If someone moves one of those glasses or re-arranges a towel, the audience might notice."

"Are they gone for lunch now?" Carla asked. "I don't see anybody else around."

Heidi nodded. "They're all in the catering tent. I planned this so you'd all get here when they were on break. That way, I can show you around before they come back."

"Can we see the rest of the sets?" Andy was curious. "There's more than this one, isn't there?"

"Yes. Daddy has five standing sets on this sound stage, and he also shoots a lot of scenes on location. When they come back, they'll finish the patio scene, and then they'll go to the nightclub set."

"There's a whole nightclub in here?" Linda looked around with awe.

"Well . . . not exactly. Daddy has four nightclub sets. One is a hallway, another's the dressing room, a third is the catwalk above the stage, and the other's the stage. I'll show you the dressing room first."

Carla followed along at Michael's side as Heidi took them to the dressing room set. It was just a room with three walls and a ledge with a long mirror behind it.

"But it's open on one side!" Linda frowned. "And that door on the wall doesn't go anywhere."

Heidi nodded. "The wall's open so the camera man can shoot from any angle. And we don't have to see the other side of that door. Follow me and I'll show you why."

"What's this?" Michael was puzzled as Heidi led them to a narrow space, open on one end with a door at the other.

"It's the hallway outside the dressing room. The actor goes out the door in the dressing room, and they pick him up coming out of this door. When you see the movie, it'll look like this hallway's right outside the dressing room. It saves money to build two separate sets rather than one big one."

Carla nodded. "I see. Where's the catwalk, Heidi?"

"Right over here." Heidi led them past a living room set and around a wall to another set. The floor of the set was painted black and there were two steps leading up to a catwalk which was built a foot above the floor.

"But you said this was over the stage!" Andy looked puzzled.

"It is . . . in the film. When the actor's on this catwalk, you'll never realize that it's only a foot from the floor. That's the magic of movies."

During the next half hour, Heidi showed them the other sets. Carla was amazed at all the tricks that were used to give the illusion of height and width. The stage itself was very small and there were only two rows of theater seats. But when Heidi explained that the seats matched those in a real theater where the audience scenes would be shot, she could see how everything would work.

The door to the sound stage opened, just as they'd taken their seats in front of the patio set. Heidi jumped up from her chair in the front and ran to hug a handsome, older man in a black polo shirt.

"Is that Heidi's father?" Carla leaned over to whisper to Michael.

"I think so. He looks like his pictures. Smile, Carla . . . here they come."

"These are my friends, Daddy." Heidi gestured to the group from Covers. "And this is my father, Ralph Robinson."

Mr. Robinson smiled. "Glad to meet you. Did Heidi explain the rules?"

"Yes, sir." Michael spoke up. "She told us to stay in our chairs and be quiet."

Mr. Robinson gazed at the group and nodded. Then he turned to Heidi. "Did I mention that we're casting for extras?"

"Yes, you did." Heidi grinned up at him. "What do you think, Daddy? Can you use some of my friends?"

"I can use all of them. Sign them up with Denise when you leave. Good work, Heidi. Now . . . aren't you going to introduce me to the young man you told me about?"

Heidi grabbed Michael's hand and practically pulled him to his feet. "Daddy? This is Michael Warden. He's the totally fantastic singer I told you about."

"Hello, Michael." Ralph Robinson stared at Michael for a moment and then he reached out to shake hands. "Heidi's right. You have the right look for the part. How about a quick audition?"

"Oh . . . sure. Whatever you say, Mr. Robinson." Michael nodded. "Do you want me to go out to the van and bring in my guitar?"

"That's not necessary. We've got a guitar around here someplace . . . Denise?"

"Yes, Mr. Robinson." A pretty dark-haired woman in her early thirties rushed over, clipboard in hand.

"Find me a guitar. And get me two copies of that love scene on the beach. We're doing a screen test."

"Yes, Mr. Robinson. Shall I find someone to read the girl's lines?"

Ralph Robinson surveyed the group from Covers for a moment, and then he shook his head. "Don't bother, Denise. We can use one of Heidi's friends."

Carla began to smile. This was wonderful! Someone from Covers would be in the screen test with Michael. Michael would be more relaxed, sharing the stage with someone he knew. And it would be a marvelous opportunity for one of the girls.

Mr. Robinson turned to Heidi. "How about it, Heidi? You know all these girls. Who should we use?"

"I'm not sure."

Carla held her breath as Heidi surveyed the group. She hoped that Heidi would choose Linda. Linda had dreams of breaking into show business, and she was very pretty. Tammy wouldn't be a bad choice, either. She'd done some acting in the drama club at school. And Nicole had starred in their last high school play. Almost all of the girls from Covers were very talented, and any one of them would love the chance to play a scene with Michael.

"I know, Daddy." Heidi gave a mean little smile and pointed to Carla. "How about . . . *her?*"

Eight

Carla could barely believe her ears. Surely Heidi couldn't be talking about her! She'd never done any acting, and she was all wrong for the part of Michael's girlfriend. Carla turned to look behind her. Heidi must be talking about someone else. But there was no one else in sight. Then Carla got it, and she blushed bright red. Heidi was making fun of her by suggesting that she play Michael's girlfriend.

But Ralph Robinson didn't laugh, as Heidi had clearly expected. He just smiled, and nodded. "You've got a good eye, Heidi. She's perfect."

Carla swallowed hard, and forced herself to ask. "Excuse me, Mr. Robinson. Are you talking about . . . uh . . . *me?*"

"That's right, young lady. Are you willing to help us out?"

"Uh . . . of course. If you want me to." Carla practically gulped out the words. "But are you sure you really want me?"

"Absolutely." Ralph Robinson turned to his assistant. "Listen carefully, Denise. Take . . . uh . . . what's your name, honey?"

Carla swallowed hard. "It's Carla Fields. But Mr. Robinson . . . I'm not an actress."

"That's a point in your favor." Mr. Robinson laughed, and turned to his assistant again. "Take Carla to make-up, and tell Mavis I want glamor plus. She should coordinate with Jessie on the costume. Something blue and sexy would be good. And I want Frank to do Carla's hair. I need something loose and kind of wild. He'll know what to do. We'll shoot the screen test right after we finish the patio scene."

Carla felt as if she were in a dream as Denise took her by the hand and led her toward the door. Was Heidi's father kidding? She couldn't act, and even worse, she was the totally wrong person to do a love scene with Michael.

"Come on, Carla." Denise tugged her along. "We don't have much time."

Carla felt like bursting into hysterical laughter. Even if they had all the time in the world, she'd never wind up looking like Michael's girlfriend. This had to be some kind of joke.

"Denise?" Carla hung back as they reached the door. "Is Mr. Robinson really serious?"

"Of course. Hurry up, Carla. It'll take them at least an hour to get you ready, and then you have to rehearse your lines."

Carla blinked as Denise opened the door, and they stepped out into the strong sunlight. "Excuse me, Denise. I suppose I shouldn't say this, but Mr. Robinson is making a horrible mistake. There's no way I can look glamorous."

"If Mr. Robinson says you can, then you can." Denise pointed to a Winnebago motor home that was parked in back of the sound stage. "Make-up's right over there."

"But, Denise . . . I'm not even *pretty!*"

Denise laughed, and propelled Carla toward the motor home. "Don't worry about it. Mavis is the best in the biz, and so are Jessie and Frank. By the time they get through with you, you won't even know yourself."

"Okay, hon. You can look now." Mavis Parker swiveled Carla's chair around to face the mirror. "Get ready for a big surprise."

Carla opened her eyes, and blinked. Another person was in the mirror, a gorgeous, mahogany-haired beauty who was wearing a low-cut silk blouse and mini-skirt. "That's . . . uh . . . that's *me?*"

"That's you, all right." Mavis patted Carla on the shoulder.

"And it wasn't all that hard, either. You've got all the right stuff in all the right places. You just don't know what to do with it."

Carla's mouth opened and closed. She was gaping like a fish out of water. "Are you sure? I mean . . . I never knew I could look like this!"

"Very nice." Jessie Coleman, the wardrobe mistress, poked her head in the doorway. "Stand up, hon. I want to see if that skirt wrinkles."

Carla stood up and smoothed the skirt down. "How could it wrinkle? It's so tight, it feels like my skin."

"When Mr. Robinson says glamorous, he means glamorous." Jessie nodded sagely. "You've got lots of great outfits to wear. Maybe you didn't know this . . . but you get to keep all the clothes when we're through shooting."

Carla's mouth dropped open in surprise. "I do?"

"You bet! That's one of the perks on Mr. Robinson's films." Jessie grinned and reached out to straighten Carla's neckline. "You look prefect for the part, hon. Go out there and knock 'em dead."

"But how about my shoes? I don't know how to walk in high heels!"

"You don't have to." Denise came in, just in time to hear Carla's comment. "It's a beach scene, and you're carrying your shoes. You're walking barefoot through the sand. Do you know your lines?"

Carla nodded. "I memorized them while they were blow-drying my hair. But really, Denise . . . I can't possibly . . ."

"Sure you can." Denise interrupted her. "Follow me. They're almost ready on the beach set."

Carla's heart was beating a million miles an hour as they walked through the sound stage and approached the beach set. She could hear Michael singing, and he sounded wonderful. That made her feel like turning around and running. She couldn't play Michael's girlfriend. There was no way. She'd spoil his screen test, and ruin his whole career!

"I knew it!" Mr. Robinson looked up with a smile as Denise

led Carla onto the set. "What do you think, Heidi? Isn't she perfect for Cheryl's part?"

Heidi turned to look at Carla, and she did a classic doubletake. Her face turned white, and she gulped. "Carla! Is that . . . *you?*"

"I think so." Carla smiled at Heidi, a sweet, innocent smile. Perhaps she could act, after all. "Thank you, Heidi. It was really nice of you to recommend me."

Mr. Robinson looked as if he were going to burst into laughter, but he cleared his throat, instead. "We'll be ready in a few minutes, Carla. Just have a seat in the front row."

Heidi looked desperately unhappy as Carla left the set.

"Look, Daddy . . . maybe I made a mistake. I really don't think that . . ."

"It's too late to worry about it." Ralph Robinson interrupted his daughter. "And I think you were absolutely right when you chose Carla. Let's shoot the test and see."

Carla watched as Denise brought in the group from Covers and seated them in a row of chairs. Everyone was staring at her. Winona's mouth was gaping open, and Tammy's eyes were wide with shock. Even Linda looked totally amazed, but she recovered enough to give Carla a friendly smile.

Carla smiled back. She felt fantastic, but she was still modest. "Don't look so shocked, everyone. It's just a new skirt and blouse, and new make-up, and a new hairstyle. I'm still me."

"But I never knew you had such beautiful eyes." Andy sighed deeply. "And I never dreamed you'd look like that in a miniskirt."

Carla was embarrassed. Andy seemed completely bowled over by the change in her appearance, but before she had time to respond to his compliment, Denise was motioning for her to take her place on the set.

"Carla? We need you up here for a lighting check." Carla felt like a princess as she took her place on the set. The floor was covered with smooth white sand dotted with deck chairs and umbrellas. Carla would have been puzzled by the blank screen in the background, but Denise had already explained it to her. They'd taken actual footage of the ocean, and they would be using rear-screen projection to run that footage during Michael's audition.

"Lights, please." Ralph Robinson made a gesture, and the lights came on. Suddenly the set was transformed to a beach at night, lit only by a full moon, hanging low over the horizon. "Are you ready, Carla?"

Carla nodded She was as ready as she'd ever be. She knew her lines, and Denise had rehearsed her.

"Mike? Take your place for the lighting check, please."

Carla felt her heart race as Michael walked onto the set, carrying a guitar. He was dressed in a black silk shirt, open at the neck and a pair of skin-tight white jeans with black lizard skin cowboy boots. He looked very sexy, and Carla was sure that every other girl from Covers was envying her.

Michael took one look at Carla and his face almost split in a smile. He mouthed the word *Wow!* and then they both stood like statues for a moment, while Heidi's father walked from camera to camera, checking their images.

"Okay. You two can relax, but don't leave the set." Heidi's father turned, and motioned to one of the grips. "Put those deck chairs closer together. And the spot directly above Carla has to be lowered a couple of inches. She's got great hair, and I want to pick up some highlights."

"Excuse me, Mr. Robinson." Michael spoke up "Could I make a quick phone call? It'll only take a second."

"Sure. Use that phone over there on the wall. Denise? I need you!"

"Yes, Mr. Robinson." Denise raced to his side, carrying her clipboard.

"Have props fix that guitar. It's too hot under these lights. And get me a couple of big hunks of driftwood. We need something for Mike to sit on when he sings."

"Right away, Mr. Robinson." Denise made a quick note and raced off, clutching her clipboard.

Carla watched all the bustle for a moment, and then Michael came back to join her. Unfortunately, Heidi was right behind him.

"Michael? I need to talk to you . . . alone." Heidi reached out and grabbed his sleeve. "Leave us for a minute, will you, Carla?"

Carla shook her head. "I can't. Your father told us we couldn't leave the set."

"Well, I'm saying you can." Heidi stamped her foot. "Get lost, Carla . . . now!"

Carla raised her eyebrows. Heidi really looked rattled. "I'll be glad to get lost . . . but only if your father says it's all right."

"Daddy?" Heidi raced over to her father who was standing a few feet away. He was busy talking to several important-looking men, but that didn't stop her from interrupting. "Tell Carla she can leave the set. I need to talk to Michael, alone."

"Later, honey. I'm busy right now."

"But Daddy!" Heidi tugged at her father's arm. "This is a real emergency!"

Carla and Michael exchanged worried glances. Heidi's voice had carried clearly, and they'd heard every word.

"What's the matter with Heidi?" Michael frowned. "She really sounds upset."

Carla shrugged. "I don't know. But I think we're going to find out."

"Those were my backers, Heidi." Mr. Robinson sounded angry. "This had better be important!"

"Oh, it is, Daddy! I wasn't going to say anything, but I think this whole scene with Carla is a big mistake. I mean . . . she looks okay, but she's never had any acting experience. She's going to make Michael look bad and ruin his whole screen test!"

"Hold it, Heidi." Mr. Robinson's voice was very stern. "You're the one who suggested that Carla do the scene."

"I know. But, Daddy . . . I was just . . . uh . . . joking around. I didn't actually think you'd pick her! Why don't you let me do the scene with Michael? I know I can do a much better job than Carla."

Mr. Robinson shook his head. "I can't do that, Heidi. Especially not with two of my biggest money men here. If I let you

do a screen test, they'll want me to audition all of their relatives."

"But, Daddy! What if Carla's really awful?"

"That's enough, Heidi!" Mr. Robinson was clearly losing his
patience. "We're doing a screen test for Mike, not for Carla.
And I'll be judging *his* performance. It won't make any difference if Carla can't act."

"But it *will*. Please, Daddy . . . can't you just . . ."

"Forget it, Heidi!" Mr. Robinson grabbed his daughter by
the arm, and led her over to a chair. "Sit and watch. And don't
say a word. If you interrupt me again, I'm going to tell Denise to
take you outside."

Michael's lips began to twitch, and he winked at Carla. "I
think Heidi's jealous. She's afraid you'll steal the show."

"*Me?*" Carla gave a bitter little laugh. "She doesn't have to
worry about that. I just hope I don't do anything wrong. This is
your big chance, Michael. I'll feel just horrible if I make you
look bad."

Michael reached out to squeeze her hand. "Don't be silly,
Carla. There's no way you could make me look bad. You heard
Mr. Robinson. He said you were perfect for the part of the girl.
And you look sensational! What did they do to you, anyway?"

"I'm not sure, but I think it was a miracle."

Michael laughed, but then he turned serious. "It wasn't a
miracle, Carla. But I feel like a fool."

"You do? Why?"

"Because I never noticed how beautiful you are."

Carla felt a current of warmth rush to her cheeks, and she
knew she was blushing. "But, Michael . . . it's just my hair, and
my make-up, and this incredible outfit. They're all gorgeous.
But I'm not."

"You could have fooled me." Michael took her hand and
squeezed it. "When we get through here, let's go down and get
you some contact lenses. Your eyes are the most beautiful shade
of violet blue."

Before Carla could think of an appropriate reply, Mr. Robertson joined them on the set. He was followed by a man carrying two huge pieces of driftwood, and they tried them out in various spots. They had just decided to place them in front of the screen, when Denise rushed up.

"Here's your guitar." Denise handed it to Michael. "They took off the strings and wiped it with something to dull the finish, but nobody in props knew how to tune it again."

As Michael began to tune the guitar, Denise turned to Carla. "Do you want to go over your lines one last time? You didn't have very long to rehearse."

"No, thanks." Carla shook her head. "I only have three, and I know them." Denise leaned over, and spoke softly in Carla's ear. "Do a fantastic job, Carla. I'd love to see Daddy's little girl eat crow."

"Me, too." Carla nodded, and glanced in Heidi's direction. She found Heidi staring at her with a sneer on her face. That sneer made Carla even more determined to do a good job. Heidi was sure she'd be awful in the part, and Carla wanted desperately to prove her wrong.

"Places, please." Ralph Robinson motioned to Carla and Michael. "Sit over here on this driftwood, Mike. Carla? I want you to enter from stage left. I'll cue you when it's time."

"Yes, Mr. Robinson." Carla nodded and went to stand where he had indicated. Her heart was beating fast, and she could feel her knees start to tremble. It must be stage fright. She'd heard Linda and some of the other girls describe how their stomachs had churned and their knees had turned to jelly before an important performance. Linda always said she used her stage-fright to work for her, but Carla had no idea how to do that. She just took a deep breath and thought about how wonderful it would be if Heidi's mean little trick backfired.

Carla was so nervous, she almost missed Mr. Robinson's cue. She could hear Michael singing, far off and very softly. It helped her to get into her character. The sound of his voice and the haunting melody made her draw closer and closer, her feet sliding silently through the sand, until she was sitting on the driftwood log, nestled close at his side.

"Hi." Michael turned to look at her, admiration in his eyes. "Do I know you?"

"No, but please don't stop." Carla smiled. "Your song is so beautiful. It's like the moonlight glistening on the water."

As Michael sang, Carla reached up to touch his face. She placed one finger gently against his cheek, and sighed as she gazed up at him.

And then the song ended, and the notes died away on the gentle breeze. The waves lapped closer as he put down his guitar. She was ready as he pulled her into his arms, and his lips met hers. Her dream lover was real and she was in his arms.

"Cut!"

Mr. Robinson's voice startled Carla out of her reverie. She pulled back, out of Michael's embrace, and blinked.

"That was fantastic!" Mr. Robinson walked over to shake their hands. "I need both of you in my movie. Do you kids have the same agent?"

"Yes, sir." Carla stared at Michael in surprise, as he nodded. What agent? She didn't have an agent. But Michael grabbed her hand and squeezed it. And then he reached into his pocket and handed Mr. Robinson a business card. "Here's his card."

"Good. That'll make things simple." Mr. Robinson glanced down at the card. "I know Jim. He's very good. Tell him to give me a call in the morning and we'll work out the details."

After Mr. Robinson had left, Carla turned to Michael in alarm. "But, Michael . . . I don't *have* an agent!"

"You do now. Remember that phone call I made, right before we did our screen test? I called Uncle Jimmy, and he said he'd represent both of us."

"You were that sure I'd get the part?"

Michael nodded. "Absolutely. I knew you'd be great. You're very talented, Carla."

There was a round of congratulations from the gang at Covers, but Heidi was conspicuously absent. Before Carla had time to take a deep breath, she found herself walking out to Andy's van in the bright sunlight.

"Hey, Carla . . . how does it feel to be a star?" Linda raced up to link arms with her.

"I . . . I don't know." Carla sighed deeply. "I still think Mr. Robinson made a mistake."

Linda shook her head. "Oh, no he didn't. You were fantastic. And you should have seen the expression on Heidi's face when he gave you that part."

"Really?" Carla began to smile. "Could you describe it?"

"It was sort of a cross between a constipated rhino, and a . . . oh, I don't know!" Linda turned around to look at Michael. "You saw Heidi's face, didn't you? How would you describe it?"

Michael grinned and shook his head. "I'm not sure, but I stepped back."

"You did?" Linda looked puzzled.

"That's right. I didn't want to get scalded. I thought steam was going to explode out of her ears any second."

Carla smiled, but she felt a very uneasy. She hoped Heidi would calm down tonight, and they could go back to being friends. Heidi was smart and she had a lot of influence. It might be very dangerous to have Heidi Robinson as a permanent enemy.

Nine

Over the next few days, Carla walked on eggshells, trying not to antagonize Heidi. Carla's part in the movie wasn't big, but she was in almost every scene with Michael. There were shots of her sitting in the audience, applauding at his performance, or waiting to hug him when he came off the stage. She danced with him at parties, and walked at his side at various locations. Carla knew she didn't have a starring role, but she had plenty of screen exposure. And every time she appeared in a scene, she was dressed in a different, totally gorgeous outfit. Her free wardrobe was growing, and Carla could hardly wait to take the clothes home when the movie wrapped. But there was a distressing downside to her new movie career. As the days went by, and Mr. Robinson praised her work with Michael, it was clear that Heidi was growing angrier and angrier.

On the fifth day, the dirty tricks started. Carla and Michael were doing a critical scene that started in the dressing room, continued down the hall, and ended with Carla joining Michael on the stage as he sang his song. Heidi was on the set as an extra, a member of the group from Covers. They'd all been cast as Michael's "groupies," the fans that followed Michael from show to show, and appeared· in the audience. Since Heidi was usually on the set with Michael and Carla, she had plenty of opportunities to try to sabotage Carla's role.

The first dirty trick almost worked. The setting was the dressing room, where Carla was keeping Michael company before his stage appearance. Carla and Michael were embracing on the couch, and she was in her stocking feet. The scene opened with a knock on the door, Michael's signal to get ready to perform. When the knock came, they were to jump up. While Michael got into his jacket and grabbed his guitar, Carla was supposed to fish her shoes out from under the couch and put them on. The first part of the scene ended as they both rushed out of the dressing room door.

There was no problem with the rehearsal, and Mr. Robinson seemed pleased. He called for a ten minute break, and Carla was hustled to make-up where her lipstick was freshened and her hair was carefully mussed to look as if she'd been locked in a passionate embrace with Michael. Crew members rushed in to redress the set, plumping cushions, rearranging several bottles and jars on the dresser, and draping clothing on the Oriental screen. By the time the ten minute break was over, the set was finished, and they were ready to shoot the scene.

The first part of the scene went exactly as Carla and Michael had rehearsed it. No problem. But when Carla slipped into her shoes, she noticed that they were a slightly different color than the ones she'd been wearing in the rehearsal. It didn't really matter. Perhaps wardrobe had changed them for some reason. She really didn't have time to think about it as Michael grabbed her hand and they raced across the floor to the dressing room door.

They had almost made it when Carla felt her feet slide out from under her. She stumbled and Michael valiantly tried to hold her up. Of course he didn't succeed and they fell to the floor in an awkward tangle of arms and legs.

"Cut!" Mr. Robinson shouted. He glared at Heidi, who was laughing hysterically, and hurried to Michael and Carla. "What happened? Are you hurt?"

"I'm okay." Michael helped Carla up and dusted her off. "Are you all right, Carla?"

Carla nodded. She was so embarrassed, her face was bright red. "I'm sorry I ruined your take, Mr. Robinson. I must have tripped."

"On what?" Denise looked down at the perfectly bare floor. Then she led Carla to a chair. "Sit down, Carla, and give me your shoes."

Carla watched as Denise examined the bottom of her shoes. There was a frown on her face. She handed them to Mr. Robinson, who examined them also, and they exchanged worried glances.

"Okay." Mr. Robinson sighed deeply. "Tell the extras they can take their lunch break, but have them back on the set by two."

Denise passed the word and the extras left, including the group from Covers. Heidi was the only one who stayed, and she was frowning as she approached her father.

"Do I have to leave, Daddy? I want to see Michael and Carla do their scene."

"Run along, Heidi." Mr. Robinson dismissed her with a wave. "Keep an eye on the extras and make sure they don't wander away from the catering tent."

Heidi was obviously disappointed, but she nodded and headed for the door. After she'd left, Mr. Robinson called for Denise again. "Get Jessie over here on the double. I want some friction tape on the bottom of these shoes. They're much too slick. Carla?"

"Yes, Mr. Robinson."

"Are these the same shoes you were wearing in rehearsal?"

Carla shook her head. "I don't think so, Mr. Robinson. When I slipped them on, I noticed that they were a slightly different shade of brown."

Mr. Robinson frowned. "Did you see who replaced your shoes, Carla?"

"No, Mr. Robinson. I was at the make-up table."

It took only a moment for Mr. Robinson to assemble the crew. No one from props had seen anything, and neither had the continuity supervisor, the assistant director, the grips, or the lighting techs. They all agreed that it would have been possible for someone to replace Carla's shoes, but no one had any idea who had done it.

"Do you think someone's trying to sabotage the film?" Denise looked very worried.

But Mr. Robinson shook his head. "It was probably just a mistake. Let's be very careful, folks. Mistakes cost time and money. We're just lucky that this was a small one."

Jessie put friction tape on the bottom of Carla's shoes, and when she was finished, they shot the scene again. This time everything went perfectly, and Carla gave a deep sigh of relief as she walked to the catering tent with Michael.

"Are you sure you're all right?" Michael looked down at her with concern.

"I'm okay. But I'm really sorry I blew that take."

"Don't worry." Michael slipped his arm around her shoulders and gave her a hug. "Mistakes happen. It wasn't anybody's fault."

As they entered the tent, Carla noticed Heidi sitting alone, at a table near the front. The moment Heidi saw them, she smiled and waved.

"Hi, Michael! I saved you a table. Get your tray and let's eat together."

"Thanks, Heidi." Michael glanced at Carla, and winked. "I'd like to join you, but I'm having lunch with Carla. We have to discuss our next scene."

Heidi's smiled faltered a bit, but then it came back, bigger and brighter than ever. "Of course. I meant Carla, too."

"Okay . . . we'll be right with you."

As they headed toward the food line, Carla glanced back at Heidi's table. She was sure Heidi hadn't wanted her to join them. There were only two chairs.

"Do you mind sitting with Heidi?" Michael turned to Carla with concern. "I figure I'd better be nice to her. After all, her father's my boss, and I don't want to get on her bad side."

Carla nodded and forced a smile. "It's fine, Michael. Heidi's father is my boss, too."

But Carla *did* mind. The less she had to do with Heidi, the better. There was only one person here who wanted her to fail, and that person was Heidi.

As they headed for Heidi's table, Carla trailed a bit behind Michael. The expression on Heidi's face was strange. She looked proud and a little smug. Heidi had laughed when she'd slipped on the set. She'd enjoyed seeing Carla stumble and ruin the take. What if the replacement shoes hadn't been a mistake? What if Heidi had substituted those slick-soled shoes deliberately, so that Carla would fall?

There were no more dirty tricks that day, and Carla actually started to relax. She was enjoying her film debut, especially since most of her scenes were with Michael. She began to think that she'd been mistaken when she'd suspected that Heidi was trying to sabotage her role. The next incident didn't occur until the next afternoon, when Carla put in her new contact lenses for a party scene with Michael. They were announcing their engagement, and Carla was supposed to look radiantly happy.

"Places, please." Mr. Robinson smiled at Michael and Carla. The scene was being shot at the studio restaurant, which had been dressed to look like a lavish and expensive bistro. This was one of Carla's speaking parts, and she'd rehearsed her lines with Denise. Michael would announce their engagement, and all the extras would clamor for a speech. That was Carla's cue to stand up and tell everyone how much she loved Michael.

Carla sat with Michael at a raised table in the front of the restaurant. There was water in the glasses, and she took a sip to moisten her mouth, which was very dry. Her face felt flushed, and she was slightly dizzy. What was the matter with her?

"Stage fright?" Michael looked concerned. "You look really pale, Carla."

Carla nodded, and put a hand to her forehead. Her forehead was clammy, the dizziness was growing worse by the second. But before she could tell Michael that she was ill, the cameras started to roll.

Michael got up to announce their engagement, and Carla

forced herself to smile. But Michael's voice sounded hollow to her ears, growing fainter and fainter as the dizziness grew.

"Speech! Speech!" The extras applauded and stared at her expectantly. "Speech! Speech!"

Carla tried to rise to her feet, but a wave of dizziness made her grasp the edge of the tablecloth to keep from falling. As the tablecloth slipped, water glasses crashed to the floor and she fell heavily back in her chair.

"Cut!" Mr. Robinson rushed up, and stared at Carla's pale face. "What happened, Carla?"

Carla burst into tears. "I'm sorry, Mr. Robinson, but I . . . I'm so dizzy, I can't stand up."

"Help her to the dressing room." Mr. Robinson motioned to Michael and Heidi. "Denise? Call for the doctor."

It took only a few minutes for the doctor to arrive. He examined Carla, and turned to Mr. Robinson with a worried expression. "Her vital signs are normal. I can't find anything wrong. But her balance is completely gone, and she can't see anything clearly."

"She can't see?" Heidi frowned as the doctor nodded. "I think I might know what's wrong. It happened to me once, when I first started wearing contacts. Let's take out Carla's lenses and see if that helps."

It only took a moment for the doctor to remove Carla's contact lenses, and drop them back in their case. Almost immediately, a little color came back to Carla's face.

"How do you feel now, Carla?" Heidi looked very concerned.

"Better." Carla blinked and took a deep breath. "I feel a lot better."

The doctor nodded, and turned to Carla. "Okay, young lady. Try to stand up for me. I'll catch you if you fall."

Carla was still a little shaky, but she managed to stand up. Her knees had stopped trembling and she took a tentative step. "I'm not dizzy anymore. What happened?"

"You had your lenses reversed." The doctor smiled at her. "The correction for your left eye is a lot stronger than your right. Reversing them threw you off balance and made you dizzy and disoriented."

Carla frowned. "But . . . how did I get them mixed up? The cases are marked."

"Oh, don't worry about that, Carla." Heidi patted her on the shoulder. "It could have happened to anyone, right Daddy?"

Mr. Robinson nodded. "Of course. I'm just glad it wasn't anything serious. You rest up for a few minutes, Carla. Heidi can fill in for you while we do another rehearsal. I'll send Denise to get you when we're ready to shoot."

After everyone had left her dressing room, Carla stared down at the cases that held her contacts. She was almost certain that she hadn't mixed them up. Was this another attempt to throw off her performance?

The dressing rooms weren't locked. It would have been easy for someone to slip in and switch the tops of the cases. And there was only one person who would be spiteful enough to pull a nasty trick like that. Heidi had known exactly what was wrong, and now her father thought she was a genius. What if Heidi had switched her lenses, and then pretended to solve the problem?

Even though Mr. Robinson had told her to rest, Carla got to her feet and made her way back to the set. She stood in the back, where no one would see her, and watched Heidi rehearse with Michael. They were very good together. Too good. Heidi had gotten exactly what she wanted, a chance to take Carla's place. Of course it was only a rehearsal, but everyone was bound to notice what a perfect couple they made.

Carla held her breath as she watched Michael put his arms around Heidi and kiss her. It was supposed to be a polite, public kiss, but Heidi made it into much more. She snuggled up against Michael so tightly, there didn't seem to be any space at all between their bodies. And Michael certainly looked to be enjoying Heidi's kiss. Their lips were glued together, and they seemed almost unwilling to break off their kiss as the extras stamped their feet and applauded.

"Cut!" Mr. Robinson was smiling as he called for a break.

There was no way he could fail to notice the attraction between Heidi and Michael. No way at all.

Suddenly, Carla felt cold and she shivered slightly. This was more than a simple rehearsal for Heidi. She was auditioning! Would Mr. Robinson reconsider and give her part to Heidi? Carla didn't think so, not this time, but he might if these nasty little incidents kept happening. Mr. Robinson was a producer, and he was concerned about the bottom line. Every time Carla blew a take, whether it was her fault or not, it cost him time and money. Carla was sure that if she wanted to keep her part in the movie, she had to watch Heidi like a hawk. Even though she couldn't prove it, Carla knew that Heidi had planted the slick pair of shoes, and switched the covers on her contact lenses. Heidi would try again. Carla was sure of it. And somehow, she had to make sure that Heidi didn't succeed in her plan to replace her.

Ten

Covers was dark on Sunday night, and Carla sat in her office and did her best to concentrate on the payroll. This past week had been a disaster, and it was all because Heidi was making a play for Michael.

Carla and Michael had planned to go to the midnight movie on Monday night. Both of them had wanted to see *They Shall Have Music*, a 1939 black and white film, with Jascha Heifetz. They'd planned to leave Covers right after the show, but Heidi had spoiled their plans. She'd told Michael that she was having trouble with a song he'd written for her, and she simply had to have some extra rehearsal time. Naturally, the only time she'd had available was that night, right after the show.

Michael had sounded very sorry when he'd told Carla that they'd have to see the film on Tuesday night. But on Tuesday, they'd had the same problem. Michael and Heidi were still working on the song, and he had re-scheduled the film for Wednesday.

As it turned out, Wednesday hadn't worked, either. Heidi had invited Michael to a Hollywood party where he could make some good contacts. Naturally, Michael had agreed to go. Carla couldn't fault him for that. She knew how important contacts were in the world of show biz.

On Thursday night, Michael had canceled again. Heidi had

car problems, and she'd asked Michael to give her a ride home. And on Friday, Heidi had presented him with two tickets for a stellar fund-raiser at the county Art Museum. She said she'd tried to get an extra ticket for Carla, but she hadn't been able to get more than two.

On Saturday, when Heidi's car was supposed to be ready, it wasn't. Naturally, Heidi had expected Michael to pick her up and take her home after the show. And tonight, the last night the movie was showing, Heidi had insisted on helping Michael choose which songs to sing at the audition she'd arranged with a record company executive.

Carla sighed, and did her best to look on the bright side. Perhaps she could rent a tape of the movie. If Michael could ever free himself from Heidi's clutches, they could watch it together at her house. But the chances of that happening were very slim. Carla was sure that Heidi would continue to monopolize all of Michael's spare time so he wouldn't be able to share an evening with her.

At least Carla had one thing to be thankful for. There hadn't been any more dirty tricks at the studio. Heidi had been too busy monopolizing Michael to think up any more ways to sabotage Carla's scenes. Despite Heidi's interference, they'd managed to shoot the last of Carla's scenes on Friday, and Jessie and Denise had helped Carla carry over thirty new outfits to her car. As the icing on the cake, Mr. Robinson had told Carla that he was so impressed with her work, he might have a part for her in his next movie.

Since Michael was still working at the studio and Carla's part was finished, they hadn't seen much of each other. In the brief time they'd managed to spend together, Michael had talked about Heidi's obsession with him. He'd said that he'd much rather be with Carla, but he really couldn't tell Heidi to get lost. He was hoping that his association with Mr. Robinson would lead to a major career move. He couldn't jeopardize that just because Heidi was making a play for him.

Carla understood. Really, she did. But she was beginning to hate the sight of Heidi's head, nestled close to Michael's chest.

Heidi had a way of hugging Michael when she walked, and making sure that her body pressed up against his in all the right places. And Michael wasn't exactly immune to her charms. He was flattered that Heidi found him so desirable.

There was the sound of the front door opening, and Carla jumped up from her chair. No one was supposed to be here tonight.

Carla switched off the lights in the office and listened as footsteps sounded on the wooden floor. Two sets of footsteps, one heavy, one light. She crept out of the office, careful not to make a sound, and almost screamed as the lights snapped on. And then she saw them, Michael and Heidi, walking across the brightly lit stage.

Michael had his arm around Heidi's shoulders, and she was smiling up at him. Carla watched as Michael placed two stools in the center of the stage, and took his guitar out of its case.

"Sing your new song first." Heidi slid onto one stool, and clasped her hands in front of her. "I think that one's your best."

Carla's heart beat faster as Michael started to play. Michael had sung his new number for her, and she thought it was wonderful. But now the words took on new meaning, as she stared at Heidi and Michael. It was about a singer who'd won the heart of a beautiful girl by writing all his songs for her.

Heidi waited until Michael had finished, and then she sighed in pleasure. "It's perfect, Michael! The best song you've ever written. I was just wondering if . . . no, it probably wouldn't work."

"What?" Michael looked interested. "Tell me, Heidi."

"I think it might be better if you had the girl join in on the last chorus. I mean . . . there he is, singing to her. And she's so enchanted, she joins in."

Michael took a moment to think it over, and then he nodded. "You're right, Heidi. It might add just the right touch. Do you want to try it?"

"Sure, if you want me to. But we've never rehearsed it, so you'll have to excuse me if I don't get it right."

Carla frowned deeply. Heidi looked like the cat that ate the canary as Michael started to sing again. She gazed up at Michael with an adoring expression, and when he came to the last chorus, she joined in, her voice rising and melding with his. The harmony was perfect, the timing was exactly right, and Carla listened in awe as they finished the song together. It really was better this way.

"That was fantastic!" Michael reached out to hug Heidi. "You're amazing. How did you manage to do it so well?"

Heidi shrugged. "It was easy. Our voices just blend together, naturally. It's almost as if we were born to sing duets together."

"Maybe we were." Michael stared deeply into Heidi's eyes. "You're . . . you're wonderful, Heidi."

Carla's breath caught in her throat as Michael pulled Heidi closer. And then he was kissing her, their lips melting, their bodies pressed tightly together.

She couldn't watch. Carla turned to go back into the office. She couldn't stand to see Michael taken in by a girl like Heidi. Denise had told Carla all about Heidi, and her series of up-and-coming boyfriends. Heidi had dated all the young stars of her father's movies, but the day after the movie premiered, she'd dropped them cold. Heidi might want Michael now, but she wasn't the type to be loyal. The moment the premiere was over, Heidi would dump Michael just like she'd dumped all those other actors.

It took only a moment to gather up her purse and car keys. There was a back door to the building, and Carla walked toward it with tears in her eyes. She'd really thought that Michael cared about her. Perhaps he did, but right now he was blinded by Heidi and his ambition for stardom. She was very afraid that Michael was in for a real let-down, but there wasn't a thing she could do about it.

As Carla locked the back door behind her, she glanced around. Michael must have parked on the street because her car was the only one in the parking lot. They hadn't known she was here, and that was good. Michael had no idea she'd seen him kissing Heidi.

Carla got into her car, but she didn't put the key in the ignition. She sat there, under the cover of darkness, and thought about Michael and Heidi. Michael was her best friend, the guy she was beginning to trust and love. Somehow she had to protect him and keep him from falling into Heidi's trap. Michael was fascinated by Heidi, and Carla couldn't blame him. Heidi was beautiful, and talented, and her family had plenty of Hollywood connections. If all things were equal, Heidi would be a perfect match for Michael, but things weren't equal at all. Heidi didn't care about Michael. All she cared about was herself. Michael might think he was dating the perfect girl, but he was bound to end up with a broken heart.

It was hot in her car, and Carla rolled down the window. It was a perfect summer night in Southern California with a full moon casting romantic shadows over the palm trees that lined the parking lot. Things would be much better if Michael broke up with Heidi. Then Michael would be with her, and he might just . . .

Carla groaned and put her romantic thoughts firmly out of her mind. Michael wasn't with her. He was with Heidi. And Heidi was the wrong girl for him. If she wanted to save Michael from future heartbreak, she had to think of a permanent way to break them up.

Heidi smiled as Michael began to sing another love song. He was so cute, and he had a wonderful voice. Heidi was sure that Doug Emery, her father's record producer friend, would love Michael. If she could get him an audition.

Naturally, Heidi had fibbed a little. She didn't really have an audition lined up. But that should be simple enough to arrange if she told Daddy that she wanted to give her new boyfriend a shot at the big time. Daddy would do anything she asked, now that she'd broken it off with Derek Peters. He'd hated Derek with a passion. But he liked Michael. He'd told her he thought that Michael was a very nice guy.

Heidi shivered a little. Daddy had been very angry when he'd found out she'd gone to a party at Derek's apartment. She guessed she really couldn't blame him. If she'd known that the police were going to raid the party, she never would have gone.

Naturally, Daddy had grounded her. He'd even threatened to hire a bodyguard to make sure she didn't get into any more trouble. But that was all in the past. Daddy liked Michael and he approved of her new romance. Of course Michael was a bit of a nerd, but it gave her great pleasure to take him away from Carla.

The song ended, and Heidi smiled up at Michael. It was a tender smile, full of promise. "I think you're going to be great, Michael. All you have to do is get more emotion in your love songs."

Michael looked a little puzzled. "Whatever you say, Heidi. But how should I do that?"

"Look at me when you sing. And pretend that you're completely in love with me."

"That shouldn't be too hard."

Heidi's smile grew wider. She was winning, and Carla was losing. There was no way Michael could think of Carla when she was coming on to him. It was a game she was playing, a test of her power to attract any guy she wanted. Keeping Michael away from Carla was a real ego trip for her.

Michael had flicked a few switches before they'd stepped out onto the stage, but he hadn't really bothered to light them like a stage act. Heidi moved her chair to a position directly under the overhead spot and got ready to sing with Michael. His face was in shadow, and he looked so handsome, she got a lump in her throat. Michael was good, and perhaps he'd make it . . . as long as she helped him. With her father's connections, they could even land a spot on television. The talk shows were always looking for musical numbers between the guests. Their television appearances could lead to bigger and better things, like their own show. Anything was possible.

As Michael sang, he gazed at her admiringly from the shadows. Heidi basked in his attention, and got ready to join in on the chorus. But just as she was about to open her mouth to sing, Michael stopped abruptly.

"Did you hear something?"

Heidi listened for a moment, and then she shook her head. "No. What's the matter?"

"I thought I heard someone moving up on the catwalk."

Heidi felt a prickle of alarm. What if someone had heard them singing and come in? "Did you lock the door behind us?"

"I think so." Michael nodded. "I'll go and check it."

Heidi began to shiver slightly as Michael got up. For some strange reason, she didn't want to be alone on the stage. She felt like a sitting duck, right here under the bright spotlight. As Michael went down the steps into the audience, she almost got up to join him. But that was silly. There was no one here except the two of them.

"It's okay. The door's locked." Michael's voice floated up from the darkness. "Wait there, Heidi. My throat's dry. I'm going to get us a couple of drinks from the kitchen. What do you want?"

Heidi took a deep breath. She still felt uneasy. "Apple juice, if they've got it."

"Okay. I'll be back in a second."

Heidi heard Michael's footsteps travel across the floor. The kitchen door creaked as it swung open, and then there was only silence. She imagined Michael flicking on the kitchen light, and rummaging around in the cooler, looking for her apple juice. Why hadn't she asked for something simple, like tap water? That would have taken much less time.

And then she heard it, stealthy footsteps high above her head. She almost screamed, but then she remembered Andy talking about the squirrels that lived in the tree by the side of the building. The noise she'd heard was probably the squirrels, scampering across the roof.

What was taking Michael so long? Heidi shivered again, and wished she'd brought a sweater. The air conditioning was on and it was cold up here on the stage with only two spots to light it.

There was another sound, and Heidi held her breath. She didn't like being out here all alone, but she knew it would be foolish to move out of the light. She might trip over a cable and hurt herself. If she sat here quietly, Michael would be back in just a moment.

And then she heard the sound of breathing. It sounded very loud in the stillness, and she began to panic.

"Michael?" Heidi's voice was low, barely more than a whisper. She didn't want him to know that she was frightened. But there was no answer. Michael was still in the kitchen.

Suddenly the spots went out, plunging the stage into darkness. Heidi jumped as she heard a loud snap, high overhead. A cable had broken! She opened her mouth to scream, but before she had time to utter a single sound, a heavy arc light hurtled down to crash on top of her head.

Eleven

It was Monday noon, and the cast and crew were sitting around the round table at Covers. Mr. Calloway had called them in, to tell them what had happened. Only one person was missing and that was Michael.

Carla shivered, and glanced around her. Although they were only a few feet from the stage, no one was looking at the spot where Heidi had died.

"Where's Michael?" Linda asked the question that was on everyone's mind.

"He should be here any moment." Mr. Calloway looked grim. "He called about fifteen minutes ago, and said he was just leaving Detective Davis's office."

"They let him go?!"

Winona looked shocked, and Carla knew that the rumors were flying again. She took a deep breath and tried to explain. "Of course they let him go. The only reason he had to go in was to give Detective Davis his statement. After all, he was a witness."

Just then the front door opened, and Michael came in. He looked tired and haggard, and Carla knew he hadn't had any sleep. She patted the empty chair next to her, and Michael sat down gratefully.

At first no one seemed to know what to say, but after a few moments of uncomfortable silence had passed, Mr. Calloway cleared his throat. "Would you like to tell us what happened, Michael?"

Michael nodded. "I'll tell you what I know, but that's not much. It's like I told Detective Davis. I was in the kitchen, pouring Heidi some apple juice, when all the lights went out. Then I heard a terrible crash, and I called out to Heidi, but she didn't answer. It took me a minute to get to the light box. It was dark, and I had to feel my way. I turned the lights back on, and then I . . . I saw what had happened."

"Oh, my God!" Linda's voice was shaking. "And you . . . you found her?"

Michael nodded, and Carla reached out to squeeze his hand. She could tell he was having trouble speaking.

"The arc light was down on the floor of the stage, smashed to pieces. And then I saw Heidi. She looked like . . ." Michael swallowed hard, ". . . like a fallen angel, all crumpled up on the stage."

Michael stopped and swallowed again. It took him a moment to gain control of his voice. "I guess I was trying to fool myself by feeling for her pulse. It was pretty clear that she was dead. The arc light was heavy and it fell right on top of her . . . her head."

"That's enough, Michael." Andy patted his shoulder. "You don't have to go into the details. You found her, felt for her pulse, and then you called the police. Is that right?"

Michael nodded. "After I made the call, I went back to her. I was going to stay right by her until the police came. That's when I noticed the arrow."

"You didn't see the arrow before?" Andy frowned slightly.

"No. But maybe I just didn't notice. I can't say for sure whether it was there or not, when I first found her."

Andy nodded. "What did you do then?"

"I just stared at the arrow for a minute. I think I was in shock. I'd thought Heidi's death was an accident, but when I saw the arrow, I knew it was murder. And then I remembered the noise we'd heard when we were singing and I panicked. I ran out the door and waited for the police on the street."

"Noise?" Mr. Calloway raised his eyebrows. "What kind of noise?"

"Footsteps. Above the stage. It sounded like someone was up on the catwalk, walking around."

"What did you do when you heard the footsteps?" Andy opened his notebook and began to write.

"I went to check the door, but it was locked and I didn't see anybody lurking around. The noise had stopped by then, and I figured that it had been caused by something natural, like an animal running across the roof, or a tree branch rubbing against the building."

"But it wasn't something natural." Linda shuddered. "What you heard was the Cupid Killer! It's a good thing you waited for the police outside. He might have come after you!"

"You're wrong, Linda! The Cupid Killer wouldn't touch Michael. He only murders Michael's girlfriends." Winona blurted out what almost everyone was thinking. Then she looked very embarrassed at what she'd said. "Sorry, Michael. I've got a big mouth."

"Maybe, but I'm afraid you're right." Michael looked grim. "I should have grabbed Heidi and ran out the door. But I didn't know that he was up there."

"Of course you didn't." Carla reached out to pat his hand. "There's one thing that puzzles me, though. How did the Cupid Killer get in if the door was locked?"

"Maybe I just thought I locked it. I've gone over it a million times in my head, but I'm just not sure."

Andy looked very sympathetic. He could tell that Michael was agonizing over whether he'd locked the door. "Hey, Michael . . . it doesn't really matter whether you locked the door or not. I'm almost sure there's a way inside without a key."

"That's right." Berto spoke up. "Andy and I are almost certain that someone's been breaking in. There's been a lot of food missing, and we think somebody's been cooking in the kitchen."

Andy nodded. "The pots and pans tipped us off. They're always washed, but sometimes we find them put back in the wrong place."

"I guess it's time to ask some questions." Mr. Calloway looked around the table, and sighed. "Look, gang . . . I expect to have some missing food, once in awhile. I don't pay that much, and I've always told you that if you're hungry, you can have a meal on me, right?"

Carla nodded along with everyone else, but she began to get terribly nervous. She held her breath as Mr. Calloway continued.

"I've never really bothered to keep a complete inventory, but lately things have really gotten out of hand. Andy and Berto told me that food has been disappearing every night. I really hate to ask, but . . . have any of you been coming in after hours to eat?"

One by one, they shook their heads. There was a long silence, and finally Carla spoke up. "Mr. Calloway?"

"Yes, Carla."

"I've noticed something, too. But I didn't want to say anything before now. Some of the petty cash has been missing, and I've been making up the losses out of my own pocket. It hasn't been much . . . only a couple of dollars a day."

"Carla!" Mr. Calloway looked shocked. "Why didn't you tell me?"

Carla sighed. She knew she should have reported the loss. "I didn't want to get anyone in trouble. And I was sure the money would be returned, sooner or later. I knew it had to be someone who worked here, because everyone knows where I keep the key to the cash drawer."

"Right." Mr. Calloway nodded, and he faced the group again. "I want you to tell me if any of you have taken money out of the cash drawer. You don't have to worry. I'll understand. And I'll let you make it up out of your paycheck."

There was another uncomfortable silence, and then Andy spoke up. "I'm sure that no one on the kitchen staff took any money. We're all friends, and we're a pretty tight group. If someone needed money, they would have asked me for a loan."

Linda, who was the unofficial leader of the talent, shook her head. "None of the talent took any money. I'm sure of it."

"And no one on the crew did." Marc Allen began to frown. "We're a tight group, too. And I would have heard about it."

Carla sighed deeply. "Someone took that money. I count the cash every night, and there's always two or three dollars missing."

"When did you notice the missing money?" Andy looked up from his notebook.

"A couple of weeks ago. At first, I thought I'd made a mistake, so I started counting the money twice. I do it once when I come in, and once when I leave at night. It's all there when I leave, but it's gone when I come in the next day."

"How about a former employee?" Michael raised the question. "Somebody who used to work here could be coming back to eat and steal money from the cash drawer."

Mr. Calloway shook his head. "That makes sense, except for one thing. There aren't any former employees. No one's ever quit. And I've never fired anyone. Most of you started when Covers opened, and you're all still here."

"But Judy's not here anymore." Vera's voice was shaking. "Judy's a former employee."

"Judy Lampert?" Carla's mouth dropped open as Vera nodded. "But Vera . . . Judy's dead! Dead girls don't eat food, and they certainly don't steal money out of petty cash."

Vera looked a little embarrassed, but she stuck to her guns. "What if Judy's like the Phantom of the Opera? Maybe we just *think* she's dead. Linda told me she found some blankets folded up in one of the dressing rooms, and it looked like someone was sleeping in there. Maybe it's Judy."

"It's not." Carla shook her head. "Judy was killed in her car. We told you it burned, remember?"

"I know. But how do we know that Judy didn't crawl out? She could be hideously deformed like the Phantom was. And she could be hiding out right here at Covers."

"Come on, Vera." Michael patted her softly. "You're not making sense."

"But I am! Judy said she was the Cupid Killer in that note she left! And then the police found an arrow in Liz's body. There was a second arrow last night, and that proves that Judy's still alive!"

"You're wrong, Vera." Andy looked very serious. "Judy's dead. We can swear to that. Michael and Carla and I saw her body. We identified her for the police."

Vera swallowed hard. Her face turned pale, and she looked absolutely horrified. "Oh, my God! That's even worse!"

"What's even worse?" Carla looked puzzled.

"If Judy's dead, then she's . . . she's *haunting* us! And she's murdering people from her grave!"

Marc Allen began to laugh. It was clear he didn't believe Vera's theory. "I love it! If Judy's spirit is hanging around, I want her to show me how to fight the backdrop for the Covers logo."

Carla could tell that Vera was ready to cry. Tears welled up in her eyes as she turned to Marc. "Don't laugh, Marc. It's scary! My aunt used to talk about ghosts and I never really believed her, but . . . but I do now!"

"Take it easy, Vera." Michael reached out to hug her. "Tell us why you're so frightened."

"I . . . I was the last one to leave on Saturday night. And I saw Judy. I know I did."

Linda frowned. "Come on, Vera. You didn't really see her. You just thought you did."

"*I did* see her!" Vera shook her head. "I left my purse in the office, and Andy let me back in to get it. The light was on in the kitchen, and I started to open the door to turn it off. That's when I saw her. Judy Lampert was sitting at the kitchen table, eating a sandwich!"

"Well, that explains where all my dill slices have been going." Andy began to chuckle. "They were Judy's favorite pickles."

"Go to hell, Andy!" Vera gave him a dirty look, and promptly burst into tears. "I don't care if any of you believe me or not. But I saw her! And it scared me half to death!"

"Maybe you saw someone who *looked* like Judy." Michael

pulled Vera close, and gave her another hug. "Think carefully, Vera. Did you get a good look at her face?"

Vera gave a deep sigh, and snuggled up against Michael's chest. "Well . . . no. Not really. She was turned away from me, but her hair was blond, and it was exactly the same length as Judy's. And she was wearing a black sweater and jeans."

"Did you talk to her?" Carla asked. "Or ask her what she was doing in the kitchen?"

Vera shivered and shook her head. "Of course not. I'm not crazy! I just turned around and ran for the door as fast as I could!"

For the next ten minutes, they all did their best to convince Vera that she'd seen a transient who just happened to look like Judy, but Vera wouldn't be swayed. She came from a very superstitious family, and they all believed in ghosts. Finally, Mr. Calloway called for order.

"Okay gang. We're wasting our breath. Vera's going to believe what she wants to believe, and we're not going to change her mind. But even if we put the problem of ghosts aside, we do have a very real problem. There's definitely someone camping out at Covers, and I'm making a new rule. No one comes in to work alone. If you get here first, wait for someone else before you unlock the door. This Judy look-alike might have friends, and one of them could be the Cupid Killer."

Michael turned to Mr. Calloway. "Then you don't think that Judy was the Cupid Killer?"

"I'm not sure what I think. But someone murdered Liz Applegate. And now Heidi's dead, too. It doesn't really matter whether this is the work of the original Cupid Killer, or a copycat. There's a serial killer out there, and we have to take precautions."

Everyone nodded solemnly. Mr. Calloway was right.

"We'll check all the windows and put on locks. And I'll have the front door re-keyed. We're going to make sure that Covers is locked up as tight as a drum. But my rule still stands. No one comes in alone."

Their meeting only lasted a few more moments, and then

everyone went off to get ready for the night's performance. Carla walked back to the office and sat down behind her desk. She was more than a little rattled, and she didn't really feel like working on the books. But she got out the ledger and opened it to the current date.

The money in the cash drawer had to be counted. Carla did it twice to make sure it was accurate, and got out her pen to record the sum in the ledger. That was when she saw the note. It was on a yellow Post-it, stuck to the page, and the handwriting looked like Judy's.

Carla stared down at the small yellow square of paper for a moment, and her mind began to spin in crazy circles. Could Vera be right? Was Judy haunting Covers? The words on the paper were ominous, and Carla closed the ledger quickly, so she wouldn't have to look at them. But their message was burned indelibly into her brain. *Carla—Tell them to leave Michael alone. He's mine!*

Twelve

The black asphalt parking lot was hot, and Carla was glad she was wearing one of her new outfits from the movie. It was a simple cotton sundress, and large, impressionistic flowers trailed over the light green background. Jessie had told her the pattern was called "Summer Garden," and the dress had been created by one of California's top designers. Carla was also wearing the accessories she'd worn in the movie. A pair of leather sandals, a matching shoulder bag, and a pair of hoop earrings that replicated in miniature one of the flowers that was printed on the dress. Carla knew she'd looked good when she'd left the house, her mirror had confirmed that fact, but standing out here in the heat was bound to take its toll.

Carla glanced at her watch, and sighed impatiently. Michael and Vera were late. She moved over to the shade of the big palm tree, and sighed again. A week had passed since Heidi's murder, but the police were no closer to solving the crime than they'd been when Liz had been killed.

Naturally, everyone was still very nervous. Mr. Calloway had called in a locksmith and they'd secured the building completely. The locks had been changed, bars had been installed on the windows, and the police had gone over every inch of Covers to make sure no one was hiding inside. But Andy still reported that food was missing, and they knew that someone had managed to get in to eat and sleep, despite their precautions. Just yesterday, Mr. Calloway had changed the locks again, to a much more expensive kind. These locks had a tamper-proof guarantee, and he'd passed out the keys after the performance last night. There was only one extra key, and Mr. Calloway and Detective Davis had locked it up in the office safe. They were the only ones who knew the combination . . . unless, as Vera had suggested, Judy's ghost was watching when they spun the dial.

Carla shivered, even though the temperature was in the eighties. No one had been able to explain the note she'd found on the yellow Post-it. Carla had shown it to the whole staff, and everyone agreed that it looked like Judy's handwriting. Of course that was impossible, unless Judy had written it before her death. But why had the yellow sticky suddenly appeared on the current date in the ledger? No one had been able to come up with a possible explanation for that. Vera still insisted that Judy's ghost was to blame, and no one had been able to convince her otherwise. Poor Vera was so nervous that Mr. Calloway had offered to let her take some time off work. But Vera had refused. She'd begged Mr. Calloway not to mention anything about Judy's ghost to her parents. They were terribly superstitious, and she was afraid they'd send her off to her grandmother's house again.

Michael had agreed to act as Vera's bodyguard until the police caught the killer. That meant he picked her up every day for work, and took her home again at night. Carla wasn't delighted with that arrangement. It meant she rarely had time to spend with Michael. But she hadn't complained. After all, Vera was their friend, and it was clear that she was badly frightened.

Carla sighed, and moved a little deeper into the shade of the palm tree. Where were they? Michael and Vera were already ten minutes late, and she had a ton of work to do this afternoon.

Long moments passed, and Carla grew more and more uncomfortable, waiting in the heat. She reached in her pocket, pulled out her new key for the front door, and thought about using it to go inside. She'd be breaking Mr. Calloway's rule, but she couldn't stand out here in the hot parking lot forever, and no one else was due to arrive for at least an hour.

Carla stepped out of the shade, and began to walk around the building, checking the doors and windows for any sign of forced entry. Everything looked perfectly normal, and she was sure she'd be in no danger if she went inside. She didn't believe Vera's crazy theory about Judy's ghost, and the person who'd murdered Heidi was probably long gone. And since Carla wasn't Michael's girlfriend, neither the Cupid Killer nor the Copycat Cupid would have any reason to attack her.

As Carla approached the front door, she heard the hum of the powerful air conditioner inside. She imagined how cool and dark the inside of Covers would be, and she made up her mind. She was going inside. It was stupid to risk a heat stroke out here in the parking lot when cool air was just a few feet away. She wouldn't be alone for long. Vera and Michael were bound to be here soon.

Carla unlocked the door and hesitated. Was she being foolish, going inside without a weapon? But she did have a weapon of sorts. She'd stopped at the bank on her way to work and there were twenty rolls of change in her purse. The change was heavy, and if anyone was lurking inside, she'd bash them with her purse and knock them out cold.

The bars on the windows cut out some of the light, and Carla held her breath as she stepped inside the cool, dimly lit building. She listened, alert for any unusual sounds, but everything seemed to be perfectly normal. She turned back and looked at the door, wishing she could leave it open. But the electricity bill was always high in the summer, and she knew it would be even higher if she let the hot air from the parking lot inside.

Reluctantly, Carla pulled the door shut. And then she listened again. There was no sound except the low humming of the air conditioner. Her eyes searched the dim shadows as she crossed the floor to switch on the lights. No movement. No one lurking in the shadows. But as she switched on the lights, she felt the hair at the back of her neck begin to prickle. Covers appeared to be deserted, but she sensed that someone was watching her, following her every move as she hurried to the office and locked the door behind her.

Carla was panting as she sank down in the chair behind her desk. She was safe. No one could get in the office unless she unlocked the door. But there had been someone out there. She was sure of it!

Carla's heart was beating a million miles a minute as she pulled the rolls of change out of her purse and retrieved her ledger from the locked drawer. By the time she'd listened to the answering machine messages, and jotted down the reservations for the night's show, she had almost managed to convince herself that her imagination had been working overtime. There was no reason to think that someone had actually been watching her. She hadn't heard anything, and she hadn't seen anyone. It was just her mind playing tricks on her. Although she was usually a very sensible person, it was hard to remain calm when everyone around her jumped at the slightest sound.

"There's no one else here." Carla said the words out loud, and then she began to work. It was impossible to imagine things that weren't there, if she was busy working. She returned four calls to confirm reservations, typed out Andy's order for kitchen supplies, and ran off copies of next week's schedule on the office Xerox machine. Then she counted the rolls of change again, and took a deep breath as she opened the ledger to the day's date to record the amount.

"Oh, my God!" Carla drew in her breath sharply as she spotted a yellow sticky on the page. But then she read the message and she laughed out loud. It was a message from Mr. Calloway, reminding her to call the locksmith for a receipt. Changing the locks and having the bars installed on the windows was a legitimate business expense, and he needed it for his tax records.

Just then the front door banged open, and Carla heard Michael call out for her.

"I'm in here!" Carla glanced at the clock on the wall as she rushed to open the office door. Michael and Vera were over forty minutes late. It was a good thing she hadn't waited for them in the parking lot. She might have died of heat stroke by now!

"Sorry we're late." Michael looked very apologetic as he hurried down the hall to greet her. "We ran into Andy and Linda at

Don's. And then Berto and Tammy and Winona came in, and we lost track of the time."

Carla nodded. She wasn't happy that they'd all gone to Don's without her, but it would sound like sour grapes if she complained.

Michael slipped his arm around her shoulders and hugged her. "We wanted you to join us. Andy tried to call you at home, but you'd already left."

"I had to go to the bank so I left early." Carla smiled at him. The fact that Michael had wanted her to join them made her feel much better.

"What were you doing here alone?" Michael began to frown. "You know that's against the rules."

"I know, but the parking lot was hot . . . and I checked the outside of the building. It was perfectly safe."

"Maybe." Michael was still frowning. "I wish you'd waited, though. It gives me the creeps to think of you alone in here. What if something had happened to you?"

Carla remembered how frightened she'd been when she'd thought that someone was watching her, and she tried not to shudder. Michael had told her he admired her for being so calm and sensible. There was no way she was going to tell him she'd run down the hall like a scared rabbit, and locked herself in the office. It would ruin her image.

"I knew I wasn't in any danger." Carla shrugged casually. "After all, I'm not your girlfriend."

The moment the words were out of her mouth, Carla wished she could take them back. Michael looked hurt, but he nodded.

"I guess you're right. You're not my formal girlfriend. But the killer might not know that. We do spend a lot of time together, and I like you a lot, Carla."

Carla felt her pulse begin to race. Michael had looked almost regretful, when he'd agreed that she wasn't his formal girlfriend. And the smile he gave her was a little sad. Did he want her to be his girlfriend? Did she dare to hope that he'd ask her someday, after the police had solved the murders and all this was over?

"I've got a favor to ask, Carla." Michael turned serious. "I know you don't believe all that stuff about Judy's ghost. I don't either. But Vera's really freaked. I took her over to her aunt's house this morning, and they did some crazy sort of spell thing."

Carla tried not to look amused, but she couldn't help it. Michael grinned, too, when he saw that she was trying not to laugh. "What kind of spell thing did they do? Tell me about it."

"Well . . . it had something to do with restless spirits, and they used candles and incense, and a couple of things that smelled awful. Vera's aunt gave her this little bag filled with stuff, and told her to sprinkle it around the outside of the building. I guess it's some kind of potion to get rid of ghosts, but it smells like roach bait."

Carla couldn't help it. She started to laugh. "The ghosts check in, but they don't check out?"

"Right." Michael chuckled. "We sprinkled that stuff around before we came in, and Vera says she feels a lot better. Don't laugh if she tells you about it . . . okay?"

"I'll do my very best to keep a straight face." Carla nodded.

"Now all she needs is something from you, and the spell's complete."

"Me?"

Michael nodded. "She needs something that belonged to Judy, and I thought maybe you had something in the office. Vera's supposed to burn it to release Judy's spirit."

"I don't think I have anything." Carla frowned. "Unless . . . how about her time card? That's still here."

"If that's all you have, it'll have to do. Could you find it for me, Carla? I know it's stupid, but Vera's determined to complete the spell."

"I'll find it right away." Carla agreed quickly. If Vera stopped being so nervous, she might tell Michael he didn't have to be her bodyguard anymore. And then Michael would be free to spend more time with her.

Michael followed her into the office, and watched as Carla got Judy's time card out of the file. But when she handed it to him, he hesitated. "There's one other thing, Carla. Vera needs two witnesses when she burns it. I told her I'd ask you."

"Okay," Carla agreed. "I'll be a witness. Do we have to do this in a graveyard at midnight, under a full moon?"

Michael laughed. "That's exactly what I asked Vera! But her aunt said that outside by the dumpster would do just fine. It has to be done at midnight, though. The spirits are more receptive then."

"Oh, great." Carla gave a deep sigh. "When does Vera want to do it?"

"Tonight, after everyone's left. It won't take long, I promise."

Carla sighed again, and then she nodded. "Okay. Count me in. But if I see Judy's ghost, I'm going to ask her where she put my best ballpoint before we banish her forever."

The ambience at Covers was eerie after everyone had left for the night. The full moon cast dark shadows across the surface of the parking lot, and the night was so still it felt as if time had stopped. Michael and Vera stood beside Carla's car until the last set of taillights had disappeared. And then Michael cleared his throat.

"Are we ready?"

"I am." Carla nodded. "Let's get this show on the road."

Carla was grinning as she followed Michael and Vera to the dumpster, but her grin changed to a frown as she caught sight of Vera's pale face. It was clear that she hadn't been sleeping well. There were dark circles under her eyes, and she looked as if she'd lost weight. And her hands were shaking as she took Judy's time card out of her pocket.

"Did Michael tell you what we have to do?" Vera turned to Carla and gave her a shaky smile.

"Not exactly. He just said you needed a witness."

"My aunt says I have to burn this, because I'm the only one who actually saw Judy's ghost. And while it's burning, you two have to chant this phrase."

Carla glanced down at the paper. She could see it clearly in the bright moonlight. The words were foreign, but Vera's aunt had written them out phonetically. "What is this? Latin?"

"No, it's Romany. My aunt's great-grandmother was a Gypsy queen. Our tradition is to pass the spells down to the oldest daughter, and my aunt has them now."

"Okay." Carla nodded. "We'll chant, you burn."

Vera's fingers were trembling as she struck a match and held it to the bottom of Judy's time card. As Carla and Michael started to chant, a dog began to howl in the distance. There was a rumbling overhead that sounded like thunder, and there was a rustling noise in the bushes. Carla knew that it was probably a lizard or small animal, but she couldn't help thinking that this was a scene straight out of a bad horror movie.

As the time card began to burn, a slight breeze picked up and extinguished the flame. Vera had to use a whole book of matches to burn the card, and by the time they had finished, Carla felt as if she'd chanted the words hundreds of times.

"That's all?" Carla looked up at Vera, and smiled. She hadn't thought it was possible, but Vera did look a lot better. A little color had come back into her face, and her hands had stopped trembling.

"That's *almost* all." Vera nodded. "I still have to prove to Judy's spirit that there's nothing left for her in the world of the living."

"How are you going to do that?" Michael looked curious.

"I have to do three things to assume Judy's place in the universe. I worked it all out with my aunt."

"Which three things?" Carla was curious. "You can't assume her job. Marc already has that."

"I know. But I was the last one to leave tonight. I pulled the door closed and tested it to make sure it was locked. That's one thing that Judy always used to do. And I punched her time card before I left. That's something she used to do, too."

Carla wasn't sure why, but suddenly she felt very uneasy. "What are you going to do for the third thing?"

"Well . . . I tried to get something of Judy's to wear, but her parents are on vacation and Marta's not there, either. And I asked Mr. Calloway if I could carry out some props, but he said he needed me to stay behind the juice bar. I called my aunt and she told me to think of something else, something that Judy had really wanted to do before she died. My aunt said that if I could fulfill a dream of Judy's, that would definitely put her spirit to rest."

Carla winced. She was pretty sure she knew what was coming. She turned to glance at Michael, but he didn't seem to be on her wavelength.

"That makes sense." Michael smiled at Vera. "Did you think of something that Judy really wanted to do?"

"I sure did. It's something that Judy told me. But I need your help. You'll help me, won't you, Michael?"

Michael nodded. "Sure. What do you want me to do?"

"Judy always wanted you to ask her out on a date. Will you ask me out on a date, Michael?"

Michael looked very uncomfortable. "Uh . . . sure. I guess I could do that. Where do you want to go?"

"To a party. My aunt owns a beach house in Malibu and it's got a private beach. She said I could throw a party there on Sunday night, and I'm going to invite everybody from Covers."

Michael nodded. "That sounds like fun. Okay, I'll take you to the party."

"Thanks, Michael." Vera reached out to hug him. "But there's one more thing you have to do. It's absolutely guaranteed to work."

"What is it?"

"You have to stay and spend the night with me. That's the one thing Judy wanted that she never got. My aunt says it's the perfect way to get rid of Judy's ghost forever!"

Thirteen

By the end of the week there wasn't one single person at Covers who hadn't heard about Vera's plan to exorcise Judy's ghost. Most of the gang thought it was silly, but the prospect of a catered party at a private beach was too tempting to resist. Everyone was coming, except Carla. Of course she hadn't told anyone that she wasn't planning to attend for fear they might guess why. The truth was, Carla couldn't bear to see Michael with Vera. She knew it would break her heart.

It was late Saturday afternoon, and everyone had gathered at Covers to rehearse for the show. The office door was open, and Carla could hear Michael singing. He sounded wonderful, and she sighed deeply. She was gazing off in space, looking sad, when Linda appeared at the office door.

"Who does Vera think she's kidding with this whole exorcism bit?" Linda was frowning as she walked into the office. "Really, Carla . . . can't you talk some sense into Michael?"

Carla shook her head. "Believe me, I tried. But Michael's convinced he's doing Vera a huge favor by being her date for the party and staying with her for the night. He told me that absolutely nothing is going to happen, but . . . well . . . I've got my doubts."

"Me, too." Linda's frown grew deeper. "What do you think,

Carla? Is Vera just using this ghost thing as an excuse to pick up on Michael?"

"I don't know. Maybe. But she seems very serious about it. She told me how her aunt had to go to Boston to stay with a man for two weeks to get rid of his dead wife's ghost."

Linda gave a very unladylike snort. "I'll bet! Did Vera's aunt have to sleep with him?"

"I don't know. I didn't have the nerve to ask. And I'm not sure I really want to know."

Linda sat down in one of the chairs in front of Carla's desk, and propped her feet up on the other. "Oh, well. The party should be fun anyway. What are you wearing?"

"I haven't really thought about it." Carla looked down at her desk and refused to meet Linda's eyes. "How about you?"

But changing the subject didn't work with Linda. She just stared until Carla had to look up. "You *are* going, aren't you, Carla?"

"Well . . . I'm not sure. My throat's been sore all day, and I'm afraid I'm coming down with a cold."

"The only cold you've got is cold feet!" Linda looked very upset. "Look, Carla. You practically have to show up. Everybody'll figure you're jealous, if you don't."

"I know. But I don't think I can do it, Linda. The thought of seeing Michael with Vera makes me positively ill."

Linda laughed. "Me, too. But don't lose hope. Maybe Michael will tumble to Vera's little scheme in time, and tell her to get lost."

"I don't think that'll happen. Michael's too nice to suspect Vera, and she's got him wrapped around her little finger."

"And that's precisely why you should be there! Michael trusts you, and I think you should make one final effort to save him from Vera's clutches. She could get him in a whole lot of trouble."

Carla nodded. "I know that. But how can you save a guy who doesn't want to be saved?"

"Well . . ." Linda looked thoughtful. "You could tell him that your car's not running right, and ask him for a ride home from the party. And then you could hogtie him and keep him with you until morning."

Carla began to laugh. It was good to have a friend, even though Linda's idea was the dumbest one she'd ever heard.

"That's better. At least I got you to laugh." Linda gave Carla a smile. "Now promise me that you'll get all dressed up, and meet me at the party. I don't have a date, either, and we can keep each other company."

"Well . . . okay." Carla caved in, against her better sense. "I'll go, but I don't think I'm going to like it."

The next evening at nine o'clock, Carla drove into the driveway of Vera's aunt's beach house. There was nowhere to park. The party had started at eight, and everyone was here already. Carla pulled in behind Vera's car, and gave one final glance in the rear-view mirror. She'd had her hair done and she was wearing a pair of loose white pants with a multi-colored floral blouse that tied at the waist. Even though she knew she looked pretty, it wouldn't help her tonight. Michael was with Vera, and he was taken for the entire night. He probably wouldn't even notice her.

The front door to the beach house opened, and Linda raced out. She was wearing blue and white cotton jeans and a matching jacket over a blue top. "Carla! I was beginning to think you'd chickened out on me."

"Maybe I should have." Carla got out of the car, and locked the door behind her. "Where is everyone?"

"Down at the beach. The caterers dug a big pit and they're roasting a whole pig."

Carla nodded as she followed Linda down the path that went around the side of the house. "Too bad they're not roasting you know who."

"I knew you'd say that."

Linda laughed and led the way to a wooden staircase that ran down the steep hill. As Carla followed her down the steps, she saw that the caterers had decorated the private beach for a Hawaiian luau. Flaming torches were stuck in the sand for light, and wooden tables and folding chairs had been set up in a circle to ring the barbecue pit. There was even a wooden bar, covered by a roof of palm fronds, at the far end of the beach.

"Where's Vera?" Carla scanned the familiar faces as she went down the stairs.

"Over there in the gold outfit." Linda gestured toward a large table right next to the edge of the water. "I've been praying for the tide to come in."

Carla frowned as she spotted Vera. She looked gorgeous, and she was surrounded by several guys from Covers, who were gazing at her with fascination. She was wearing a gold bikini top with a long gold skirt and tiny gold sandals. Her bare skin gleamed like copper in the light of the torches, and Carla could understand why the guys were so attentive. Vera's black hair fell past her shoulders in a shower of shimmering waves, and the gold bracelets on her arms made her look like an exotic Gypsy princess.

"She makes you feel undressed, doesn't she?" Linda shook her head in disgust. "She told us all to dress casually on purpose, so she'd look really good. See? There's Tammy. She's wearing a denim skirt and a cotton sweater. And there's Winona over there in shorts and a blouse."

Carla nodded, but she was too busy looking for Michael to pay much attention to what Linda was saying. And then she spotted him, sitting on a stool at the bar, firelight from the torches casting flickering shadows across his handsome face. "At least he's not with her."

Carla didn't realize she'd spoke aloud, until Linda nodded.

"That's true. And he doesn't look like he's enjoying himself. Let's go over and say hello."

"I'm not really sure that's a good idea. After all, he's Vera's date."

"Don't be an idiot!" Linda grabbed Carla's hand and pulled her across the sandy beach. "Somebody's got to cheer him up. Michael looks like he's just lost his best friend."

"Hi, Carla." Michael stood up and waved as they approached. "I was wondering when you'd get here."

Before Carla could even say hello, Linda jumped into the

conversation. "Carla had a little car trouble, but it's probably nothing that serious. I'm going to get us a plate of appetizers, and she can tell you all about it."

"But, Linda . . ."

Carla started to object, but Linda gave her a warning look. "That's okay . . . I don't need any help. Just tell Michael about your car and I'll be right back."

Carla smiled, and let Michael pull her up on a stool next to his. And then she met his eyes. Michael looked almost desperate, and he didn't let go of her hand. It was clear he was beginning to feel trapped by Vera.

"I ordered this for you when I saw you coming down the stairs." Michael placed a drink in a coconut shell in front of Carla, and smiled at her. "Tell me . . . what's wrong with your car?"

Carla made up her mind. Linda's plan was stupid, but she owed it to Michael to try. "Well . . . I'm not sure. It started to sputter about halfway here. It's probably nothing."

"It sounds like a carburetor problem to me. You came here alone?"

Carla nodded. Maybe Linda's stupid idea wasn't so stupid, after all.

"You can't drive home by yourself." Michael began to frown. "It might conk out on you, and you'd be stuck."

Carla nodded again, and managed to look worried. "That's true. I'd hate to get stuck on one of those mountain roads at night. It might be dangerous."

"Don't worry, Carla." Michael slipped his arm around her shoulders and gave her a friendly squeeze. "I'll take care of it for you, I promise."

"Thank you, Michael." Carla smiled and he smiled back, but then his friendly expression turned to a frown. He was staring at something over her shoulder, and Carla turned to see what it was. It didn't take her long to spot the cause of Michael's discomfort. Vera was heading across the sand toward them, so fast she was almost running.

"Hello, Carla!" Vera had a bright smile on her face, but her eyes were glittering dangerously. "I'm so glad you could make it to our little party. We're going to have fun, aren't we, Michael?"

Michael nodded. "Sure. Carla was just telling me that she had car trouble on the way here. I told her it wouldn't be safe to drive home alone."

"Of course not!" Vera shook her head. "Andy lives close to you, doesn't he, Carla?"

"Well . . . not exactly. His place is more than five miles away."

"That's not very far. I'll ask him, and I'm sure he'll be glad to follow you home. We can't have you out there on the road by yourself . . . right, Michael?"

"Right."

Michael nodded, and Carla's spirits took a nose dive. She was sure that Michael had been about to offer to give her a ride, before Vera had appeared on the scene.

"The band's almost ready to play." Vera put her hand on Michael's arm. "You'll dance the first set with me, won't you?"

"Uh . . . sure. But I don't want to leave Carla sitting here by herself."

"Oh, she won't be alone for long." Vera smiled her very best smile. "Marc promised me he'd ask her to dance. Let's go, Michael. I want to tell the band to play something slow and romantic."

Carla knew it wasn't very nice of her, but she couldn't help staring daggers at Vera's back as she walked away with Michael in tow. If Vera was really as terrified of Judy's ghost as she claimed she was, she certainly shouldn't be trying to snare Michael! In the letter that Judy had left, she'd confessed that she was the Cupid Killer. Carla didn't believe that Judy's ghost had come back to kill the girls who dated Michael, but she almost wished it were true . . . especially since Vera was setting herself up as the next target!

"Oh, no!" Carla sighed softly as she spotted Marc, walking toward her across the sand. He didn't look happy about asking her to dance, and Carla wasn't happy, either. Although Marc was a very nice guy, he had two left feet and no sense of rhythm. But Carla was trapped and she knew it. She had to dance with Marc because her refusal might hurt his feelings.

"Do you want to dance, Carla?"

Marc smiled, but it was very clear his heart wasn't in it. He expected her to make some excuse, but Carla was too kind-hearted to do that.

"Thanks, Marc. I'd love to."

"You *would?*" The expression on Marc's face was almost comical, he was so shocked. "Are you sure?"

Carla got up, and took his arm. "Of course I'm sure. But I'm not sure you want to dance with me. I've got two left feet, and no sense of rhythm."

"Me, too!" Marc grinned at her happily. "What do you say we sit this one out and save our feet from certain destruction?"

"Great idea." Carla sat back down, and patted the stool that Michael had vacated. "Sit down, Marc. Linda's coming with a plate of appetizers, and I'll buy you a drink."

The rest of the evening passed by Carla in a painful blur. The appetizers were divine, the barbecued pig was crisp and succulent, and the fruit drinks were tasty and refreshing. The band was excellent and Carla was asked to dance almost every set, but there was a pall over the evening that no amount of good food and great music could cure. Michael was with Vera, and she couldn't think of any way to rescue him.

It was one in the morning when the band packed up, and shortly after that, the party guests began to leave. Carla and Linda had moved to a table, and Carla knew they'd have to go soon. It would look strange if they were the last ones to leave.

"Are you ready, Carla?" Andy was frowning as he approached their table. He'd been trying to pick up on Tammy all night, but he'd obviously struck out.

Carla nodded, and reached for her purse. "I'm ready. But you don't really have to follow me, Andy. There's nothing wrong with my car. I was just trying to give Michael an excuse to leave, if he didn't want to stay with Vera."

"I don't think Michael minds staying."

Andy gestured toward the deserted stretch of beach that had been set aside as a dance floor, and Carla turned to look. Michael was still dancing with Vera, even though the band had stopped playing over ten minutes ago.

"You're right." Carla sighed as she watched them dance to the nonexistent music. Michael didn't look trapped now. His arms were around Vera's waist and he was holding her very close. There was a dreamy expression on his face, and he was smiling down into Vera's eyes.

"He's bombed." Andy leaned close to whisper in Carla's ear. "The bartender said he's been spiking Michael's drinks with vodka. Vera told him to do it. I guess she really wants him to stay."

"I guess so." Carla got up, and started for the stairs with Linda and Andy. She didn't want to say goodbye to Vera, and there was no reason to say anything to Michael. He was so torqued, he wouldn't remember it anyway.

Andy seemed to be oblivious to Carla's disappointment. He even whistled a little tune as they climbed up the stairs. When they reached Carla's car, he opened the door and grinned at her. "Nice party, huh?"

Carla didn't bother to reply. She just got inside her car, started the engine, and backed out onto the highway. It hadn't been a nice party. It had been horrible.

As Carla drove down the highway toward home, she found herself wishing that she were more like Judy. What Judy had done was wrong, but Carla was beginning to understand why she'd done it. She was almost as angry as Judy had been, when she'd seen Michael falling under Vera's spell.

"Where are you when I need you, Judy?" Carla let the wind from her open window blow her words away. Then she gave a bitter laugh. She almost wished that Judy were still alive. If Judy had seen Vera spiking Michael's drinks, she would have taken action. Judy wouldn't have sat by idly and watched as Vera set her trap for Michael. She would have armed herself with another arrow and gotten rid of Vera, once and for all!

Fourteen

Vera was having the time of her life. She'd seen Carla sitting at the table, looking heartsick, and it hadn't bothered her a bit. Carla'd had her chance with Michael and she'd blown it. She never should have let him get away.

A soft laugh escaped Vera's lips. Her father's passion was fishing, and he was always talking about something called "catch and release." If her father caught a fish, he took out the hook and put it back into the water so the next fisherman could have his fun. Vera knew that Carla had landed Michael, hook, line and sinker. He'd certainly seemed to be crazy about her. But Carla had lacked the courage to keep him. She'd let Michael go, and that had been her big mistake. Now Vera had caught him, and she intended to keep him until she got exactly what she wanted. Michael was her trophy, and this party had been an excuse to show him off.

"What's so funny?"

Michael's words were slurred and Vera giggled. She hoped she hadn't spiked his drinks with too much vodka. She had big plans for him later. She patted his back, and smiled up into his eyes. "I'm just happy, that's all."

"Me, too." Michael gave her a silly grin. "The music's stopped."

"I know. Does it make any difference?"

"Not really."

Michael pulled her a little closer, and Vera molded her body to his. The vodka didn't seem to be affecting him where it counted, and she'd give him a little time to sober up, after they got inside the beach house. She'd worked out all the times with her older brother. He'd come crashing in the bedroom door at precisely three A.M., and he'd find them in a very compromising position. Michael's parents would pay to keep it quiet. Vera was sure of that. Mr. and Mrs. Warden already had to live with the fact that Michael was a former mental patient. They certainly wouldn't want him charged with rape, on top of everything else!

"It's cold out here." Vera smiled up at Michael and gave a little shiver. "Let's go inside where it's warm."

Michael nodded. "Okay . . . whatever you say, Vera. Can we make coffee? My head's spinning around in circles."

"Of course we can." Vera clamped her arm around Michael's waist and led him to the staircase. "Come on, Michael. Climb the steps."

"Right."

Michael almost missed the first step, but Vera caught him before he fell. He was really whacked out of his mind. Maybe a little coffee was a good idea. She wanted him to remember making love to her so he could convince his parents that it had actually happened.

It took almost ten minutes to get Michael up the stairs, and Vera was panting by the time they reached the beach house. She guided Michael to the couch, and pushed him down on the soft cushions. "Wait right here, Michael. I'll make the coffee and bring you a cup."

Michael shook his head and tried to clear it. He felt awful, and he needed some air. Dimly, he remembered Vera telling him that she was going to the kitchen to make coffee. That was good. A cup of coffee might make him feel better.

Even though all he wanted to do was sink back against the couch cushions and go to sleep, Michael forced himself to get up. His head was throbbing painfully, and he wondered whether he was coming down with the flu. He'd felt just fine when he'd arrived at the party, but now he was as sick as a dog.

Maybe some air would help. Michael staggered out through the door, and stumbled to the railing overlooking the beach. The breeze blowing in from the ocean helped a little, and he took deep breaths of the cool night air.

The caterers had left the chairs and tables. They'd probably pick them up in the morning. They'd left the bar, too. Michael moistened his dry lips, and frowned slightly. He was terribly thirsty, and a fruit drink would taste good right now. Had they left the bottles of juice behind the bar?

There was only one way to find out. Michael took another deep breath and made his way to the staircase. The steps were steep and they seemed to stretch out for miles until they finally ended at the edge of the beach. Was it worth the effort? He wouldn't know unless he tried to walk down them.

Cautiously, Michael walked down the first step. That wasn't so bad. His hands gripped the rail as he climbed down another step, and then another. He didn't think about how steep the staircase was, he just thought about the prize at the other end. A cold glass of pineapple juice, or maybe some orange and banana mixed together. The bartender had come up with all sorts of tasty combinations, and all of them had been wonderful.

It seemed to take forever, but at last Michael reached the bottom step. Then his feet hit the beach, and he smiled. He'd made it. The wet sand stuck to the side of his shoes, and he took them off to walk barefoot across the beach to the bar.

The bottles of juice were right where he'd expected them to be, in the tubs of ice behind the bar. Michael found a leftover bottle of orange juice and he swigged it down, right out of the bottle. The tangy juice made his taste buds tingle, and he searched through the watery ice for more. That was when he found it, a bottle of vodka that was almost empty.

Michael stared down at the bottle and frowned. Since almost everyone at the party had been underage, Vera had promised that no booze would be served. But here was a bottle of vodka, and it was almost gone. Someone had been drinking. But who?

There was a name on the bottle, and Michael held it up to read it in the bright moonlight. It said, *Michael Warden,* and Michael was sure it was Vera's handwriting. But he hadn't brought any booze to the party. And he hadn't had anything to drink, unless . . .

Michael groaned as his head throbbed again. Now he knew why he felt so sick. The bartender had been spiking his fruit drinks with vodka all night. Vera had deliberately tried to get him drunk, and he didn't like that at all. No wonder he'd had trouble climbing down the staircase! He'd finished almost a whole bottle of vodka!

But why had Vera spiked his drinks? Michael frowned deeply. He was in no condition to think about it now. All he knew was that he didn't want to be anywhere near Vera. If he'd been sober, he would have climbed in his car and gone straight home, but Michael knew he was in no shape to drive. Hell, he couldn't even walk very well, or he'd seriously think about setting out on foot.

What to do? Michael's mind spun in crazy circles. Carla had given him a perfect excuse to leave when she'd told him she'd had car trouble. Now he wished he'd insisted on driving her home, instead of staying here with Vera. Even though he was still suffering from the effects of the vodka, Michael knew one thing for sure. He certainly wasn't going back to the beach house. Vera must have had some reason to spike his drinks, and there was no way he'd be a willing participant in whatever it was that she'd planned.

The bartender had left his jacket, and Michael slipped it on to stay warm. Then he found a stack of clean towels behind the bar, and he bunched them up for a pillow. As he curled up behind the bar on his makeshift bed, Michael gave a lopsided grin. Vera didn't know where he was. She was probably still in the kitchen, making the coffee. He'd stay right here and sack out behind the bar until he was sober enough to drive home.

It took a long time to make the coffee. Vera had to search through the cupboards to find the coffee, and figure out how to use her aunt's coffeemaker. It was the old-fashioned percolator type, and she stood at the kitchen counter for what seemed like hours, listening to the coffee perk, and waiting until it was strong enough.

Finally, the coffee was ready, and Vera poured out two cups. She set them on a tray, and carried them out to the living room.

"Here it is. I made you some nice, strong . . ." Vera stopped in her tracks as she saw the empty couch. "Michael? Where are you?"

The bathroom. The minute Vera thought of it, she raced to the bathroom to look. But Michael wasn't there. The room was deserted.

The bedroom? Vera climbed the steps to the second floor to check all three of the bedrooms, but they were empty. She even looked in the closets, but Michael was nowhere in the beach house.

"Oh, my God!" Vera's face turned pale. Had Michael driven home? She rushed to the window to peer out and gave a deep sigh of relief as she saw Michael's car. He was still here . . . somewhere. A glance at the clock told her she had over an hour to find him. There was no need to panic. He'd probably gone for a walk on the beach. But what if she couldn't find him in time? She was counting on the money she'd get from Michael's parents to pay for modeling school. All her plans would be ruined if her brother crashed through the bedroom door and Michael wasn't in bed with her!

"Michael?" Vera tried to keep the panic out of her voice, as she ran out to check Michael's car. Perhaps he'd climbed into the backseat and passed out. But Michael's car was locked up tight and she could see that there was no one inside. He wasn't inside her car, either, and that meant he had to be somewhere on the beach.

Vera retraced her steps, and went out on the patio to survey the empty beach. There was no one in sight, but she could see two objects at the bottom of the steps. She ran down the staircase and began to smile as she saw what they were. Michael's shoes. He'd kicked them off and gone for a walk. He'd probably be back any minute, but she couldn't count on that. She had to find him . . . now!

Since the beach was private, it was fenced off all the way to the water line. But her aunt owned a half mile of beach front, and Michael could be anywhere inside the perimeter.

Vera had thought it was great when her aunt had bought the expensive beach house. It just proved that there were lots of gullible people who were eager to part with their money. Aunt Luba, who didn't have a drop of Gypsy blood in her, had set herself up as a Gypsy psychic. She'd raked in the cash for giving readings, healing all sorts of ailments, and putting people in touch with their dead loved ones. Of course Aunt Luba was a fake, but only Vera's family knew that.

Right now Vera wished that her aunt hadn't made quite so much money, or bought such a big beach front property. If Aunt Luba had settled for a little bungalow in Van Nuys, Vera could have found Michael in no time flat.

"Michael?" Vera started off on her walk along the shore, calling out softly. "Michael? Where are you?"

But there was no answer, and Vera sighed. He'd probably passed out somewhere, and she'd have to look behind every bush and palm tree to find him.

Vera had been searching for almost ten minutes, when she heard it. There was a rustling sound that seemed to be coming from a huge clump of sea grass behind her. She turned and started back, intending to part the grass and see if Michael was there. But the rustling stopped abruptly as she approached.

The breeze blowing off the ocean was chilling. Vera shivered a little as she arrived at the edge of the tall sea grass. There had been something very ominous about that rustling noise, something that made her want to turn and run back to the safety of the beach house.

Vera told herself to stop being silly. There was nothing frightening out here at the beach. There were no wild animals, and the sea birds couldn't hurt her. She had just started to search the grass, when the wind picked up, and blew a gust of salty spray directly into her face.

"Damn!" Vera turned away from the spray, and wiped her eyes on the edge of her skirt. When she opened her eyes again, she realized that the night had grown much darker. A bank of clouds had moved to cover the moon, and she could no longer see the gentle waves lapping up against the sand.

As Vera parted the tall grass, she began to shiver. It was scary, out here at night. A moment ago, the waves had been gentle, sliding into the wet sand like a soft caress. But now that the wind had picked up, the ocean was becoming turbulent, and the waves were rolling in much faster.

There was a crash, and Vera almost screamed. But it was only the waves, beating against a large rock at the ocean's edge. As Vera stood there, they pelted the shore in a staccato burst of sound, crashing and slapping against the rocks lining the shore. There was no doubt about it. A storm was blowing in. Ocean gales came up quite suddenly in the summer, and it sounded as if they were in for some nasty weather.

Vera knew she should turn around and go back to the beach house. She had to make sure the shutters were fastened, and the windows were tightly closed. But Michael might be sleeping out here in the open. She had to find him before the rain started pelting down.

As she knelt down to part the sea grass again, the wind whipped and howled around her face. That was when she heard it, a high eerie voice that called out to her. *Vera . . . come closer, Vera. I need you.*

Vera jumped back, startled. And then she laughed. For a moment the voice had sounded like Judy, but it must have been her imagination. Judy was dead, and Vera wasn't the least bit superstitious. She'd only said she believed in Judy's ghost as part of her plan to lure Michael away from Carla.

She was about to part the sea grass again, when she saw a dark shape loom up behind her, and a hand touched her shoulder. Michael was back. Thank goodness for that! There was still time to put her plan into effect. All she had to do was get him inside the house and lure him to bed.

"Michael! I've been looking all over for you!"

Vera stood up and dusted off her skirt. Then she turned, a

welcoming smile on her face. But Vera's smile quickly turned into an expression of terror as her eyes were drawn to the glittering shape of an arrow.

"No!" Vera screamed once, but her cry was lost in the howling wind. She kicked out as hard as she could, and the heel of her sandal connected solidly. But before she could whirl and run, something big and heavy crashed down on her head, plunging her into eternal darkness.

Fifteen

It was eleven o'clock on Monday morning when Carla turned into the driveway of the beach house again. Almost twelve hours had passed since she'd left the party, and the parking area was still crowded with cars. Vera's old Honda was still there, right next to Michael's Lincoln, but with the exception of a pickup truck she didn't recognize, all the rest of the cars belonged to the police.

Carla parked behind Michael's Lincoln, and got out of her car. Yellow tape with black lettering blocked off the path around the side of the house. It was printed with the legend, DO NOT ENTER—POLICE CRIME SCENE.

"Carla! Wait up!"

Carla turned to see Andy pulling into the driveway. Linda was with him, and she was frowning as she jumped out of the van. "Isn't it awful? Andy says they found another arrow!"

"I know." Carla nodded. "Andy told me when he called. But why do the police want to see us?"

Andy came up just in time to hear her question. "My uncle needs to interview everyone who was at the party. He's in charge now, and he's the one who decided to do the interviews here."

"But, why?" Carla was curious.

"He thought that bringing everyone to the scene of the party might jog our memories about what happened last night."

"They don't think Michael had anything to do with it, do they?" Carla held her breath as she waited for Andy to answer.

"I don't know. My uncle didn't tell me much on the phone. He just said to call everyone and tell them to come here. That's all I know, Carla . . . really."

When they knocked on the front door, a young rookie answered. They gave him their names, and he checked them off on a list. Then he motioned to them to follow him. "Right this way. They're meeting in the living room."

The living room was large, and there were several couches and chairs. Carla felt her eyes fill with tears as she saw Michael sitting alone on a couch. He looked pale, and there were dark circles under his eyes.

"Carla?"

Michael looked up and met her eyes. He didn't say any more, but Carla knew exactly what he wanted. She sat down next to him, and gave him a big hug. And then she motioned for Andy and Linda to join them. Michael needed his friends around him.

Just then Detective Davis came out of the dining room, and motioned to a stranger who was sitting in a chair across the room. The stranger got up to follow Detective Davis, and the door closed behind them.

The minute they were gone, Linda turned to Michael. "Who was that? I didn't notice him at the party."

"That was Vera's brother. He got here at three a.m. He's the one who found Vera and called the police. I didn't even know there was anything wrong until I heard the sirens and woke up."

"Woke up where?" Carla held her breath. She hoped it wasn't where she thought it was.

"Out on the beach. I went to sleep behind the bar. I guess Vera came out to look for me, because her brother found her about fifty yards away."

"But why were you sleeping outside?" Linda was clearly puzzled. "There was a storm last night."

"That's what they told me. But I slept through it. Actually, I was . . . uh . . . it's kind of embarrassing, but I guess I was passed out cold."

"The vodka." Andy nodded. "You drank a lot of it. Vera told the bartender to spike your drinks. I tried to warn you, but you were too drunk to listen to me."

"I wish I had!"

Carla nodded. She wished the same thing. But it was too late to think about that. Michael hadn't listened, and now he was in big trouble.

"Let me get this straight." Andy began to add up the facts. "You were passed out behind the bar, and Vera went out to look for you. But the Cupid Killer found her and killed her. And then her brother just happened to come out here at three in the morning, looking for her?"

Michael nodded. "That's what he said."

"There's something strange going on." Andy looked very serious. "Did you tell Vera you'd spend the night with her?"

"That's right. I promised her I'd stay after the party."

"Then why did she have to spike your drinks to keep you here? And why did her brother show up at three o'clock? It just doesn't make sense unless . . . wait a second! Think carefully, Michael. Do you think Vera was setting you up for the badger game?"

"The what?" Michael frowned.

"The badger game. A girl gets a guy in bed with her, and then her husband, or some other member of her family catches them. It's all set up ahead of time, but the guy doesn't know that. He's scared, so he pays them off. That would explain why Vera spiked your drinks."

"Huh?" Michael winced and held his head. "Sorry. I'm not thinking very well right now. You'd better explain it again."

"Let me put this another way. What would you have said if Vera had asked you to go to bed with her? Be honest."

Michael frowned. "I would have told her thanks, but no thanks. Vera was a nice girl, but I wasn't interested in her that way. When I promised I'd stay the night with her, I made it very clear that nothing was going to happen between us."

"Ah-ha!" Andy looked excited. "Vera knew you wouldn't cooperate, so she spiked your drinks to get you in bed! She probably figured you'd go along with her if you were drunk. And then her brother was supposed to find you, and raise the roof."

"But, why? I don't have any money."

"Your parents do." Carla sighed deeply. She was beginning to understand exactly where Andy's questions were leading. "Vera must have thought that your parents would pay to keep the whole thing quiet. I know she was desperate for money. She borrowed fifty dollars from me just last week."

Linda gave a little groan, and they turned to look at her. She was clearly upset. "This is my fault! I never realized that Vera would take me seriously. But she must have!"

"What are you talking about?" Andy put his arm around Linda's shoulder and gave her a little shake. "Tell us!"

"Well . . . Vera told me they wouldn't let her enroll in modeling school unless she could raise a thousand dollars by the first of September. She said she'd already borrowed from everybody at Covers, but she was still five hundred short."

Andy looked surprised. "So that's where the money was going! She borrowed fifty from me, too."

"She was really worried about it." Linda gave a little sigh. "She told me she'd die if she couldn't get into that modeling course. She said she didn't know how she was going to raise the money, and I . . . I told her to go out and find a rich boyfriend!"

"Okay, I get the picture." Andy stood up and squared his shoulders. "Excuse me, guys. I've got to talk to my uncle."

They watched as Andy marched in the dining room door, and then Carla turned to Michael. "Do you think your parents would have paid Vera five hundred dollars?"

"Maybe." Michael looked thoughtful. "They might have done it, I'm just not sure. But I can't believe Vera would set me up for something like that. There has to be some other explanation!"

Carla and Linda exchanged glances. They didn't have any trouble believing that Vera had set Michael up. They knew how desperate she'd been for money, and they'd never thought that Vera had been serious about exorcising Judy's ghost. Vera and her brother had planned the whole thing to take advantage of

Michael's good nature. That made Carla so mad, she was almost glad that Vera was dead.

"Well . . ." Linda sighed deeply. "We'll never know for sure unless Vera's brother talks. Right, Carla?"

Carla nodded, but her mind wasn't really on Vera's brother. She was thinking about a problem that had occurred only to her, and she certainly didn't want to share her concerns with Linda and Michael. Vera could have planned to extort money from Michael's parents. That made perfect sense. But if Michael had tumbled to her scheme, it would have given him the perfect motive to kill her!

The interviews with the police took up most of the day. Mr. Calloway offered to cancel the performance at Covers that evening, but no one wanted that to happen. Covers had a perfect record for the two years it had been in existence. They'd never canceled a performance before, and they weren't about to do it now.

Carla sighed as she glanced out at the audience. A full house. And everyone who came in, wanted to know about how Vera had died. Of course they hadn't given out any information, but rumors were flying.

"Carla?" Linda tapped her on the shoulder. "Michael wants to see you. He's in the dressing room."

"How is he?"

"Shaky. Very shaky. I think he needs a pep talk before he goes out on stage."

Carla nodded, and headed for the dressing room. Of course Michael was shaky. They all were. But he had more reason to be upset than any of them. He was definitely a suspect. Andy had told her that. Even though Michael claimed he'd been behind the bar sleeping, there were no witnesses to prove that it was true. And since he admitted to being right there on the beach when Vera had been murdered, the police had interviewed him for hours before they'd finally let him go.

"Michael?" Carla knocked on the door, and Michael called out for her to come in. She pushed open the door, and gasped as she saw him sitting on a chair in front of the makeup table. In the harsh lights, his face looked haggard, and no amount of stage makeup could conceal the dark circles under his eyes or the pale cast to his skin.

"Carla. Boy, am I glad to see you!" Michael patted the chair next to him. "They think I did it, you know."

"Who thinks you did it?"

"Everybody. The police, Vera's relatives, everybody here at Covers. And I didn't, Carla! I didn't kill Vera!"

"I know you didn't." Carla put her arm around Michael's shoulders and hugged him tightly. But Michael pulled away.

"You'll doubt me, too, when I tell you what I told the police. But I have to tell you. It's the truth. And I can't hold anything back from you. It wouldn't be right."

Carla frowned slightly. What was Michael talking about? "You can tell me, Michael. It won't make any difference. I'm sure you didn't kill Vera, and nothing's going to change my mind."

"When I went down to the bar, I found the bottle of vodka. My name was on it in Vera's handwriting, and I knew she'd been spiking my drinks. I didn't know why, but I was mad enough to kill her. And then I passed out."

Carla nodded. "That's just it, Michael. You passed out. There's no way you could have killed Vera if you were passed out cold."

"What if I woke up? I was so drunk, I might not remember. What if I heard Vera come down to the beach, looking for me? And what if I was still so mad about that bottle of vodka that I . . . I killed her?"

Carla sighed, and slipped her arm around Michael's shoulder again. This time he didn't pull away and she was glad. "Look, Michael . . . those are all *what ifs*. Sure, you could have killed her. But you didn't."

"Then who did?"

"Maybe I did. What if I knew that Vera was up to something? I knew you were drunk and Andy told me that she was spiking your drinks. What if I didn't drive home? What if I came back, looking for you, and found Vera on the beach? What if I hit her over the head with a rock and killed her? And stuck that arrow in her chest so it would look like the Cupid Killer had done it?"

"But you didn't do that." Michael pulled Carla close. "I know you didn't."

Carla nodded. "Of course I didn't. But I could have, just like you could have. Think about it, Michael. I'm trying to make an important point. You don't believe that I'm the killer, and I don't believe that you are. It's all a matter of trust."

"I guess you're right." Michael began to smile, and he hugged her tightly. "I trust you, and you trust me. I'm a lucky guy, Carla."

But after Michael had left to go out on stage, Carla sat there for a moment, with a puzzled expression on her face. How could Michael possibly consider himself lucky? Most of the girls he'd dated had been murdered, the police suspected him of being the Cupid Killer, and almost all of his friends had turned against him. If that was luck, Carla hoped she'd be very unlucky in the days to come!

Sixteen

Carla wasn't intending to eavesdrop on anyone's private conversation, but when she let herself in the front door of Covers at four on Saturday afternoon, she couldn't help but hear every word that was coming from the kitchen. Tammy, Winona, and Berto were arguing, and their voices were so loud, they could have roused the dead. Actually, that's what they were arguing about. The dead . . . as in, Judy Lampert's ghost.

The swinging door to the kitchen was open, and Carla didn't want to walk past it. Then they'd know that she had overheard. But she didn't want to turn around and go back outside, either. It was hot in the parking lot, and she had a lot of work to do before they opened for the evening.

Carla sighed. Since she was here, she might as well stay. She was about to sit down on a chair and wait for the end of the argument, when the front door opened and Michael came in.

"What's going on?" Michael looked puzzled as he saw her standing there.

Carla gestured toward the kitchen. "I'm not sure. It sounds like Berto, and Tammy, and Winona are arguing about the existence of Judy's ghost."

"Again?" Michael chuckled. "Maybe we ought to bill them as a comedy routine. They've been doing this for over a week."

"Well, I say it's true!" Tammy was so excited, her voice

squeaked. "There were two packs of French fries gone this morning, and you know how much Judy always loved French fries!"

When Berto spoke, he sounded disgusted. "What did you do? Count the whole carton?"

"Yes! And Winona helped me, didn't you, Winona?"

"It's true. I did." Winona didn't sound quite as excited as Tammy. "You've got to face facts, Berto. Somebody's been eating our food. And somebody's been sitting in our chairs. They're all out of place when we come in."

Tammy took up the argument again. "And somebody's been sleeping in the girls' dressing room! What do you have to say about that?"

"Goldilocks." Michael spoke softly in Carla's ear as he slipped his arm around her shoulders. "I wonder if Berto'll pick up on that."

"Come on, girls. You sound like the three bears."

Berto sounded amused, and Michael and Carla began to laugh. Berto must have heard them, because the argument abruptly stopped, and he stuck his head out the door. "Hi, guys. Why don't you come in here, and beat some sense into Tammy and Winona's pointed little heads? They're still blabbering on and on about Judy's ghost."

Tammy and Winona looked embarrassed as Carla and Michael trooped into the kitchen. Tammy was the first to recover, and she gave a nervous little laugh. "Berto doesn't believe us, but there's more stuff missing. Look at this!"

Michael and Carla looked where Tammy was pointing. There was a plate on the table with two limp French fries, sitting in a gob of dried mustard.

"Judy always dipped her french fries in mustard." Winona explained. "Everybody else I know uses ketchup. There's something going on here, and I don't like it."

Michael nodded. "I don't like it, either. And neither does Mr. Calloway. He's losing money on all this missing food. I don't suppose you've been keeping a list?"

"I have." Berto opened the kitchen drawer, and took out a

notebook. He opened it, and handed it to Michael with a frown. "Twenty-three hamburgers with buns, a bunch of French fries, four packs of sliced cheese, and six gallons of strawberry ice cream."

"That's your proof!" Tammy pointed to the last item on the list. "Strawberry ice cream is Judy's favorite!"

Berto frowned. "Don't be an idiot, Tammy. Strawberry ice cream is a lot of people's favorite. We sell at least four gallons a night."

"With chocolate sauce?" Tammy pointed to the container of chocolate sauce on the counter. "I filled that up last night, and now there's some missing. I just wish Vera had gone through with that exorcism, no matter how stupid it sounds. I'd feel a whole lot better."

There was silence for a moment, and then Carla cleared her throat. She could tell that Tammy's careless comment had disturbed Michael. He still didn't like to talk about Vera, especially since her brother had confessed that they'd planned to extort money from Michael's parents. "Look, Tammy . . . do you *really* think Judy's ghost is eating this food?"

"I . . . I don't know." Tammy hesitated. "All I know is, it scares me to come in and find all this stuff missing. Somebody's been here. You can't deny that."

"I don't deny it. I think someone's been staying here, too. But I don't think it's a ghost. I think it's a real live person."

"That's impossible." Winona shook her head. "Mr. Calloway changed all the locks and put bars on the windows. Nobody can get in."

"So it's got to be a ghost because ghosts can walk through walls?"

Tammy frowned. "Exactly!"

"Then tell me how I got in." Carla started to smile.

"You used your key." Winona looked at Carla like she was crazy. "That's obvious."

"But I didn't. I didn't have to use my key because the door was open. We don't lock it behind us in the daytime. And that's probably how our food thief got in. He or she could have opened the door and walked right past the kitchen while we were arguing."

"Oh, my God! You're right!" Tammy gave a little shiver. "I never thought of that! The food thief could be sneaking in during the daytime, and hiding out until we leave for the night. And that means there's no ghost. Judy's really dead."

Carla turned to wink at Michael. Proving a point to Tammy and Winona was a lot like teaching a kindergarten class. You had to spell everything out, and it took infinite patience. But Michael didn't look amused. He just looked very sad, and Carla knew he was thinking about the awful way that Judy had died.

"Hello? Is anyone here?" A voice floated out from the main room, and everyone jumped.

"We're in here!" Carla frowned slightly. It wasn't a voice she recognized, but it could be someone Mr. Calloway had signed up to appear as a guest in tonight's show.

The owner of the voice stepped into the kitchen. She was a gorgeous brunette in her early twenties, wearing shorts and a halter top. Her skin was golden, her hair fell to her waist in a shining curtain of mahogany silk, and her face was something a model would die for. As she spotted Michael, her deep brown eyes began to sparkle, and she rushed across the room to hug him tightly.

"Scooter!" Her voice was low-pitched and breathless. "Your mother told me you'd be here, so I rushed right over."

Michael looked dazed as he glanced down at the gorgeous creature in his arms. "Stinky? Is that you?"

"In the flesh." The girl laughed, and stood on tiptoe to kiss his cheek. "I'll make a deal with you. If you promise you won't call me Stinky, I won't call you Scooter."

"Deal." Michael laughed and hugged her again. Then he turned to introduce her to the rest of the group. "This is my sort-of cousin, Angela Price. She used to live next door to me until her parents moved away. Angela . . . meet Berto, and Tammy, and Winona, and Carla."

Angela's beautiful lips parted and she smiled, showing her perfect teeth. "Hi. I'm glad to meet you. Aunt Ginnie told me all about Covers, and I could hardly wait to see it."

"Will you be in town long?" Michael draped a friendly arm around Angela's shoulders.

"Forever!" Angela smiled up at him. "At least it seems like forever. I just got accepted at U.C.L.A., and I'm transferring here."

"Great!"

Michael sounded really pleased, and Carla felt an unwelcome stab of jealousy. She tried to stifle it by telling herself that she was being ridiculous. Angela was so beautiful, she probably had hundreds of boyfriends. It was perfectly understandable that she'd wanted to look up her former neighbor. She'd do the same thing herself, if she went back to her old home town.

"What's your major, Angela?" Berto did his best to make polite conversation.

"Theater Arts. I went to Washington State for my first two years, but everyone told me I'd be better off coming down here. After all, this is the capital of show biz, and I want to be where the action is."

"Are you a performer?" Tammy asked the question that was on everyone's mind, Carla's included.

Angela laughed. "You couldn't keep me off a stage if you tried. I sing and dance, and I can get by on a guitar or a keyboard, but that's about it."

"That's plenty." Michael sounded impressed. "Wait until Mr. Calloway comes in. If he likes you, he might give you a guest shot. You probably need the extra cash."

Angela laughed again, a wonderfully musical laugh that set Carla's teeth on edge. No one should have such a marvelous laugh. It just wasn't fair.

"Cash is no problem, Scoot . . . I mean, Michael. My grandfather left me a trust fund that covers all my expenses. But I'd love to do it for the experience."

"Come on, Carla." Michael motioned to her. "Let's go show Angela around. You've got time, haven't you?"

"Uh . . . sure!" Carla gave him a blinding smile that she knew wasn't as pretty as Angela's. She didn't have the time, and she'd have to work her tail off to get everything done by the time Mr.

Calloway arrived, but she didn't want to leave Angela alone with Michael.

They walked out of the kitchen and across the floor, and climbed the steps to the stage. Angela shivered a little as she stepped out on the boards. "I hope I don't run into that girl again. She was very strange. I asked her if you were here, and she turned around and ran."

"What girl?" Carla began to frown. She hadn't heard anyone come in.

"The girl who was up on the stage. She was a blonde, a little taller than I am, and she was dressed all in black."

Carla turned to meet Michael's eyes. He looked just as startled as she was. A blonde dressed in black was the exact description Vera had given when she'd told them about seeing Judy's ghost!

Seventeen

Carla and Michael had insisted that Angela tell Mr. Calloway about the girl she'd seen, and they'd made a thorough search of the building. Mr. Calloway had even called the police to look for the intruder, but the girl had vanished into thin air. Everyone hoped that they'd frightened her away, but the girl was bolder than they'd thought. On Tuesday, Andy had reported that there was more missing food, and on Wednesday, Marc had found a bedroll tucked into a corner of the prop closet. Just yesterday, Linda had discovered that several costumes were no longer on the rack in the dressing room, and Carla had come up short when she'd counted petty cash. It was clear that the girl was hiding out in the building, but no one had caught a glimpse of her since Angela had startled her on Monday afternoon.

It had been a miserable week at Covers, and everyone was very nervous. Linda, who was usually calm and collected, had broken down in tears at their after-show meeting when she'd told Mr. Calloway that she thought someone was watching her. Phil had admitted he'd had the same feeling, and so had most of the Covers staff. Even Carla had felt uneasy when she worked alone in the office. She'd almost jumped out of her skin last night, when a squirrel had scampered across the roof.

And then there was the problem of Angela. Everyone at Covers was wild about her, and they all thought it was only a matter of time before she'd be discovered. Angela danced, and sang. She played several musical instruments, including the guitar, and she'd done a couple of comedy sketches with Michael that had left the audience in convulsions. Everyone thought that Angela was an incredible talent, and Carla agreed. But Angela seemed to think that being Michael's old neighbor entitled her to monopolize all his time.

Michael and Angela had been practically inseparable, and he seemed to enjoy playing tour guide. They'd gone to a tourist attraction every day. Even though Michael always invited her to come along, Carla couldn't help but feel excluded. When Michael and Angela weren't re-living their childhood escapades, they were talking about how they were going to set the show biz world on fire after they graduated from U.C.L.A.

Carla had hoped that one of Mr. Calloway's contacts would discover Angela, and whisk her away to a new career far away from Covers. But most of Mr. Calloway's high-powered friends were on vacation, and no one had come to see Angela perform. She was a big hit with the regular Covers audience, but she hadn't received one single offer.

"We're here." Angela pulled into Don's parking lot, and shut off the engine of her bright blue convertible. Carla sighed as she got out of the back seat, and followed Angela and Michael to the side entrance. She'd suggested having lunch at Don's, and she had an ulterior motive. Carla knew that the studio people hung out at Don's, and she was hoping she'd run into a friend of Mr. Calloway's who knew her from Covers. She had several guest tickets in her purse, and Mr. Calloway had given her permission to pass them out. Carla knew that everyone at Covers was absolutely right. Angela was an undiscovered talent, and Carla was determined to find someone to discover her.

Michael led the way to a vacant table in the center of the patio, and pulled out a chair for Angela. "Well . . . what do you think?"

"This place is wonderful!" Angela gave Carla a friendly

smile. "It looks like somebody snatched it up from a lake shore in Wisconsin, and plunked it down right here."

Carla nodded, but her mind wasn't on what Angela was saying. She was too busy looking for studio executives. She spotted several men wearing Universal Studio tee-shirts, but they looked like grips or carpenters. And there were two older guys, dressed in three-piece suits, who had to be local businessmen. Studio executives didn't wear suits. They wore expensive, but casual clothes. Three-piece suits were reserved for accountants, or money men from New York.

There were two women at a table in the back, who looked much more promising. Although they were both older women, they were dressed in very trendy clothes, and their makeup and their hair were perfect. Executive assistants? Studio secretaries? Carla just wasn't sure. But then, one of the women laughed, and Carla recognized her laugh. She'd heard it at Covers, less than a year ago.

"Carla? What are you going to have?"

Michael smiled at her across the table, and Carla realized that the waitress was there to take their order. "Sorry. I'll have a single cheeseburger and an order of onion rings."

"To drink?" Michael prompted her.

"An iced tea."

"Do you know those two ladies over there?" Angela smiled. "You were staring at them so hard, you didn't even hear the waitress."

Carla nodded. "I think I know them, but I can't quite place them. The one with the short dark hair was at Covers last year. I recognized her laugh. I seated her at a two-person table in the front."

"Are you sure it was a table in the front?" Michael raised his eyebrows. He knew that the front tables were reserved for Mr. Calloway's contacts.

"I'm positive. But I can't remember who was with her."

"I'm sure it'll come to you." Angela smiled. "Michael says you have an incredible memory. And speaking about memories . . .

remember the time we rode our bicycles all the way out to the airport?"

The moment Angela began to re-live old times with Michael, Carla tuned her out and concentrated on the dark-haired lady. When she had come to Covers, she'd been wearing a forest green designer sweatsuit. Her hair had been longer then, and she'd pulled it back with a green leather barrette. The whole impression had been one of understated elegance, and Carla had admired her outfit. She'd also admired the man who'd been with her. Tall, with silver hair worn a little long around the ears, chinos and a soft pink cotton shirt. She remembered thinking that a man had to be very sure of himself to wear a pink shirt. But Mr. Calloway had told her the pink shirt was the man's trademark. He always wore them because his name was . . .

Just then the man appeared, and Carla drew in her breath sharply as he walked across the patio to join the two women. It was Nate Rose and he was one of the biggest casting agents at Mirage Studios! Would he remember her? She had to go over to try to jog his memory. And then she had to invite him to Covers.

Carla took the guest tickets out of her purse, and stood up before she lost her nerve. There was no need to ask Michael and Angela to excuse her. They were so busy talking, they hadn't even noticed she'd left her chair.

"Excuse me, Mr. Rose." Carla arrived at the table, breathless. Her hands were trembling slightly, and she hoped she looked more composed than she felt. "I'm Carla Fields, Mr. Calloway's assistant manager at Covers."

Nate Rose looked up, and frowned slightly. And then he smiled. "Oh, yes. I remember you, but you look a lot different. I seem to recall that you wore glasses."

"I did. I have contact lenses now." Mr. Rose was staring at her so hard, Carla felt like giggling. It was a wonder he recognized her at all. She knew she looked completely different, now that Mr. Robinson's makeup people at the studio had shown her how to make the most of herself. Her new wardrobe helped, too, and she was wearing one of her most stylish outfits, loose cotton trousers in a lovely shade of cobalt blue, a matching short-sleeved cotton sweater, and a cobalt blue blazer with wild geometric patterns on the lapels.

"So how's Stan doing?" Nate Rose gave her a friendly smile. "I've been on vacation, and I haven't heard from him in awhile."

Carla smiled back. "Oh, he's fine. As a matter of fact, he tried to get in touch with you earlier in the week. He wanted to give you tickets to see one of our new talents."

"Stan's never brought me in for anything less than star material." Nate Rose looked thoughtful as he turned to the brunette with the short hair. "Do you remember the night we saw Deana Burroughs?"

The brunette nodded. "I'll never forget it. You were about to sign her when we got the call that she'd been murdered. Such a pity."

"Yes, it was." Carla put on an appropriately solemn expression. Deana had been a bitch, but she had been talented. "This new singer's even better, Mr. Rose. She dances and does comedy, too. Her name's Angela Price, and she's sitting right over there at the table with Michael Warden."

The brunette glanced over at the table, and smiled. "Michael Warden . . . You tried to sign him last year, but he wanted to finish school."

"Right." Nate Rose nodded, and turned to Carla. "Do you think he'd be interested now?"

"I'm not sure. You'd have to ask. Michael just finished doing a cameo in Ralph Robinson's new movie."

"That's a very good start!" The brunette looked impressed. "Most of Ralph's discoveries go on to bigger and better things."

Carla tried not to look disappointed. Here she was, trying to talk up Angela, and they seemed to be much more interested in Michael. She had to do something to get the conversation back on track.

"I'll make sure you get a chance to talk to Michael when you come to see Angela perform." Carla steered the conversation right back to her objective. "I think you'll be very impressed with her."

"They'd make a hell of a team." Nate Rose began to smile. "She looks like she might have Madonna charisma, and she's prettier than Mariah Carey. When am I free, Lottie?"

The brunette reached into her purse and took out a pocket organizer. She flipped through a few pages until she found one with less writing than the rest. "Monday night? You've got early dinner with Maggie, but then you're free."

"Monday would be perfect." Carla gave her a big smile, and then she turned back to Nate Rose. "How many tickets would you like?"

"Two. Just give them to Lottie. She keeps track of things like that. Nice seeing you . . . uh . . ."

"Carla." Carla smiled.

"Carla." Nate Rose smiled back. "Don't worry, sweetie . . . I won't forget your name a second time. Tell those two to work up something together, okay?"

Carla nodded and headed back out through the entrance, to the ladies room at the side of the building. She was blinking back tears, and she didn't think she could face Michael and Angela right now. She was just too disappointed. Her plans had backfired in the worst way possible. She'd done such a good job of selling Angela to Nate Rose, he wanted to team her up with Michael and take both of them away!

"I really messed up this time!" Carla stared down at the calendar blotter on her desk, and blinked back tears. "Nate Rose wants both of them!"

Linda looked properly sympathetic. "I know, but it's not the end of the world. Maybe Michael will refuse to sign."

"Oh, sure." Carla's tone was sarcastic. "Nate Rose is just the biggest casting director in the biz."

"But he tried to sign Michael once before, and Michael refused. He's always said that he wanted to finish college before he started in on his career."

Carla gave a bitter laugh. "Angela's his oldest friend. She'll talk him into it. She'll probably say that she can't make it alone. And Michael will do it. He's crazy about her!"

"That's true." Linda sighed as she nodded. "But there's no sense in borrowing trouble. Maybe their duet will be awful. That happens, sometimes, when two good soloists get together. You've never heard them try to sing together."

Carla nodded, but she wasn't encouraged. She'd heard Michael sing duets with most of the female singers at Covers, Linda included. He always managed to inspire his singing partners, and he usually made them sound better than they actually were. Angela was terrific on her own, and Carla had no doubt that her duet with Michael would be nothing short of fantastic.

"Are you sorry you told Michael to sing a duet with Angela?" Linda probed gently.

"No. I had to tell them. It wouldn't have been fair, if I hadn't. And they would have found out, anyway. Nate Rose would have asked them why they didn't do it."

"True." Linda nodded. "Well . . . I guess you can always pray that Michael comes down with a cold so he can't sing. Barring death, that's about the only thing that'll keep him off the stage."

Carla sat and stared out the window long after Linda had left the office. Linda's words came back to her, and she gave a bitter smile. Only death would keep Michael from singing that duet with Angela, but she certainly didn't want Michael to die! Angela, however, was another matter. Carla did her best to resist the turn her thoughts were taking, but she couldn't help giving an ironic grin. Angela was trying to pick up on Michael. Carla was sure of it. And if Angela became Michael's new girlfriend, the Cupid Killer could solve all of her problems in one fell swoop.

Eighteen

It was ten o'clock on Sunday night, and Angela wished that Carla would get tired of hearing them practice and go home. Of course that wouldn't happen. Angela knew that Carla was in love with Michael. What other reason could she have for tagging along? Angela was getting very tired of having to be polite to Carla, when she really wanted to tell her to buzz off.

Angela thought about saying it now, and a smile played over her lips. But if she did, Michael would look hurt, and he'd hurry off to comfort Carla. Angela couldn't for the life of her understand why Michael seemed so concerned about Carla. Carla was pretty, in an ordinary sort of way, but she wasn't as beautiful as Angela was. And she certainly didn't have Angela's talents. Carla was the strangest competition that Angela had ever had, but she had worked out a plan. It would take a while, but Angela intended to show Michael exactly how much nicer life would be with her. She had looks, talent, and money. What more could a guy like Michael want?

Angela joined Michael on the chorus and she gave it her all. When the last note had faded away, she turned toward the audience and smiled at Carla. "What do you think, Carla? Was that better?"

"I thought it was good before." Carla smiled back. "You two sing very well together."

"Thank you. The fact that you think so, is a real compli . . ." Angela stopped, without finishing her sentence, and began to cough. It was deliberate.

"Are you all right?"

Michael looked concerned, but Angela just shrugged. "It's really nothing serious. I just strained my voice a little on that last note."

Now Michael looked positively panic-stricken, and Angela had all she could do to keep from laughing. She coughed again, just to see if Michael's face could get any paler. It did.

"Can I get you some water or something?" Michael sounded anxious.

"No thanks." Angela shook her head. "I've had this before and water only makes it worse. The only thing that really seems to help is cranberry juice."

Michael jumped up from his stool. "I'll get you some, but you'll have to come along. We still haven't caught that intruder, and I don't want to leave you girls here alone."

"Well . . . okay." Angela agreed reluctantly. "But I'd really rather stay here and practice my guitar. "That intro for my second song needs work."

"No problem. I'll go." Carla stood up. "Would you like plain cranberry, or one of those combinations like Cran-apple or Cran-raspberry?"

Angela thought fast. The combinations would be harder to find, especially if she made up one that didn't exist. Carla would drive around, looking for it, and she'd have plenty of time, alone with Michael.

"Cran-lemon worked the best." Angela gave a sweet little smile. "But don't go out of your way. Practically anything'll do just fine."

"Cran-lemon? I've never seen that one before." Carla looked mystified.

"Oh, I'm sure they've got it. It was in practically every store when I lived in Washington."

"Okay." Carla headed for the door.

"Are you sure you'll be all right, alone?" Michael called out after her. "We could all go."

"I'll be fine. There's a Von's Market about ten blocks away. I'll be back just as soon as I can."

Angela waited until the door had closed behind Carla, and then she turned to Michael with a smile. "She's just wonderful, Michael. I can see why you're in love with her."

"In love?" Michael looked uncomfortable. "I like Carla a lot, but I'm not sure I'm in love with her."

"Of course you are! If you weren't in love with Carla, you would have kissed me by now. After all, I want you to." Michael looked even more uncomfortable, but Angela went right on with her plan. "How about one kiss for your best pal?"

Before Michael could say yes or no, Angela moved in. She wound her arms around his neck, and stood on tiptoe to kiss him. At first Michael was hesitant, but the heat of Angela's lips began to thaw his resolve, and Angela almost laughed out loud as he began to respond to her.

"Angela . . ." Michael looked uncertain as Angela pulled him toward the couch at the back of the stage. "I don't think we'd better . . ."

Angela silenced him with another kiss, and this time she let her tongue slide over his lips in a very sensual way. Everything began to happen very fast then, everything that Angela had wanted to happen, and exactly according to her plan.

Carla gave an exasperated sigh as she headed back toward the entrance. She couldn't believe she'd walked off without her purse. It was a good thing she realized it before she'd gone more than a couple of blocks, but she felt like an idiot for forgetting it in the first place.

The door was unlocked, and that was another thing she'd forgotten to do. Carla sighed again, as she turned the knob. She was obviously rattled and she knew the reason why. Just as she'd feared, Angela and Michael had sounded wonderful together. And that meant that Nate Rose was bound to sign both of them.

Carla hesitated, her hand on the doorknob. What if she came back and said she couldn't find any Cran-lemon juice? Without it, Angela's voice might be strained tomorrow night and she wouldn't be able to audition for Nate Rose.

No, she couldn't do that. Carla knew she'd feel terribly guilty if she told an outright lie. She'd have to get the juice, and she'd have to give it to Angela. She'd promised she would, and she'd never broken a promise in her life.

Carla pushed open the door and stepped inside. And then she realized that there was no music. Angela's guitar was propped up against a stool, and Michael's was in its case. They must have stopped practicing. The stage was deserted, except for . . .

Carla's eyes were drawn to the back of the stage, where Marc had stored the old couch they used in one of the comedy routines. As she stared in terrible fascination, Angela's blouse slithered over the back, and fell in a heap on the floor. Her bra came next. And then her wrap-around skirt. Carla didn't wait for the next item of clothing to fall. She just turned on her heel and ran through the door, heading for her car.

It took her several minutes to stop crying. But as her tears dried, a raging anger took their place. Angela had duped her. She hadn't needed Cran-lemon juice for her throat. She'd just wanted Carla out of the way so that she could make love to Michael!

Carla wiped away her tears, and stared out at the palm tree at the back of the parking lot. Angela was a bitch. She'd pretended to be so sweet and friendly, but all the time she'd been planning to make a move on Michael. A girl like Angela didn't deserve Michael's love. There had to be something that she could do to make sure that Angela didn't succeed.

There was a rustling in the bushes at the side of the building, and Carla reached out to lock her doors. Was someone out there? And would that someone sneak into the building, thinking it was deserted for the night? Carla had a sudden mental picture of the Cupid Killer taking revenge on Angela, and she shivered a bit. Perhaps it wasn't fair, but she found herself hoping that the killer would strike again, and make Angela the next victim!

*   *   *

"What was that?!" Michael sat up, startled, and glanced out over the back of the couch. "Hurry up, Angela. Put on your clothes! I think I heard somebody!"

Angela laughed, a deep throaty sound that she knew was incredibly sexy. "It's just your imagination, Michael. Take off your clothes and come here."

"That's not a good idea." Michael stood up, and began to button his shirt. "Carla could come back any second."

Angela laughed, and made a grab for his arm, but Michael stepped back. She pouted, and then she licked her lips. "She won't be back for hours. I personally guarantee it. So come on back here, and show me what an incredible lover you are."

"What do you mean, she won't be back?" Michael began to frown. "The grocery store's only a few blocks away."

"But she won't find any Cran-lemon juice there."

Michael's frown deepened. "Why not?"

"Because there's no such thing. I sent her on a wild goose chase so we could be alone. If I know Carla, she'll go to at least three different stores before she comes back and tells us she can't find it."

Michael's eyes were hard as he stared at Angela. "That was a rotten thing to do!"

"Maybe." Angela shrugged, and then she smiled again. "But all's fair in love and war. And I want you to love me, Michael."

The expression on Michael's face was fierce, and Angela shuddered slightly. He really looked mad about the dirty trick she'd played, and she was afraid she'd underestimated his feelings for Carla.

"Hey . . . I'm sorry." Angela managed to look contrite. "I'll apologize when she comes back. But Carla was in the way. Can't you understand? I really needed to be alone with you."

"You don't need to be alone with me. You just need to be alone, period." Michael grabbed his guitar case, and climbed down the steps that led from the stage. When he got to the door, he turned and glared at Angela. "I'm going to wait for Carla outside. And when she comes, I'm going to ask her for a ride home."

Angela sighed, and grabbed her clothes from the back of the couch. Michael was stubborn, but that made him even more of a challenge. Now she had to find a way to get back in his good graces.

It didn't take long for Angela to dress again. She'd purposely worn clothes that were easy to take on and off. As she was climbing down the steps to go out and placate Michael, she remembered the deli food they'd picked up on their way to Covers. Her mother had always said that the best way to a man's heart was through his stomach. She'd fix Michael a sandwich, and take it to him as a peace offering. That should put him in a much better mood. And after he'd eaten, she'd appeal to his male ego. She'd promise him that she'd do her absolute best to resist him, even though he was terribly sexy.

Angela was smiling as she opened the packages she'd bought at the deli. There was rare roast beef, Black Forest ham, and three kinds of imported cheese. She slathered two thick slices of freshly baked rye bread with hot German mustard, and began to make a sandwich that Michael wouldn't be able to resist. When she was through, she arranged it all on a paper plate and popped it in the microwave for a few seconds.

The microwave beeped, and Angela reached out for the catch to release the door. But as her finger touched the lever, all the lights went out. What rotten luck! She'd blown a fuse!

Angela reached into the interior of the microwave, and picked up the sandwich. At least it was hot. Dim light from the parking lot filtered in through the high kitchen window, and Angela carried the sandwich across the kitchen floor. But she stopped and gave a little gasp of fright as she came to the kitchen door. It was closed, and she distinctly remembered leaving it open.

That was when she heard it, soft breathing coming from the dark shadows near the walk~in cooler. Angela shivered, and stepped back so far, she bumped against the wall. Suddenly she remembered the stories she'd heard about the food thief and the Cupid Killer, and she began to panic. Someone was in the kitchen with her!

"Michael?" Angela's voice was shaking, she was so frightened. "Is that you?"

But no one answered. There was only silence and that terrible breathing. In, out. In, out. The breathing got faster and faster. Angela felt her hands begin to tremble, and she flung the sandwich toward the darkest shadow as she turned and ran toward the other kitchen door, the one that led outside.

Her hands found the knob and she twisted desperately, but the door wouldn't pull open. She knew there must be a second lock, but where? Her shaking fingers had just located the deadbolt, when strong arms grabbed her from behind. It was too dark to see the arrow, and she didn't even have time to scream before something hard and heavy crashed down on her head, and endless darkness closed in.

Nineteen

"And you found her?!" Linda looked shocked as Carla nodded. "Was Michael with you?"

Carla nodded again. "Michael was waiting for me when I drove up. Von's didn't have any Cran-lemon juice, so I bought a quart of Cran-apple."

"Cran-lemon?" Linda looked puzzled. "I didn't know they made that kind."

"They don't. It was just Angela's excuse to get me out of the way so she'd have time to put her moves on Michael."

Linda sighed. "I know it isn't nice to say, under the circumstances, but Angela was really a bitch."

"That's true. I knew all that when I went out for the juice, but I'd promised, so I did it. The trip to the store helped. I needed the time to cool off."

"I'll bet!" Linda raised her eyebrows. Carla had already told her how she'd gone back inside and discovered Angela and Michael on the couch. "I don't think I would have gone back."

"I wasn't going to, at first. I felt like driving straight home, but then I remembered that I'd only seen *Angela's* clothes draped over the back of the couch."

Linda nodded. "And you were hoping that maybe she was just changing into another outfit?"

"I knew better than that." Carla gave a small laugh. "But I

decided it was only fair to give Michael the benefit of the doubt. After all, I didn't see any of *his* clothes. As it turned out, I was right. Angela did her best to seduce Michael, but he got so mad when she admitted that she'd tricked me, he grabbed his guitar and left."

"And he forgot his keys?"

"That's right. The door locked behind him, and he couldn't get back in. That's the reason he was waiting outside."

"Did Michael know what was happening inside?" Linda winced a little.

"No. He didn't even know that the lights were off, until I unlocked the front door."

"Were you scared?" Linda shivered again.

"Of course. Michael remembered how the lights had gone off when Heidi was killed, and neither one of us really wanted to go inside."

"But you did."

"Only after we called out for Angela, and she didn't answer. That's when we knew that something was wrong. I got the flashlight from my car, and Michael picked up a big branch to use as a club. And then . . ." Carla stopped and swallowed hard. "And then we went inside."

Linda looked worried as she saw how pale Carla was. "You don't have to tell me any more if you don't want to."

"Thanks, Linda." Carla smiled at her friend. "But I don't mind telling you. I've already gone over it twice for the police, and once more won't matter. But I'll never forget how scared I was, shining that flashlight around in the dark."

"Did you find Angela right away?"

"No. We went straight to the light box, and Michael turned on the lights. The killer had turned them off with the master switch."

"Just like he did the last time!" Linda took a deep breath, and let it out with a shuddering sigh. "That was when you knew, right?"

"That was when we *suspected*. But we were still hoping that

Angela was all right. We looked on the stage, and she wasn't there, and then we went to . . . to the kitchen to see if she'd run out that way."

"And you found her there, by the outside door?"

"That's right." Carla nodded. "We thought maybe she was still alive, but then Michael saw the shaft of the arrow, and we knew for sure that she wasn't."

Linda reached out to pat Carla's shoulder. "This is going to sound strange, but I'm glad you were there with Michael. At least the police can't suspect him this time."

"Oh, yes they can!" Carla's voice was bitter. "Don't forget that I was gone for at least twenty minutes, getting that juice. All they have is Michael's word that he was outside when Angela was killed. There was no one else there to verify it."

"So he's a suspect again?"

Carla nodded. "I'm afraid so. I know that Michael didn't kill Angela, but the police think he did."

"Are they going to arrest him?"

"Andy says it's only a matter of time. His uncle told him they're ninety-nine percent sure that Michael's the Cupid Killer."

"That's awful! What are you going to do?" Linda looked nervous.

"I'm not sure, but I have to do something." Carla shivered, although the hot afternoon sun was streaming through the office window. "I'm going to prove that Michael's innocent, even if I have to catch the Cupid Killer myself!"

Somehow, the word got out and though Nate Rose cancelled, Covers was packed for the Monday night show. It was a good audience. They applauded wildly for every act. But when Michael got out on the stage, people were very quiet. They listened to him sing, and they clapped politely, but Carla could tell they were seeing Michael in a new light. Everyone thought that he could be the Cupid Killer.

The same thing happened on Tuesday, and it kept on happening all through the week. The audience applauded, but they looked very nervous during Michael's sets, and they whispered to each other while he was performing.

Late Sunday afternoon, Carla met Michael at Covers. She had book work to do, and she'd asked him to be there with her. It wasn't for her protection. It was for his. If the Cupid Killer struck again, Carla was determined to be Michael's alibi. But Carla was almost sure that the killer wouldn't surface for quite some time. Michael wasn't dating any new girls, and that meant the Cupid Killer didn't have any new targets.

Carla had just finished making out the paychecks when Michael stuck his head in the office door. "Do you have time to listen to a song I just wrote?"

"I'd love to hear it." Carla smiled and motioned to the huge leather couch in her office. Michael had written four new songs this week, and he'd asked her to listen to all of them. The only time he seemed truly relaxed was when he was singing, and his new songs were all very good. Carla was glad he'd found some way to cope with his frustration.

But when Michael started to sing, Carla drew in her breath sharply. His new song was all about a guy who was accused of crimes he hadn't committed. Tears came to Carla's eyes as he sang of his loneliness, and how much it hurt when all his friends had abandoned him. There was only one ray of hope, and that was the girl who had stuck by his side, loyal and loving, even though everyone else had stopped believing in him.

The last note died away, and Michael looked at Carla. "Well? What do you think?"

"It's . . . it's beautiful, Michael." Carla spoke the words that were in her heart. "But it's so sad, it makes me want to cry."

"That's why I wrote it. It's my way of crying. Sometimes I wish I was a little kid again, so I could bawl my eyes out."

"I know." Carla got up and walked to the couch where she sat down beside him. She put her arm around his shoulders and patted his back. "It'll all work out. Don't worry. There's going to be a lot of embarrassed people at Covers, when the police catch the real Cupid Killer, and they realize that it's not you."

"You've never doubted me, have you, Carla?" Michael pulled her close and hugged her.

"No, I haven't." Carla's voice was shaking. It felt so good to be in Michael's arms. "But maybe that's because I know you better than anyone else."

"Maybe that's it. But I was kind of hoping it was because you loved me more than anyone else."

Carla held her breath. It was suddenly very quiet, and she could hear her heart beating fast. She *did* love Michael. And this was the perfect time to tell him. She'd been afraid that he'd back away if she said it before, but tonight he seemed to want the closeness that they could share.

"I do love you." Carla raised her eyes to his. "I've loved you for a long time, Michael. But I didn't think it was right to say it back then."

Michael reached down and wiped a tear off her cheek. He looked very serious. "I love you, too, Carla. And it's not just because you're the only friend I have left. I think I started loving you right after Judy died. It was like a nightmare, and you were right there for me. You kept me from going crazy."

"Maybe you're confusing being grateful with being in love." Carla voiced her worst fear. She hoped that Michael wouldn't deny it, but she had to ask. "Are you really sure you love me, Michael?"

Michael nodded. "I've never been surer of anything in my life. That's why I was so angry at Angela for tricking you. I never wanted her. I wanted you."

Carla didn't say anything. She was too happy to speak. Michael reached out very gently, and tipped up her face to his. And then he kissed her softly.

His kiss was gentle, and Carla sighed softly. Her dream was coming true. Michael loved her, and she loved him. She'd never been so happy in her life.

"You're my girl, Carla." Michael bent down to kiss her

again. And then he took the fraternity ring off his finger, and slipped it on hers. "Here. I want you to have this. I never really wanted to give it to anyone but you."

Carla looked down at the ring on her finger. He'd put it on the third finger of her left hand, and she had to ask, even if her whole dream dissolved right in front of her eyes. She took a deep breath and blurted out the question. "What does it mean, Michael?"

"It means that we're engaged to be engaged." Michael smiled at her tenderly. "Is that all right with you?"

"Oh, yes!" Carla felt her spirits rise to the ceiling, burst through the plaster, and float freely up to the stars.

"We'll tell my parents tomorrow night. They went to Palm Springs for the weekend, but they'll be back tomorrow. How about your family? Do you want to tell them now?"

Carla glanced at the clock on the wall. It was past ten and everyone would be in bed. "I think we'd better wait until tomorrow. They have to get up early for work."

"We should tell someone." Michael grinned at her. "It's not official if we don't."

Carla reached up to kiss him again. And then she gave him a happy smile. "It's official if we tell a friend, and we did that."

"We did?" Michael looked puzzled, as Carla nodded.

"You told me, and I told you. That means we both told our best friends."

Michael laughed softly and pulled her close again. And then Carla lost track of the time, because Michael was kissing her again. His lips were warm and very gentle at first, and Carla loved his tender kisses. But she had waited a lifetime for this moment, and she felt a rush of compelling urgency. The police could arrest Michael any day. And then she'd be without him again! She wrapped her arms around Michael's neck, and molded her body to his, letting him know that she belonged to him completely.

Michael groaned, deep in his throat. He knew Carla was his for the taking. But he wanted much more than this one night with her, and as tempting as her kisses were, he held himself in check.

"Not now, Carla." Michael's voice was trembling with emotion. "And not here. We've got a whole lifetime to love each other."

Carla nodded, and gave him a shaky smile. She wanted Michael to make love to her, but she knew this wasn't the right time or place. Michael knew, too, and she loved him even more for reminding her that they had a future. They didn't have to cling to each other in desperation. The police would catch the Cupid Killer and everything would work out.

Suddenly Carla felt the hair on the back of her neck stand up. She felt as if disapproving eyes were watching them, eyes that burned with an almost fanatical anger.

Michael felt her shiver, and he looked concerned. "What's the matter, Carla?"

"I just felt a little chill, that's all." Carla smiled quickly, to cover her distress. It was only her imagination, and she didn't want to cast any sort of pall over this happy night. And then both of them heard it, the sound of the front door banging closed. Someone was here!

"Hello? Is anyone here?"

The voice had a heavy Spanish accent, and Carla began to laugh. It was only the cleaning crew, coming in to work. Mr. Calloway had hired a service to re-surface the stage. Carla had made all the arrangements, and they'd picked up the key on Friday morning.

"We're in here!" Carla called out, and then she turned to explain to Michael. "It's the crew Mr. Calloway hired to wax the floors. I forgot they were coming in tonight. We'd better leave, Michael. I don't want to get in their way."

Michael stood up and pulled her to her feet, giving her one last kiss. "Love makes me hungry. Don's is closed, but do you want to stop at Hamburger Heaven on the way home?"

"I'd love to!" Carla grabbed her purse. She'd been too upset to eat very much for the past couple of days, and she'd been losing sleep, worrying about whether Michael would be arrested or not. She remembered reading that people who suffered from food and sleep deprivation were prone to hallucinations. That was probably why she'd imagined that someone was watching them. Food and a good night's sleep would fix her up just fine.

Twenty

It was eleven-thirty by the time they left Hamburger Heaven. Michael had kissed her goodbye in the parking lot, and Carla was floating on air as she drove home. She had just pulled into the driveway, when she glanced down at her finger and noticed that Michael's fraternity ring wasn't there. "Oh, no!" Carla stared down at her hand, willing that the ring would suddenly reappear, but no such thing happened. She forced herself not to panic, and tried to remember the last time she'd seen it. They were on the couch when Michael had slipped it on her finger. Of course it had been too large, and Carla clearly remembered taking it off and placing it on the table by the couch. Michael's kisses had driven all practical thoughts out of her mind, and she'd forgotten it when they'd left.

Carla put her car in reverse, and backed out of the driveway again. The ring was precious, and she wanted to put it on a chain to wear around her neck, until she could have it sized to fit her finger. She'd drive back to Covers, and pick it up right now. She'd be perfectly safe. The cleaning crew would still be there, and she didn't want to take the chance that they'd find it and misplace it.

But there were no cars in the parking lot when Carla arrived at Covers. The crew must have finished and left. Carla shivered a bit as she got out of her car and walked toward the front door.

Should she go in alone? It would be breaking Mr. Calloway's rule.

But the ring was much more important than a rule, and Carla stuck her key in the lock. It would only take a moment to get the ring. She'd run straight back to the office to get it, and then she'd leave. There was really no need to worry.

Carla opened the door and stepped into the inky blackness inside. The scent of fresh wax was so strong, it almost made her light-headed. She switched on the lights by the door, and raced back to the office to get her ring. But the ring wasn't where she'd left it! Someone had taken Michael's ring!

As Carla stood there, uncertain what to do, the lights clicked off with a loud snap, and the office was plunged into total darkness. Carla didn't take time to think about what she should do. She just ran out the office door, and pressed herself flat against the side of the hallway.

Her only hope was to be perfectly quiet. Carla's mind spun in dizzying circles. She hadn't been imagining things when she'd been on the couch with Michael. Angry eyes *had* been watching her. And those eyes belonged to the Cupid Killer!

Carla took a deep, silent breath for courage, and began to inch along the hallway toward the back door. She couldn't just stand here and wait to be murdered like the rest of Michael's girlfriends. She had too much to live for. Somehow she had to get out and call the police.

She was almost to the end of the hallway when she heard the sound of laughter. It was soft at first, as if in response to a funny joke, but then it grew louder and louder until it reached a screaming pitch. And then a voice called out from the stage.

"Car . . . la. Where are you, Carla? You were my friend, Carla. And I'm sorry that I have to kill you. But I do. You can see that, can't you? Come here and I'll make this easy. You won't feel a thing, I promise."

Carla's mouth dropped open in a silent scream. Her blood ran cold, as she recognized the eerie voice. It was Judy! It was impossible, but Judy was still alive! And Judy Lampert was the Cupid Killer!

Silently, Carla drew back the deadbolt on the back door. Then she pushed it open, hoping it wouldn't squeak. But just as she was about to hurl herself out, into the welcome darkness outside, strong arms tightened like steel bands around her shoulders. Carla didn't struggle. She knew it was useless. Judy had always been as strong as an ox.

"It's not nice to fool your friend, Carla."

Judy's voice was low and menacing, and Carla racked her brain for something to say. She knew she had to throw Judy off-balance, and keep her talking.

"I asked you to come, and you tried to run. Now I'm going to have to . . ."

"Judy!" Carla put all the warmth she could muster into her voice. "I'm so glad you're alive!"

There was a long silence, and Judy relaxed her grip slightly. It wasn't enough for Carla to make her break, but she'd managed to confuse her.

"I'm sorry I tried to run." Carla did her best to sound friendly. "But I didn't know it was you. Everybody thinks you're dead. Except for Vera, of course. She was convinced that you were a ghost."

Judy laughed, a high-pitched giggle that was on the verge of hysteria. "I know. But she didn't really think I was a ghost. That was just a trick to trap Michael."

"You're kidding!" Carla managed to laugh. "Well, she had me fooled. I thought she was perfectly serious. How did you catch on?"

"My eyes and ears are everywhere. I heard Vera call her brother from the pay phone in the hallway. That's how I knew what she was planning. But Vera doesn't matter now. All that matters is . . ."

"Let's get some juice." Carla interrupted her smoothly. "You scared me so much, my throat's dry. I need a glass of orange juice and I've just *got* to find out how you got out of that car!"

There was another long silence, and then Judy whirled Carla around so fast, she stumbled. "Okay. You walk ahead of me.

There's juice behind the bar, and you can pour it. But I've got my eye on you, so don't try to run."

"I won't," Carla promised, and it was the truth. When Judy had whirled her around, she'd noticed the sharp knife she held in her hand. Running right now would be the same as suicide. But if she could keep Judy talking, there was bound to be a chance for escape. All she had to do was recognize it, and go for the element of surprise.

As Carla walked back down the hallway with Judy directly behind her, she began to form a plan. Maybe she wouldn't be able to escape, but she might be able to save Michael. The sound system was rigged so that Mr. Calloway could make tapes of all the shows. If she could manage to switch it on, she could record everything that Judy said. All she had to do was make sure Judy didn't realize that she was flicking the switch. And the switch was right next to the . . .

"Is it okay if I turn on the air-conditioner?" Carla hesitated as they came to the edge of the stage. "It's really stifling in here, and the smell of that wax they put on the floor is making me sick to my stomach."

Judy nodded. "Okay. But don't try to pull anything, Carla. I'm right behind you with this knife."

"I know. I saw it. But that's Andy's favorite chef knife. He's going to be royally pissed if you bend that blade."

Judy laughed, and she sounded almost like the old Judy as she guided Carla toward the switch for the air-conditioner. But her next comment made Carla know that she was completely insane.

"Maybe I should save this knife. I could use it on Andy. Wouldn't that be choice? They'd find him with his favorite knife sticking out of his back."

Carla reached out with her right hand and turned on the air-conditioner. As it whirred into life with a clatter, she also flicked the switch for the tape to record through the sound system. She held her breath, but Judy didn't seem to notice. Tomorrow night, when Mr. Calloway got ready to tape the show, he would be bound to notice that the recorder was on. And when he played the tape, he'd be able to hear every word that Judy had said.

"Do you want orange juice, too?" Carla turned and headed for the bar. Judy was still on her heels and she tried to make her voice sound natural. Would the tape pick up all the way over here? All she could do was hope.

"No. I'm tired of orange juice. What else is there?"

"I'm not sure. I can't make out the labels in the dark. Is it okay to turn on a light?"

"No!" Judy sounded angry. "Light one of those little candles they've got on the tables, and put it on top of the bar."

Carla did exactly as Judy asked. This was going very well. Judy didn't seem quite as determined to kill her as she'd been, earlier. But then she saw Michael's fraternity ring, glittering on Judy's finger, and she knew she was in big trouble. And when she caught sight of Judy's face in the flickering light, she almost lost hope. Judy's eyes glittered dangerously, and she looked almost demonic.

"What kind of juice is there?" Judy's voice sounded hard and stem, as if she were correcting a recalcitrant child.

"Apple, mango, banana-pineapple, peach, strawberry-coconut, and spicy tomato."

"Pour me some spicy tomato. I like that."

As Carla poured the juice, she had an inspiration, and she made herself giggle. "Too bad there's no Cran-lemon. Right, Judy?"

Judy laughed. It was her old laugh, full of mirth, and Carla was heartened by the sound. If she played her cards just right, she might be able to talk Judy into letting her go. But Judy's laughter stopped as suddenly as it had started, and she looked angry again. "That Angela was a bitch. I really enjoyed smashing her head in and watching her bleed."

"How about Vera?" Carla tried to make her voice casual and conversational, as if she were talking about a dance or a movie, instead of cold-blooded murder.

"That was fun, too. I used a rock, you know. That's why the police never found a weapon. I tossed it back into the ocean when I was through."

"That was smart." Carla did her best to sound impressed. "And you used the arc light with Heidi. That was very clever. At first they thought it was an accident, you know . . . until they found the arrow."

"That's my calling card." Judy looked pleased.

"Which one was the hardest?" Carla tried to sound interested, although talking about these murders was so unnerving, her hands began to shake.

"I don't know." Judy frowned. "Liz, I guess. I had to hold her under the water so long, my arms began to cramp. It reminded me of the time I went deep-sea fishing, and I hooked a big tuna."

Carla nodded, and put an understanding smile on her face, but mentally, she was trying to think of who she'd missed. She had to get Judy to confess to every one of the Cupid Murders. "Deana must have been easy. She was small."

"It was a snap. I hit her over the head with that tire iron before she knew what was happening. Becky was harder, but I managed. She tried to run, you know."

"I didn't know that." Carla raised her eyebrows. "How about Mary Beth? Did she suspect that something was wrong?"

Judy laughed. "Mary Beth was funny. Do you know, she was actually glad to see me? She was nervous, all alone in the house, and she greeted me with that big, dumb smile of hers. I was laughing so hard, I had trouble killing her. But Ingrid was the most fun of all. I got to stalk her. It was like a game, you know? The whole thing reminded me of hide and seek."

"You must have felt that way about Nita, too."

"I did."

Judy smiled as she nodded, but she was gazing at the knife in her hand. Carla knew she had to say something fast. "How did you stage your own death? That must have been very difficult."

Judy laughed, long and hard. It wasn't a nice laugh. "It was simple. I just picked up a hitchhiker with blond hair. She was a runaway, and I told her I'd take her home with me, and give her some clothes and a hot meal. She trusted me completely, so it was easy. I killed her and drove to the edge of the lookout. Then I doused her with gas, and pushed the car over the cliff."

Carla shuddered. She didn't want to think of the poor, terrified teenager that Judy had murdered. "How did you get her to switch clothes with you?"

"Oh, I did that after she was dead. It was easier that way. And then I hitchhiked back here, and I've been here ever since."

Judy sounded very proud of herself, and Carla shivered. She picked up the bottle of spicy tomato, and held it out to Judy. "More juice?"

"No, thanks. It's time to kill you now."

Judy moved like lightning, and Carla screamed as she lunged toward her. The bottle of juice dropped from Carla's startled hands, and it crashed to the floor. The sound of breaking glass threw Judy slightly off-balance, but Carla felt a blinding pain as the knife plunged into her body and she fell backwards, behind the bar.

The pain was so intense that Carla couldn't move. She was stunned and helpless, lying amidst the shards of broken glass, with spicy tomato juice splattered all over the front of her white blouse.

Judy grabbed the candle and leaned over the bar for a closer look. What she saw in the flickering light must have convinced her that Carla was dead, because she set the candle back on the top of the bar, and sighed deeply. "Sorry, Carla. I liked you. Really I did. But I couldn't let you have Michael."

Carla wanted to groan, but she didn't. The knife wound hurt like blazing fire, but she didn't make a sound. If Judy thought she was still alive, she'd stab her again.

"It's over, Carla. You're my last female victim." Judy sounded almost cheerful. "I can't go around killing off Michael's girlfriends anymore. I know they're going to catch me, sooner or later. It's time to finish up and go."

Carla held her breath as Judy pushed back her stool. And then she felt something hard and cold hit her forehead. It was Michael's ring! Judy had thrown it on top of what she'd assumed was Carla's dead body.

"I'll leave this with you. Somebody might spot it if I wear it. And here's your arrow, just like all the rest."

It was the hardest thing that Carla had ever done, but she didn't flinch as Judy leaned over her with an arrow. She felt a dull thud as the arrow struck her chest, but no pain. How odd . . . was the pain of the knife wound so great, that it had cancelled out everything else? And then Judy was standing up again, smiling in satisfaction.

"That ought to do it. You're the tenth and last victim of the Cupid Killer. The police are going to think that Michael killed you, too, right before he committed suicide."

Carla's head was whirling, and she knew she was close to losing consciousness. But she was sure she'd heard Judy clearly. She'd said that Michael was going to commit suicide. What did that mean?

"I know his parents are gone, and I've got a key to his house. Mrs. Warden gave it to Marta when they went on vacation last year. Poor Michael's going to end up just like that little hitchhiker. I've got it all planned out. And I'm the only one who'll ever know that he wasn't really the Cupid Killer."

Judy began to laugh as she blew out the candle, plunging the interior of Covers into darkness. And then her laughter grew louder and louder, until Carla was afraid she'd scream. Judy laughed all the way past the tables, and she didn't stop until she had reached the front door. And then her voice floated out through the darkness again.

"Goodbye, Carla. It was nice knowing you. And don't worry about Michael. He'll be joining you much sooner than he thinks."

The moment she was sure that Judy was gone, Carla attempted to get to her feet. But she was much too weak to stand, and her wound throbbed painfully with every breath she took.

Only one thought ran through Carla's mind. She had to warn Michael. There was a telephone up on the stage, and she had to reach it!

Slowly, painfully, Carla managed to crawl to the stairs. There were only four steps to climb, but it seemed to take forever to drag herself to the floor of the stage. Just a few feet to go. The telephone was next to the light box. It took precious minutes, and a lot of courage, but at last Carla made it.

The telephone was much to high for her to reach, but Carla pulled herself up on the stool that Marc used between the acts. Her fingers felt numb as she dialed Michael's number. It rang several times, but at last he answered, sounding groggy.

"It's me . . . Carla." Carla felt herself weaken, and she made a conscious effort to keep from fainting. "Judy's alive and she's on her way to your house. She's got a key!"

"Carla? Are you dreaming?"

Michael sounded as if he didn't believe her, and Carla began to cry. "Please, Michael . . . get out of the house and call the police. Judy's going to kill you!"

"It's okay, Carla. It's just a bad dream. Do you want me to come over and keep you company?"

"Listen to me!" Carla tried to scream her warning into the phone, but her voice was a weak as she was. "Do you love me, Michael?"

"Of course I do." Michael's voice was warm with emotion.

"Then run straight to the police! Judy tried to kill me, and now she's coming for you!"

There was a brief silence, and then Michael spoke again. This time he sounded urgent. "Where are you?"

"At Covers. Judy stabbed me, but I'm okay. Please believe me, Michael! Get out of there right now!"

"Okay, Carla. I'm gone."

There was a click. Michael had listened to her warning, and he was leaving the house. Carla smiled and let the phone drop from her hand. She knew she should call for an ambulance, but she was just too tired. And then the soft blackness closed in, and her thoughts disappeared in a thick comforting fog that knew no pain.

Epilogue

One by one, the cars pulled into the parking lot at Covers. It was the Sunday before Christmas and Mr. Calloway was hosting his annual Christmas party for the cast and crew of Covers. Late last night, after the show, everyone had stayed to set up the Christmas tree and decorate the building for the holiday season. They'd all slept late this morning, had a leisurely day, and now they were arriving, dressed for the party and bearing brightly wrapped gifts.

Carla and Michael were the first to arrive, and they chatted with Mr. Calloway until the other guests began to troop in the door. Andy arrived with Linda, Berto, Tammy, and Winona. Phil and Rob rode with Marc Allen, and Jerry Maxwell brought the Alway Brothers and Gina and Nicole in his band bus. There were many familiar faces, and some who would become familiar. Mr. Calloway had hired ten new acts to audition tonight. The regulars would be the audience, and they'd get the chance to enjoy the show from the floor.

"Are you cold, Carla?" Michael looked concerned as Carla pulled her beaded sweater around her shoulders.

"No, I'm fine. But I wish I hadn't worn a low-cut dress. I'm still a little embarrassed about my scar."

"I love your scar." Michael bent over to kiss the top of her head. "And I especially love where it is. Another couple of inches lower, and you wouldn't be here with me now."

"I know." Carla nodded. She'd been very lucky in many ways, lucky that the tape recorder had worked to record all of Judy's confession, lucky that Michael had rushed right over to Covers immediately after he'd called the police to tell them about Judy, lucky that he'd asked the paramedics to meet him there, and lucky that Judy had been caught just as she was unlocking Michael's front door. She knew that Michael was right about her scar. The doctors had promised that it would fade in time, but she still shivered every time she saw it in the mirror. It was a tangible reminder of the terrible danger that they had been in.

The scar from the knife wound was the only one she had. There was no scar from the arrow at all, and there was a good reason why she'd felt no pain when Judy had thrust it into her chest. Carla had been wearing a blouse with pockets, and the arrow had pierced the telephone message pad she'd forgotten to return to her desk drawer. The message pad had been ruined, but the arrow hadn't even scratched Carla.

"Are you happy, Carla?"

Michael's eyes were shining as he looked at her, and Carla knew that he loved her.

"Yes. I'm very happy." Carla leaned over and gave him a light kiss on the cheek. "I just wish that everyone could have been here."

Michael nodded, and hugged her again. He knew exactly what she was thinking. Ten members of the Covers' cast and crew were gone forever.

Andy approached their table with Linda in tow. He looked worried, and he was frowning. "I don't like this. What if the caterers mess up my kitchen? It'll take me weeks to get it back in shape. I think I'll take a peek, and make sure they're not using my new set of pans."

"I'll go with you, if you'll go with me." Linda grinned at him.

"I've got to check out the dressing room. Those new girls'll never be able to figure out the light for the makeup table."

As Michael and Carla watched, everyone began to get up. Berto and Tammy went to make sure there was a supply of clean glasses, Winona decided to check out the bar and make sure there was plenty of juice on hand, Marc went off to give final instructions to his new assistant who was lighting the show, and every other performer suddenly decided to make sure their props were intact.

"Don't you want to check out the office?" Michael turned to Carla with a smile.

"No. It's all locked up and I'm the only one with the key. How about you? Are you worried about your dressing room?"

Michael shook his head. "The other guys'll check it out. I'd rather stay right here with you."

The first half of the show was excellent, and Carla and Michael applauded wildly at intermission. There was a lot of new talent out there, and some of them would be invited back to become regular performers. Appetizers were served, and fruit drinks were refilled, and then the lights dimmed again, for the second half of the show.

"And now we have a special Christmas surprise." Mr. Calloway beamed at the audience, and Carla noticed that he was carrying Michael's guitar. "Michael's written a new song for the holiday season, and he's agreed to sing it for us tonight. Michael?"

Michael reached out and grabbed Carla's hand. "I told Marc to bring out two stools. This song's for you, and I won't sing it unless you come up and sit with me."

"All right." Carla blushed, but she nodded. She wasn't as shy as she'd been last summer. As the audience applauded, she took her place on the stool and smiled at Michael as he started to play.

Michael's song was about Christmas wishes, and how all he wanted was love. Material things didn't mean a thing, unless there was someone to share them. Carla's eyes glistened with happy tears as Michael sang. Every word he was singing was true. Love was the most important gift of all, and life wasn't worth living without it.

The song ended and the audience applauded. Michael took Carla's hand and he led her from the stage. When they were back at their table again, he pulled her close and kissed her.

"Am I right?" Michael's voice was a soft whisper.

"Yes," Carla whispered back. "Love is the most important gift of all. In a way, it's a shame that Judy never learned that. She tried to take love, and you have to wait for it to be given."

Michael kissed her again, and then Carla asked the question that had been running through her mind all night. "Do you think she'll ever get out?"

"No. I talked to Andy's uncle today, and he told me that Judy would be there for life. We're safe, Carla. We're safe, forever."

Judy shivered in the chill night air, and slipped on her jacket. It was nippy out tonight, and Christmas was coming. She knew exactly what she was giving herself for Christmas this year. It was the one thing she wanted more than anything else, her freedom.

At first, they'd locked her up like a rat in a cage, but good old Buddy and Pamela had come through for her. They'd moved her to this expensive sanitarium where the food was excellent and she had a private suite with cable television. It looked more like a health spa than a prison, but the bars on the windows had been a continual reminder that she was a prisoner.

Judy had formulated her escape plan on the very first day. She'd been a model patient, unfailingly polite to the staff of ugly nurses, and very cooperative with the young doctor who was assigned to her case. She'd insisted that she couldn't remember anything about the murders, and when the doctor had told her exactly what she had done, she'd broken down in tears of remorse.

Naturally, she'd been hoping for a plea of temporary insanity, and Judy was sure that she would have triumphed. But the process had been much too slow, and she'd quickly tired of acting sweet and innocent. All she'd been able to think about was how she'd failed to kill Carla and Michael. That mistake had to be rectified soon.

Judy had started with the nurses. It was always good to get them on your side. She'd told Marta to bring flowers for them every week when she visited, and expensive boxes of candy from a gourmet chocolate shop. At Judy's suggestion, Pamela and Buddy had donated a giant-screen television and a VCR for the nurses' lounge. Then Judy had told Marta to purchase tapes of first-run movies, and that had made Judy the darling of the nursing staff.

The doctor had been harder to win over than the nurses. He was smarter, and he'd been immune to Judy's charms for several weeks. But Judy had managed to fool him, too, the minute she'd found out that he was writing a book. She'd asked to read it, and she'd been full of praise for the dull, technical passages. Then, as the icing on the cake, Judy had talked Buddy into buying the manuscript for one of the publishing houses he owned.

It had taken Judy less than two months to earn unlimited privileges. She could go out on the grounds any time she wished, and that was also a part of her plan. Judy had taken a walk every night, and the nurses were used to seeing her go out and come back with her jacket on.

Tonight, she'd yawned all through dinner. When the head nurse had asked her what was wrong, Judy had said she'd stayed up late the night before, reading a novel. She'd told the head nurse that she was going to take her nightly walk, and then she planned to turn in early.

After that, it had been simple. Judy had taken the movies that Marta had brought, three new releases she knew the nurses were dying to see, and left them in the lounge. Then she'd gone back to her room and piled pillows in a row under her blankets. The nurses always opened her door to do a bed check at night, but Judy's status had been changed to nonviolent, and all they did was glance at the bed. The pillows would fool them into thinking that she was there, sleeping peacefully, with the covers pulled over her head.

Next, Judy had checked her supply of cash. Pamela and Buddy always sent plenty of money with Marta on her weekly visits. They thought Judy used it to buy snacks and magazines and little gifts for the other patients. Since Buddy and Pamela had no idea how much to send, and money seemed to mean nothing to them, Judy had managed to squirrel away over a thousand dollars.

Judy had stuffed the cash into her jacket pocket, and waved at the nurses as she'd walked past the desk. And now she was out on the grounds in the moonlight, only a few feet from the high fence running around the perimeter. She knew she wouldn't have much trouble getting over the fence. She was athletic, and she wasn't doped up on tranquilizers like the rest of the patients.

There was a tree, close to the fence. Judy grinned as she climbed up the thick branches, and dropped easily over the top of the fence. They wouldn't start looking for her until morning, and by then she'd be hundreds of miles away.

Judy slipped on the black wig Marta had bought for her, and walked confidently to the nearest road. It didn't take long to wave down a passing motorist, and the man was very sympathetic when she told him how she decided to walk back to town when her friends started drinking. She got him to drop her off at a truck stop, where she could supposedly call her parents, and Judy was on her way.

The waitress brought her coffee, and Judy smiled as she tasted her first dose of caffeine in months. She checked her appearance in the mirror behind the counter, and smiled in satisfaction. The denim jacket and jeans she'd bought in the trucker's shop next to the restaurant were a good disguise. She'd changed clothes in the ladies' room, and dropped her old things in a Salvation Army box. By the time they were discovered, she'd be long gone.

The truckers sitting in the back of the restaurant were a friendly bunch. Judy won their sympathy immediately, when she told them that her boyfriend had deserted her and left her here in Northern California, miles from her home in San Diego. A

trucker who was high-balling it to Los Angeles said he'd be glad
to take her that far.

Los Angeles would be perfect. Judy gave him a teary smile as
she followed him out to the parking lot and swung herself up
into his truck. Of course she wasn't actually planning to go
home. That was the first place they'd look for her. But she had
some unfinished business in Burbank, and she'd disappear into
the street scene and get herself another identity. That shouldn't
be so hard. Money could buy anything and she had plenty of
that.

Judy sank back, into the comfortable passenger's seat, and relaxed. Then she watched the miles click off on the odometer and
listened to country western music on the trucker's radio. The
song they were playing reminded her of one that Michael had
written, and she sighed softly. She still loved Michael, and she'd
decided to give him one more chance. She'd kill Carla first, and
then she'd concentrate all her energies on Michael. If he still refused to cooperate, she'd just have to cut out his unfaithful
heart.

"You got a job waiting for you at home, honey?" The trucker
glanced over at her with a friendly smile.

Judy nodded. She'd just thought of the perfect answer, and
she didn't even have to lie. "I sure do. I work, for an extermina-
tor service."

WHERE INNOCENCE DIES . . .

Expectant parents Karen and Mike Houston are excited about restoring their old rambling Victorian mansion to its former glory. With its endless maze of rooms, hallways, and hiding places, it's a wonderful place for their nine-year-old daughter Leslie to play and explore. Unfortunately, they didn't listen to the stories about the house's dark history. They didn't believe the rumors about the evil that lived there.

. . . THE NIGHTMARE BEGINS.

It begins with a whisper. A child's voice beckoning from the rose garden. Crying out in the night. It lures little Leslie to a crumbling storm door. Down a flight of broken stairs. It calls to their unborn child. It wants something from each of them. Something in their very hearts and souls. Tonight, the house will reveal its secret. *Tonight, the other child will come out to play . . .*

Please turn the page for an exciting sneak peek of Joanne Fluke's THE OTHER CHILD coming in August 2014!

Prologue

The train was rolling across the Arizona desert when it started, a pain so intense it made her double over in the dusty red velvet seat. Dorthea gasped aloud as the spasm tore through her and several passengers leaned close.

"Just a touch of indigestion." She smiled apologetically. "Really, I'm fine now."

Drawing a deep steadying breath, she folded her hands protectively over her rounded stomach and turned to stare out at the unbroken miles of sand and cactus. The pain would disappear if she just sat quietly and thought pleasant thoughts. She had been on the train for days now and the constant swaying motion was making her ill.

Thank goodness she was almost to California. Dorthea sighed gratefully. The moment she arrived she would get her old job back, and then she would send for Christopher. They could find a home together, she and Christopher and the new baby.

She never should have gone back. Dorthea pressed her forehead against the cool glass of the window and blinked back bitter tears. The people in Cold Spring were hateful. They had called Christopher a bastard. They had ridiculed her when Mother's will was made public. They knew that her mother had never forgiven her and they were glad. The righteous, upstanding citizens of her old hometown were the same cruel gossips they'd been ten years ago.

If only she had gotten there before Mother died! Dorthea was certain that those horrid people in Cold Spring had poisoned her mother's mind against her and she hated them for it. Her dream of being welcomed home to her beautiful house was shattered. Now she was completely alone in the world. Poor Christopher was abandoned back there until she could afford to send him the money for a train ticket.

Dorthea moaned as the pain tore through her again. She braced her body against the lurching of the train and clumsily made her way up the aisle, carefully avoiding the stares of the other passengers. There it started and she slumped to the floor. A pool of blood was gathering beneath her and she pressed her hand tightly against the pain.

Numbness crept up her legs and she was cold, as cold as she'd been in the winter in Cold Spring. Her eyelids fluttered and her lips moved in silent protest. Christopher! He was alone in Cold Spring, in a town full of spiteful, meddling strangers. Dear God, what would they do to Christopher?

"No! She's not dead!" He stood facing them, one small boy against the circle of adults. "It's a lie! You're telling lies about her, just like you did before!"

His voice broke in a sob and he whirled to run out the door of the parsonage. His mother wasn't dead. She couldn't be dead! She had promised to come back for him just as soon as she made some money.

"Lies. Dirty lies." The wind whipped away his words as he raced through the vacant lot and around the corner. The neighbors had told lies before about his mother, lies his grandmother had believed. They were all liars in Cold Spring, just as his mother had said.

There it was in front of him now, huge and solid against the gray sky. Christopher stopped at the gate, panting heavily. Appleton Mansion, the home that should have been his. Their lies had cost him his family, his inheritance, and he'd get even with all of them somehow.

They were shouting his name now, calling for him to come back. Christopher slipped between the posts of the wrought-iron fence and ran into the overgrown yard. They wanted to tell him more lies, to confuse him the way they had confused Grandmother Appleton, but he wouldn't listen. He'd hide until it was dark and then he'd run away to California where his mother was waiting for him.

The small boy gave a sob of relief when he saw an open door-way. It was perfect. He'd hide in his grandmother's root cellar and they'd never find him. Then, when it was dark, he'd run away.

Without a backward glance Christopher hurtled through the opening, seeking the safety of the darkness below. He gave a shrill cry as his foot missed the steeply slanted step and then he was falling, arms flailing helplessly at the air as he pitched forward into the deep, damp blackness.

Wade Comstock stood still, letting the leaves skitter and pile in colored mounds around his feet, smiling as he looked up at the shuttered house. His wife, Verna, had been right, the Appleton Mansion had gone dirt cheap. He still couldn't understand how modern people at the turn of the century could take stock in silly ghost stories. He certainly didn't believe for one minute that Amelia Appleton was back from the dead, haunting the Appleton house. But then again, he had been the only one ever to venture a bid on the old place. Amelia's daughter Dorthea had left town right after her mother's will was read, cut off without a dime—and it served her right. Now the estate was his, the first acquisition of the Comstock Realty Company.

His thin lips tightened into a straight line as he thought of Dorthea. The good people of Cold Spring hadn't been fooled one bit by her tears at her mother's funeral. She was after the property, pure and simple. Bringing her bastard son here was bad enough, but you'd think a woman in her condition would have sense enough to stay away. And then she had run off, leaving the boy behind. He could make a bet that Dorthea was never planning to send for Christopher. Women like her didn't want kids in the way.

Wade kicked out at the piles of leaves and walked around his new property. As he turned the corner of the house, the open root cellar caught his eye and he reached in his pocket for the padlock and key he'd found hanging in the tool shed. That old cellar should be locked up before somebody got hurt down there. He'd tell the gardener to leave the bushes in that area and it would be overgrown in no time at all.

For a moment Wade stood and stared at the opening. He supposed he should go down there, but it was already too dark to be able to see his way around. Something about the place made him uneasy. There was no real reason to be afraid, but his heart beat faster and an icy sweat broke out on his forehead as he thought about climbing down into that small dark hole.

The day was turning to night as he hurriedly hefted the weather-beaten door and slammed it shut. The door was warped but it still fit. The hasp was in workable order and with a little effort he lined up the two pieces and secured them with the padlock. Then he jammed the key into his pocket and took a shortcut through the rose garden to the front yard.

Wade didn't notice the key was missing from his pocket until he was out on the sidewalk. He looked back at the overcast sky. There was no point in going back to try to find it in the dark. Actually he could do without the key. No one needed a root cellar anymore. It could stay locked up till kingdom come.

As he stood watching, shadows played over the windows of the stately house and crept up the crushed granite driveway. The air was still now, so humid it almost choked him. He could hear thunder rumbling in the distance. Then there was another noise—a thin hollow cry that set the hair on the back of his arms prickling. He listened intently, bent forward slightly, and balanced on the balls of his feet, but there was only the thunder. It was going to rain again and Wade felt a strange uneasiness. Once more he looked back, drawn to the house . . . as though something had been left unfinished. He had a vague sense of foreboding. The house looked almost menacing.

"Poppycock!" he muttered, and turned away, pulling out his watch. He'd have to hurry to get home in time for supper. Verna liked her meals punctual.

He started to walk, turning back every now and then to glance at the shadow of the house looming between the tall trees. Even though he knew those stories were a whole lot of foolishness, he felt a little spooked himself. The brick mansion did look eerie against the blackening sky.

"Mama!" He awoke with a scream on his lips, a half-choked cry of pure terror. It was dark and cold and inky black. Where was he? The air was damp, like a grave. He squeezed his eyes shut tightly and screamed again.

"Mama!" He would hear her footsteps coming any minute to wake him from this awful nightmare. She'd turn on the light and hug him and tell him not to be afraid. If he just waited, she'd come. She always came when he had nightmares.

No footsteps, no light, no sound except his own hoarse breathing. Christopher reached out cautiously and felt damp earth around him. This was no dream. Where was he?

There was a big lump on his head and it hurt. He must have fallen . . . yes, that was it.

He let his breath out in a shuddering sigh as he remembered. He was in his Grandmother Appleton's root cellar. He'd fallen down the steps trying to hide from the people who told him lies about his mama. And tonight he was going to run away and find her in California. She'd be so proud of him when he told her he hadn't believed their lies. She'd hug him and kiss him and promise she'd never have to go away again.

Perhaps it was night now. Christopher forced himself to open his eyes. He opened them wide but he couldn't see anything, not even the white shirt he was wearing. It must be night and that meant it was time for him to go.

Christopher sat up with a groan. It was so dark he couldn't see the staircase. He knew he'd have to crawl around and feel for the steps, but it took a real effort to reach out into the blackness. He wasn't usually afraid of the dark. At least he wasn't afraid of the dark when there was a lamppost or a moon or something. This kind of darkness was different. It made his mouth dry and he held his breath as he forced himself to reach out into the inky depths.

There. He gave a grateful sigh as he crawled up the first step of the stairs. He didn't want to lose his balance and fall back down again.

Four . . . five . . . six . . . he was partway up when he heard a stealthy rustling noise from below. Fear pushed him forward in a rush, his knees scraping against the old slivery wood in a scramble to get to the top.

He let out a terrified yell as his head hit something hard. The cover—somebody had closed up the root cellar!

He couldn't think; he was too scared. Blind panic made him scream and pound, beating his fists against the wooden door until his knuckles were swollen and raw. Somehow he had to lift door.

With a mighty effort Christopher heaved his body upward, straining against the solid piece of wood. The door gave a slight, sickening lurch, creaking and lifting just enough for him to hear the sound of metal grating against metal.

At first the sound lay at the back of his mind like a giant pendulum of horror, surging slowly forward until it reached the active part of his brain. The Cold Spring people had locked him in.

The thought was so terrifying he lost his breath and slumped into a huddled ball on the step. In the darkness he could see flashed of red and bright gold beneath his eyelids. He had to get out somehow! *He had to!*

"Help!" the sound tore through his lips and bounced off the earthen walls, giving a hollow, muted echo. He screamed until his voice was a weak whisper but no one came. Then his voice was gone and he could hear it again, the ominous rustling from the depths of the cellar, growing louder with each passing heartbeat.

God, no! This nightmare was really happening! He recognized the scuffling noise now and shivered with terror. Rats. They were sniffing at the air, searching for him, and there was nowhere to hide. They'd find him even here at the top of the stairs and they would come in a rush, darting hurtling balls of fur and needle teeth . . . the pain of flesh being torn from his body . . . the agony of being eaten alive!

He opened his throat in a tortured scream, a shrill hoarse cry that circled the earthen room then faded to a deadly silence. There was a roaring in his ears and terror rose to choke him, squeezing and strangling him with clutching fingers.

"Mama! Please, Mama!" he cried again, and then suddenly he was pitching forward, rolling and bumping to the black pit below. He gasped as an old shovel bit deeply into his neck and a warm stickiness gushed out to cover his face. There was a moment of vivid consciousness before death claimed him and in that final moment, one emotion blazed its way through his whole being. Hatred. He hated all of them. They had driven his mother away. They had stolen his inheritance. They had locked him in here and left him to die. He would punish them . . . make them suffer as his mother had suffered . . . as he was suffering.

One

The interior of the truck was dusty and Mike opened the wing window all the way, shifting on the slick plastic-covered seat, Karen had wanted to take an afternoon drive through the country and here they were over fifty miles from Minneapolis, on a bumpy country road. It wasn't Mike's idea of a great way to spend a Sunday. He'd rather be home watching the Expos and the Phillies from the couch in their air-conditioned Lake Street apartment.

Mike glanced uneasily at Karen as he thought about today's game. He had a bundle riding on this one and it was a damn good thing Karen didn't know about it. She'd been curious about his interest in baseball lately but he'd told her he got a kick out of watching the teams knock themselves out for the pennant. The explanation seemed to satisfy her.

Karen was death on two of his pet vices, drinking and gambling, and he'd agreed to reform three years ago when they were married. Way back then he'd made all the required promises. Lay off the booze. No more Saturday-night poker games. No betting on the horses. No quick trips to Vegas. No office pools, even. The idea of a sportsbook hadn't occurred to her yet and he was hoping it wouldn't now. Naturally Mike didn't make a habit of keeping secrets from his wife but in this case he'd chosen the lesser of two evils. He knew Karen would hit the roof if he told her he hadn't gotten that hundred-dollar-a-month bonus after all, that the extra money came from his gambling winnings on the games. It was just lucky that he took care of all the finances. What Karen didn't know wouldn't hurt her.

"Cold Spring, one mile." Leslie was reading the road signs again in her clear high voice. "Oh, look Mike! A church with a white steeple and all those trees. Can't we just drive past before we go home?"

Mike had been up most of the night developing prints for his spread in *Homes* magazine and he wasn't in the mood for extensive sightseeing. He was going to refuse, but then he caught sight of his stepdaughter's pleading face in the rearview mirror. Another little side trip wouldn't kill him. He'd been too busy lately to spend much time at home and these Sunday drives were a family tradition.

"Oh, let's, Mike." Karen's voice was wistful. Mike could tell by her tone that she'd been feeling a little neglected lately, too. Maybe it had been a mistake insisting she quit her job at the interior decorating firm. Mike was old-fashioned sometimes, and he maintained that a mother's place was at home with her children. When he had discovered that Karen was pregnant he'd put his foot down insisting she stay home. Karen had agreed, but still she missed her job. He told himself that she'd be busy enough when the baby was born, but that didn't solve the problem right now.

Mike slowed the truck, looking for a turnoff. A little sightseeing might be fun. Karen and Leslie would certainly enjoy it and his being home to watch the game wouldn't change the outcome any.

"All right, you two win." Mike smiled at his wife and turned left at the arrowed sign. "Just a quick run through town and then we have to get back. I still have to finish the penthouse prints and start work on that feature."

Leslie gave Mike a quick kiss and settled down again in the back seat of their Land-Rover. When she was sitting down on the seat, Mike could barely see the top of her blond head over the stacks of film boxes and camera cases. She was a small child for nine, fair-haired and delicate like the little porcelain shepherdesses his mother used to collect. She was an exquisite child, a classic Scandinavian beauty. Mike was accustomed to being approached by people who wanted to use Leslie as a model. Karen claimed she didn't want Leslie to become self-conscious, but Mike noticed how she enjoyed dressing Leslie in the height of fashion. Much of Karen's salary had gone into designer jeans, Gucci loafers, and Pierre Cardin sweaters for her daughter. Leslie always had the best in clothes and she wore them beautifully, taking meticulous care of her wardrobe. Even in play clothes she always looked every inch a lady.

Karen possessed a different kind of beauty. Hers was the active, tennis-pro look. She had long, dark hair and a lithe, athletic body. People had trouble believing that she and Leslie were mother and daughter. They looked and acted completely different. Leslie preferred to curl up in a fluffy blanket and read, while Karen was relentlessly active. She was a fresh-air-and-exercise fanatic. For the last six years Karen had jogged around Lake Harriet every morning, dragging Leslie with her. That was how they'd met, the three of them.

Mike had been coming home from an all-night party, camera slung over his shoulder, when he spotted them. He was always on the lookout for a photogenic subject and he'd stopped to take a few pictures of the lovely black-haired runner and her towheaded child. It had seemed only natural to ask for Karen's address and a day later he was knocking at her door with some sample prints in one hand and a stuffed toy for Leslie in the other. The three of them had formed an instant bond.

Leslie had been fascinated by the man in her mother's life. She was five then, and fatherless. Karen always said Leslie was the image of her father—a handsome Swedish exchange student with whom Karen had enjoyed a brief affair before he'd gone back to his native country.

They made an unlikely trio, and Mike grinned a little at the thought. He had shaggy brown hair and a lined face. He needed a shave at least twice a day. Karen claimed he could walk out of Saks Fifth Avenue, dressed in the best from the skin out, and still look like an unemployed rock musician. The three of them made a striking contrast in their red Land-Rover with MIKE HOUSTON, PHOTOGRAPHER painted on both doors.

Mike was so busy thinking about the picture they made that he almost missed the house. Karen's voice, breathless in his ear, jogged him back to reality.

"Oh, Mike! Stop, please! Just look at that beautiful old house!"

The house was a classic; built before the turn of the century. It sprawled over half of the large, tree-shaded lot, yellow brick gleaming in the late afternoon sun. There was a veranda that ran the length of the front and around both sides, three stories high with a balcony on the second story. A cupola graced the slanted roof like the decoration on a fancy cake. It struck Mike right away: here was the perfect subject for a special old-fashioned feature in *Homes* magazine.

"That's it, isn't it, Mike?" Leslie's voice was hushed and expectant as if she sensed the creative magic of this moment. "You're going to use this house for a special feature, aren't you?"

It was more a statement than a question and Mike nodded. Leslie had a real eye for a good photograph. "You bet I am!" he responded enthusiastically. "Hand me the Luna-Pro, honey, and push the big black case with the Linhof to the back door. Grab your Leica if you want and let's go. The sun's just right if we hurry."

Karen grinned as her husband and daughter made a hasty exit from the truck, cameras in tow. She'd voiced her objections when Mike gave Leslie the Leica for her ninth birthday. "Such an expensive camera for a nine-year-old?" she'd asked. "She'll probably lose it, Mike. And it's much too complicated for a child her age to operate."

But Mike had been right this time around. Leslie loved her Leica. She slept with it close by the side of her bed, along with her fuzzy stuffed bear and her ballet slippers. And she'd learned how to use it, too, listening attentively when Mike gave her instructions, asking questions that even Karen admitted were advanced for her age. Leslie seemed destined to follow in her stepfather's footsteps. She showed real talent in framing scenes and instinctively knew what made up a good photograph.

Her long hair was heavy and hot on the back of her neck and Karen pulled it up and secured it with a rubber band. She felt a bit queasy but she knew that was natural. It had been a long drive and she remembered getting carsick during the time she'd been carrying Leslie. Just a few more months and she would begin to show. Then she'd have to drag out all her old maternity clothes and see what could be salvaged.

Karen sighed, remembering. Ten years ago she was completely on her own, pregnant and unmarried, struggling to finish school. But once Leslie was born it was better. While it had been exhausting—attending decorating classes in the morning, working all afternoon at the firm, then coming home to care for the baby—it was well worth any trouble. Looking back, she could honestly say that she was happy she hadn't listened to all the well-meaning advice from other women about adoption or abortion. They were a family now, she and Mike and Leslie. She hadn't planned on getting pregnant again so soon after she met Mike, but it would all work out. This time it was going to be different. She wasn't alone. This time she had Mike to help her.

Karen's eyes widened as she slid out of the truck and gazed up at the huge house. It was a decorator's paradise, exactly the sort of house she'd dreamed of tackling when she was a naïve, first-year art student.

She found Leslie around the side of the house, snapping a picture of the exterior. As soon as Leslie spotted her mother she pointed excitedly toward the old greenhouse.

"Oh, Mom! Look at this! You could grow your own flowers in here! Isn't it super?"

"It certainly is!" Karen gave her daughter a quick hug. Leslie's excitement was contagious and Karen's smile widened as she let her eyes wander to take it all in. There was plenty of space for a children's wing on the second floor and somewhere in that vast expanse of rooms was the perfect place for Mike's studio and darkroom. The sign outside said FOR SALE. The thought of owning this house kindled Karen's artistic imagination. They *had* mentioned looking for a house only a week ago and here it was. Of course it would take real backbreaking effort to fix it up, but she felt sure it could be done. It would be the project she'd been looking for, to keep her occupied the next six months. With a little time, patience, and help from Mike with the heavy stuff, she could turn the mansion into a showplace.

They were peeking in through the glass windows of the greenhouse when they heard voices. Mike was talking to someone in the front yard. They heard his laugh and another, deeper voice. Karen grabbed Leslie's hand and they hurried around the side of the house in time to see Mike talking to a gray-haired man in a sport jacket. There was a white Lincoln parked in the driveway with a magnetic sign reading COMSTOCK REALTY.

Rob Comstock had been driving by on his way home from the office when he saw the Land-Rover parked outside the old Appleton Mansion. He noticed the painted signs on the vehicle's door and began to scheme. Out-of-towners, by the look of it. Making a sharp turn at the corner he drove around to pull up behind the truck, shutting off the motor of his new Continental. He'd just sit here and let them get a nice, long look.

This might be it, he thought to himself as he drew a Camel from the crumpled pack in his shirt pocket. He'd wanted to be rid of this white elephant for years. It had been on the books since his grandfather bought it eighty years ago. Rob leased it out whenever he could but that wasn't often enough to make a profit. Tenants never stayed for more than a couple of months. It was too large, they said, or it was too far from the Cities. Even though the rent was reasonable, they still made their excuses and left. He'd been trying to sell it for the past ten years with no success. Houses like this one had gone out of style in his grandfather's day. It was huge and inconvenient, and keeping it up was a financial disaster. It seemed nobody wanted to be stuck with an eight-bedroom house . . . especially a house with a reputation like this one.

Rob finished his cigarette and opened the car door. Maybe, just maybe, today would be his lucky day. He put on his sincerest, most helpful smile and cut across the lawn to greet the owner of the Land-Rover. He was ready for a real challenge.

Leslie and Karen came around the corner of the house in time to catch the tail end of the sales pitch. Mike was nodding as the older man spoke.

"It's been vacant for five years now, but we check it every week to make sure there's no damage. It's a real buy, Mr. Houston. They don't build them like this anymore. Of course it would take a real professional to fix it up and decorate it but the price is right. Only forty-five even, for the right buyer. It's going on the block next week and that'll drive the price up higher, sure as you're standing here. These old estate auctions bring people in from all over; you'd be smart to put in a bid right now. Get it before someone buys the land and decides to tear it down and put in a trailer court."

"That'd be a real shame." Mike was shaking his head and Karen instantly recognized the thoughtful expression on his face. She'd seen it enough times when he was in the market for a new camera. He really was interested. Of course she was, too, she thought, giving the house another look. They'd already decided to get out of the Twin Cities and Mike could work anywhere as long as he had a studio and darkroom. The price was fantastically low and there was the new baby on the way. They couldn't stay in their two-bedroom apartment much longer. Out here she could raise flowers and enjoy working on the house. They might even be able to swing a tennis court in a couple of years and Leslie would have lots of room to play.

"I'd really have to think about it for a while," Mike said, shrugging his shoulders. "And I'd have to see the inside, of course. If it needs a lot of work, the price would have to come down."

"No problem, Mr. Houston." The real estate agent turned to smile at Karen and Leslie. "Glad to meet you, ladies. I'm Rob Comstock from Comstock Realty and I've got the keys with me, if you folks would like to take a look. We've got at least an hour of daylight left."

Karen had a sense of inevitability as she followed Leslie and Mike inside. She'd been dying to see the interior and here she was. One look at the huge high-ceilinged living room made her gasp. This room alone was bigger than their whole apartment! Stained-glass panes graced the upper sections of the floor-length windows and the hardwood floors were virtually unblemished.

"Oh . . . lovely," Karen murmured softly. Her voice was hushed as if she were in a museum. She began to smile as she followed Rob Comstock up the circular staircase and viewed the second floor. Huge, airy bedrooms with polished oak moldings, a separate dressing room in the master suite with an ancient claw-footed dresser dominating the space—-the interior was just as she had imagined. If only they could afford it.

"The furniture on the third floor is included." He was speaking to her now and Karen smiled. Rob Comstock could see she was interested. There was no denying Karen's excitement as she stepped up on the third-floor landing and saw what must have been the original ballroom, filled with old furniture covered by drop-cloths. What she wouldn't give to poke under the shrouded shapes and see the intriguing pieces that were stored and forgotten in this enormous shadowed space.

A small staircase with a door at the top led to the cupola and Leslie was scrambling up before Karen could caution her to be careful. The steps were safe enough. The whole house seemed untouched by time, waiting for some new owners to love and nourish it, to bring it back to life again. Karen could imagine it was almost the same as it had been when the original occupants left, with only a bit of dust and cobwebs covering its intrinsic beauty.

"Plenty of real antiques up here, I'll bet!" Rob Comstock was speaking to her, but Karen only half heard him. She anticipated squeals of delight from Leslie over the view that stretched in all directions from the windowed cupola. Strange that there was only silence overhead.

Karen excused herself reluctantly. "I'd better go up and check on Leslie." A prickle of anxiety invaded her mind as she started up the narrow staircase into the dusty silence.

Karen was convinced there was something wrong when she reached the landing and pushed open the door to the cupola. Leslie was standing at one of the twelve narrow windows, staring out blankly. She looked preoccupied and started as Karen spoke her name.

"Kitten? What's the matter?" The still, stiff way Leslie was standing made Karen terribly nervous. She rushed to put her arms around her daughter.

"Huh? Oh . . . nothing, Mom." Leslie gave her a funny, lopsided smile. She looked miserable. "I'm afraid Mike won't buy it!" There was a quaver in her voice. "This house is perfect for us, Mom. We just have to live here!"

"Now, don't be silly, darling." Karen gave her a quick squeeze. "This is the first house we've seen and it really is awfully large for us. We'll probably see other houses you like just as much."

"No! We have to live here in this house!" Leslie's voice was stronger now and pleading. "You know it's the right house, Mom. We can't live anywhere else. This house was built just for us!"

"I think you should have Mr. Comstock's job." Karen said, smiling down indulgently. "You're an even better salesman than he is. But really, kitten, we have to be sensible. I know you love this old house and I do, too, but the final decision is Mike's."

Karen was firm as she turned Leslie around and guided her toward the stairs. "Come on now, honey. We have to get back downstairs before it gets dark. The power's not turned on, you know."

"But you'll help me convince Mike to buy it, won't you, Mom?" Leslie asked insistently, stopping at the top step. "You know it would be perfect for us."

"Yes, I'll help you, silly," Karen promised, brushing a wisp of silvery-blond hair out of Leslie's eyes. She breathed a sigh of relief as her daughter smiled fully and hurried down the stairs in front of her. Leslie would be persistent and she might just manage to convince Mike. Leslie was right. It was almost as if the house had been waiting all this time just for them.